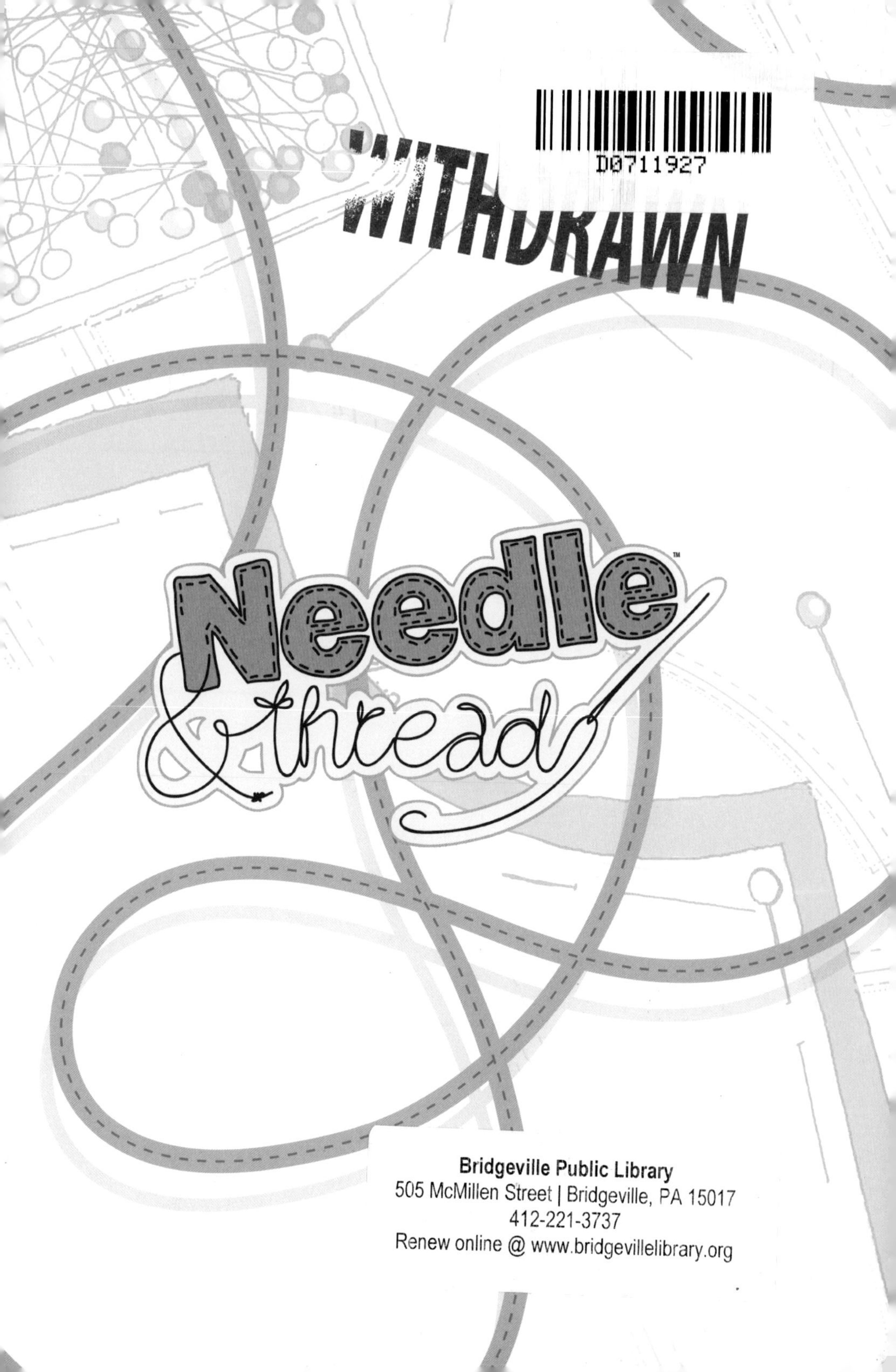
Needle™
&thread

LAURA CHACÓN
FOUNDER

MARK LONDON
CEO AND CHIEF CREATIVE OFFICER

GIOVANNA T. OROZCO
VP OF OPERATIONS

CHRIS FERNANDEZ
PUBLISHER

CHRIS SANCHEZ
EDITOR-IN-CHIEF

CECILIA MEDINA
CHIEF FINANCIAL OFFICER

MANUEL CASTELLANOS
DIRECTOR OF SALES AND RETAILER
RELATIONS MANAGER

ALLISON POND
MARKETING DIRECTOR

MIGUEL ANGEL ZAPATA
DESIGN DIRECTOR

DIANA BERMÚDEZ
GRAPHIC DESIGNER

DAVID REYES
GRAPHIC DESIGNER

ADRIANA T. OROZCO
INTERACTIVE MEDIA
DESIGNER

NICOLÁS ZEA ARIAS
AUDIOVISUAL PRODUCTION

FRANK SILVA
EXECUTIVE ASSISTANT

STEPHANIE HIDALGO
EXECUTIVE ASSISTANT

Printed in Canada
ISBN: 978-1-952303-23-4

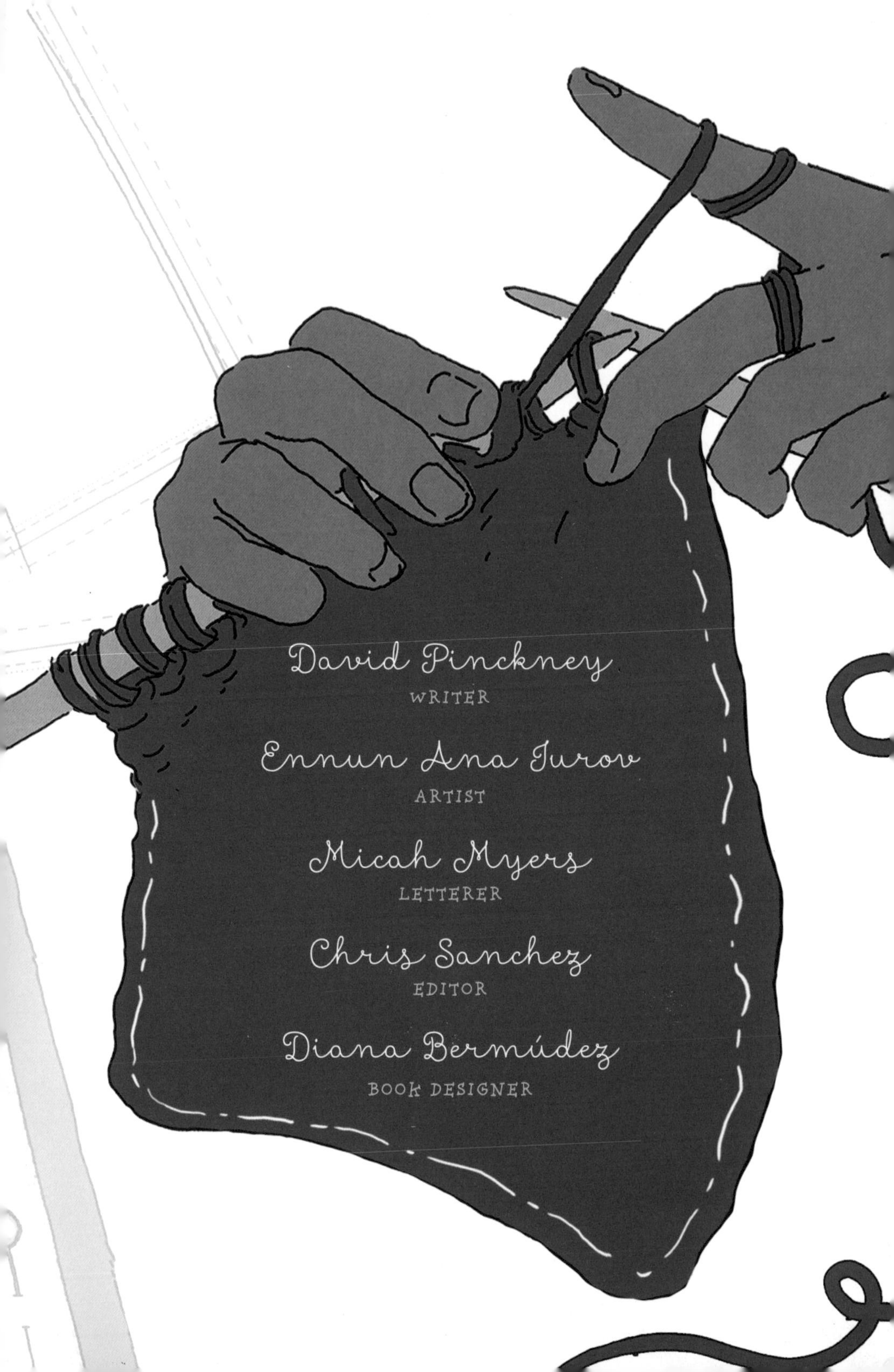

David Pinckney
WRITER

Ennun Ana Iurov
ARTIST

Micah Myers
LETTERER

Chris Sanchez
EDITOR

Diana Bermúdez
BOOK DESIGNER

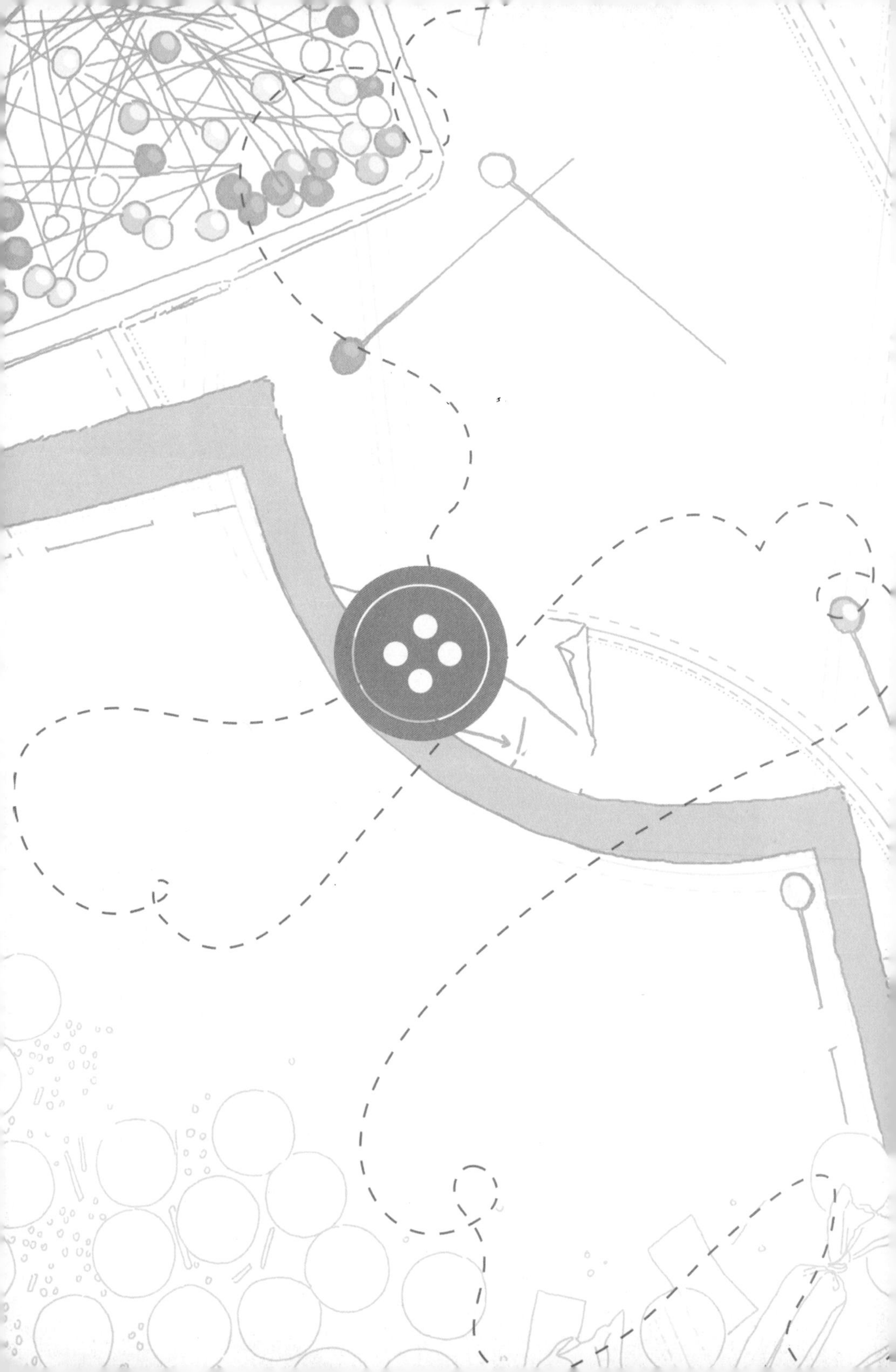

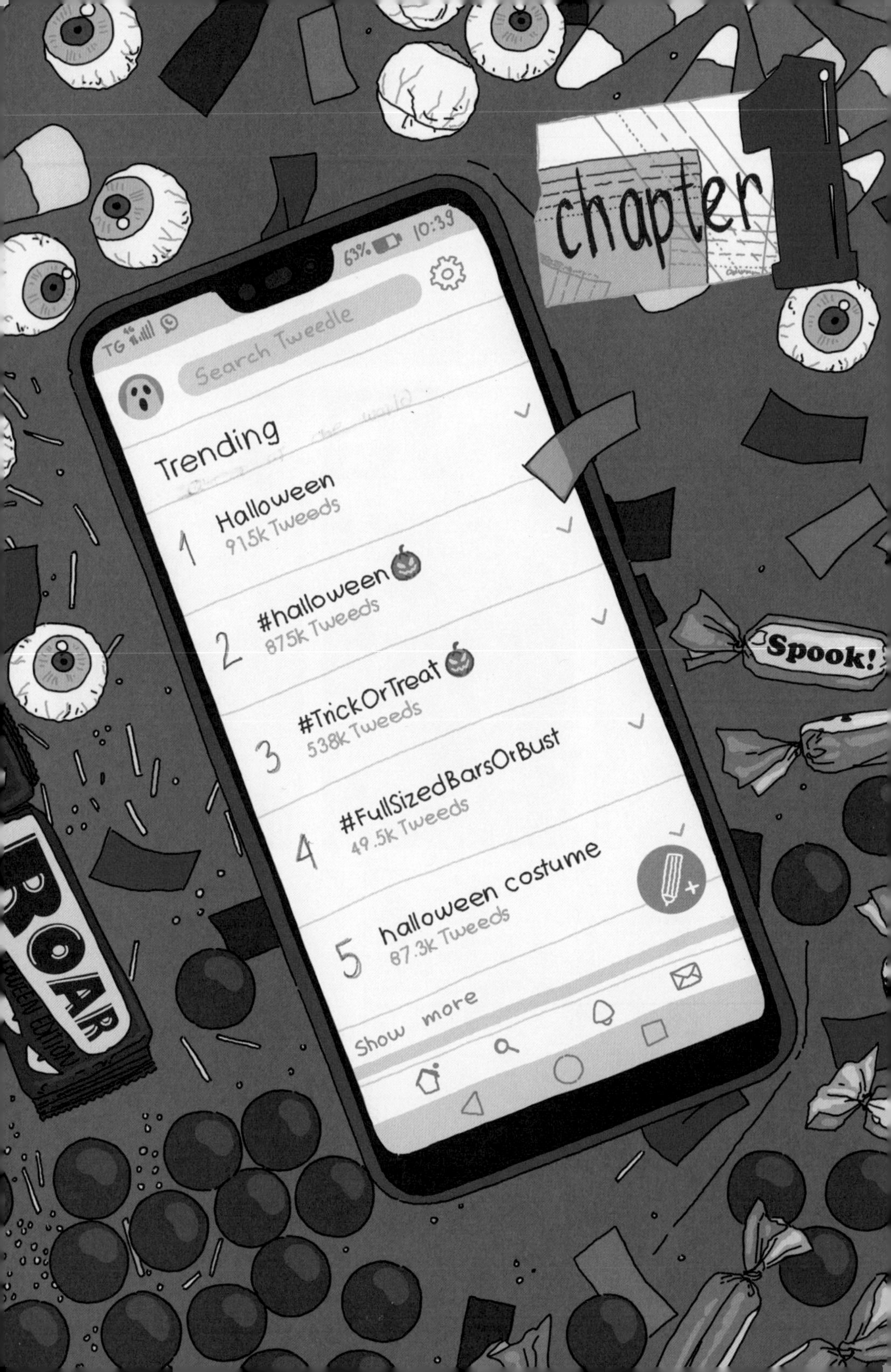
chapter 1
TG
63%
10:39
Search Tweedle
Trending
1 Halloween
915k Tweeds
2 #halloween
875k Tweeds
3 #TrickOrTreat
538k Tweeds
4 #FullSizedBarsOrBust
49.5k Tweeds
5 halloween costume
87.3k Tweeds
Show more
Spook!
BOAR

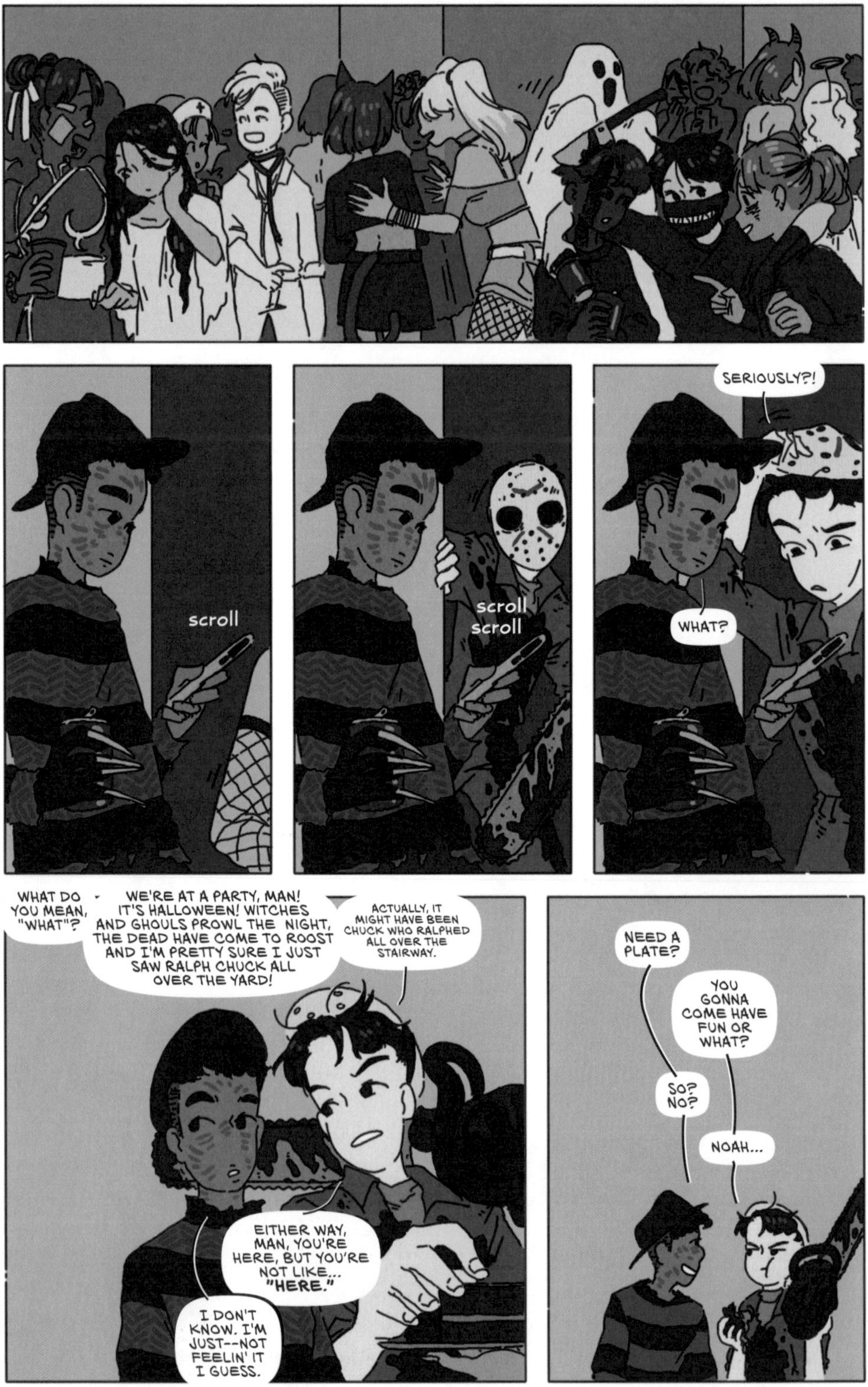

scroll
scroll
scroll
SERIOUSLY?!
WHAT?
WHAT DO YOU MEAN, "WHAT"?
WE'RE AT A PARTY, MAN! IT'S HALLOWEEN! WITCHES AND GHOULS PROWL THE NIGHT, THE DEAD HAVE COME TO ROOST AND I'M PRETTY SURE I JUST SAW RALPH CHUCK ALL OVER THE YARD!
ACTUALLY, IT MIGHT HAVE BEEN CHUCK WHO RALPHED ALL OVER THE STAIRWAY.
EITHER WAY, MAN, YOU'RE HERE, BUT YOU'RE NOT LIKE... **"HERE."**
I DON'T KNOW. I'M JUST--NOT FEELIN' IT I GUESS.
NEED A PLATE?
YOU GONNA COME HAVE FUN OR WHAT?
SO? NO?
NOAH...

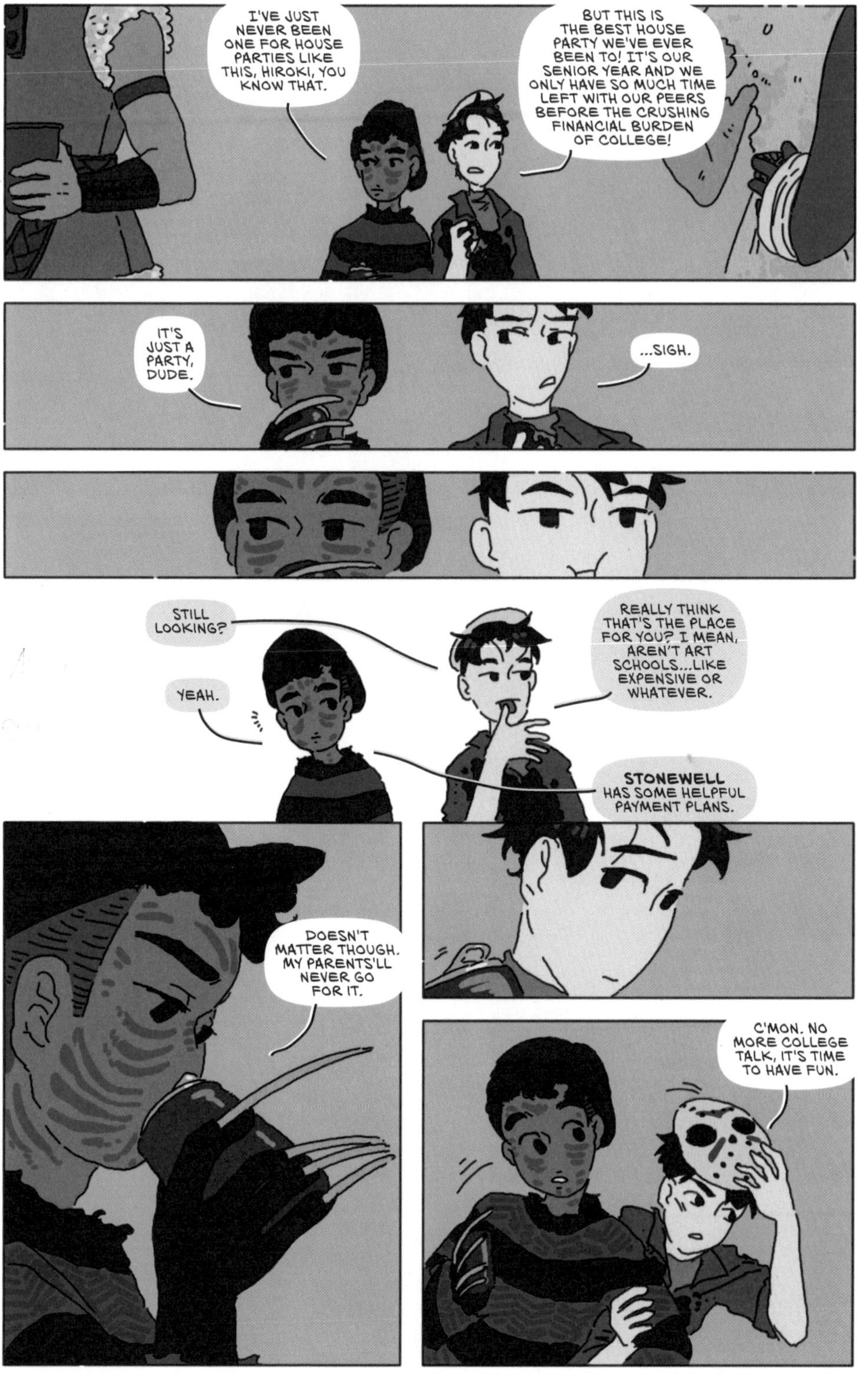
I'VE JUST NEVER BEEN ONE FOR HOUSE PARTIES LIKE THIS, HIROKI, YOU KNOW THAT.
BUT THIS IS THE BEST HOUSE PARTY WE'VE EVER BEEN TO! IT'S OUR SENIOR YEAR AND WE ONLY HAVE SO MUCH TIME LEFT WITH OUR PEERS BEFORE THE CRUSHING FINANCIAL BURDEN OF COLLEGE!
IT'S JUST A PARTY, DUDE.
...SIGH.
STILL LOOKING?
YEAH.
REALLY THINK THAT'S THE PLACE FOR YOU? I MEAN, AREN'T ART SCHOOLS...LIKE EXPENSIVE OR WHATEVER.
STONEWELL HAS SOME HELPFUL PAYMENT PLANS.
DOESN'T MATTER THOUGH. MY PARENTS'LL NEVER GO FOR IT.
C'MON. NO MORE COLLEGE TALK, IT'S TIME TO HAVE FUN.

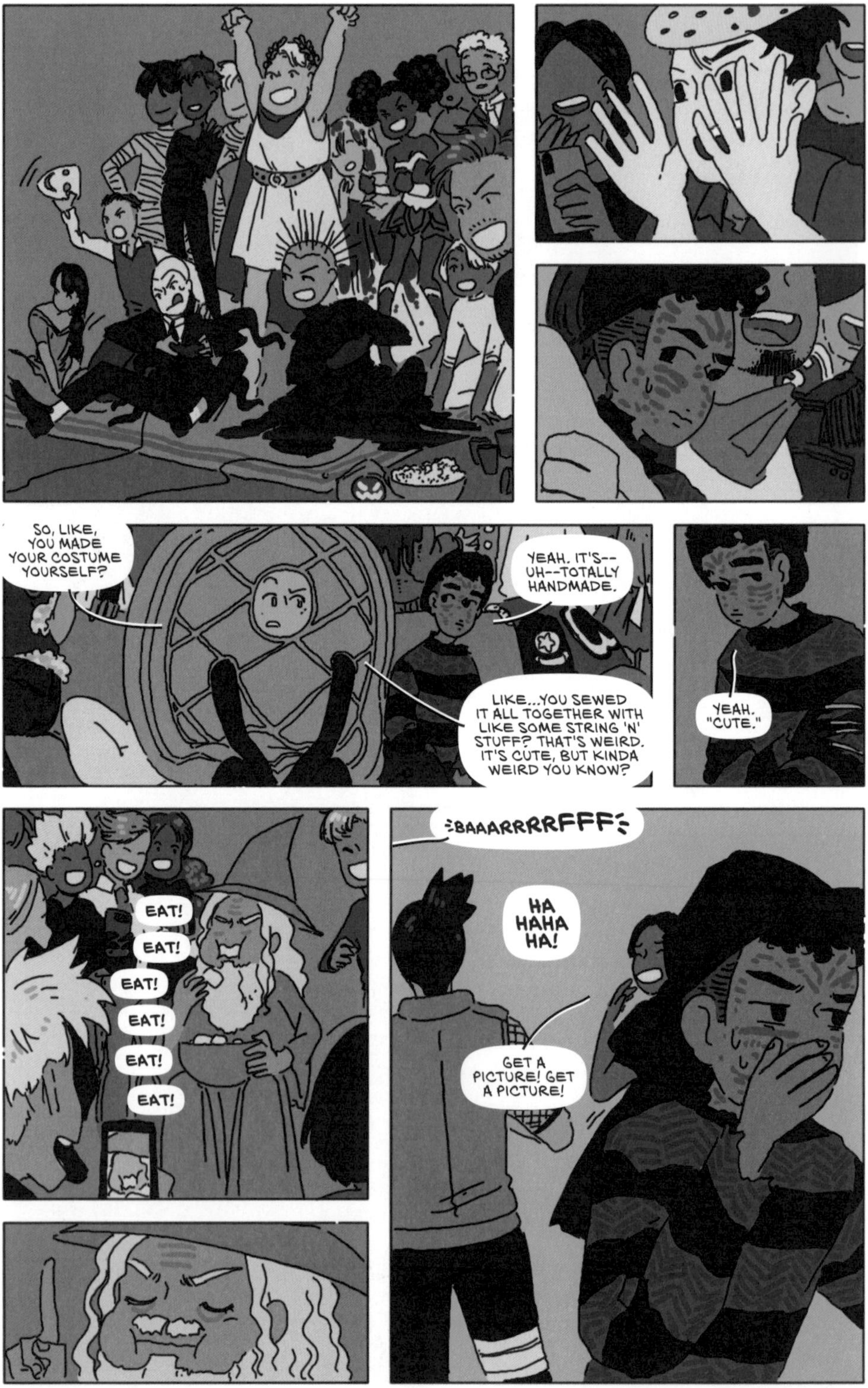
SO, LIKE, YOU MADE YOUR COSTUME YOURSELF?
YEAH. IT'S-- UH--TOTALLY HANDMADE.
LIKE...YOU SEWED IT ALL TOGETHER WITH LIKE SOME STRING 'N' STUFF? THAT'S WEIRD. IT'S CUTE, BUT KINDA WEIRD YOU KNOW?
YEAH. "CUTE."
EAT!
EAT!
EAT!
EAT!
EAT!
EAT!
BAAARRRRFFF
HA HAHA HA!
GET A PICTURE! GET A PICTURE!

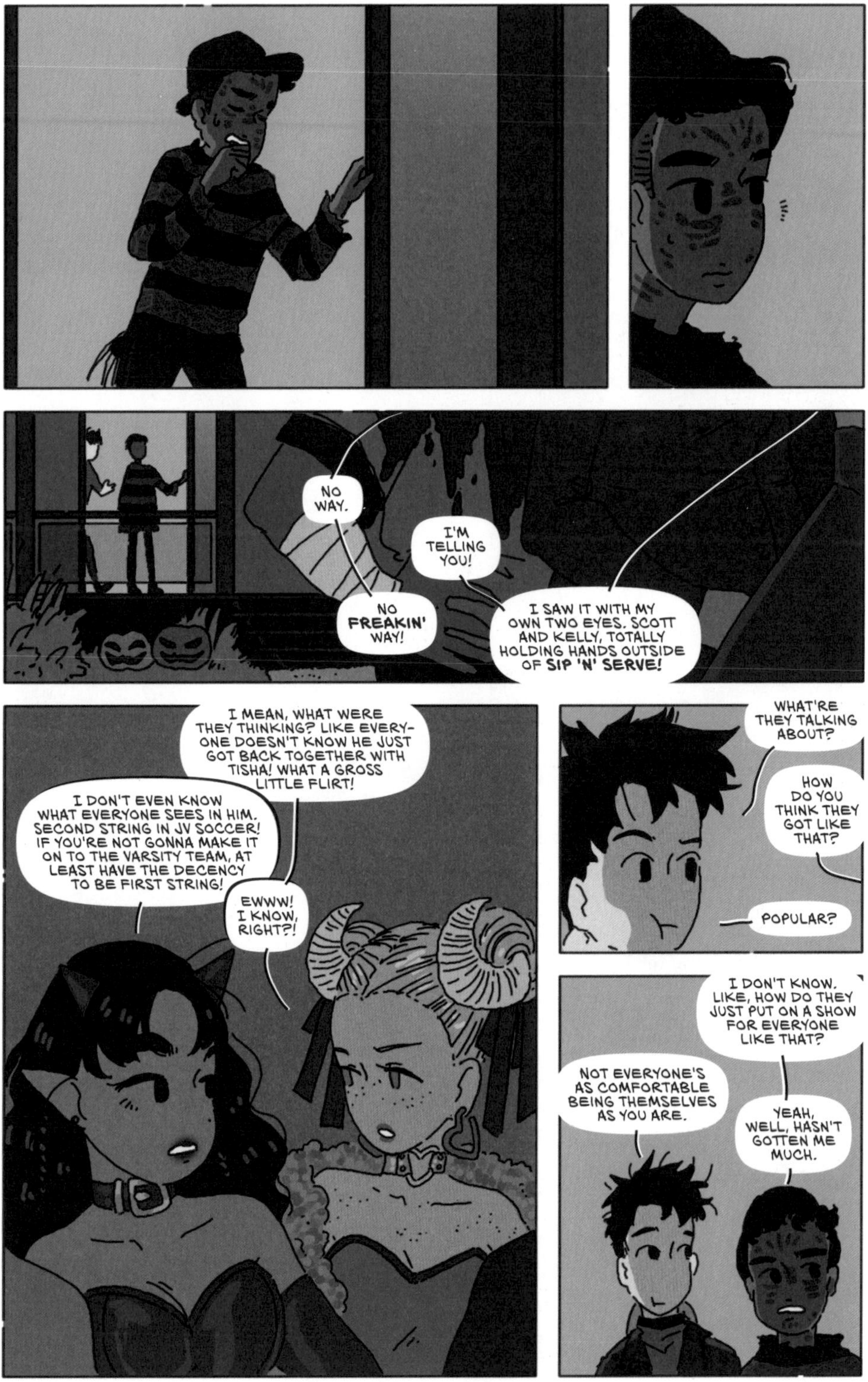
NO WAY.
I'M TELLING YOU!
NO **FREAKIN'** WAY!
I SAW IT WITH MY OWN TWO EYES. SCOTT AND KELLY, TOTALLY HOLDING HANDS OUTSIDE OF **SIP 'N' SERVE!**
I MEAN, WHAT WERE THEY THINKING? LIKE EVERY-ONE DOESN'T KNOW HE JUST GOT BACK TOGETHER WITH TISHA! WHAT A GROSS LITTLE FLIRT!
I DON'T EVEN KNOW WHAT EVERYONE SEES IN HIM. SECOND STRING IN JV SOCCER! IF YOU'RE NOT GONNA MAKE IT ON TO THE VARSITY TEAM, AT LEAST HAVE THE DECENCY TO BE FIRST STRING!
EWWW! I KNOW, RIGHT?!
WHAT'RE THEY TALKING ABOUT?
HOW DO YOU THINK THEY GOT LIKE THAT?
POPULAR?
I DON'T KNOW. LIKE, HOW DO THEY JUST PUT ON A SHOW FOR EVERYONE LIKE THAT?
NOT EVERYONE'S AS COMFORTABLE BEING THEMSELVES AS YOU ARE.
YEAH, WELL, HASN'T GOTTEN ME MUCH.

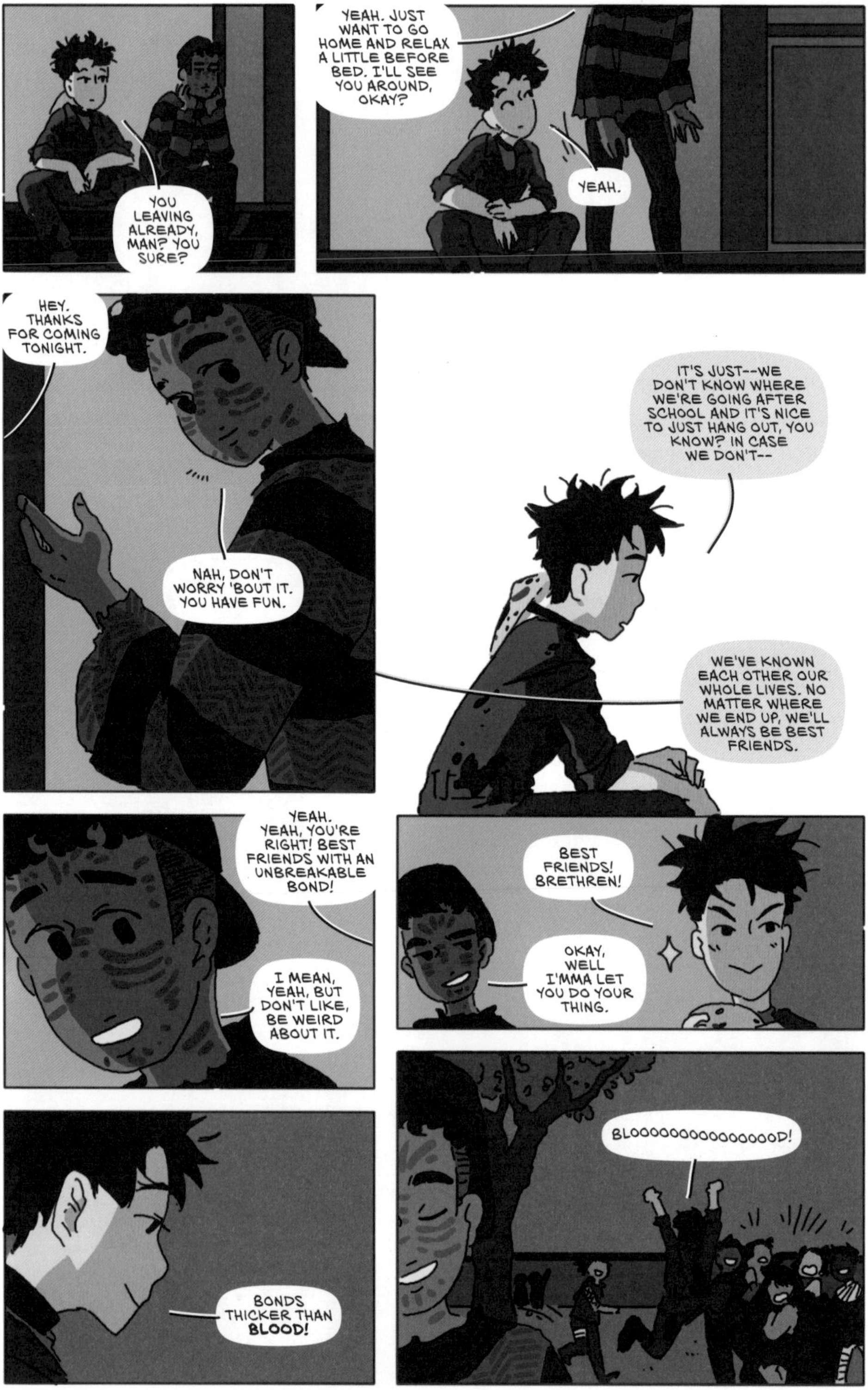
YOU LEAVING ALREADY, MAN? YOU SURE?
YEAH. JUST WANT TO GO HOME AND RELAX A LITTLE BEFORE BED. I'LL SEE YOU AROUND, OKAY?
YEAH.
HEY. THANKS FOR COMING TONIGHT.
NAH, DON'T WORRY 'BOUT IT. YOU HAVE FUN.
IT'S JUST--WE DON'T KNOW WHERE WE'RE GOING AFTER SCHOOL AND IT'S NICE TO JUST HANG OUT, YOU KNOW? IN CASE WE DON'T--
WE'VE KNOWN EACH OTHER OUR WHOLE LIVES. NO MATTER WHERE WE END UP, WE'LL ALWAYS BE BEST FRIENDS.
YEAH. YEAH, YOU'RE RIGHT! BEST FRIENDS WITH AN UNBREAKABLE BOND!
I MEAN, YEAH, BUT DON'T LIKE, BE WEIRD ABOUT IT.
BEST FRIENDS! BRETHREN!
OKAY, WELL I'MMA LET YOU DO YOUR THING.
BONDS THICKER THAN **BLOOD!**
BLOOOOOOOOOOOOOOOD!

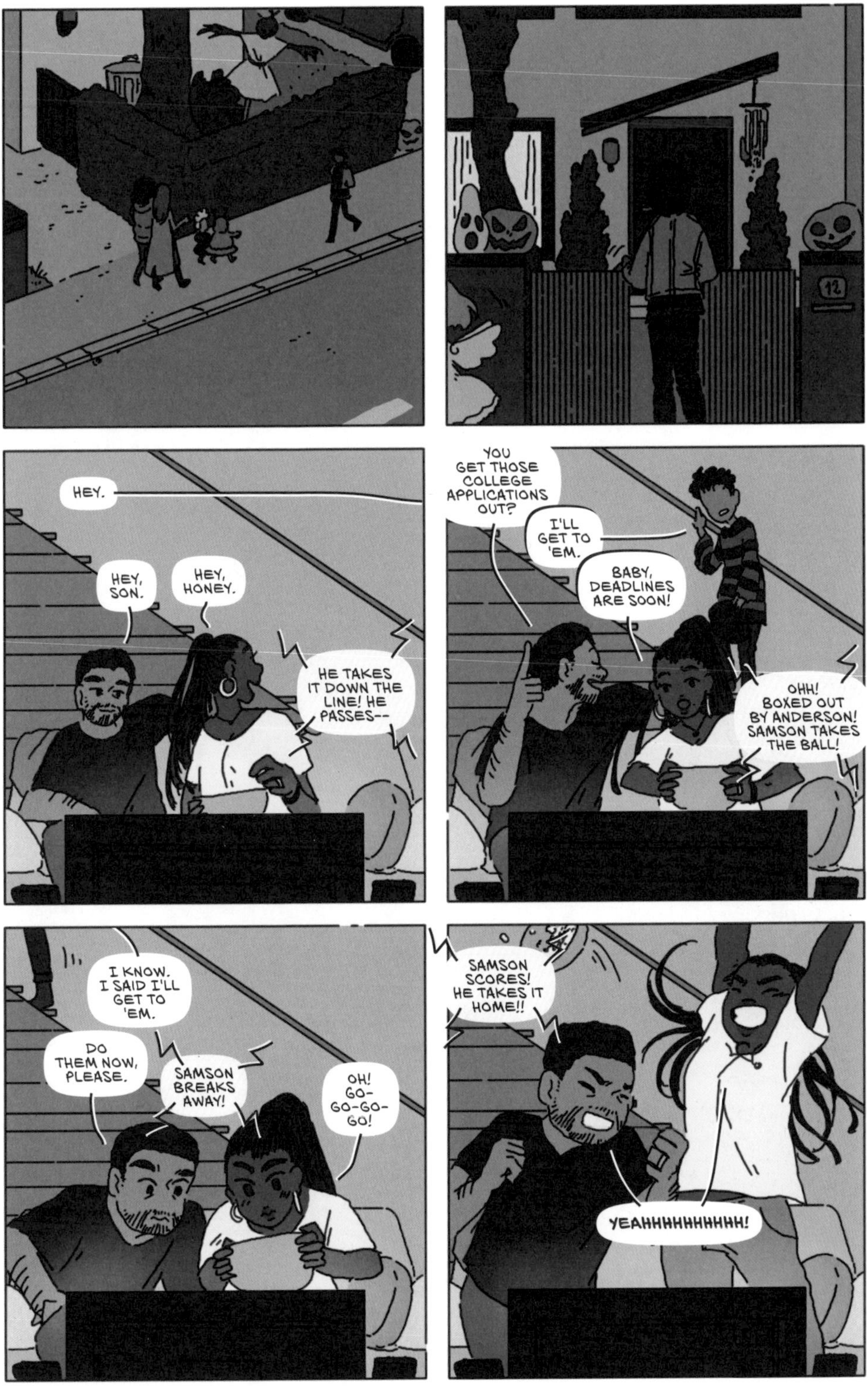
12
HEY.
HEY, SON.
HEY, HONEY.
HE TAKES IT DOWN THE LINE! HE PASSES--
YOU GET THOSE COLLEGE APPLICATIONS OUT?
I'LL GET TO 'EM.
BABY, DEADLINES ARE SOON!
OHH! BOXED OUT BY ANDERSON! SAMSON TAKES THE BALL!
I KNOW. I SAID I'LL GET TO 'EM.
DO THEM NOW, PLEASE.
SAMSON BREAKS AWAY!
OH! GO-GO-GO-GO!
SAMSON SCORES! HE TAKES IT HOME!!
YEAHHHHHHHHHH!

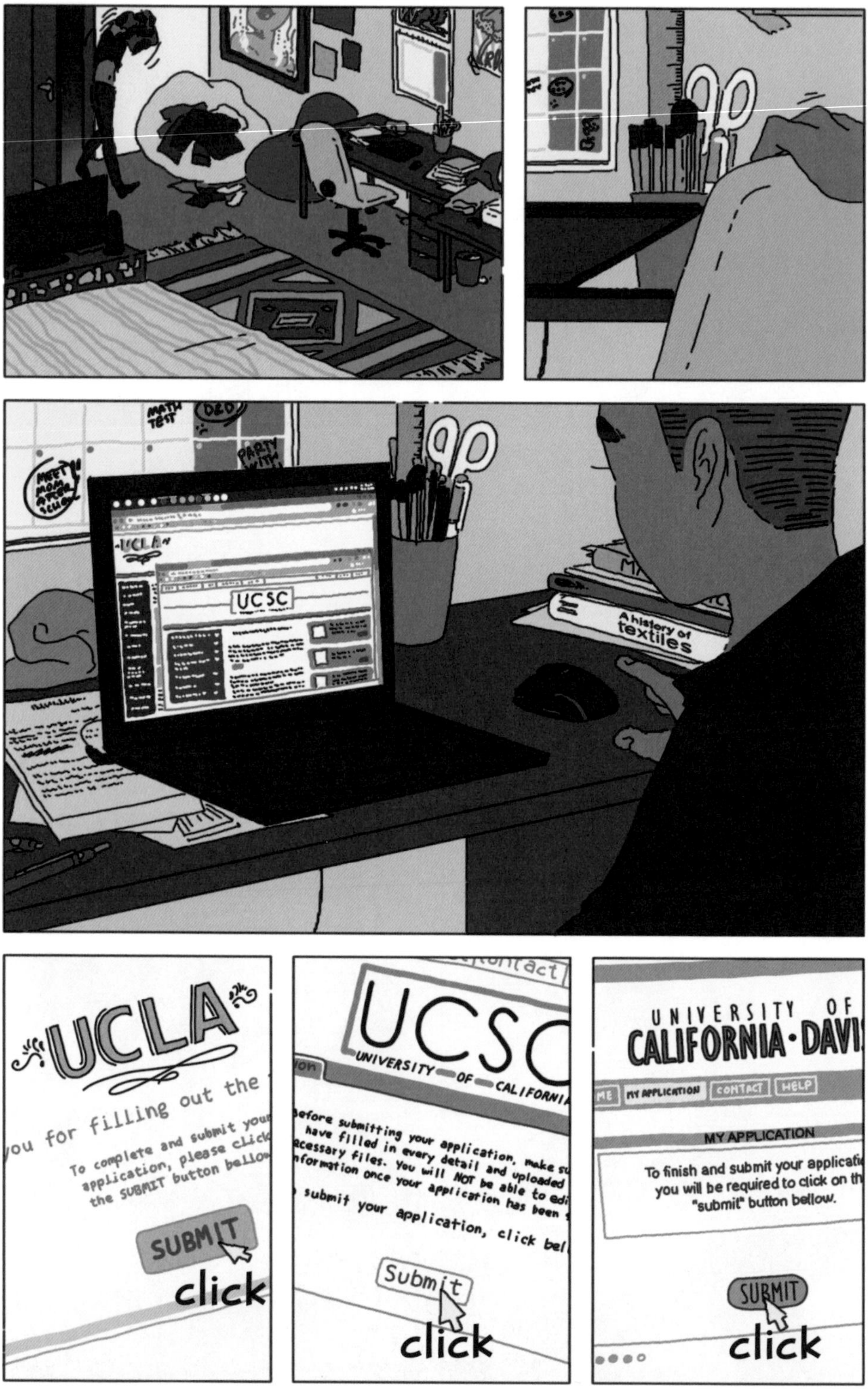
MATH TEST
D&D
PARTY WITH
UCLA
UCSC
A history of textiles
UCLA
you for filling out the
To complete and submit your
application, please click
the SUBMIT button bellow
SUBMIT
click
contact
UCSC
UNIVERSITY OF CALIFORNIA
Before submitting your application, make su
have filled in every detail and uploaded
necessary files. You will NOT be able to edi
information once your application has been
submit your application, click bel
Submit
click
UNIVERSITY OF
CALIFORNIA · DAVIS
ME
MY APPLICATION
CONTACT
HELP
MY APPLICATION
To finish and submit your applicati
you will be required to click on th
"submit" button bellow.
SUBMIT
click

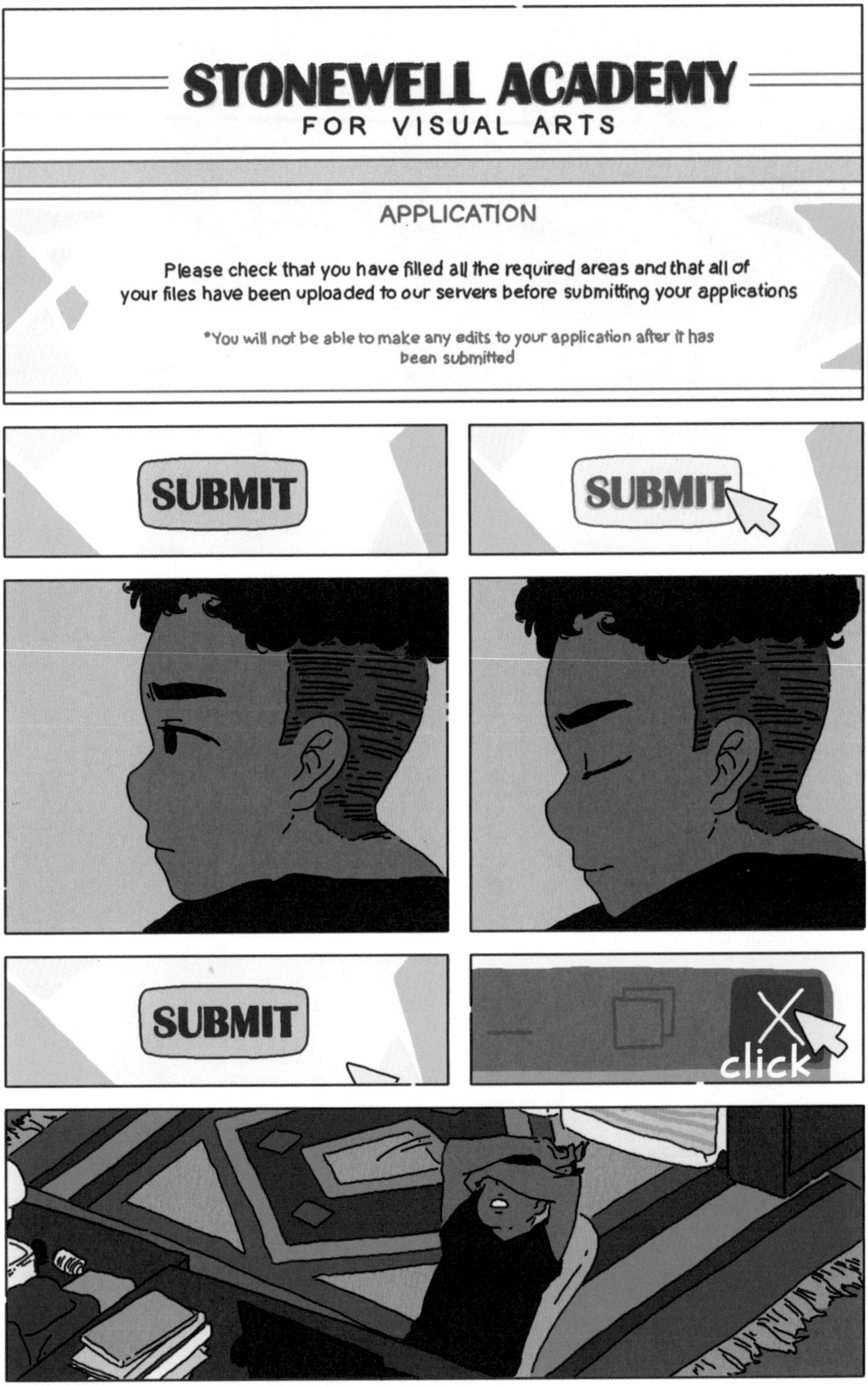
STONEWELL ACADEMY
FOR VISUAL ARTS
APPLICATION
Please check that you have filled all the required areas and that all of your files have been uploaded to our servers before submitting your applications
*You will not be able to make any edits to your application after it has been submitted
SUBMIT
SUBMIT
SUBMIT
click

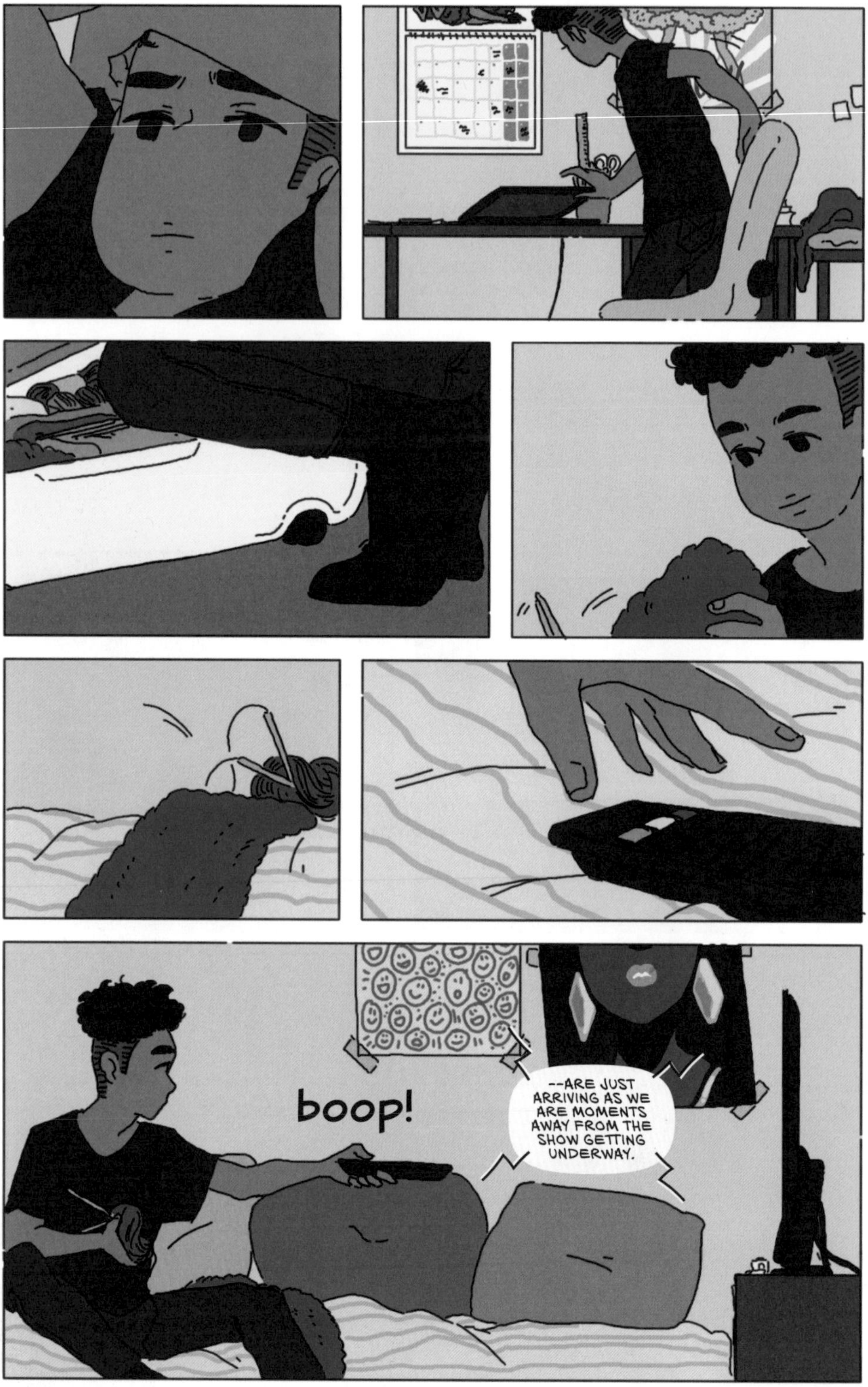
boop!
--ARE JUST ARRIVING AS WE ARE MOMENTS AWAY FROM THE SHOW GETTING UNDERWAY.

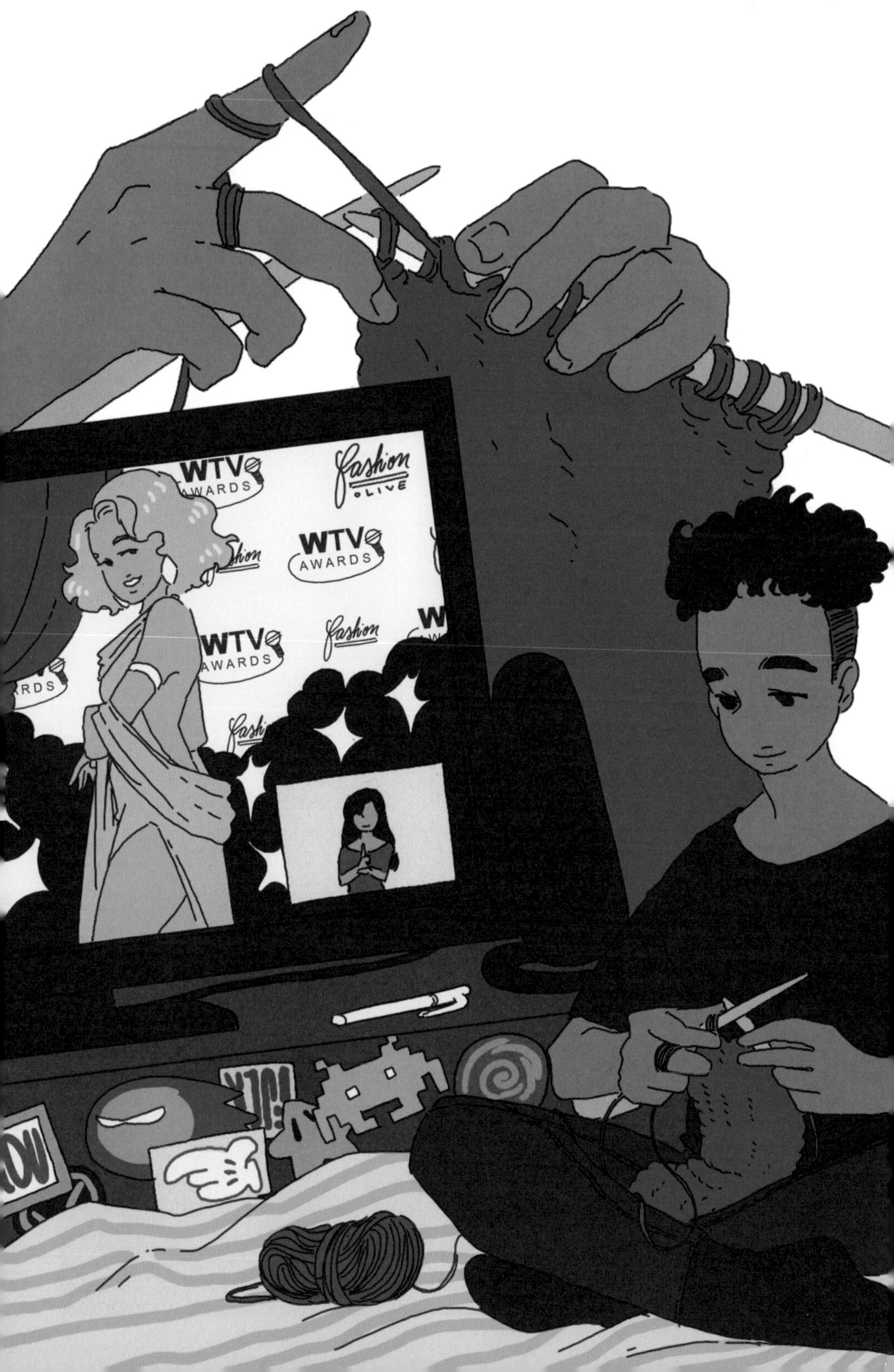
WTV AWARDS
fashion LIVE
WTV AWARDS
WTV AWARDS

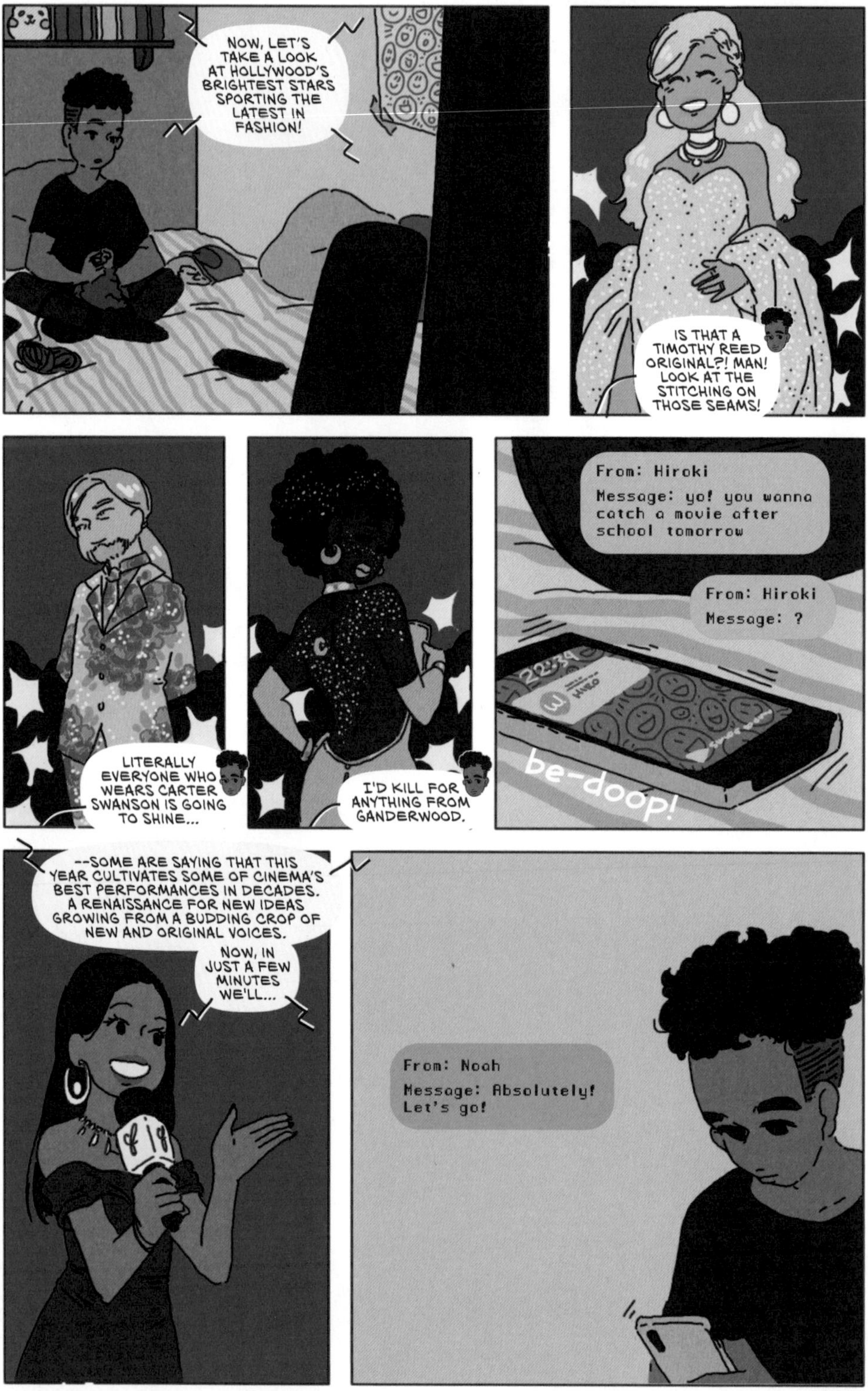
NOW, LET'S TAKE A LOOK AT HOLLYWOOD'S BRIGHTEST STARS SPORTING THE LATEST IN FASHION!
IS THAT A TIMOTHY REED ORIGINAL?! MAN! LOOK AT THE STITCHING ON THOSE SEAMS!
LITERALLY EVERYONE WHO WEARS CARTER SWANSON IS GOING TO SHINE...
I'D KILL FOR ANYTHING FROM GANDERWOOD.
From: Hiroki
Message: yo! you wanna catch a movie after school tomorrow
From: Hiroki
Message: ?
be-doop!
--SOME ARE SAYING THAT THIS YEAR CULTIVATES SOME OF CINEMA'S BEST PERFORMANCES IN DECADES. A RENAISSANCE FOR NEW IDEAS GROWING FROM A BUDDING CROP OF NEW AND ORIGINAL VOICES.
NOW, IN JUST A FEW MINUTES WE'LL...
From: Noah
Message: Absolutely! Let's go!

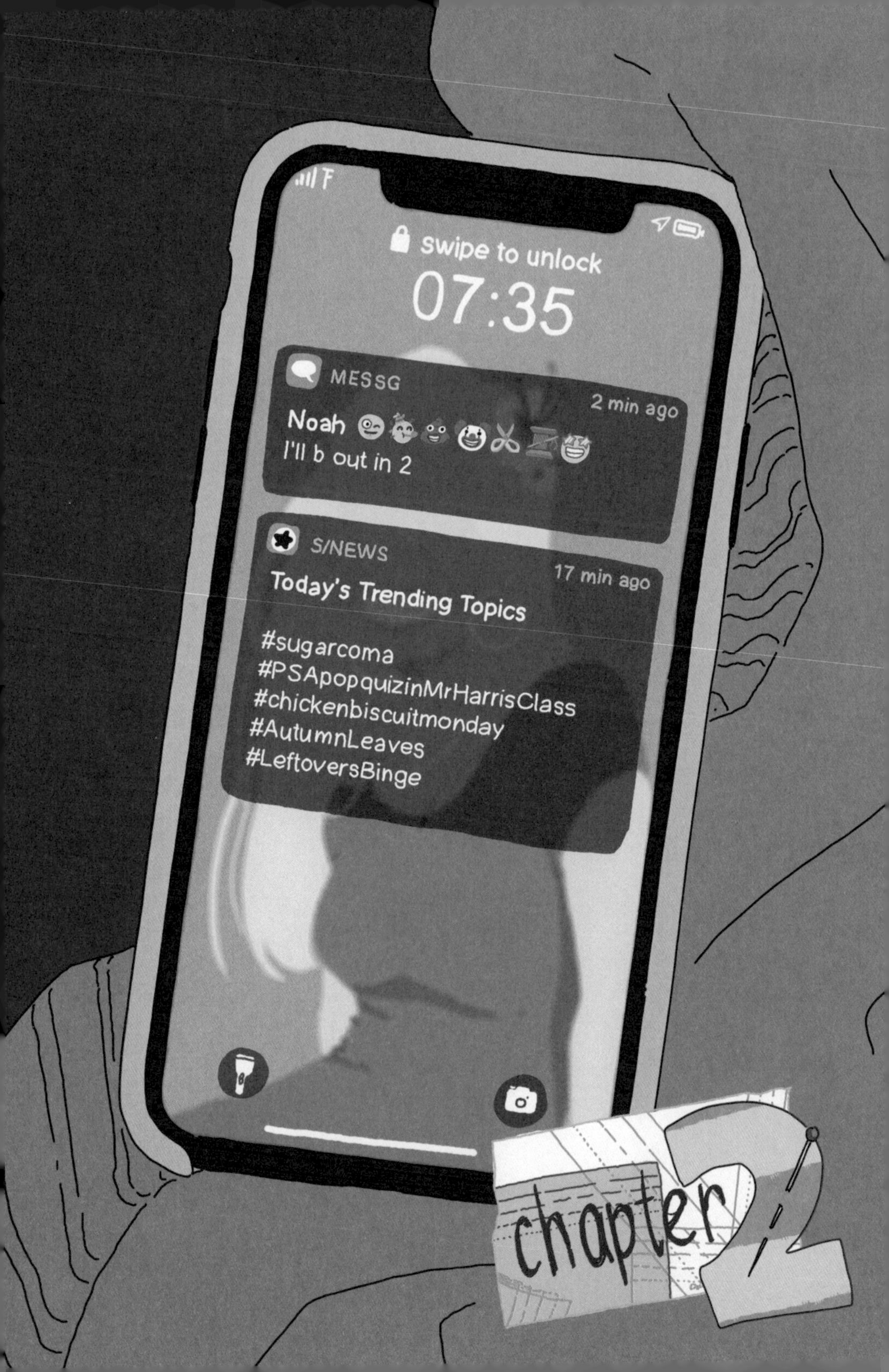
swipe to unlock
07:35
MESSG
2 min ago
Noah
I'll b out in 2
S/NEWS
17 min ago
Today's Trending Topics
#sugarcoma
#PSApopquizinMrHarrisClass
#chickenbiscuitmonday
#AutumnLeaves
#LeftoversBinge
chapter 2

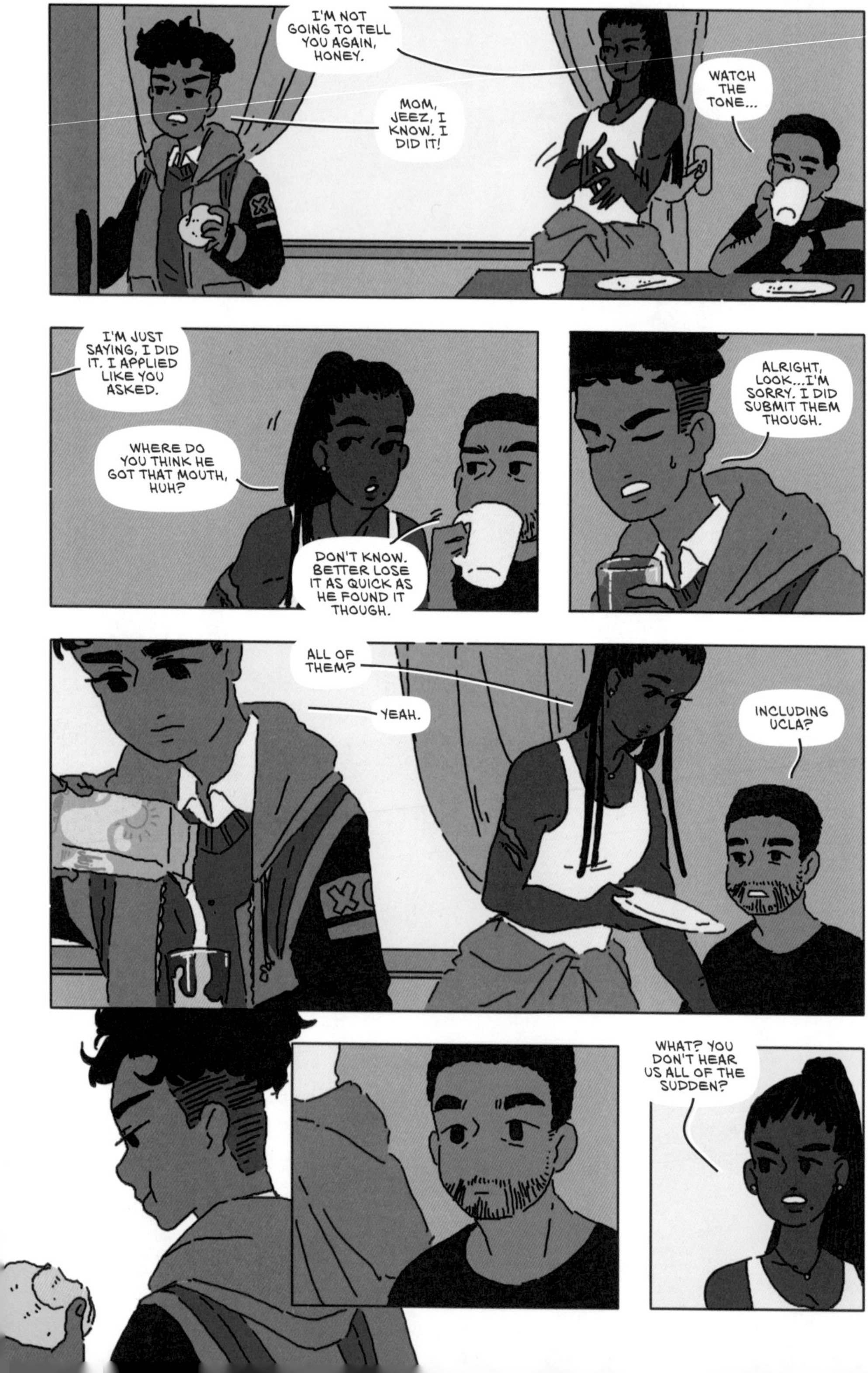
I'M NOT GOING TO TELL YOU AGAIN, HONEY.
MOM, JEEZ, I KNOW. I DID IT!
WATCH THE TONE...
I'M JUST SAYING, I DID IT. I APPLIED LIKE YOU ASKED.
WHERE DO YOU THINK HE GOT THAT MOUTH, HUH?
DON'T KNOW. BETTER LOSE IT AS QUICK AS HE FOUND IT THOUGH.
ALRIGHT, LOOK...I'M SORRY. I DID SUBMIT THEM THOUGH.
ALL OF THEM?
YEAH.
INCLUDING UCLA?
WHAT? YOU DON'T HEAR US ALL OF THE SUDDEN?

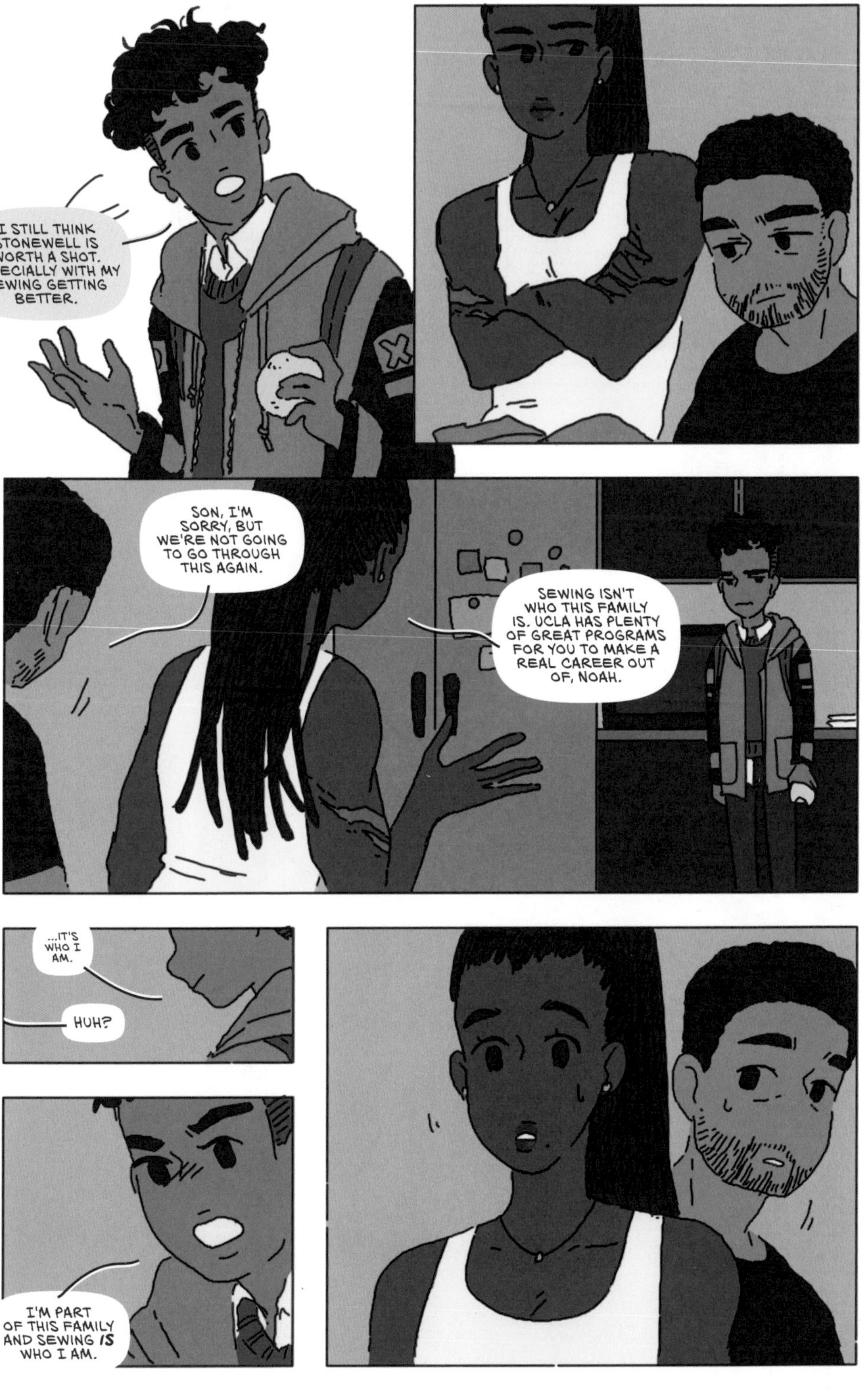
I STILL THINK STONEWELL IS WORTH A SHOT. ESPECIALLY WITH MY SEWING GETTING BETTER.
SON, I'M SORRY, BUT WE'RE NOT GOING TO GO THROUGH THIS AGAIN.
SEWING ISN'T WHO THIS FAMILY IS. UCLA HAS PLENTY OF GREAT PROGRAMS FOR YOU TO MAKE A REAL CAREER OUT OF, NOAH.
...IT'S WHO I AM.
HUH?
I'M PART OF THIS FAMILY AND SEWING *IS* WHO I AM.

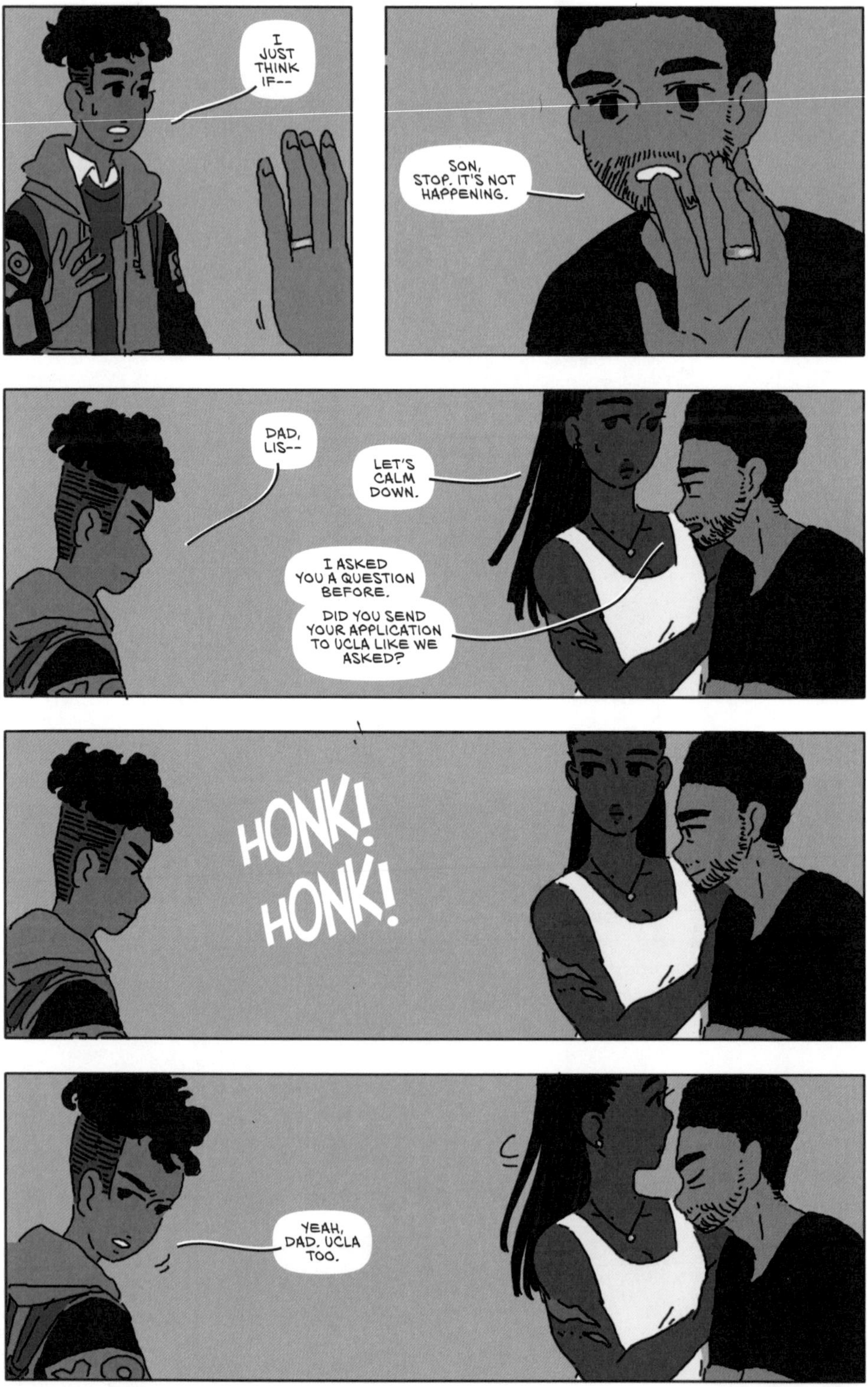
I JUST THINK IF--
SON, STOP. IT'S NOT HAPPENING.
DAD, LIS--
LET'S CALM DOWN.
I ASKED YOU A QUESTION BEFORE.
DID YOU SEND YOUR APPLICATION TO UCLA LIKE WE ASKED?
HONK! HONK!
YEAH, DAD. UCLA TOO.

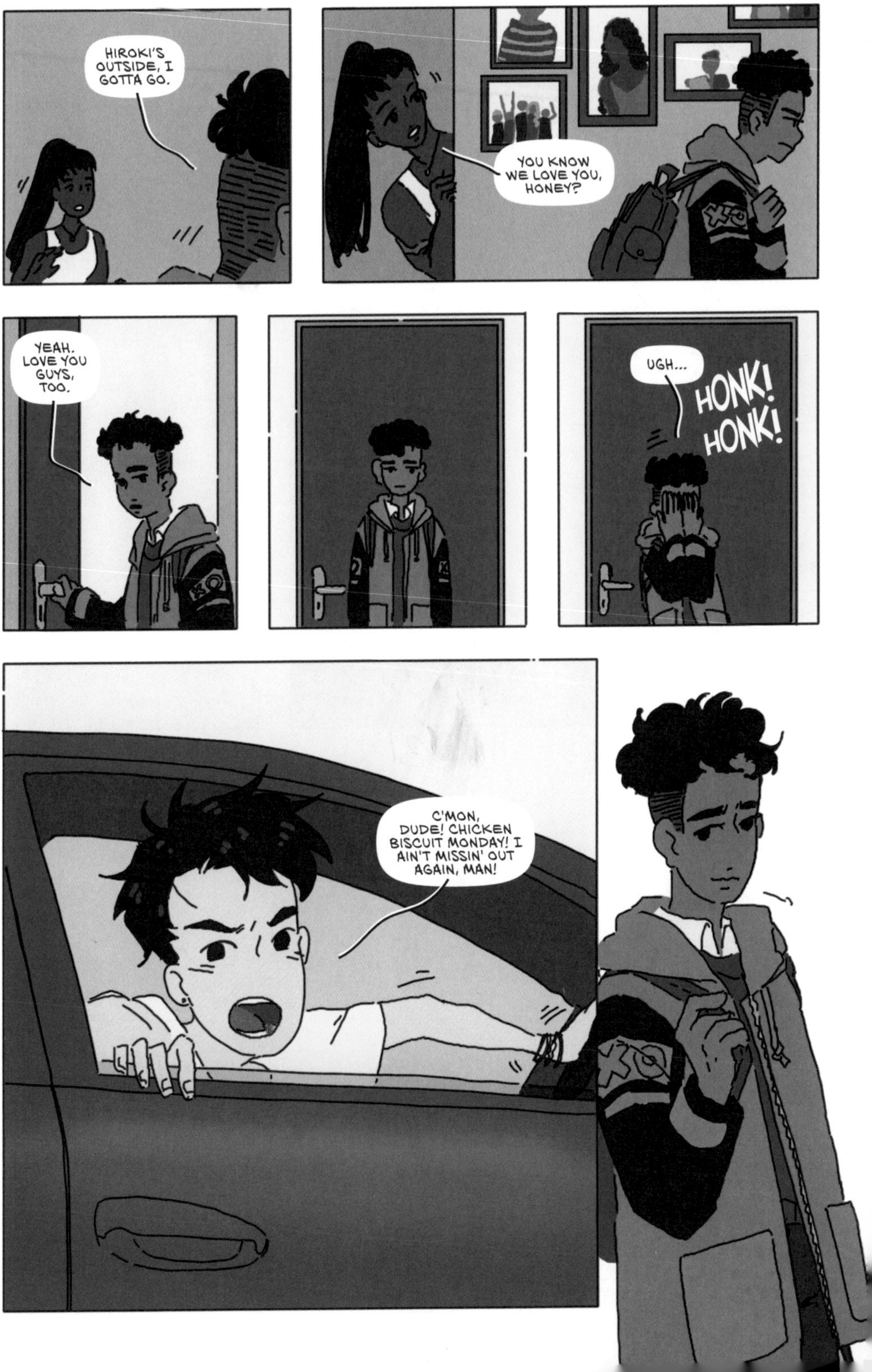

HIROKI'S OUTSIDE, I GOTTA GO.
YOU KNOW WE LOVE YOU, HONEY?
YEAH. LOVE YOU GUYS, TOO.
UGH...
HONK! HONK!
C'MON, DUDE! CHICKEN BISCUIT MONDAY! I AIN'T MISSIN' OUT AGAIN, MAN!

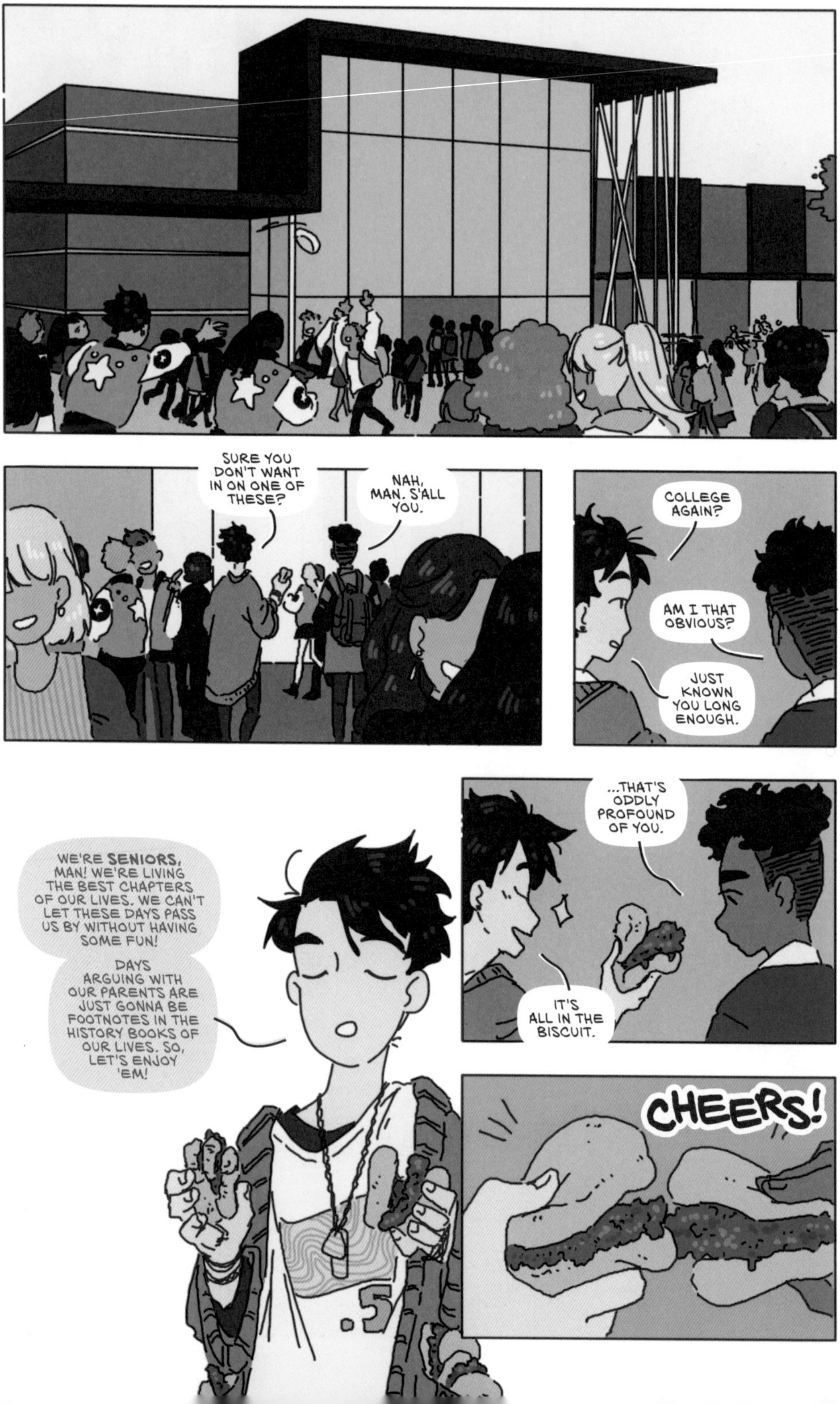
SURE YOU DON'T WANT IN ON ONE OF THESE?
NAH, MAN. S'ALL YOU.
COLLEGE AGAIN?
AM I THAT OBVIOUS?
JUST KNOWN YOU LONG ENOUGH.
WE'RE SENIORS, MAN! WE'RE LIVING THE BEST CHAPTERS OF OUR LIVES. WE CAN'T LET THESE DAYS PASS US BY WITHOUT HAVING SOME FUN!
DAYS ARGUING WITH OUR PARENTS ARE JUST GONNA BE FOOTNOTES IN THE HISTORY BOOKS OF OUR LIVES. SO, LET'S ENJOY 'EM!
...THAT'S ODDLY PROFOUND OF YOU.
IT'S ALL IN THE BISCUIT.
CHEERS!

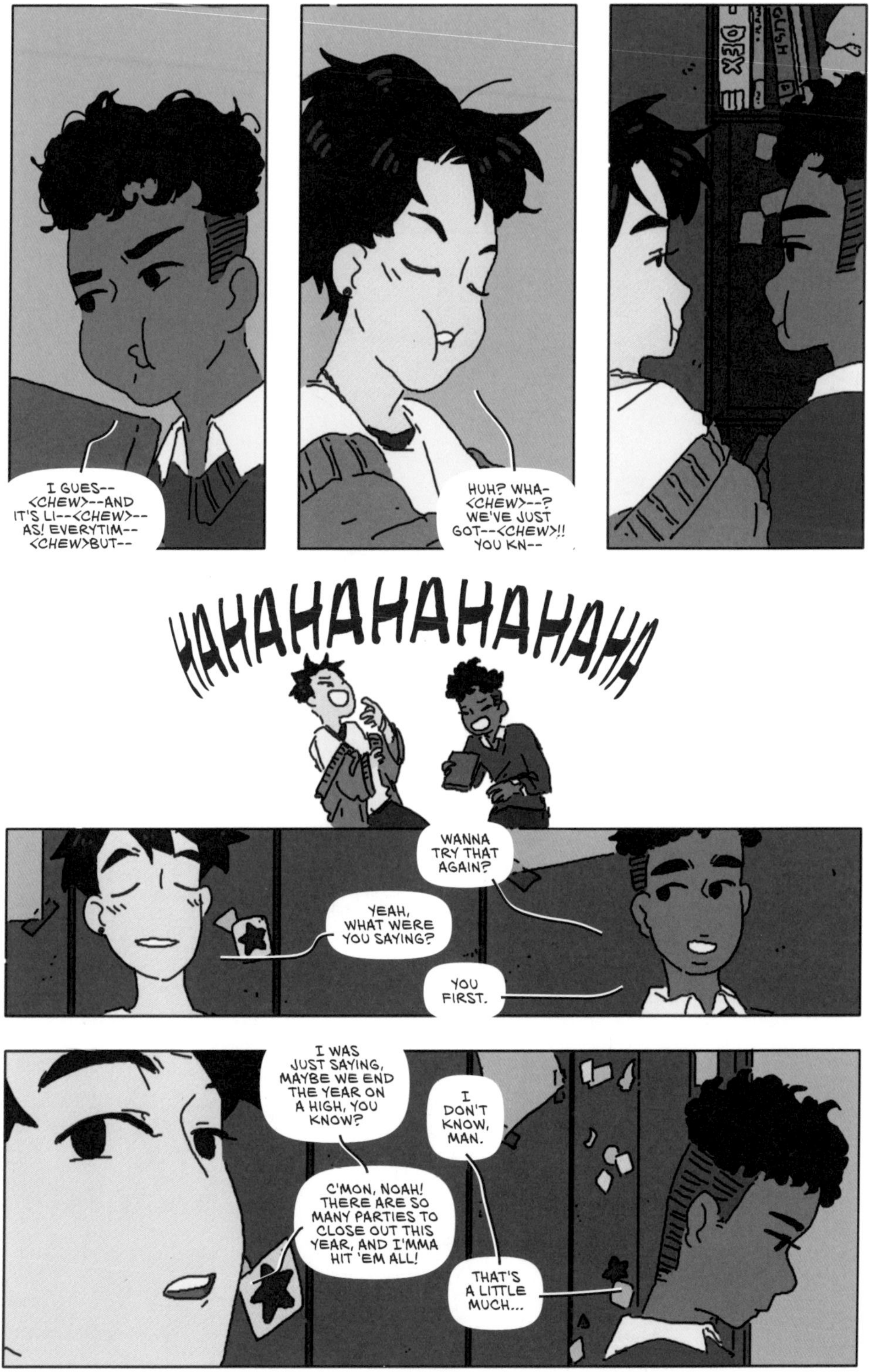

I GUES-- <CHEW>--AND IT'S LI--<CHEW>-- AS! EVERYTIM-- <CHEW>BUT--
HUH? WHA- <CHEW>--? WE'VE JUST GOT--<CHEW>!! YOU KN--
HAHAHAHAHAHAHAHA
WANNA TRY THAT AGAIN?
YEAH, WHAT WERE YOU SAYING?
YOU FIRST.
I WAS JUST SAYING, MAYBE WE END THE YEAR ON A HIGH, YOU KNOW?
I DON'T KNOW, MAN.
C'MON, NOAH! THERE ARE SO MANY PARTIES TO CLOSE OUT THIS YEAR, AND I'MMA HIT 'EM ALL!
THAT'S A LITTLE MUCH...

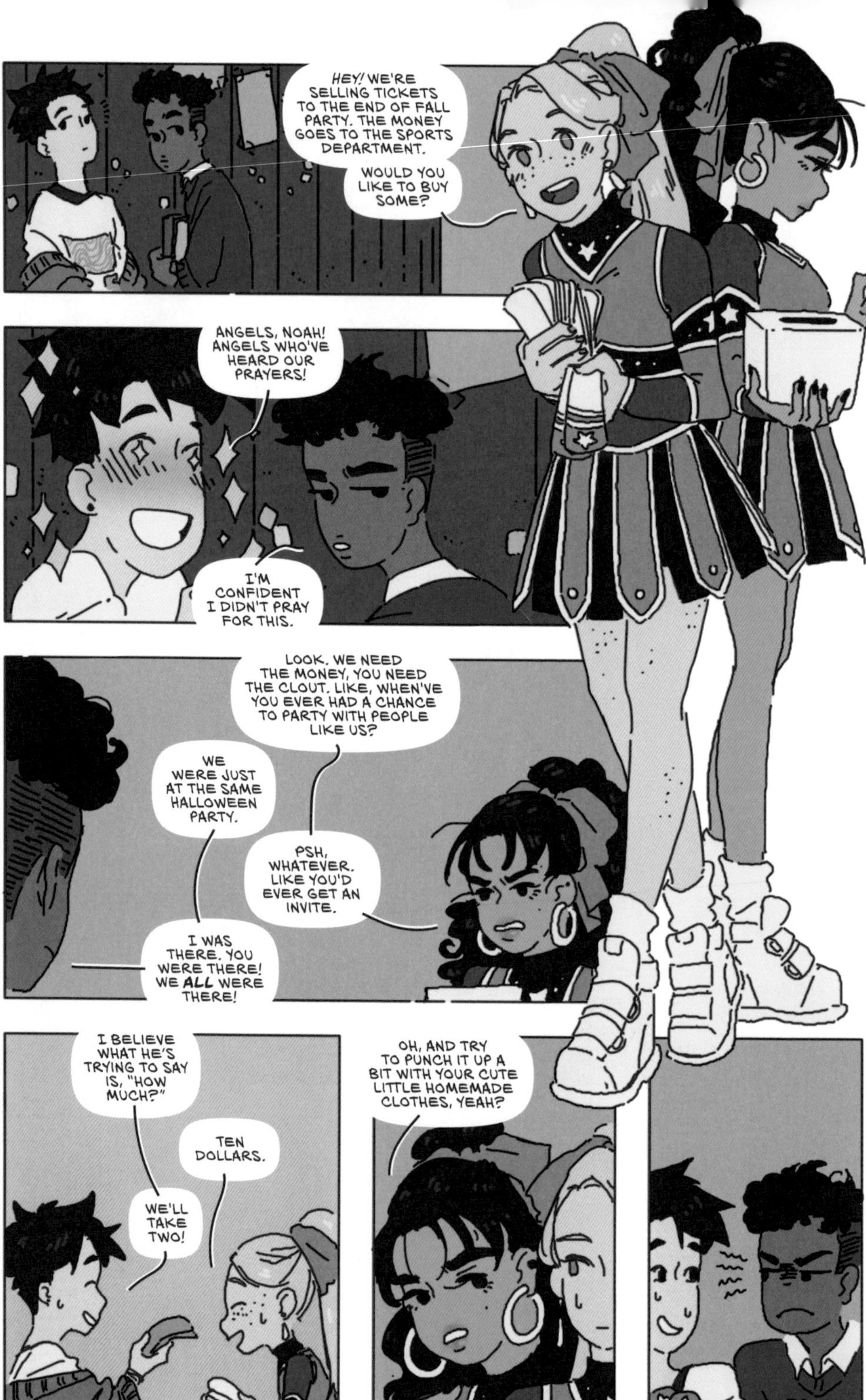
HEY! WE'RE SELLING TICKETS TO THE END OF FALL PARTY. THE MONEY GOES TO THE SPORTS DEPARTMENT.
WOULD YOU LIKE TO BUY SOME?
ANGELS, NOAH! ANGELS WHO'VE HEARD OUR PRAYERS!
I'M CONFIDENT I DIDN'T PRAY FOR THIS.
LOOK. WE NEED THE MONEY, YOU NEED THE CLOUT. LIKE, WHEN'VE YOU EVER HAD A CHANCE TO PARTY WITH PEOPLE LIKE US?
WE WERE JUST AT THE SAME HALLOWEEN PARTY.
PSH, WHATEVER. LIKE YOU'D EVER GET AN INVITE.
I WAS THERE. YOU WERE THERE! WE **ALL** WERE THERE!
I BELIEVE WHAT HE'S TRYING TO SAY IS, "HOW MUCH?"
TEN DOLLARS.
WE'LL TAKE TWO!
OH, AND TRY TO PUNCH IT UP A BIT WITH YOUR CUTE LITTLE HOMEMADE CLOTHES, YEAH?

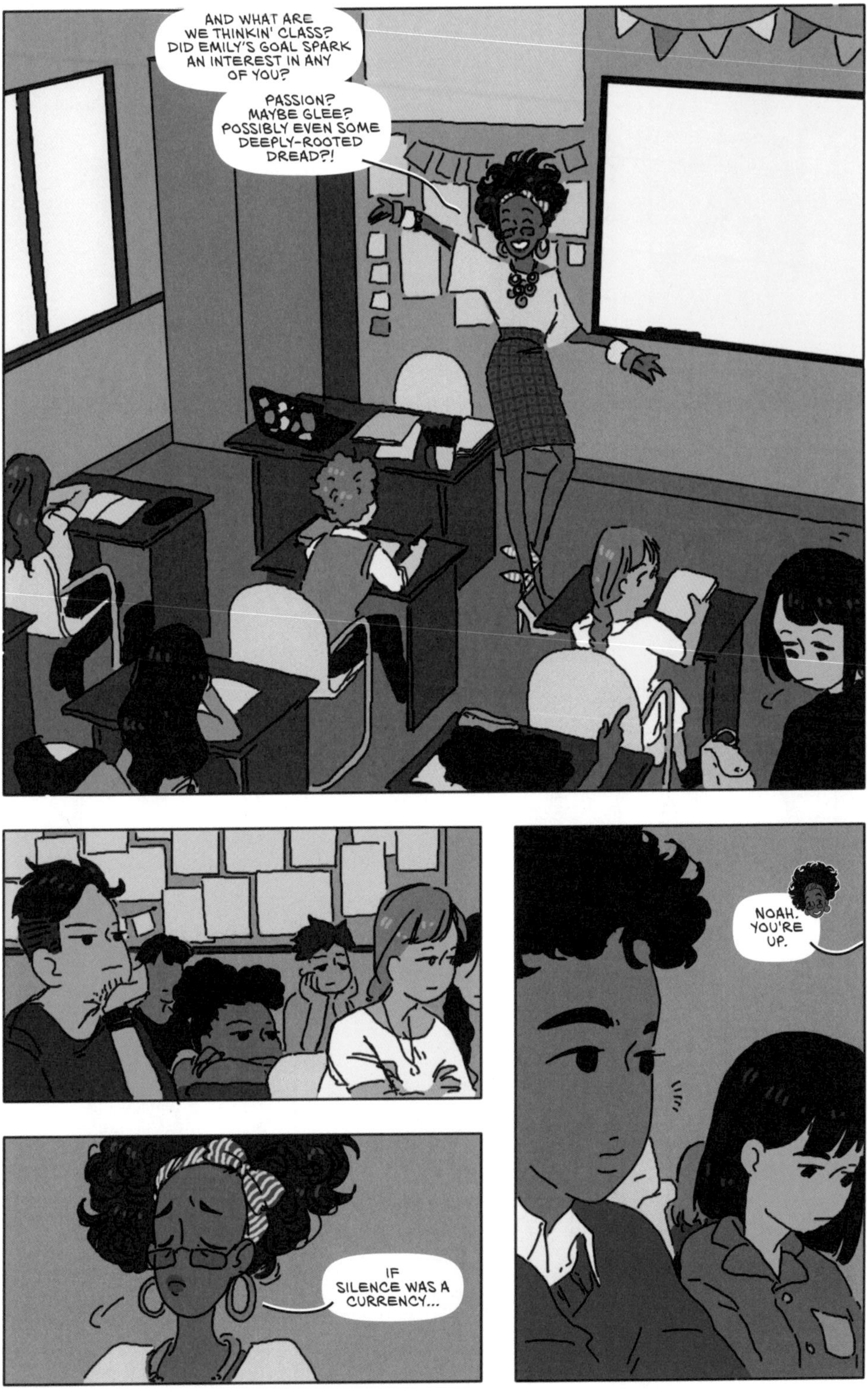
AND WHAT ARE WE THINKIN' CLASS? DID EMILY'S GOAL SPARK AN INTEREST IN ANY OF YOU?
PASSION? MAYBE GLEE? POSSIBLY EVEN SOME DEEPLY-ROOTED DREAD?!
IF SILENCE WAS A CURRENCY...
NOAH. YOU'RE UP.

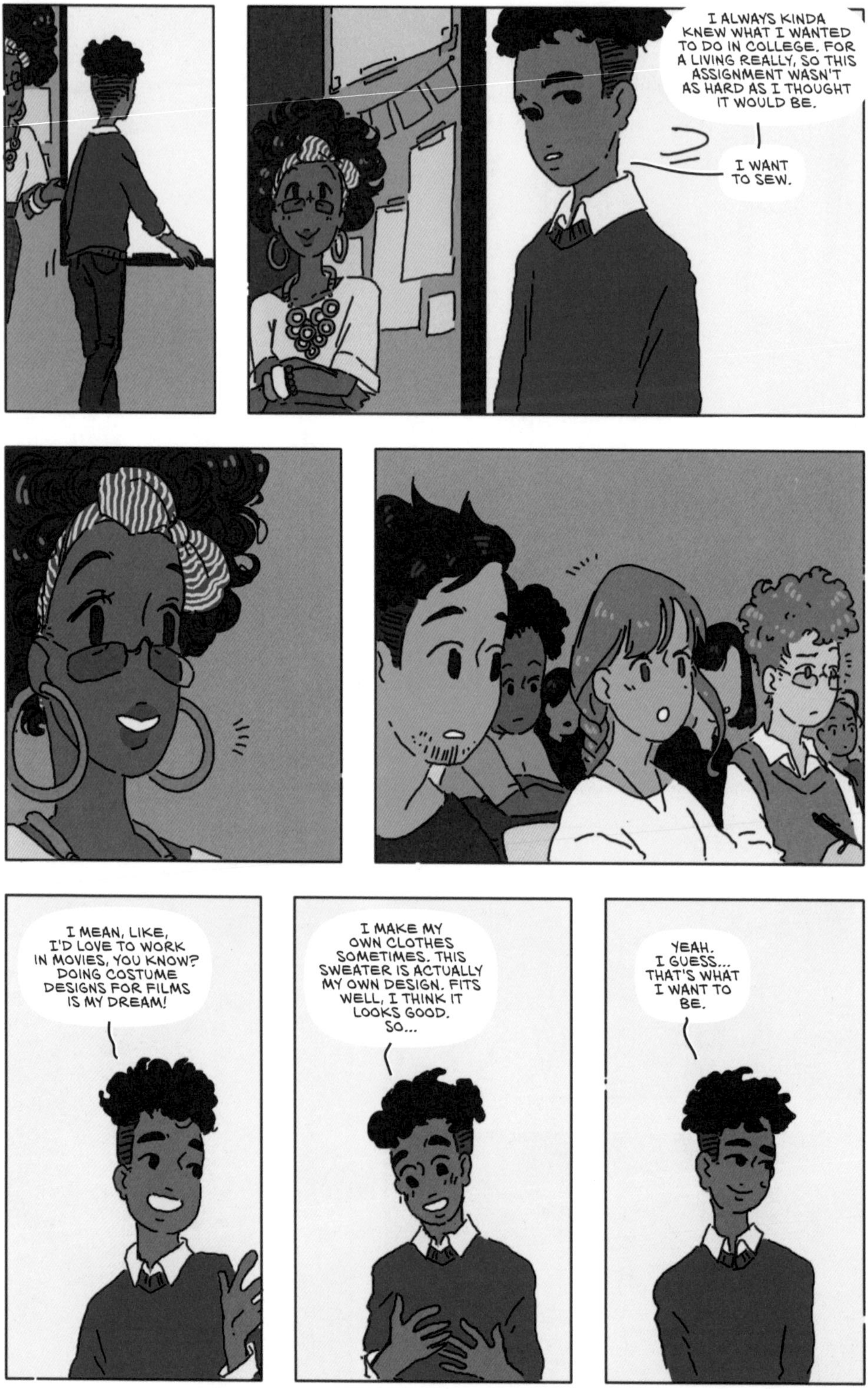
I ALWAYS KINDA KNEW WHAT I WANTED TO DO IN COLLEGE. FOR A LIVING REALLY, SO THIS ASSIGNMENT WASN'T AS HARD AS I THOUGHT IT WOULD BE.
I WANT TO SEW.
I MEAN, LIKE, I'D LOVE TO WORK IN MOVIES, YOU KNOW? DOING COSTUME DESIGNS FOR FILMS IS MY DREAM!
I MAKE MY OWN CLOTHES SOMETIMES. THIS SWEATER IS ACTUALLY MY OWN DESIGN. FITS WELL, I THINK IT LOOKS GOOD. SO...
YEAH. I GUESS... THAT'S WHAT I WANT TO BE.

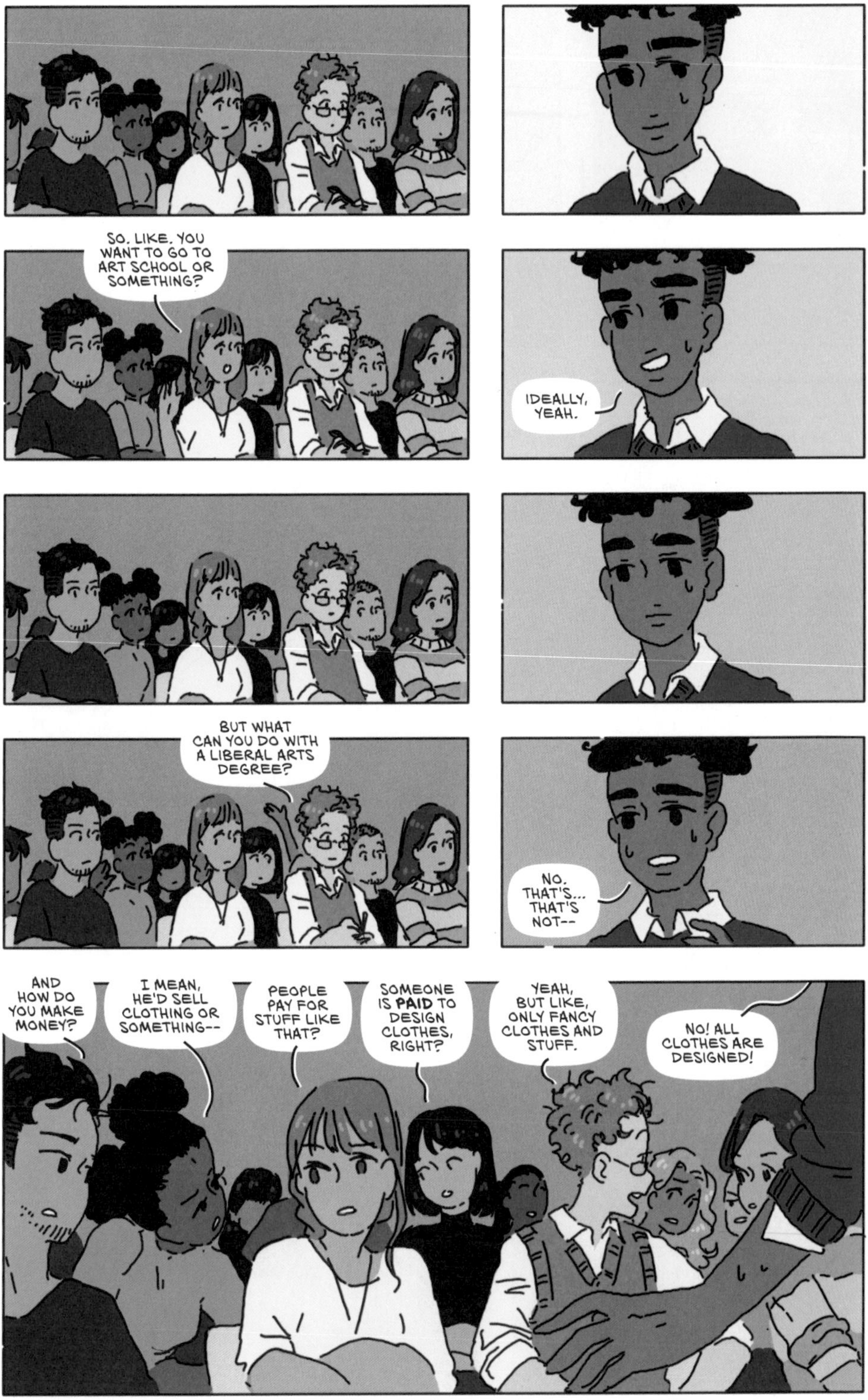
SO. LIKE. YOU WANT TO GO TO ART SCHOOL OR SOMETHING?
IDEALLY, YEAH.
BUT WHAT CAN YOU DO WITH A LIBERAL ARTS DEGREE?
NO. THAT'S... THAT'S NOT--
AND HOW DO YOU MAKE MONEY?
I MEAN, HE'D SELL CLOTHING OR SOMETHING--
PEOPLE PAY FOR STUFF LIKE THAT?
SOMEONE IS **PAID** TO DESIGN CLOTHES, RIGHT?
YEAH, BUT LIKE, ONLY FANCY CLOTHES AND STUFF.
NO! ALL CLOTHES ARE DESIGNED!

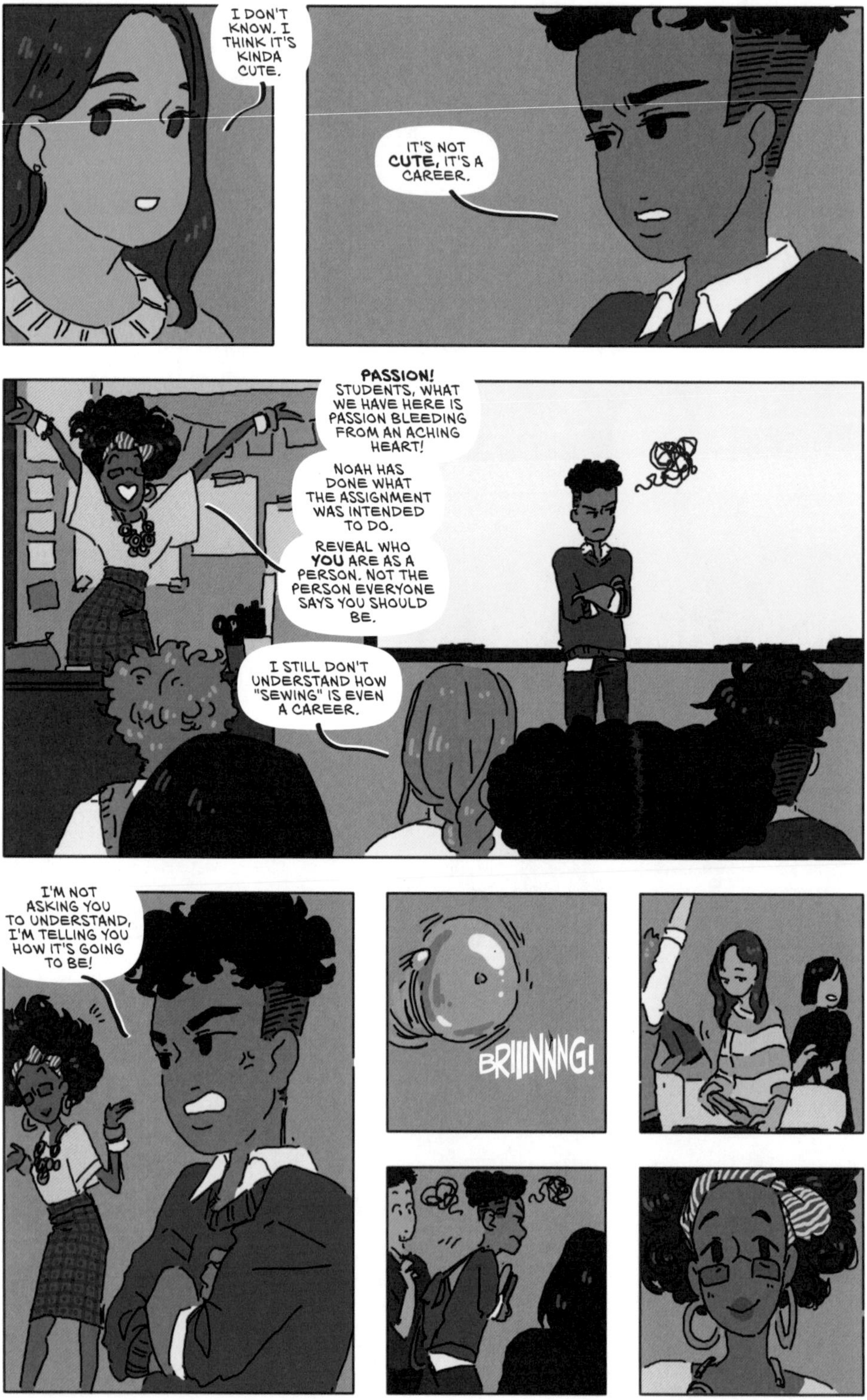
I DON'T KNOW. I THINK IT'S KINDA CUTE.
IT'S NOT **CUTE**, IT'S A CAREER.
PASSION! STUDENTS, WHAT WE HAVE HERE IS PASSION BLEEDING FROM AN ACHING HEART!
NOAH HAS DONE WHAT THE ASSIGNMENT WAS INTENDED TO DO.
REVEAL WHO **YOU** ARE AS A PERSON. NOT THE PERSON EVERYONE SAYS YOU SHOULD BE.
I STILL DON'T UNDERSTAND HOW "SEWING" IS EVEN A CAREER.
I'M NOT ASKING YOU TO UNDERSTAND, I'M TELLING YOU HOW IT'S GOING TO BE!
BRIIINNNG!

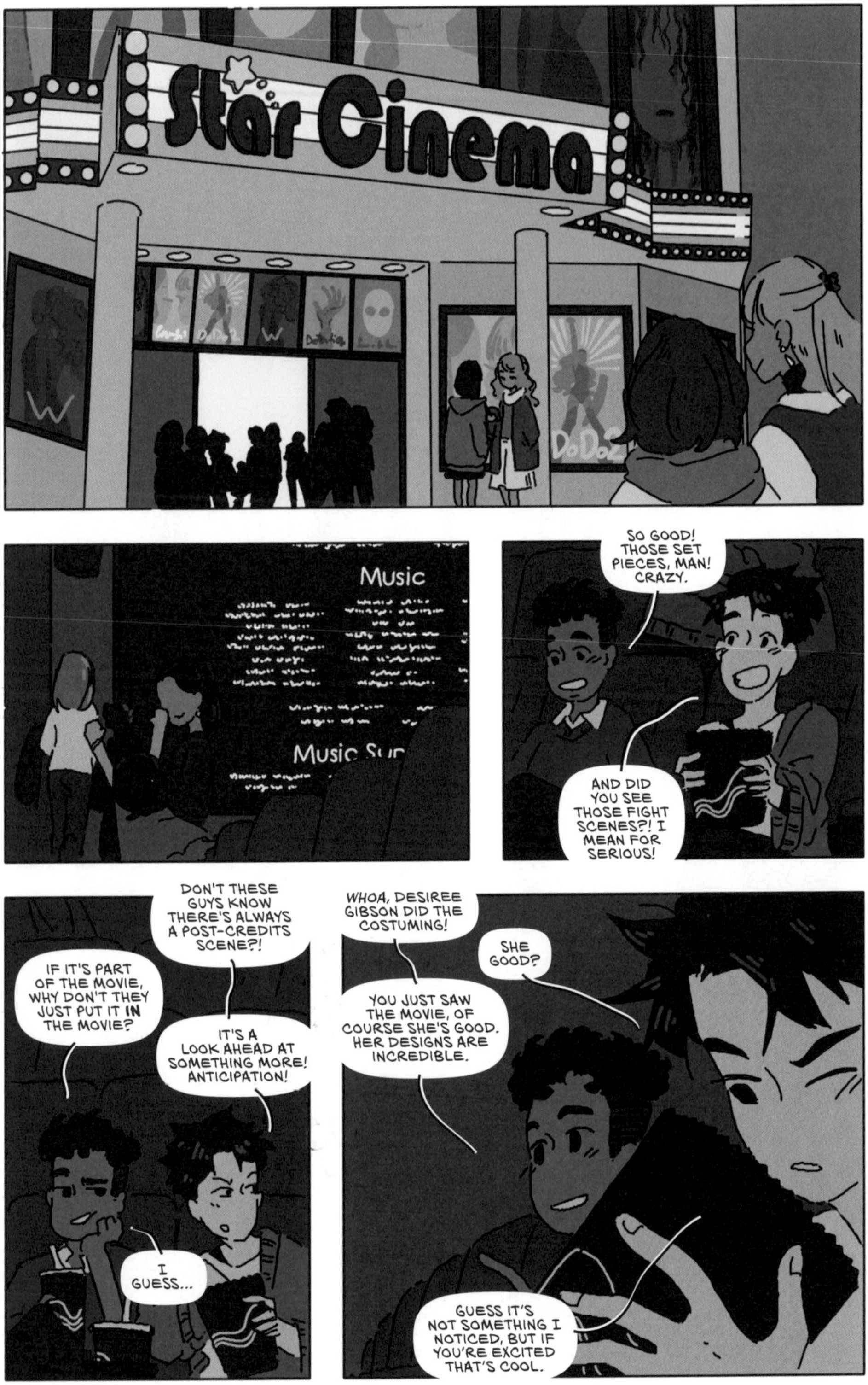

Star Cinema
Music
Music Sup
SO GOOD! THOSE SET PIECES, MAN! CRAZY.
AND DID YOU SEE THOSE FIGHT SCENES?! I MEAN FOR SERIOUS!
DON'T THESE GUYS KNOW THERE'S ALWAYS A POST-CREDITS SCENE?!
IF IT'S PART OF THE MOVIE, WHY DON'T THEY JUST PUT IT **IN** THE MOVIE?
IT'S A LOOK AHEAD AT SOMETHING MORE! ANTICIPATION!
I GUESS...
WHOA, DESIREE GIBSON DID THE COSTUMING!
SHE GOOD?
YOU JUST SAW THE MOVIE, OF COURSE SHE'S GOOD. HER DESIGNS ARE INCREDIBLE.
GUESS IT'S NOT SOMETHING I NOTICED, BUT IF YOU'RE EXCITED THAT'S COOL.

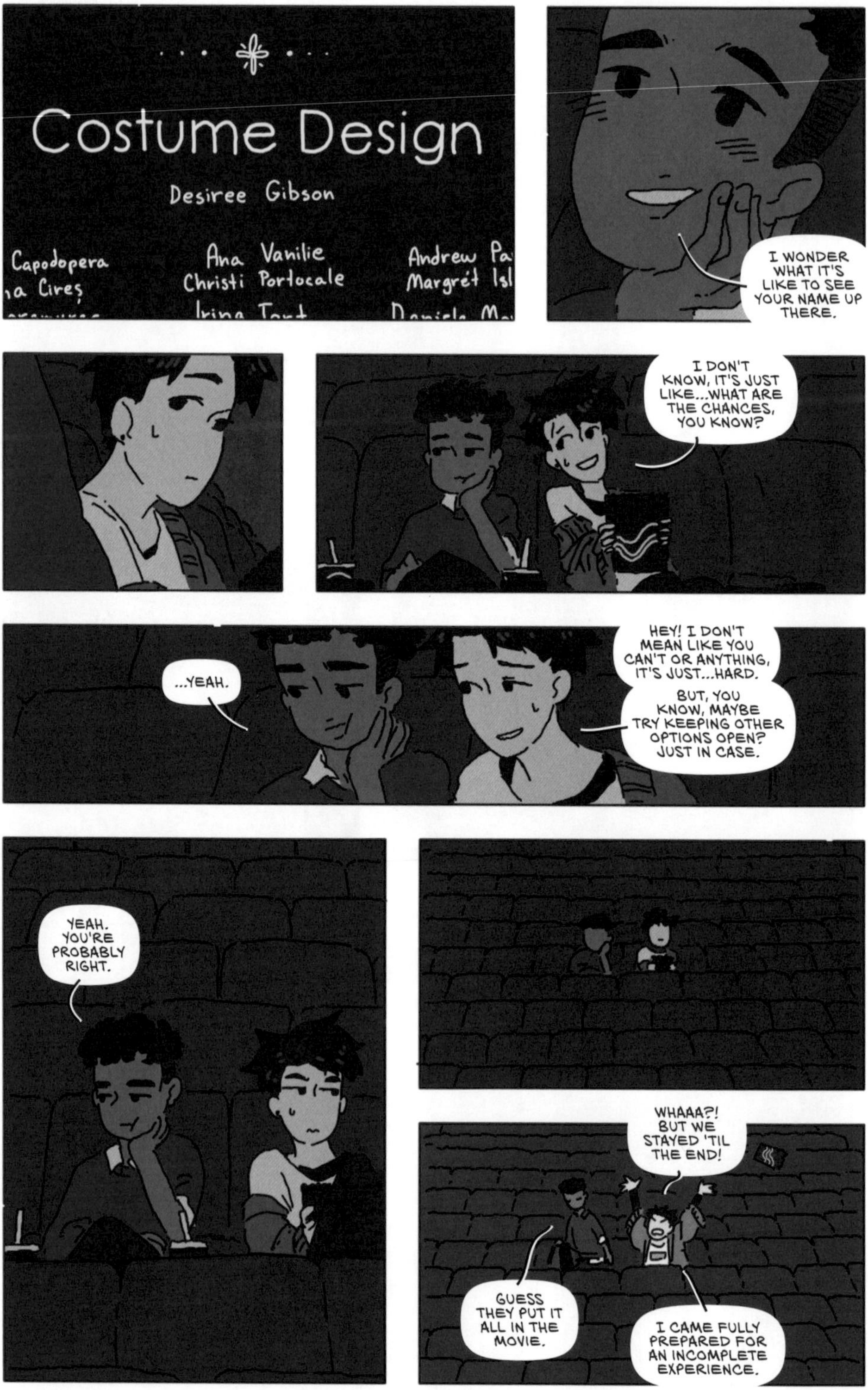
Costume Design
Desiree Gibson
Capodopera
Ana Vanilie
Christi Portocale
Andrew
Margrét
I WONDER WHAT IT'S LIKE TO SEE YOUR NAME UP THERE.
I DON'T KNOW, IT'S JUST LIKE...WHAT ARE THE CHANCES, YOU KNOW?
...YEAH.
HEY! I DON'T MEAN LIKE YOU CAN'T OR ANYTHING, IT'S JUST...HARD.
BUT, YOU KNOW, MAYBE TRY KEEPING OTHER OPTIONS OPEN? JUST IN CASE.
YEAH. YOU'RE PROBABLY RIGHT.
WHAAA?! BUT WE STAYED 'TIL THE END!
GUESS THEY PUT IT ALL IN THE MOVIE.
I CAME FULLY PREPARED FOR AN INCOMPLETE EXPERIENCE.

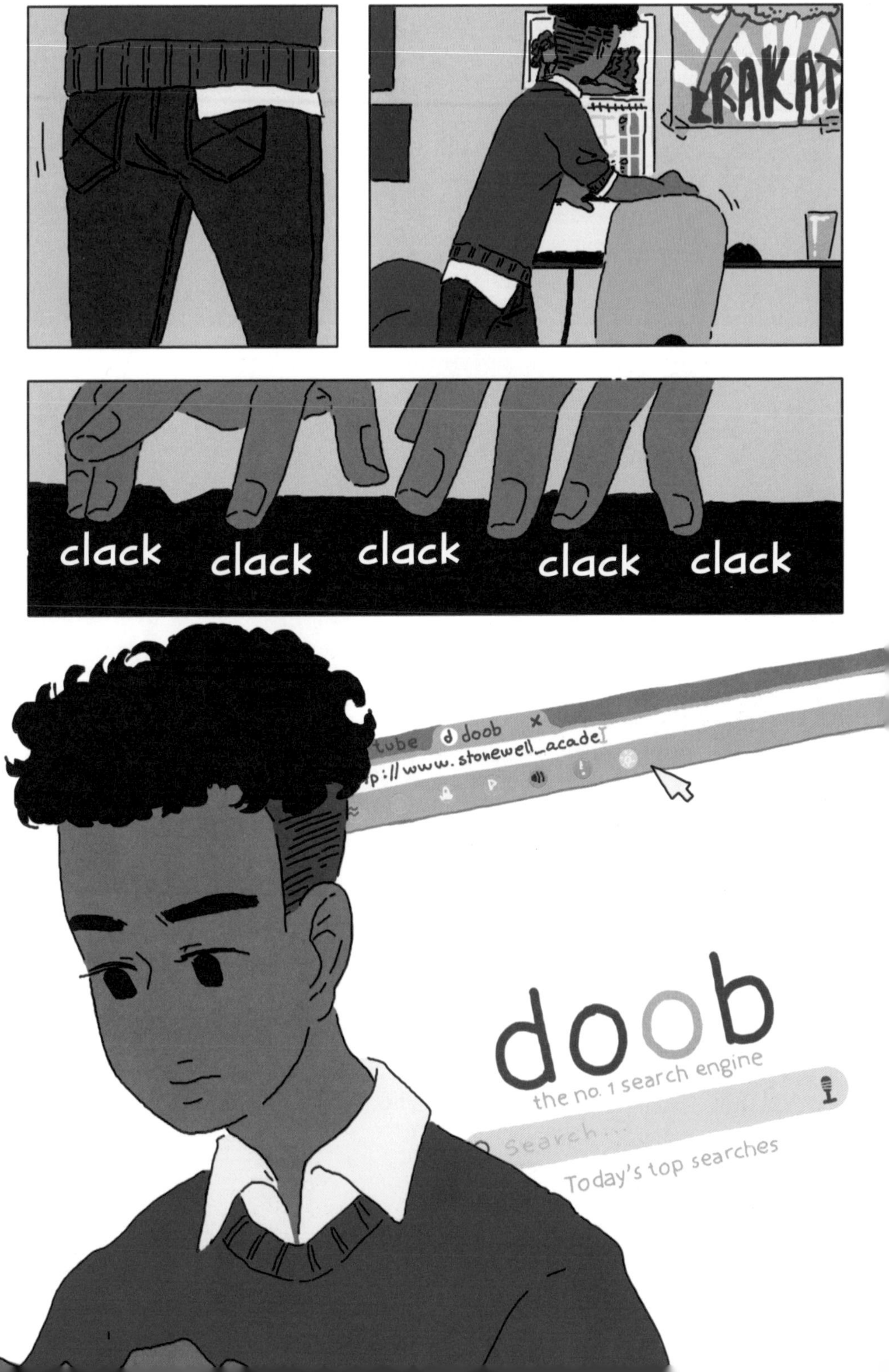
clack
clack
clack
clack
clack
tube
doob
p://www.stonewell_acade
doob
the no. 1 search engine
Search...
Today's top searches

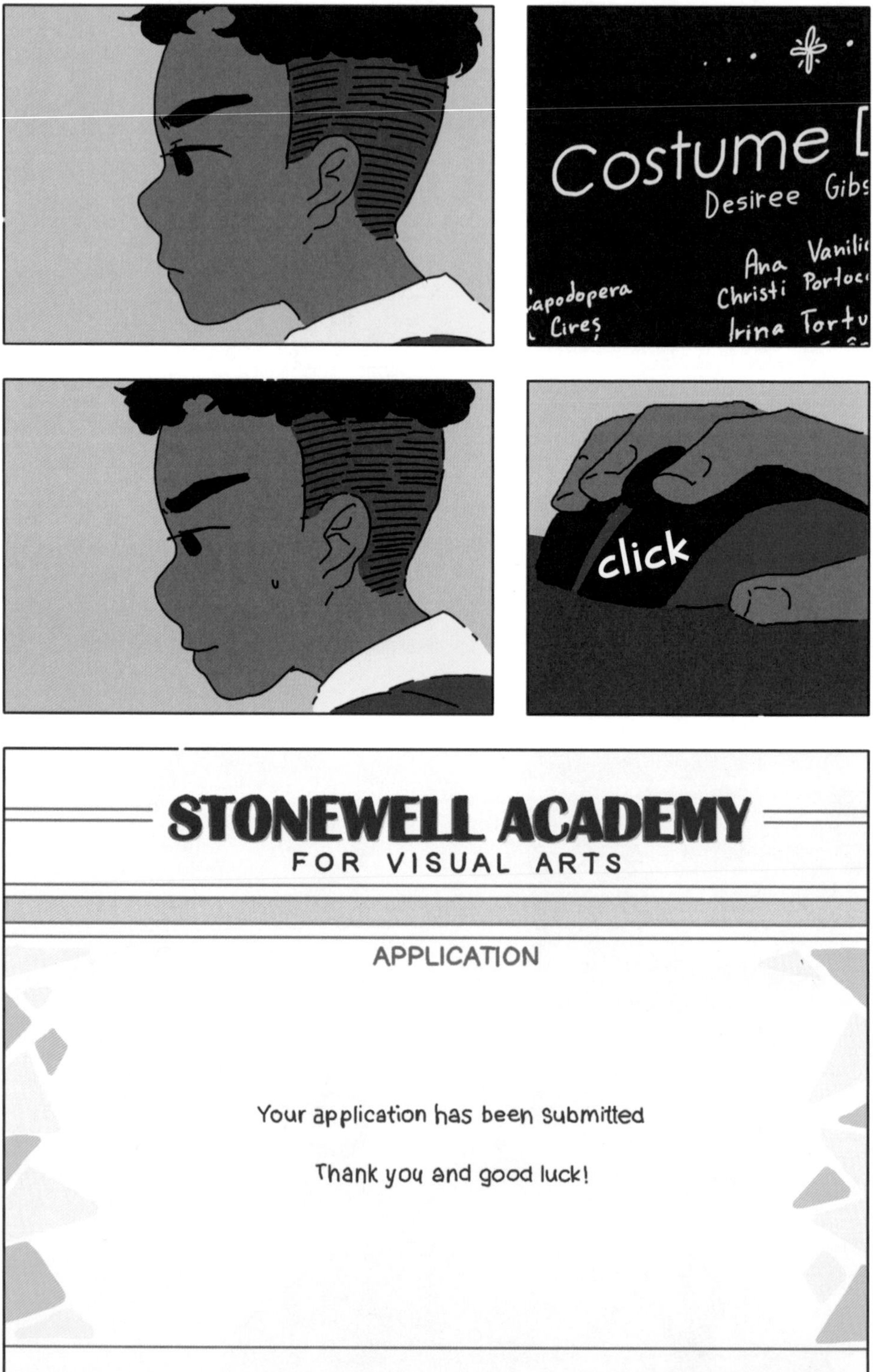
Costume D
Desiree Gibs
Ana Vanili
Christi Portoc
Irina Tortu
apodopera
Cireș
click
STONEWELL ACADEMY
FOR VISUAL ARTS
APPLICATION
Your application has been submitted
Thank you and good luck!

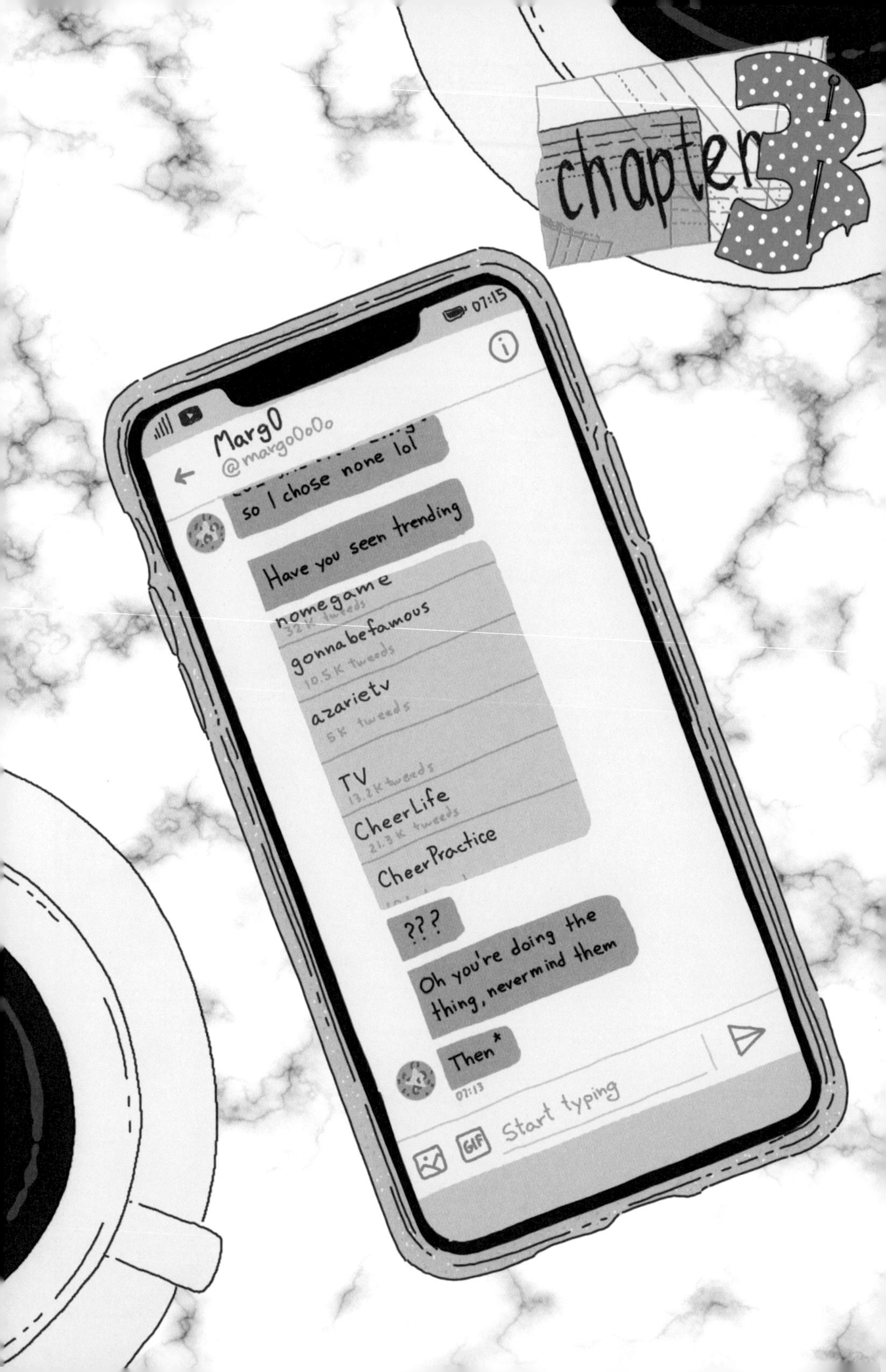
chapter 3
07:15
MargO
@margo0o0o
so I chose none lol
Have you seen trending
nomegame
gonnabefamous
10.5K tweeds
azarietv
5K tweeds
TV
13.2K tweeds
CheerLife
21.3K tweeds
CheerPractice
???
Oh you're doing the thing, nevermind them
Then*
07:13
Start typing
GIF

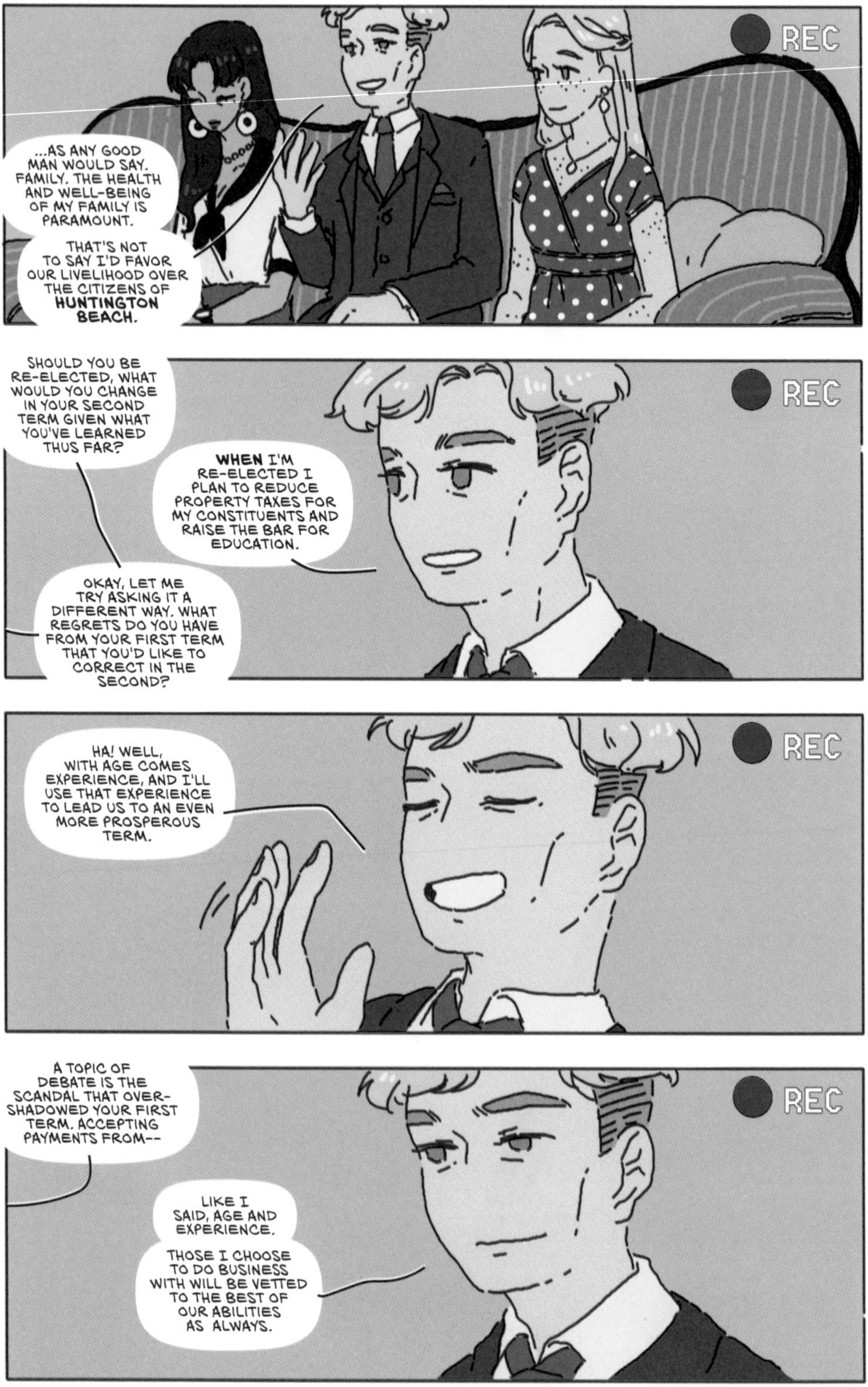
REC
...AS ANY GOOD MAN WOULD SAY. FAMILY. THE HEALTH AND WELL-BEING OF MY FAMILY IS PARAMOUNT.
THAT'S NOT TO SAY I'D FAVOR OUR LIVELIHOOD OVER THE CITIZENS OF **HUNTINGTON BEACH**.
REC
SHOULD YOU BE RE-ELECTED, WHAT WOULD YOU CHANGE IN YOUR SECOND TERM GIVEN WHAT YOU'VE LEARNED THUS FAR?
WHEN I'M RE-ELECTED I PLAN TO REDUCE PROPERTY TAXES FOR MY CONSTITUENTS AND RAISE THE BAR FOR EDUCATION.
OKAY, LET ME TRY ASKING IT A DIFFERENT WAY. WHAT REGRETS DO YOU HAVE FROM YOUR FIRST TERM THAT YOU'D LIKE TO CORRECT IN THE SECOND?
REC
HA! WELL, WITH AGE COMES EXPERIENCE, AND I'LL USE THAT EXPERIENCE TO LEAD US TO AN EVEN MORE PROSPEROUS TERM.
REC
A TOPIC OF DEBATE IS THE SCANDAL THAT OVER-SHADOWED YOUR FIRST TERM. ACCEPTING PAYMENTS FROM--
LIKE I SAID, AGE AND EXPERIENCE.
THOSE I CHOOSE TO DO BUSINESS WITH WILL BE VETTED TO THE BEST OF OUR ABILITIES AS ALWAYS.

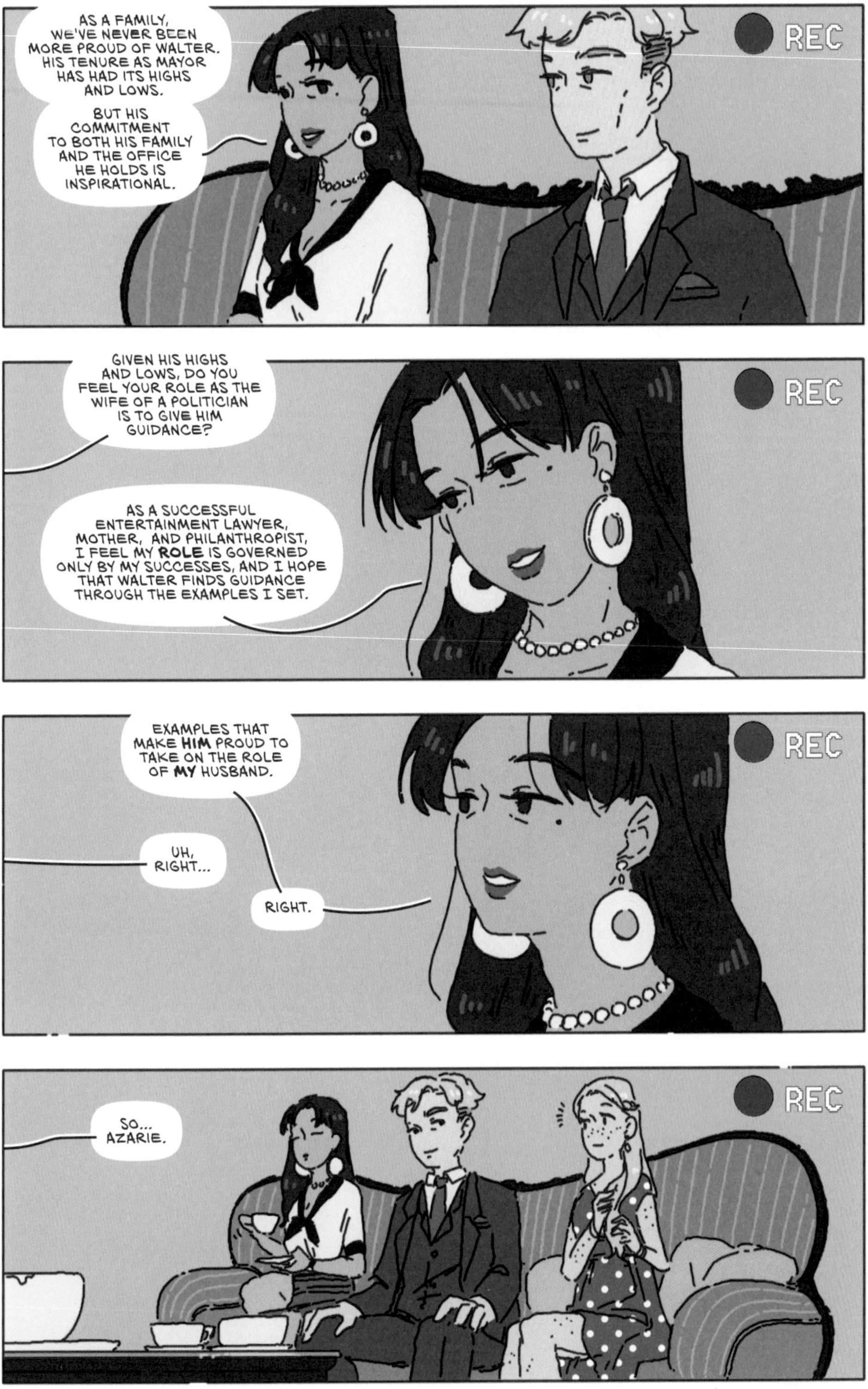
REC
AS A FAMILY, WE'VE NEVER BEEN MORE PROUD OF WALTER. HIS TENURE AS MAYOR HAS HAD ITS HIGHS AND LOWS.
BUT HIS COMMITMENT TO BOTH HIS FAMILY AND THE OFFICE HE HOLDS IS INSPIRATIONAL.
REC
GIVEN HIS HIGHS AND LOWS, DO YOU FEEL YOUR ROLE AS THE WIFE OF A POLITICIAN IS TO GIVE HIM GUIDANCE?
AS A SUCCESSFUL ENTERTAINMENT LAWYER, MOTHER, AND PHILANTHROPIST, I FEEL MY **ROLE** IS GOVERNED ONLY BY MY SUCCESSES, AND I HOPE THAT WALTER FINDS GUIDANCE THROUGH THE EXAMPLES I SET.
REC
EXAMPLES THAT MAKE **HIM** PROUD TO TAKE ON THE ROLE OF **MY** HUSBAND.
UH, RIGHT...
RIGHT.
REC
SO... AZARIE.

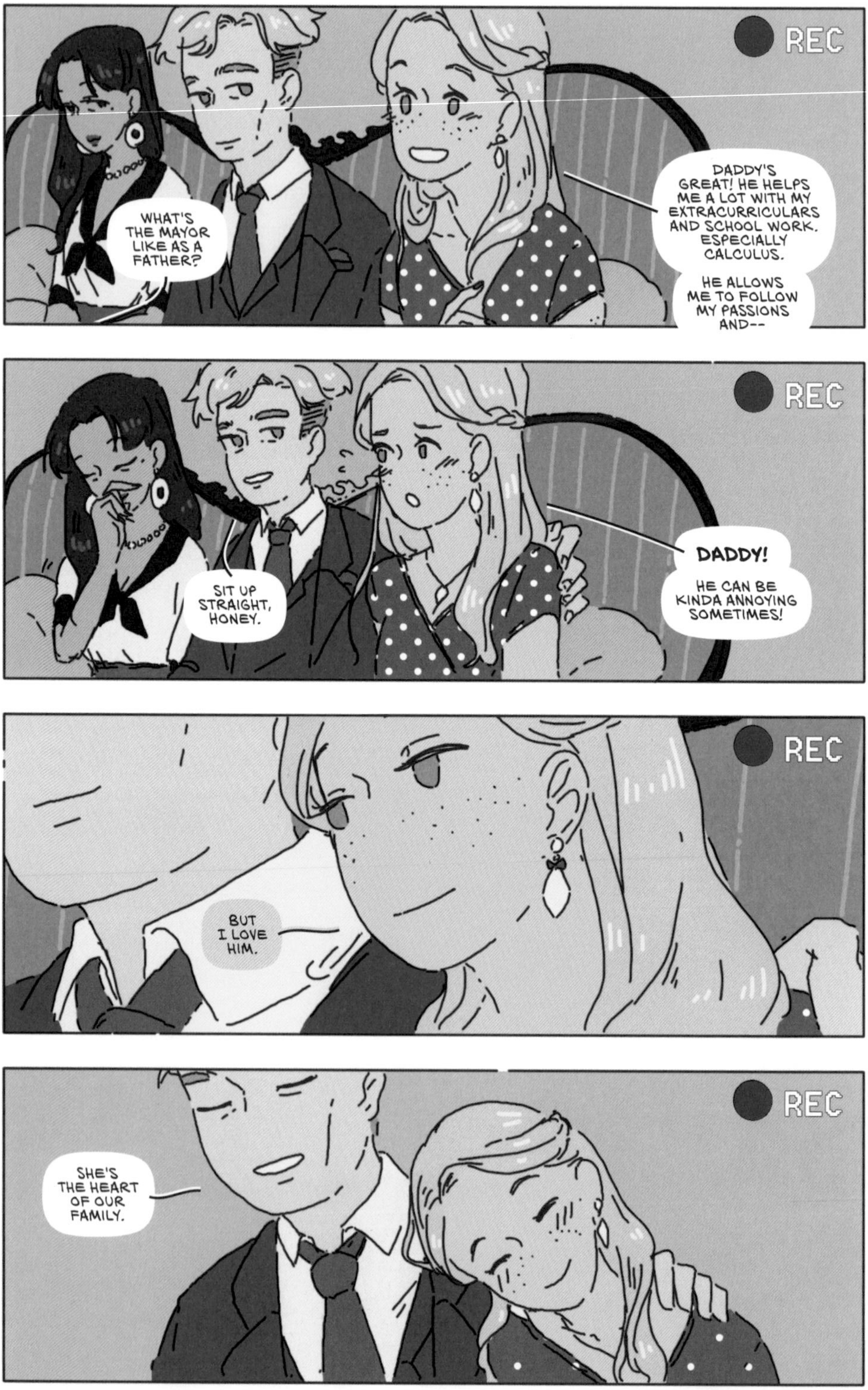
REC
WHAT'S THE MAYOR LIKE AS A FATHER?
DADDY'S GREAT! HE HELPS ME A LOT WITH MY EXTRACURRICULARS AND SCHOOL WORK. ESPECIALLY CALCULUS.
HE ALLOWS ME TO FOLLOW MY PASSIONS AND--
REC
SIT UP STRAIGHT, HONEY.
DADDY!
HE CAN BE KINDA ANNOYING SOMETIMES!
REC
BUT I LOVE HIM.
REC
SHE'S THE HEART OF OUR FAMILY.

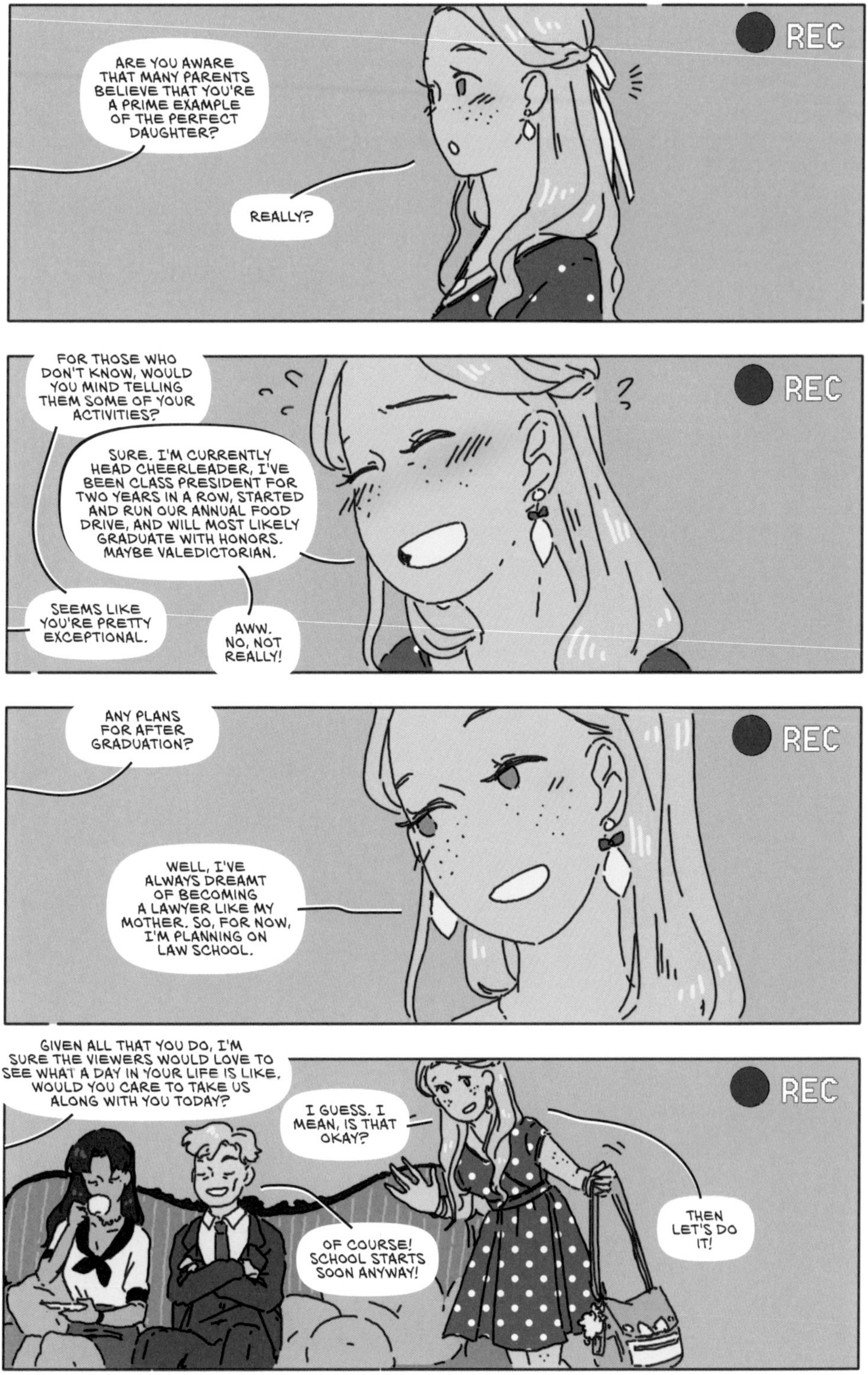
REC
ARE YOU AWARE THAT MANY PARENTS BELIEVE THAT YOU'RE A PRIME EXAMPLE OF THE PERFECT DAUGHTER?
REALLY?
REC
FOR THOSE WHO DON'T KNOW, WOULD YOU MIND TELLING THEM SOME OF YOUR ACTIVITIES?
SURE. I'M CURRENTLY HEAD CHEERLEADER, I'VE BEEN CLASS PRESIDENT FOR TWO YEARS IN A ROW, STARTED AND RUN OUR ANNUAL FOOD DRIVE, AND WILL MOST LIKELY GRADUATE WITH HONORS. MAYBE VALEDICTORIAN.
SEEMS LIKE YOU'RE PRETTY EXCEPTIONAL.
AWW. NO, NOT REALLY!
REC
ANY PLANS FOR AFTER GRADUATION?
WELL, I'VE ALWAYS DREAMT OF BECOMING A LAWYER LIKE MY MOTHER. SO, FOR NOW, I'M PLANNING ON LAW SCHOOL.
REC
GIVEN ALL THAT YOU DO, I'M SURE THE VIEWERS WOULD LOVE TO SEE WHAT A DAY IN YOUR LIFE IS LIKE. WOULD YOU CARE TO TAKE US ALONG WITH YOU TODAY?
I GUESS. I MEAN, IS THAT OKAY?
OF COURSE! SCHOOL STARTS SOON ANYWAY!
THEN LET'S DO IT!

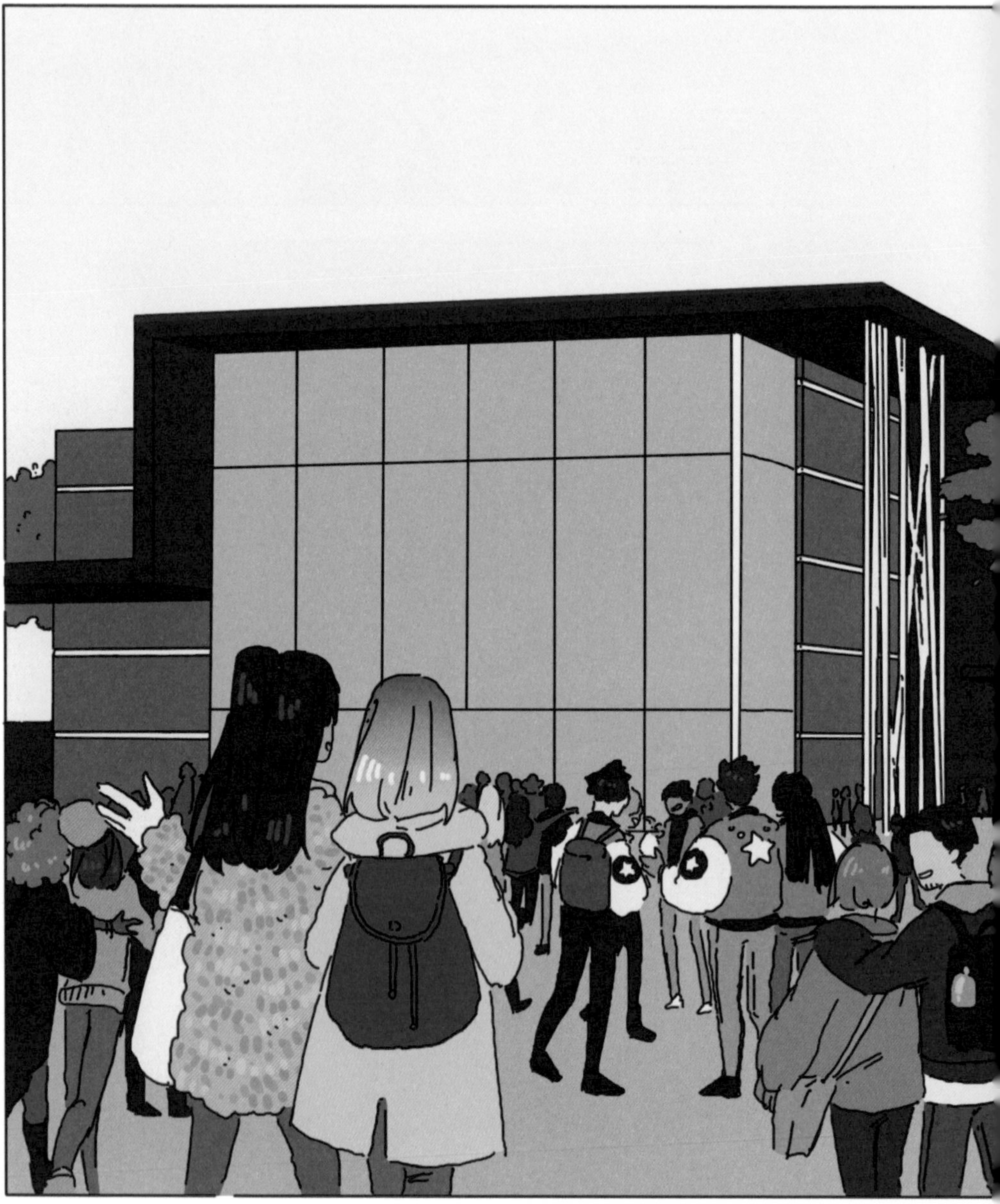

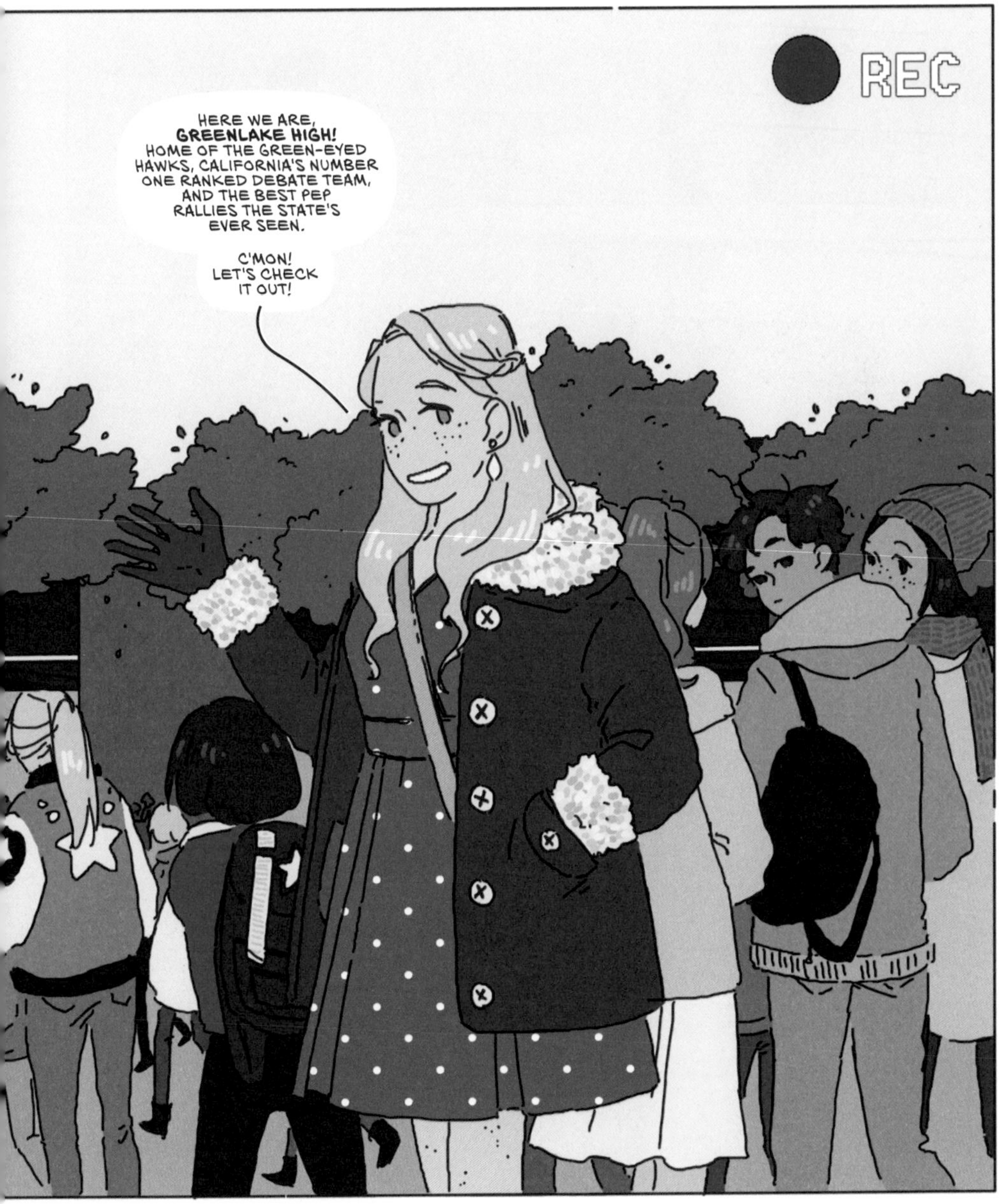
REC
HERE WE ARE, **GREENLAKE HIGH!** HOME OF THE GREEN-EYED HAWKS, CALIFORNIA'S NUMBER ONE RANKED DEBATE TEAM, AND THE BEST PEP RALLIES THE STATE'S EVER SEEN.
C'MON! LET'S CHECK IT OUT!

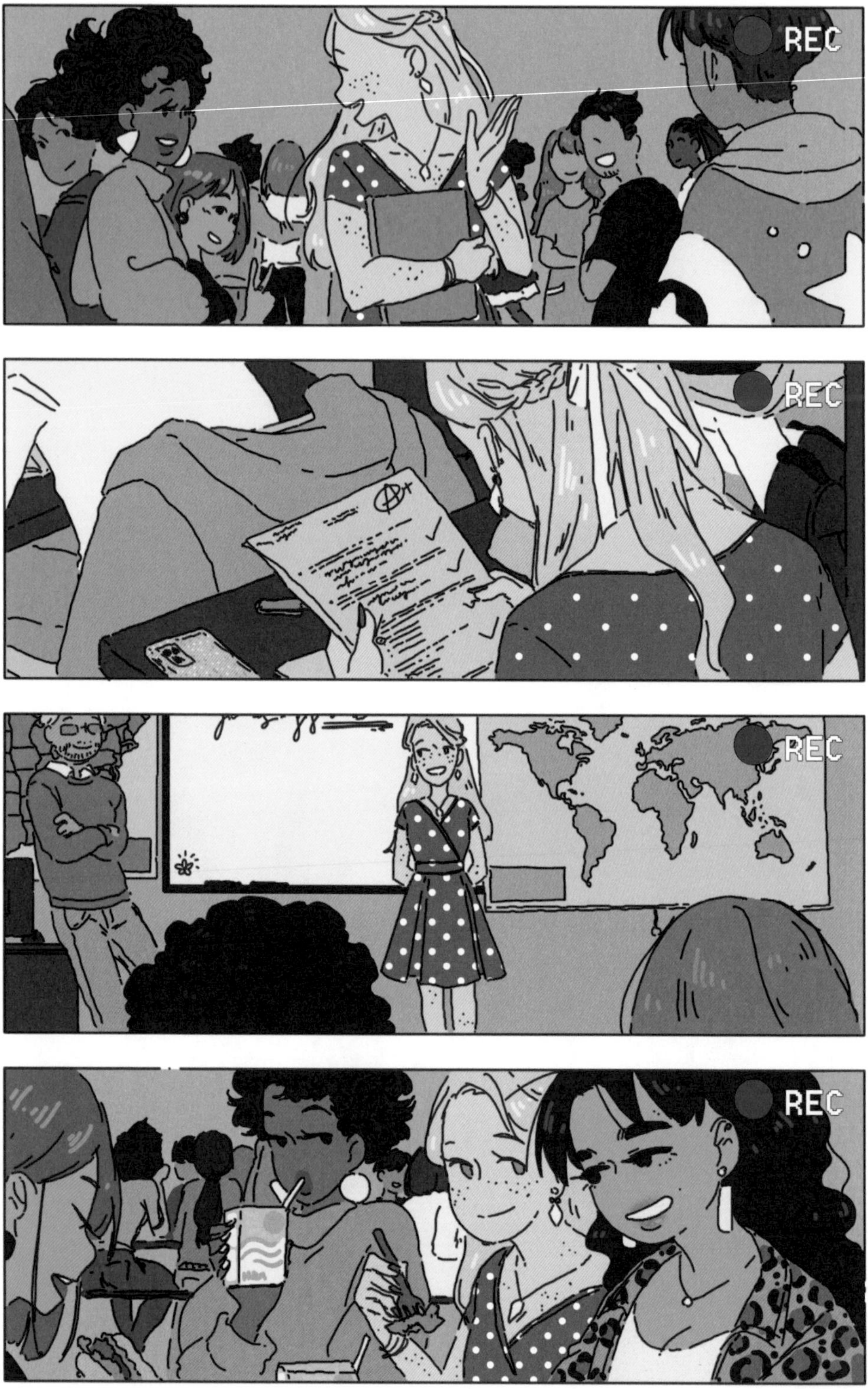
REC
REC
REC
REC

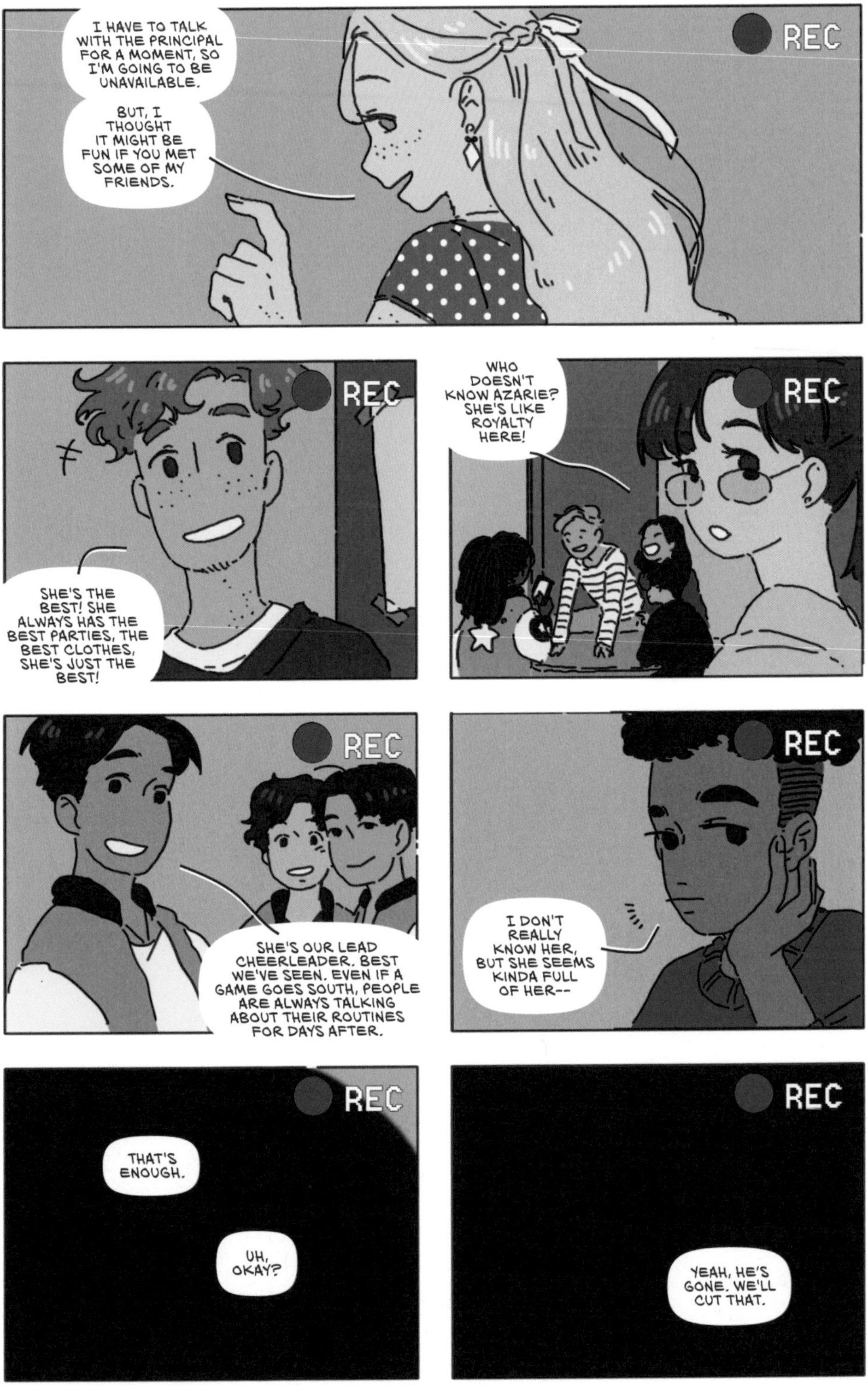
REC
I HAVE TO TALK WITH THE PRINCIPAL FOR A MOMENT, SO I'M GOING TO BE UNAVAILABLE.
BUT, I THOUGHT IT MIGHT BE FUN IF YOU MET SOME OF MY FRIENDS.
REC
SHE'S THE BEST! SHE ALWAYS HAS THE BEST PARTIES, THE BEST CLOTHES, SHE'S JUST THE BEST!
REC
WHO DOESN'T KNOW AZARIE? SHE'S LIKE ROYALTY HERE!
REC
SHE'S OUR LEAD CHEERLEADER. BEST WE'VE SEEN. EVEN IF A GAME GOES SOUTH, PEOPLE ARE ALWAYS TALKING ABOUT THEIR ROUTINES FOR DAYS AFTER.
REC
I DON'T REALLY KNOW HER, BUT SHE SEEMS KINDA FULL OF HER--
REC
THAT'S ENOUGH.
UH, OKAY?
REC
YEAH, HE'S GONE. WE'LL CUT THAT.

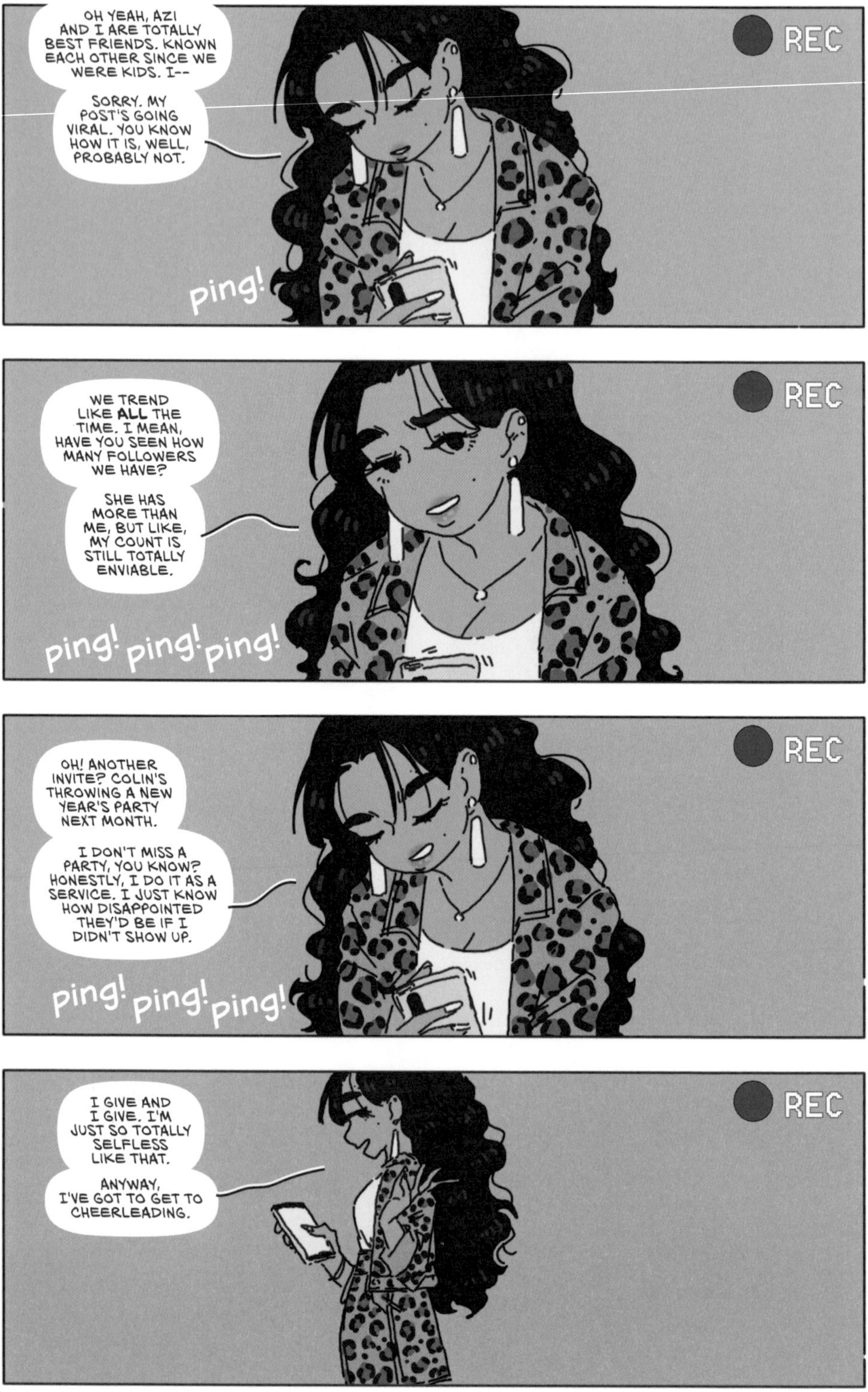
REC
OH YEAH, AZI AND I ARE TOTALLY BEST FRIENDS. KNOWN EACH OTHER SINCE WE WERE KIDS. I--
SORRY. MY POST'S GOING VIRAL. YOU KNOW HOW IT IS, WELL, PROBABLY NOT.
ping!
REC
WE TREND LIKE **ALL** THE TIME. I MEAN, HAVE YOU SEEN HOW MANY FOLLOWERS WE HAVE?
SHE HAS MORE THAN ME, BUT LIKE, MY COUNT IS STILL TOTALLY ENVIABLE.
ping! ping! ping!
REC
OH! ANOTHER INVITE? COLIN'S THROWING A NEW YEAR'S PARTY NEXT MONTH.
I DON'T MISS A PARTY, YOU KNOW? HONESTLY, I DO IT AS A SERVICE. I JUST KNOW HOW DISAPPOINTED THEY'D BE IF I DIDN'T SHOW UP.
ping! ping! ping!
REC
I GIVE AND I GIVE. I'M JUST SO TOTALLY SELFLESS LIKE THAT.
ANYWAY, I'VE GOT TO GET TO CHEERLEADING.

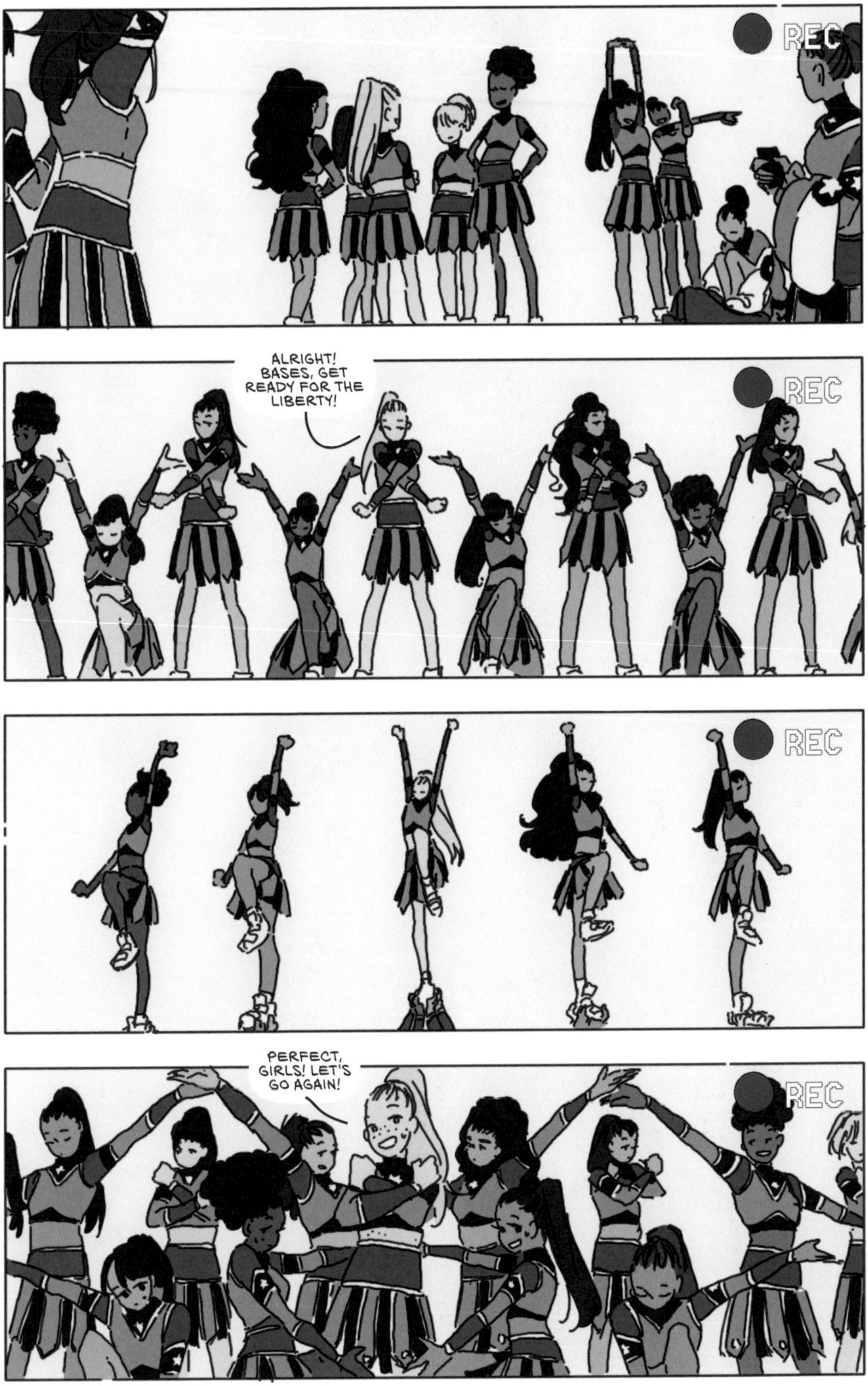
REC
REC
ALRIGHT! BASES, GET READY FOR THE LIBERTY!
REC
REC
PERFECT, GIRLS! LET'S GO AGAIN!

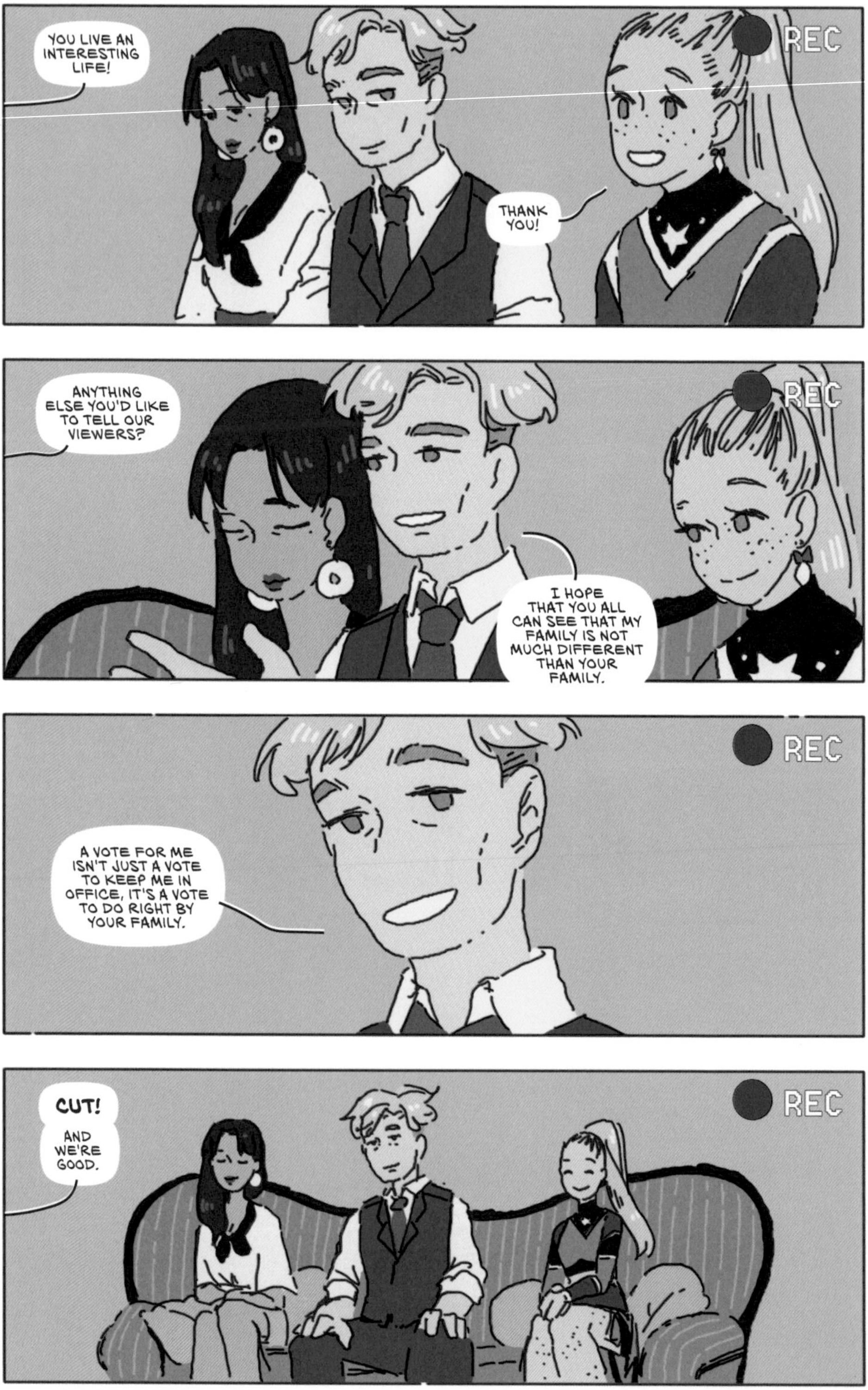
REC
YOU LIVE AN INTERESTING LIFE!
THANK YOU!
REC
ANYTHING ELSE YOU'D LIKE TO TELL OUR VIEWERS?
I HOPE THAT YOU ALL CAN SEE THAT MY FAMILY IS NOT MUCH DIFFERENT THAN YOUR FAMILY.
REC
A VOTE FOR ME ISN'T JUST A VOTE TO KEEP ME IN OFFICE, IT'S A VOTE TO DO RIGHT BY YOUR FAMILY.
REC
CUT!
AND WE'RE GOOD.

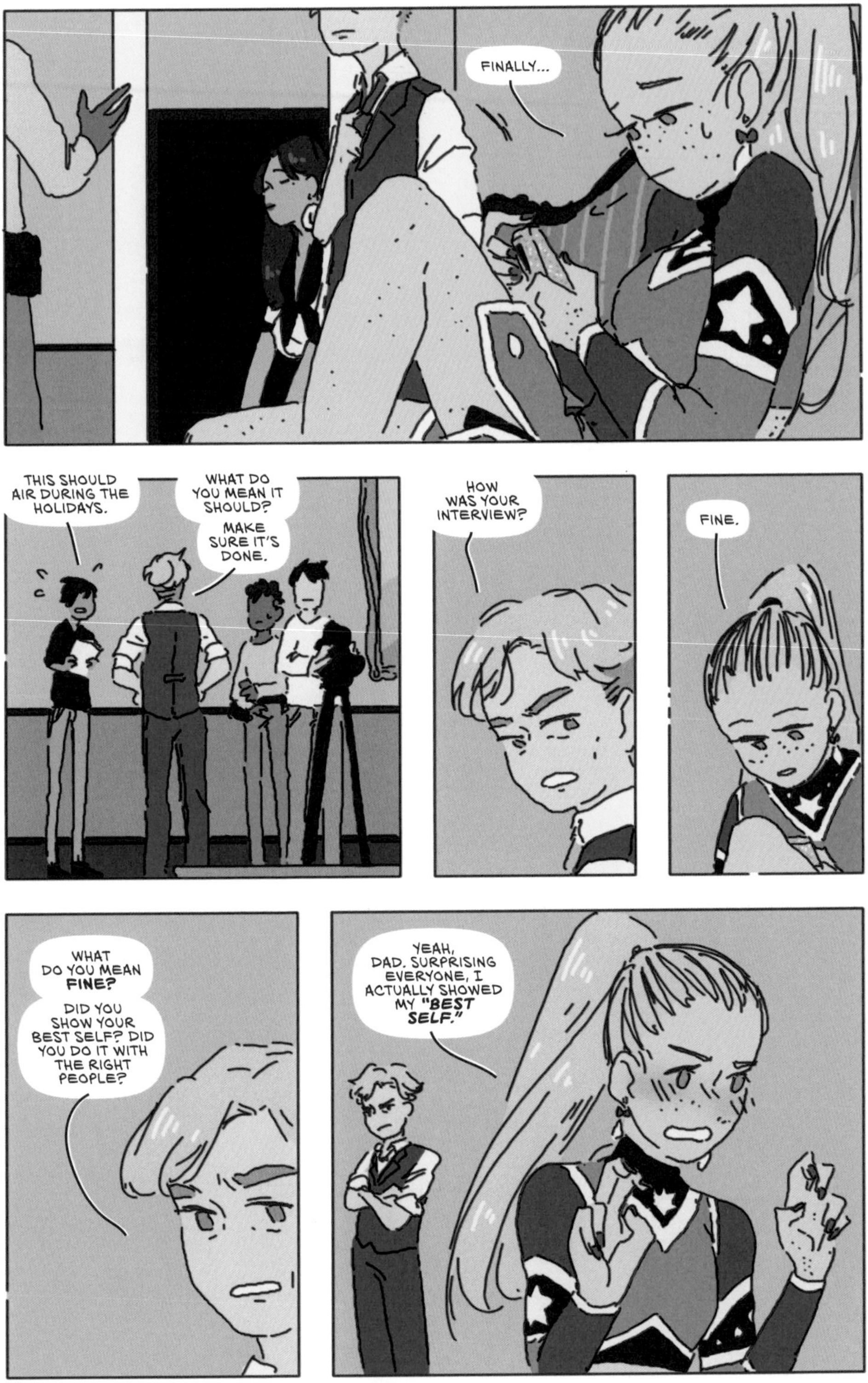
FINALLY...
THIS SHOULD AIR DURING THE HOLIDAYS.
WHAT DO YOU MEAN IT SHOULD?
MAKE SURE IT'S DONE.
HOW WAS YOUR INTERVIEW?
FINE.
WHAT DO YOU MEAN **FINE?**
DID YOU SHOW YOUR BEST SELF? DID YOU DO IT WITH THE RIGHT PEOPLE?
YEAH, DAD. SURPRISING EVERYONE, I ACTUALLY SHOWED MY ***"BEST SELF."***

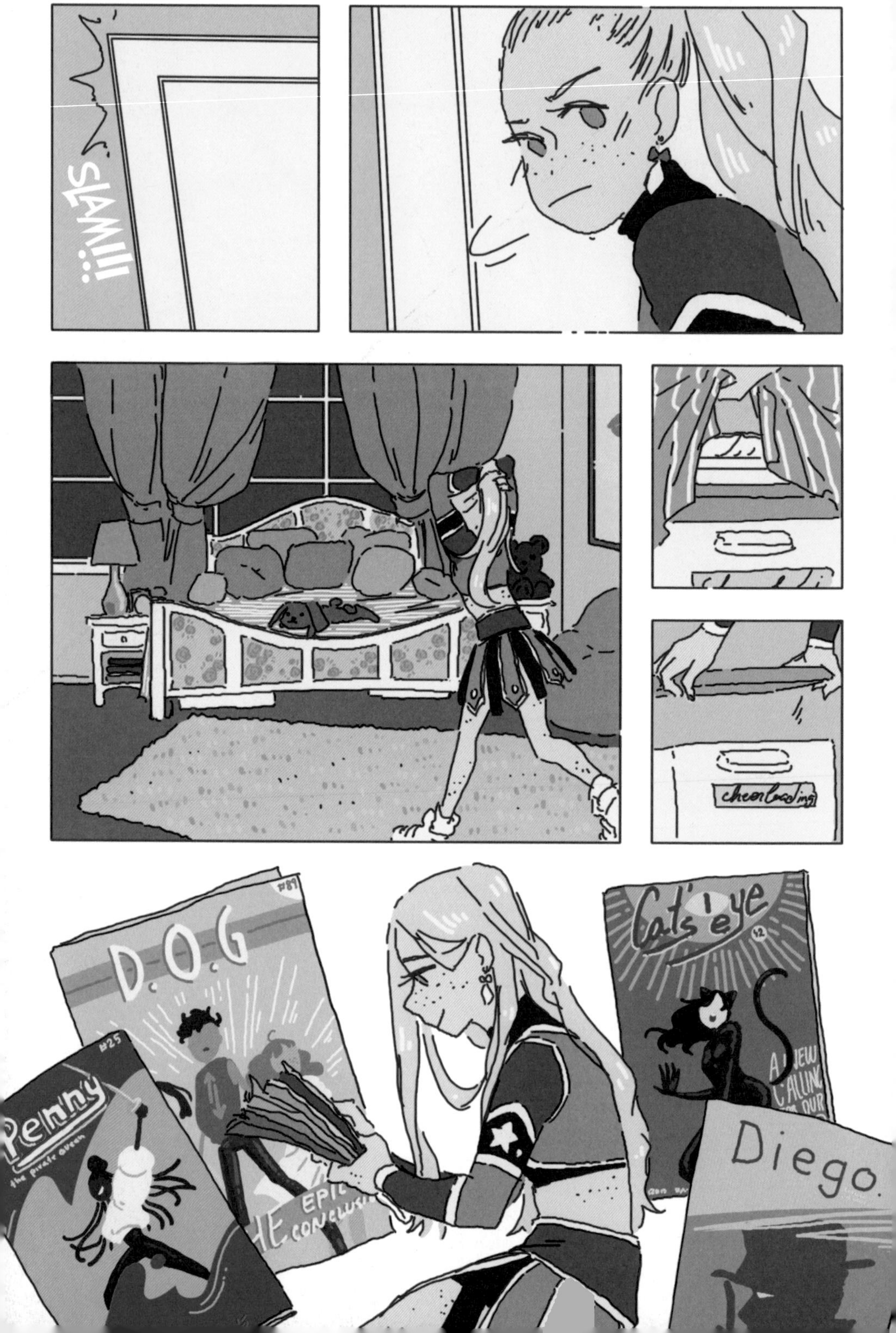
SLAM!!!
cheerleading
#89
D.O.G
#25
Penny
the pirate queen
EPIC
Cat's eye
Diego.

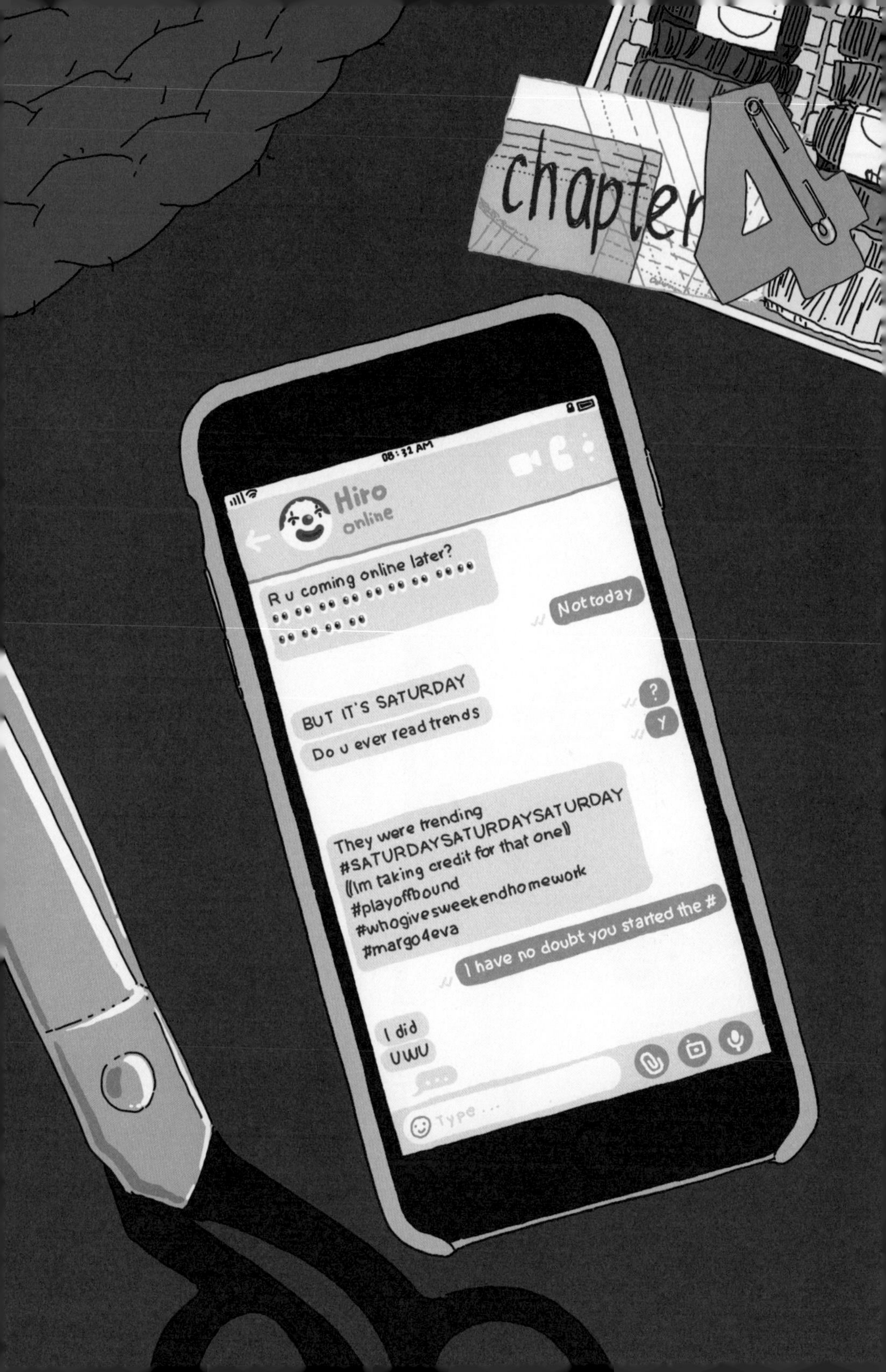
chapter 4
08:32 AM
Hiro
online
R u coming online later?
Not today
BUT IT'S SATURDAY
Do u ever read trends
?
Y
They were trending
#SATURDAYSATURDAYSATURDAY
((Im taking credit for that one))
#playoffbound
#whogivesweekendhomework
#margo4eva
I have no doubt you started the #
I did
UWU
Type ...

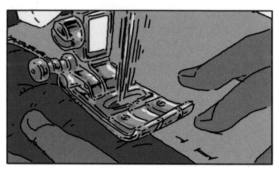

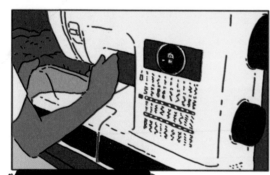

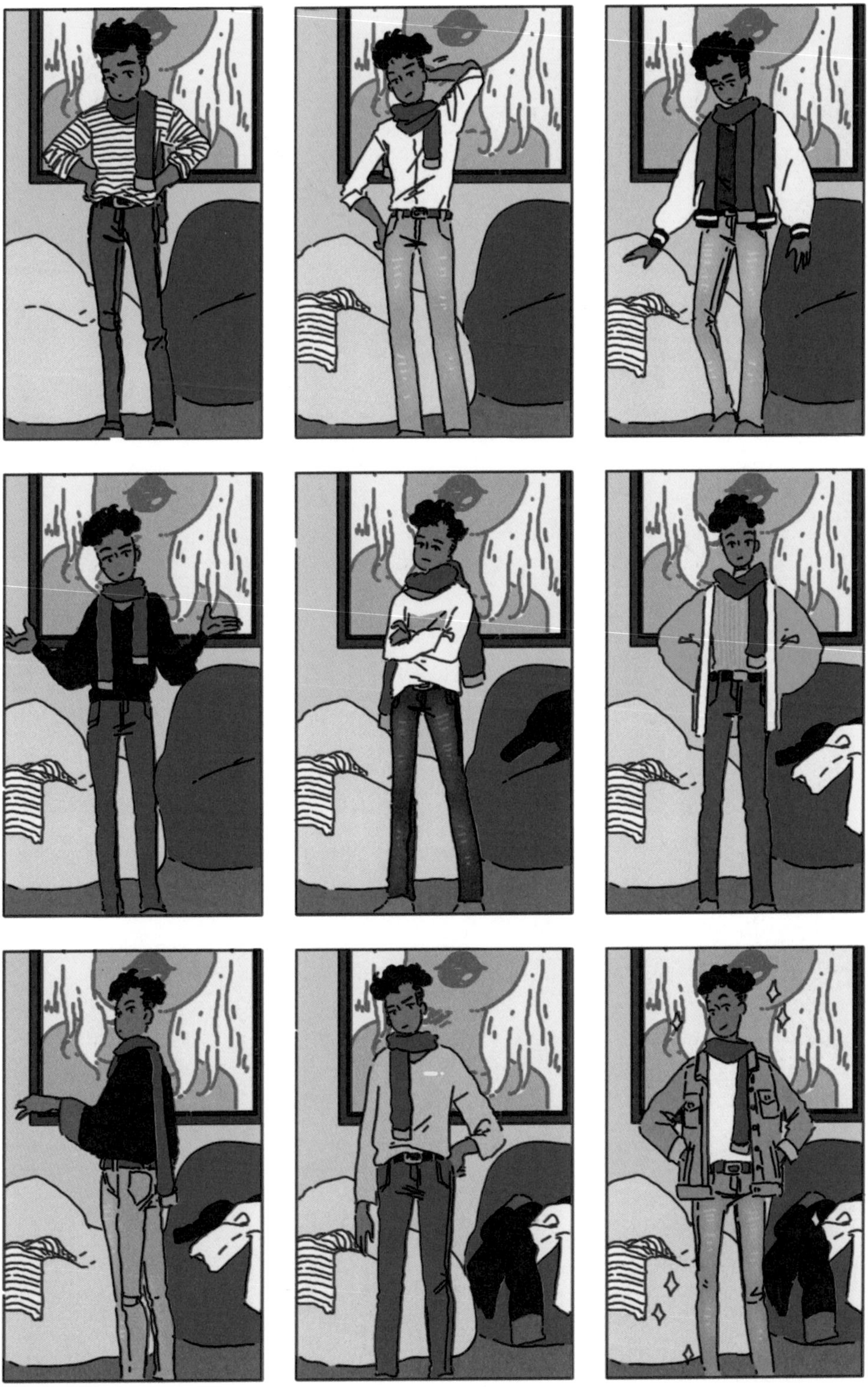

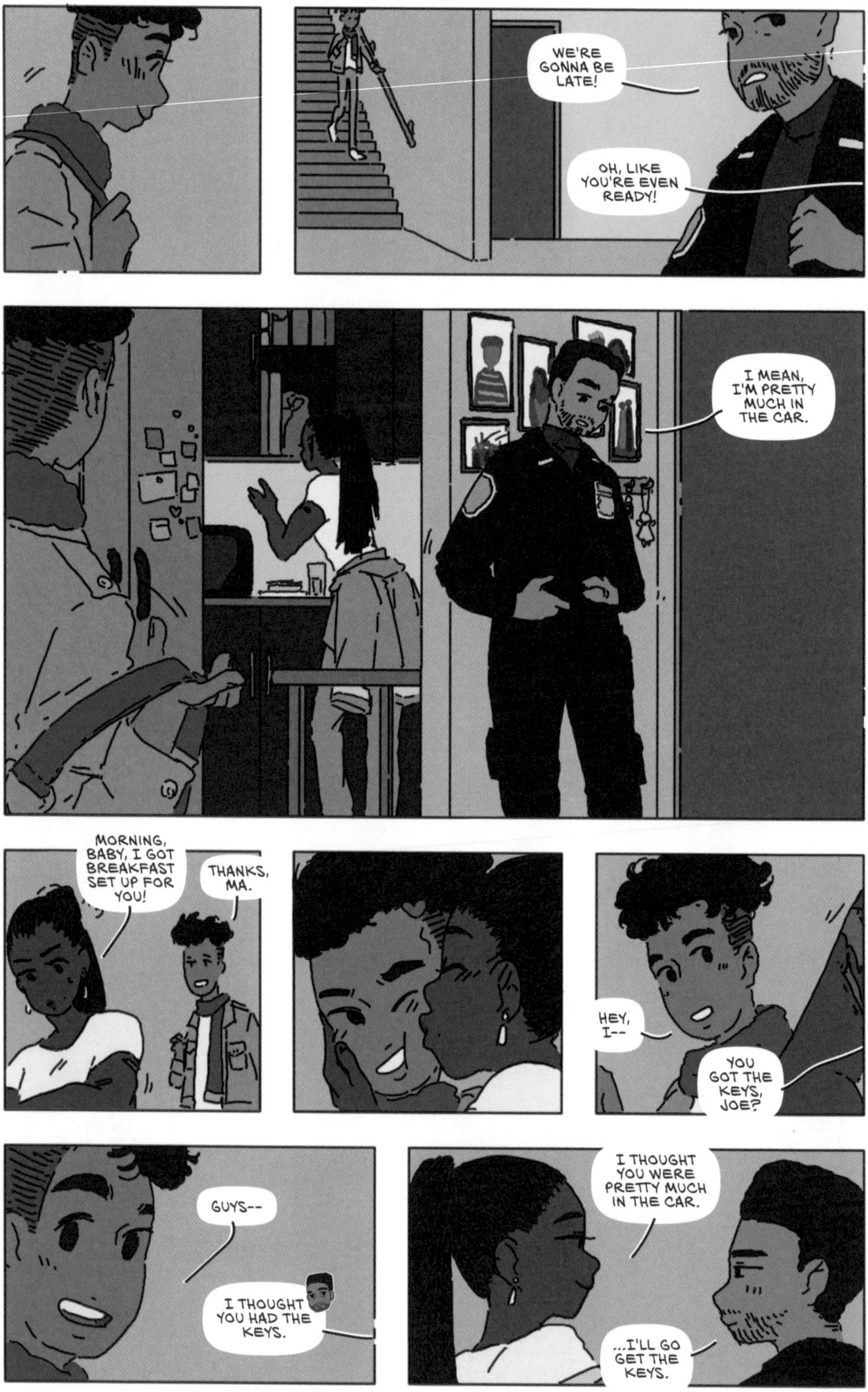
WE'RE GONNA BE LATE!
OH, LIKE YOU'RE EVEN READY!
I MEAN, I'M PRETTY MUCH IN THE CAR.
MORNING, BABY, I GOT BREAKFAST SET UP FOR YOU!
THANKS, MA.
HEY, I--
YOU GOT THE KEYS, JOE?
GUYS--
I THOUGHT YOU HAD THE KEYS.
I THOUGHT YOU WERE PRETTY MUCH IN THE CAR.
...I'LL GO GET THE KEYS.

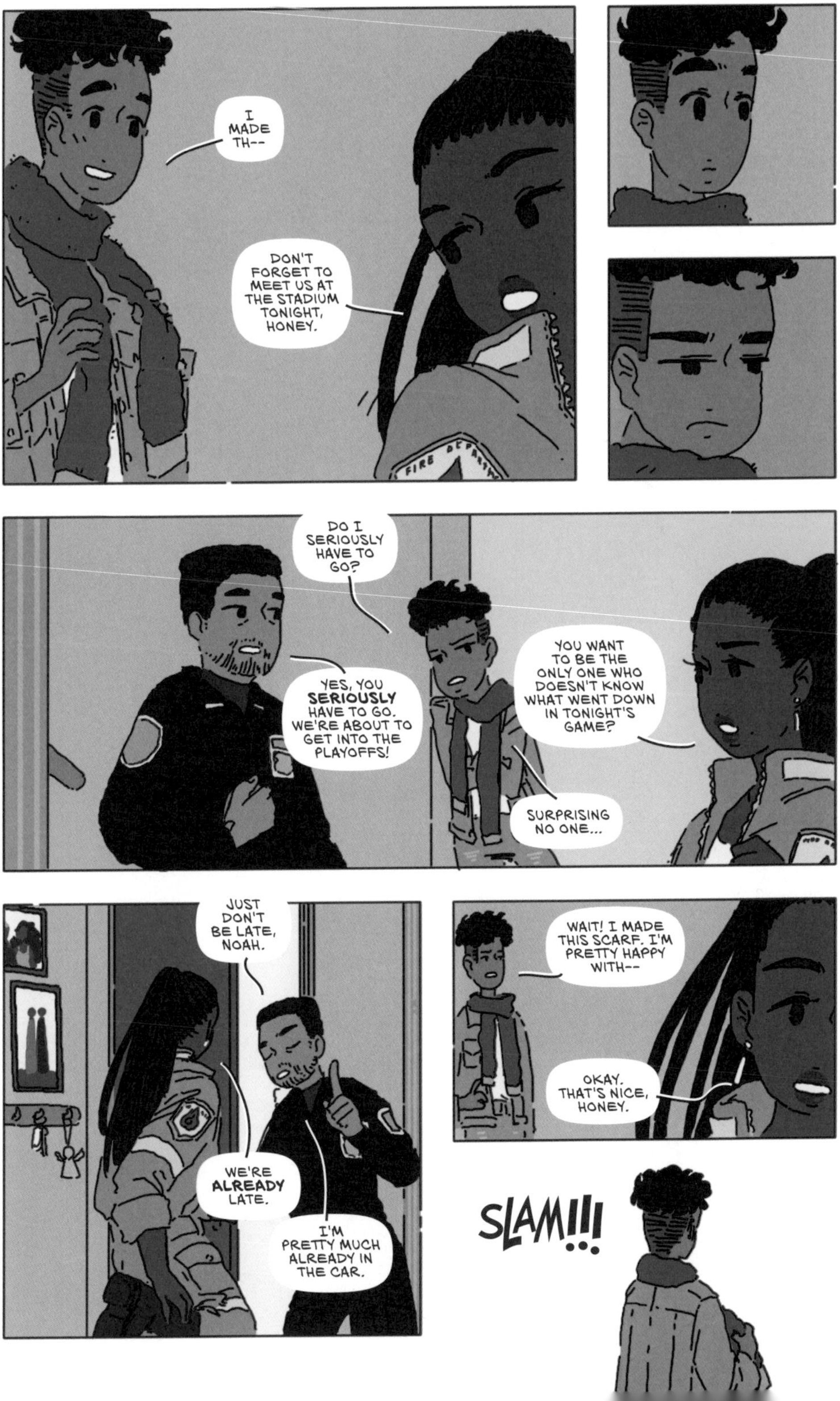
I MADE TH--
DON'T FORGET TO MEET US AT THE STADIUM TONIGHT, HONEY.
FIRE DEPT
DO I SERIOUSLY HAVE TO GO?
YES, YOU **SERIOUSLY** HAVE TO GO. WE'RE ABOUT TO GET INTO THE PLAYOFFS!
YOU WANT TO BE THE ONLY ONE WHO DOESN'T KNOW WHAT WENT DOWN IN TONIGHT'S GAME?
SURPRISING NO ONE...
JUST DON'T BE LATE, NOAH.
WE'RE **ALREADY** LATE.
I'M PRETTY MUCH ALREADY IN THE CAR.
WAIT! I MADE THIS SCARF. I'M PRETTY HAPPY WITH--
OKAY. THAT'S NICE, HONEY.
SLAM!!!

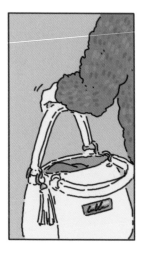

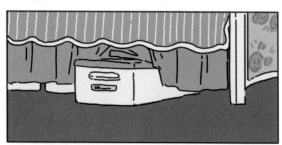

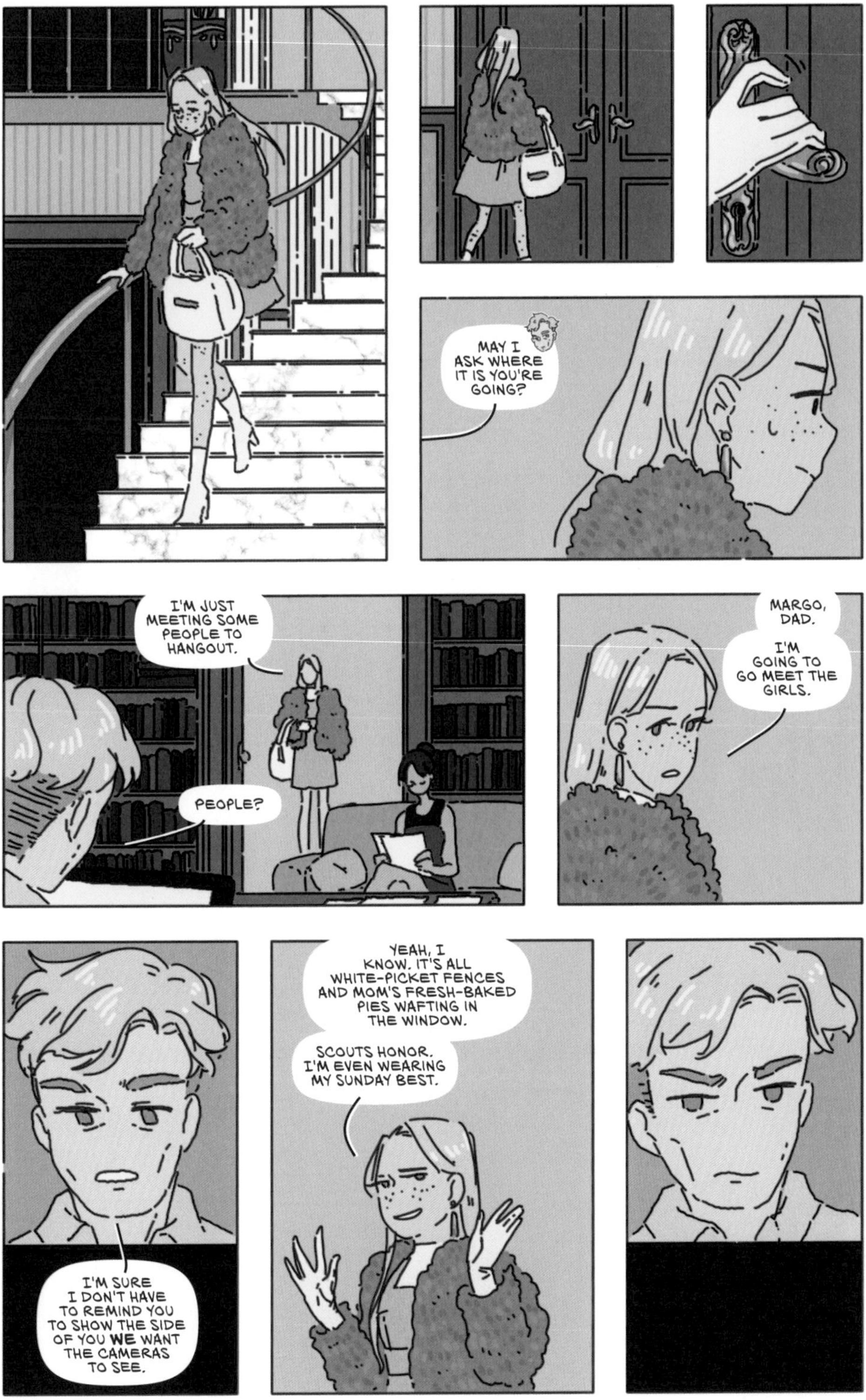
MAY I ASK WHERE IT IS YOU'RE GOING?
I'M JUST MEETING SOME PEOPLE TO HANGOUT.
PEOPLE?
MARGO, DAD.
I'M GOING TO GO MEET THE GIRLS.
I'M SURE I DON'T HAVE TO REMIND YOU TO SHOW THE SIDE OF YOU WE WANT THE CAMERAS TO SEE.
YEAH, I KNOW. IT'S ALL WHITE-PICKET FENCES AND MOM'S FRESH-BAKED PIES WAFTING IN THE WINDOW.
SCOUTS HONOR. I'M EVEN WEARING MY SUNDAY BEST.

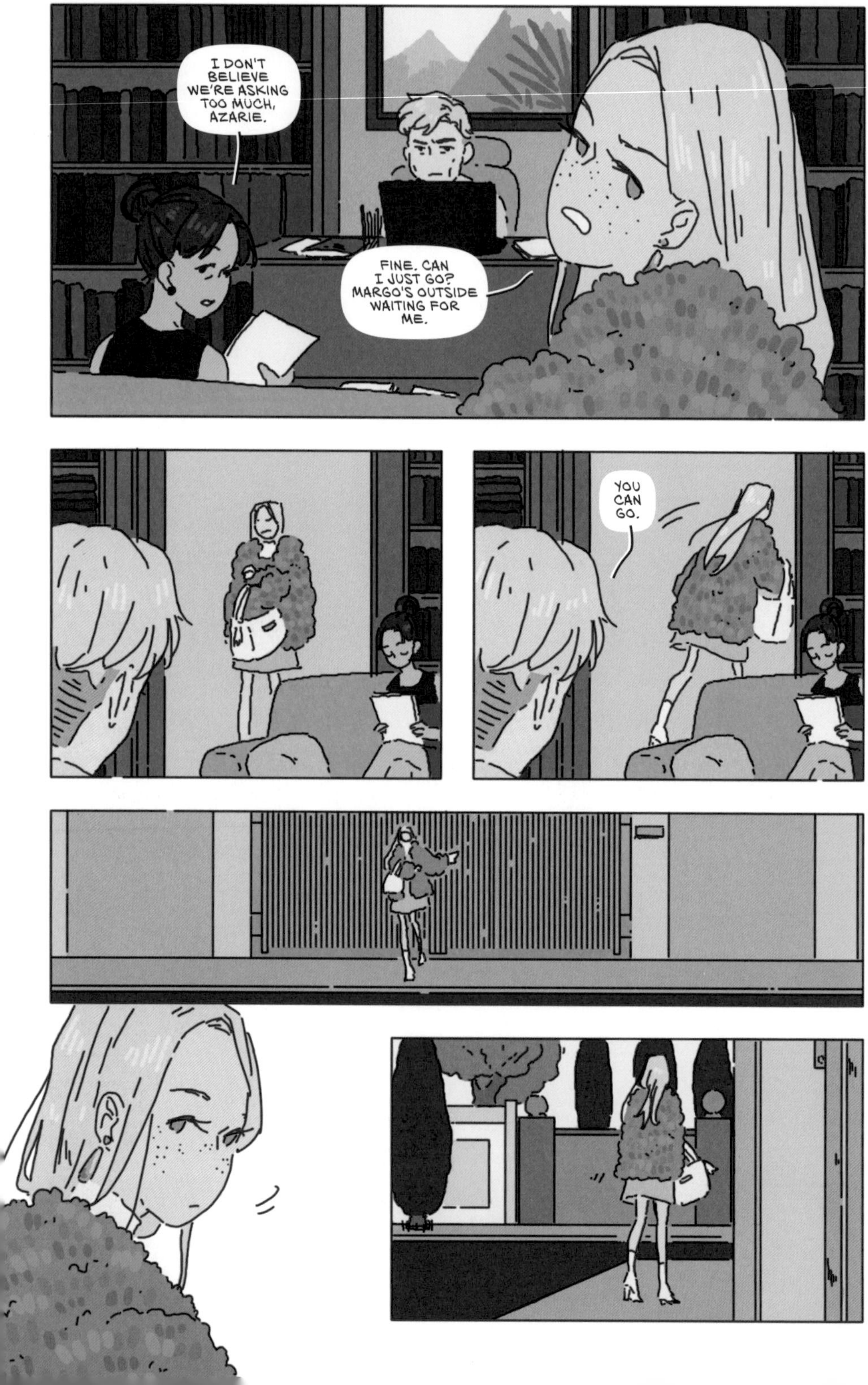
I DON'T BELIEVE WE'RE ASKING TOO MUCH, AZARIE.
FINE. CAN I JUST GO? MARGO'S OUTSIDE WAITING FOR ME.
YOU CAN GO.

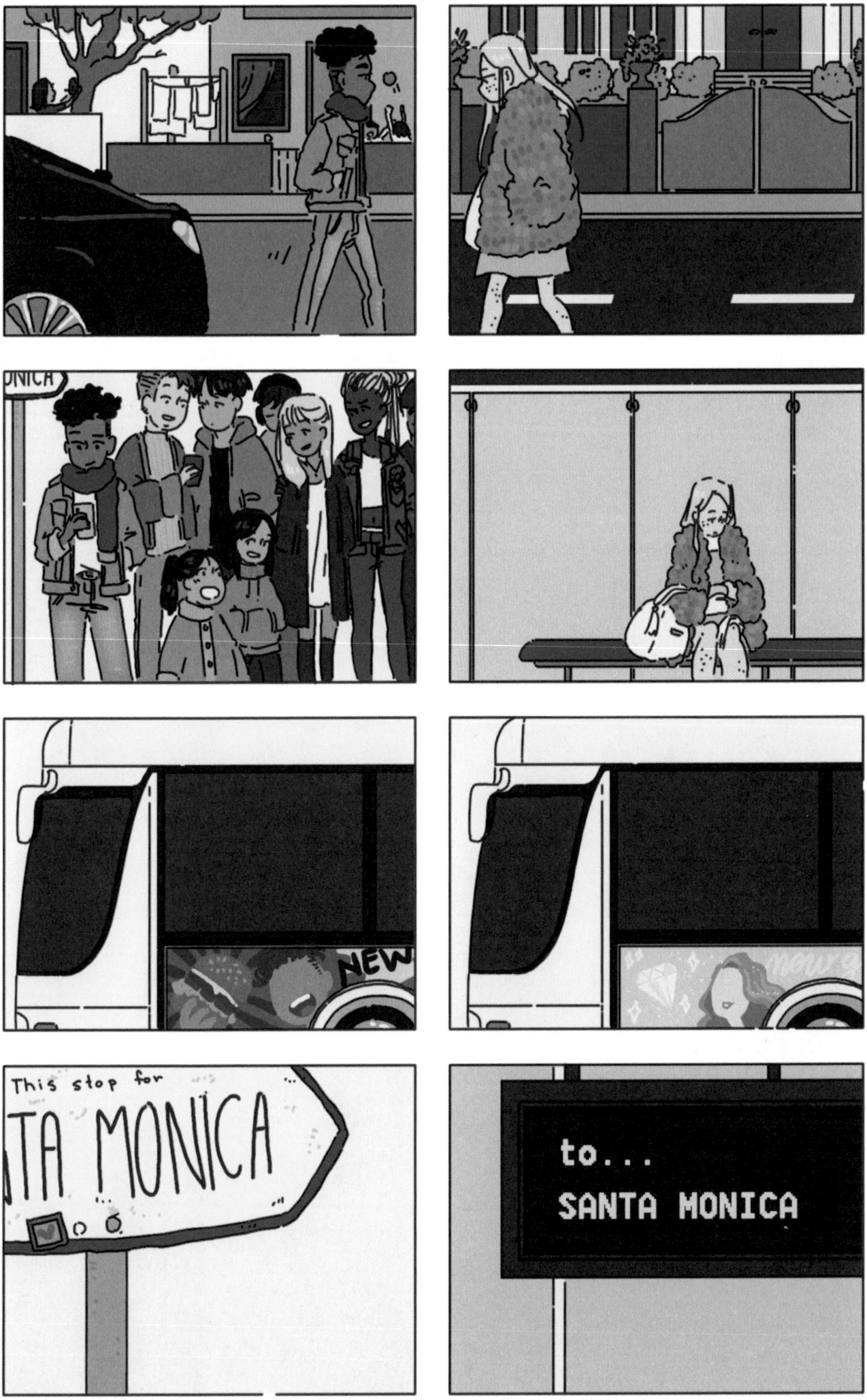

NICA
NEW
This stop for
TA MONICA
to...
SANTA MONICA

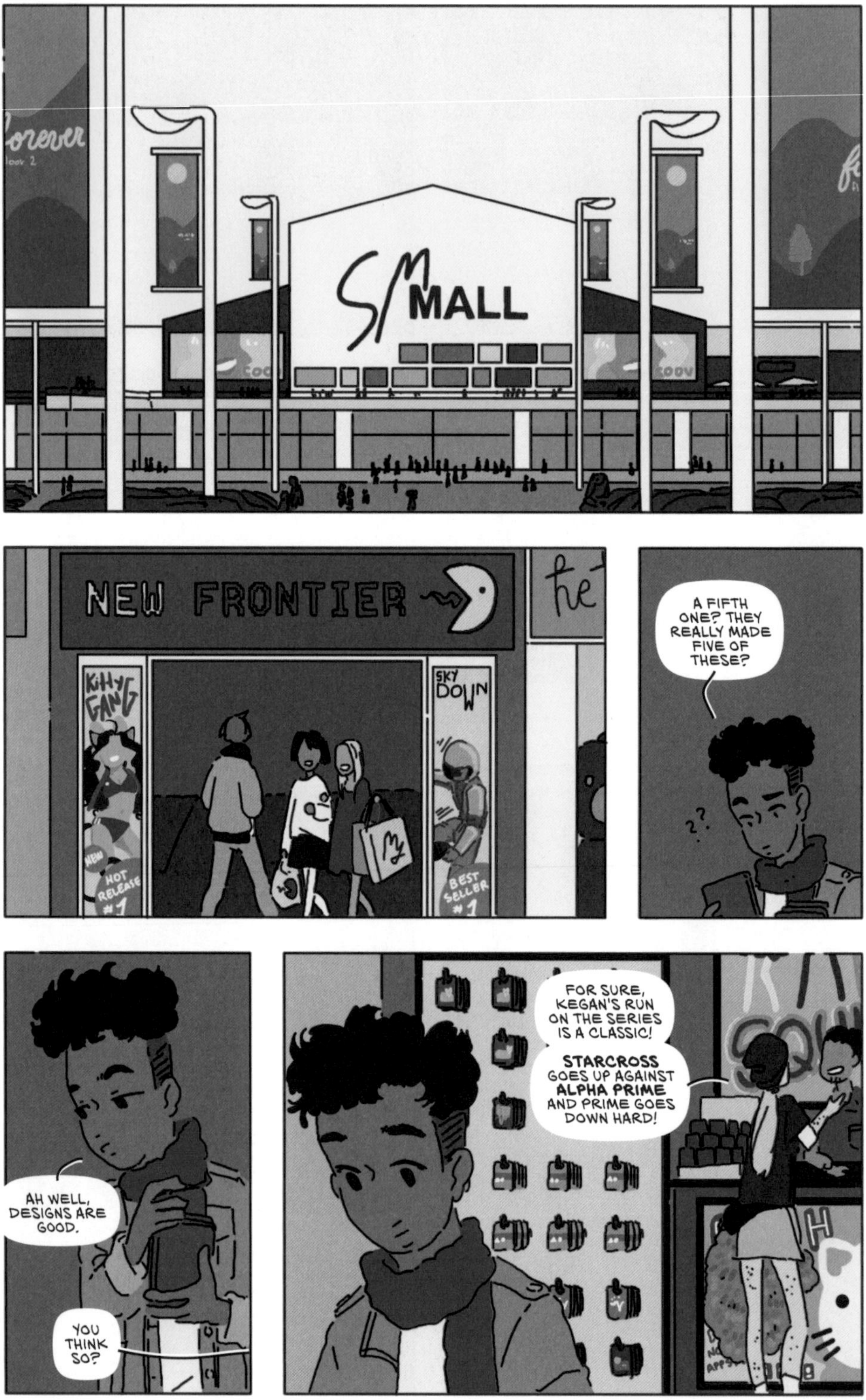
Forever
Floor 2
SM MALL
NEW FRONTIER
Kitty GANG
NEW
HOT RELEASE #1
SKY DOWN
BEST SELLER #1
A FIFTH ONE? THEY REALLY MADE FIVE OF THESE?
AH WELL, DESIGNS ARE GOOD.
YOU THINK SO?
FOR SURE, KEGAN'S RUN ON THE SERIES IS A CLASSIC!
STARCROSS GOES UP AGAINST **ALPHA PRIME** AND PRIME GOES DOWN HARD!

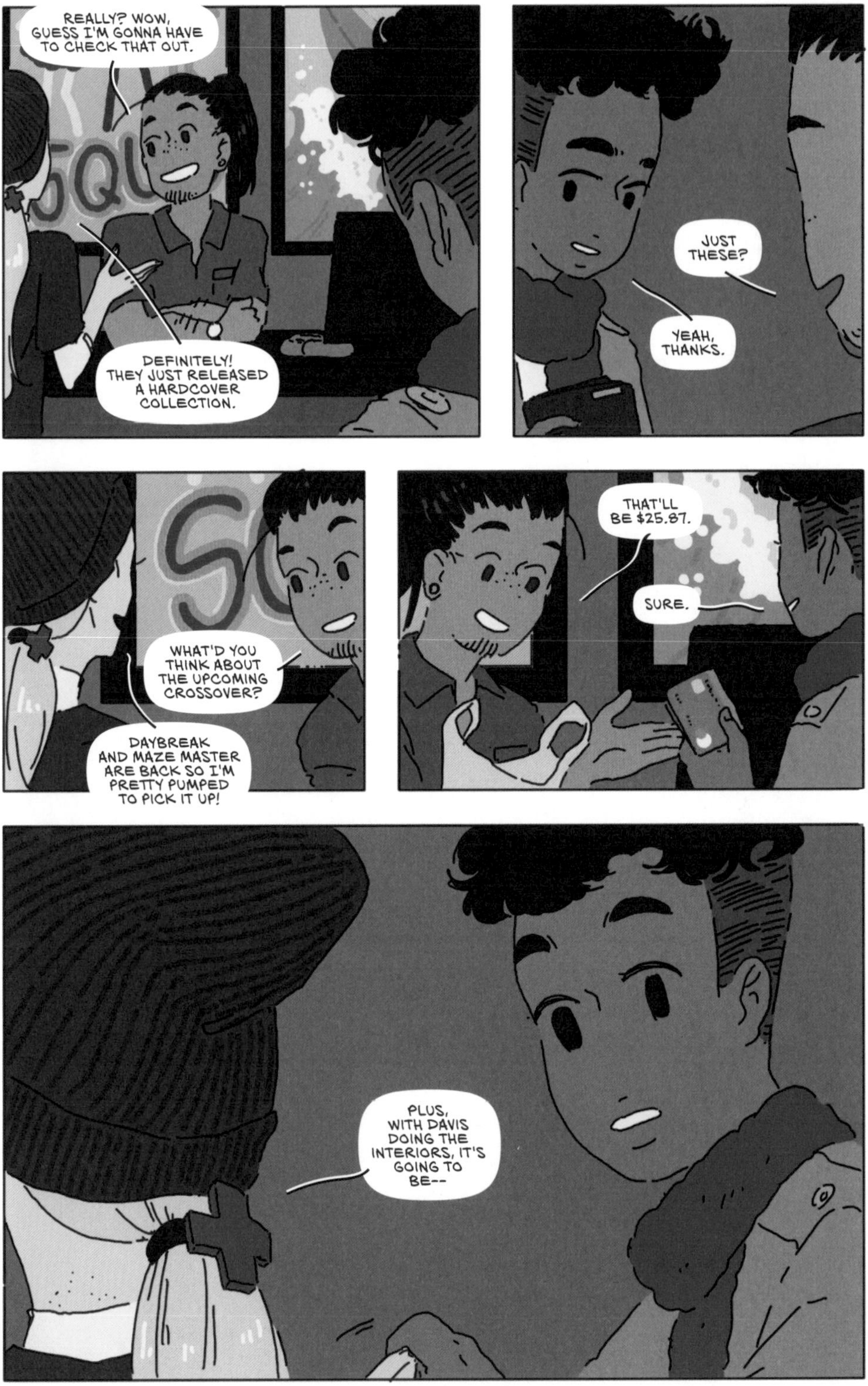
REALLY? WOW, GUESS I'M GONNA HAVE TO CHECK THAT OUT.
DEFINITELY! THEY JUST RELEASED A HARDCOVER COLLECTION.
JUST THESE?
YEAH, THANKS.
WHAT'D YOU THINK ABOUT THE UPCOMING CROSSOVER?
DAYBREAK AND MAZE MASTER ARE BACK SO I'M PRETTY PUMPED TO PICK IT UP!
THAT'LL BE $25.87.
SURE.
PLUS, WITH DAVIS DOING THE INTERIORS, IT'S GOING TO BE--

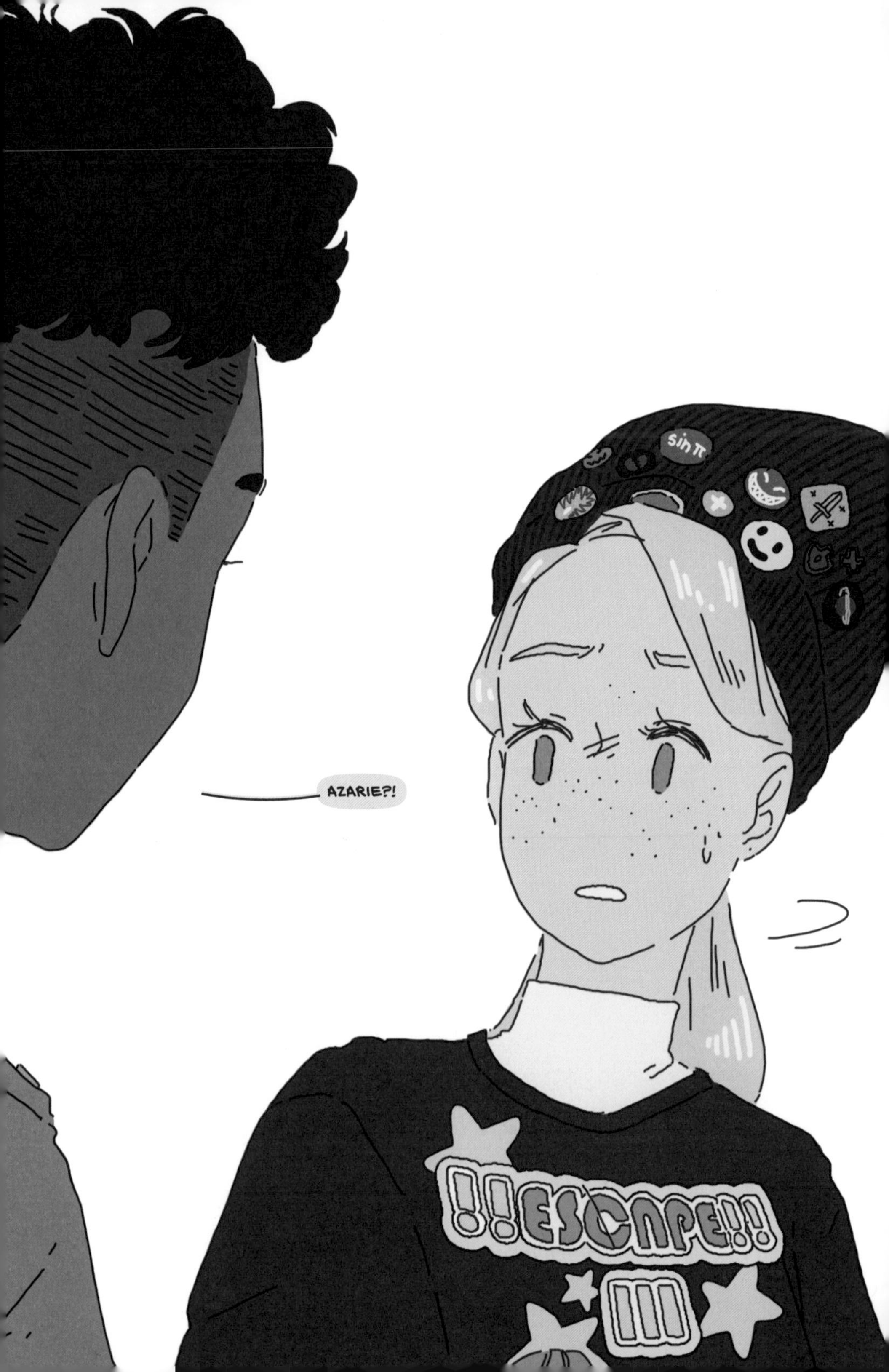
AZARIE?!
sin π
!!ESCAPE!!
III

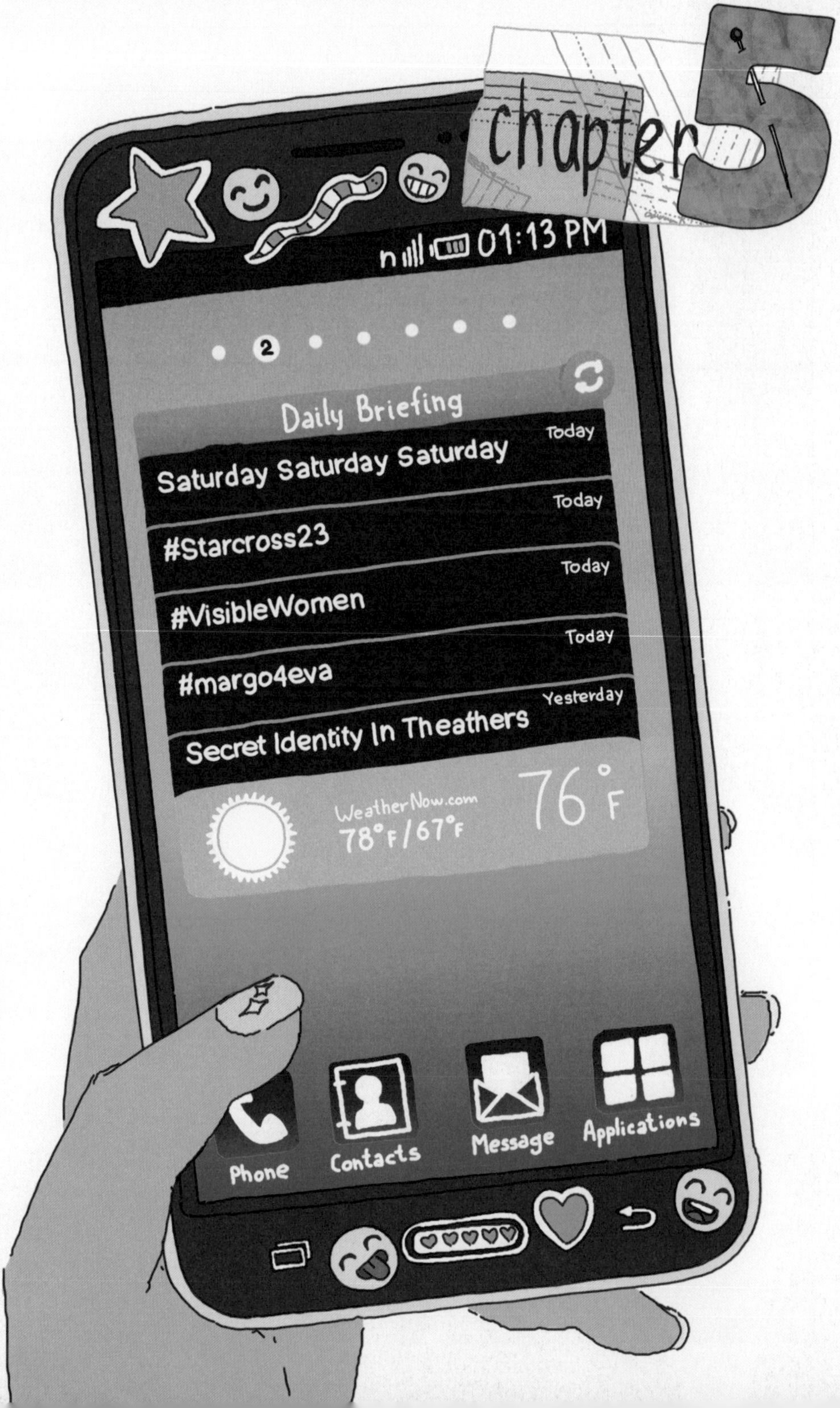
chapter 5
01:13 PM
2
Daily Briefing
Saturday Saturday Saturday
Today
#Starcross23
Today
#VisibleWomen
Today
#margo4eva
Today
Secret Identity In Theathers
Yesterday
WeatherNow.com
78°F/67°F
76°F
Phone
Contacts
Message
Applications

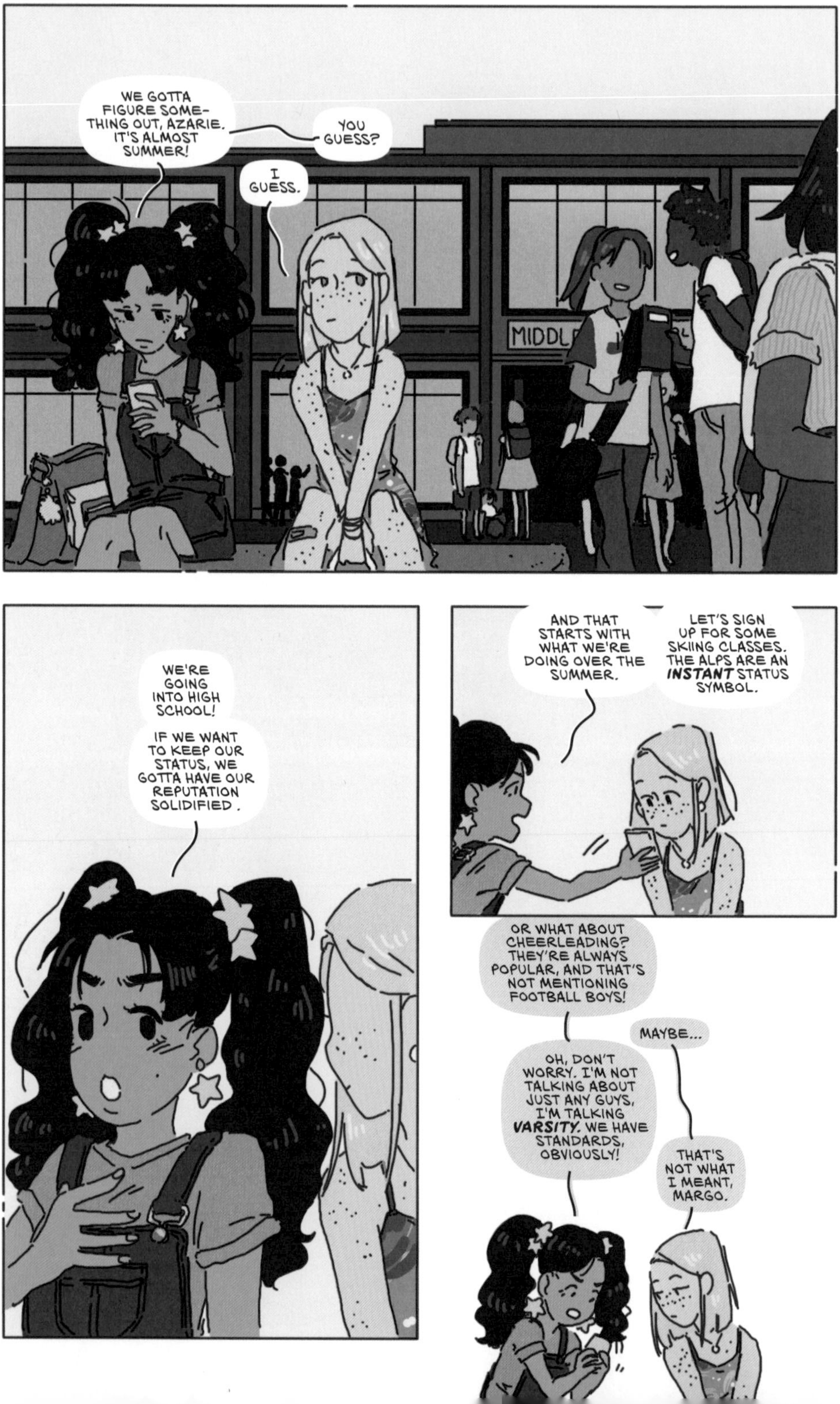
WE GOTTA FIGURE SOMETHING OUT, AZARIE. IT'S ALMOST SUMMER!
YOU GUESS?
I GUESS.
MIDDL
WE'RE GOING INTO HIGH SCHOOL!
IF WE WANT TO KEEP OUR STATUS, WE GOTTA HAVE OUR REPUTATION SOLIDIFIED.
AND THAT STARTS WITH WHAT WE'RE DOING OVER THE SUMMER.
LET'S SIGN UP FOR SOME SKIING CLASSES. THE ALPS ARE AN ***INSTANT*** STATUS SYMBOL.
OR WHAT ABOUT CHEERLEADING? THEY'RE ALWAYS POPULAR, AND THAT'S NOT MENTIONING FOOTBALL BOYS!
MAYBE...
OH, DON'T WORRY. I'M NOT TALKING ABOUT JUST ANY GUYS, I'M TALKING ***VARSITY.*** WE HAVE STANDARDS, OBVIOUSLY!
THAT'S NOT WHAT I MEANT, MARGO.

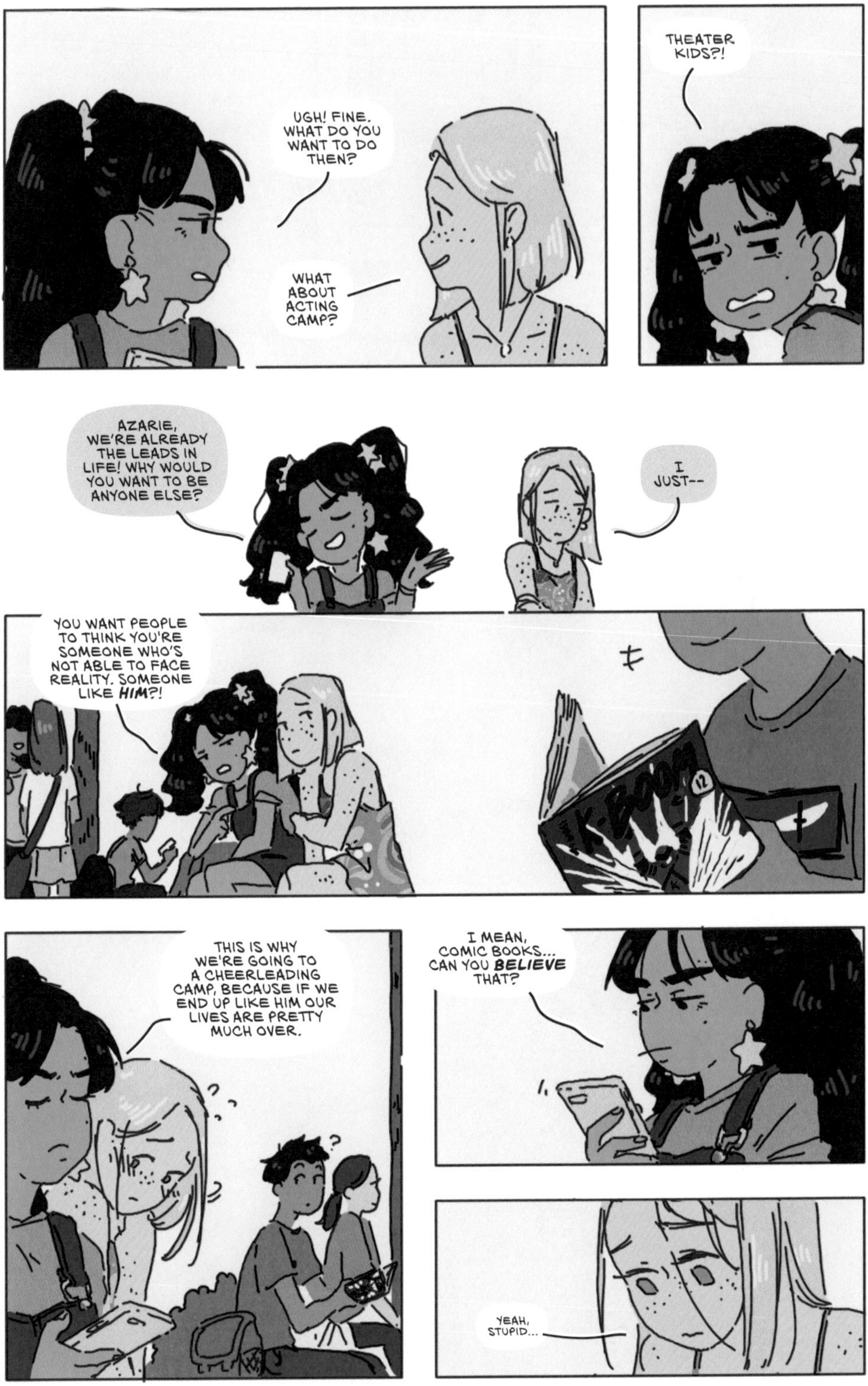
UGH! FINE. WHAT DO YOU WANT TO DO THEN?
WHAT ABOUT ACTING CAMP?
THEATER KIDS?!
AZARIE, WE'RE ALREADY THE LEADS IN LIFE! WHY WOULD YOU WANT TO BE ANYONE ELSE?
I JUST--
YOU WANT PEOPLE TO THINK YOU'RE SOMEONE WHO'S NOT ABLE TO FACE REALITY. SOMEONE LIKE **HIM**?!
K-BOOM
THIS IS WHY WE'RE GOING TO A CHEERLEADING CAMP, BECAUSE IF WE END UP LIKE HIM OUR LIVES ARE PRETTY MUCH OVER.
I MEAN, COMIC BOOKS... CAN YOU **BELIEVE** THAT?
YEAH, STUPID...

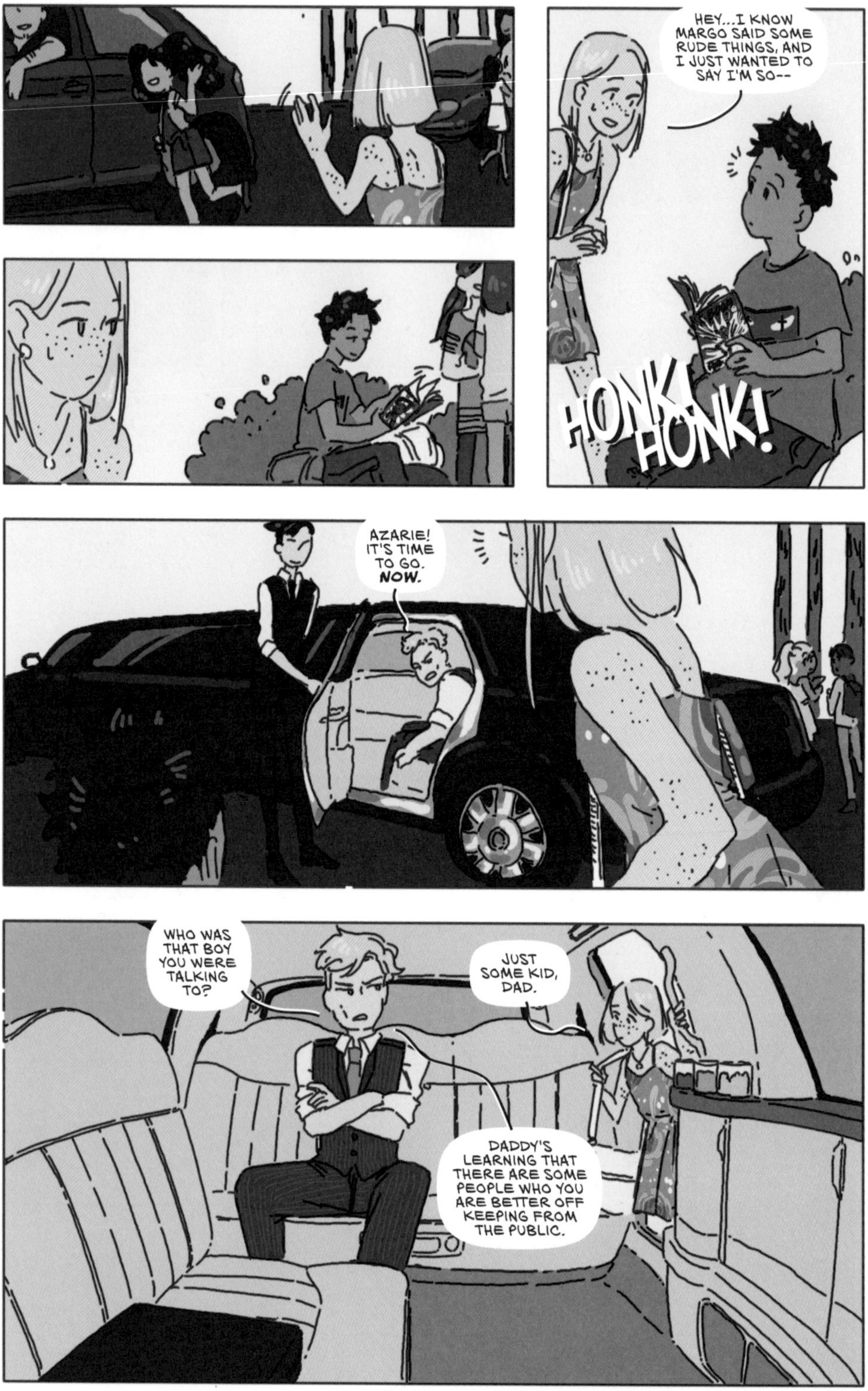
HEY...I KNOW MARGO SAID SOME RUDE THINGS, AND I JUST WANTED TO SAY I'M SO--
HONK! HONK!
AZARIE! IT'S TIME TO GO. NOW.
WHO WAS THAT BOY YOU WERE TALKING TO?
JUST SOME KID, DAD.
DADDY'S LEARNING THAT THERE ARE SOME PEOPLE WHO YOU ARE BETTER OFF KEEPING FROM THE PUBLIC.

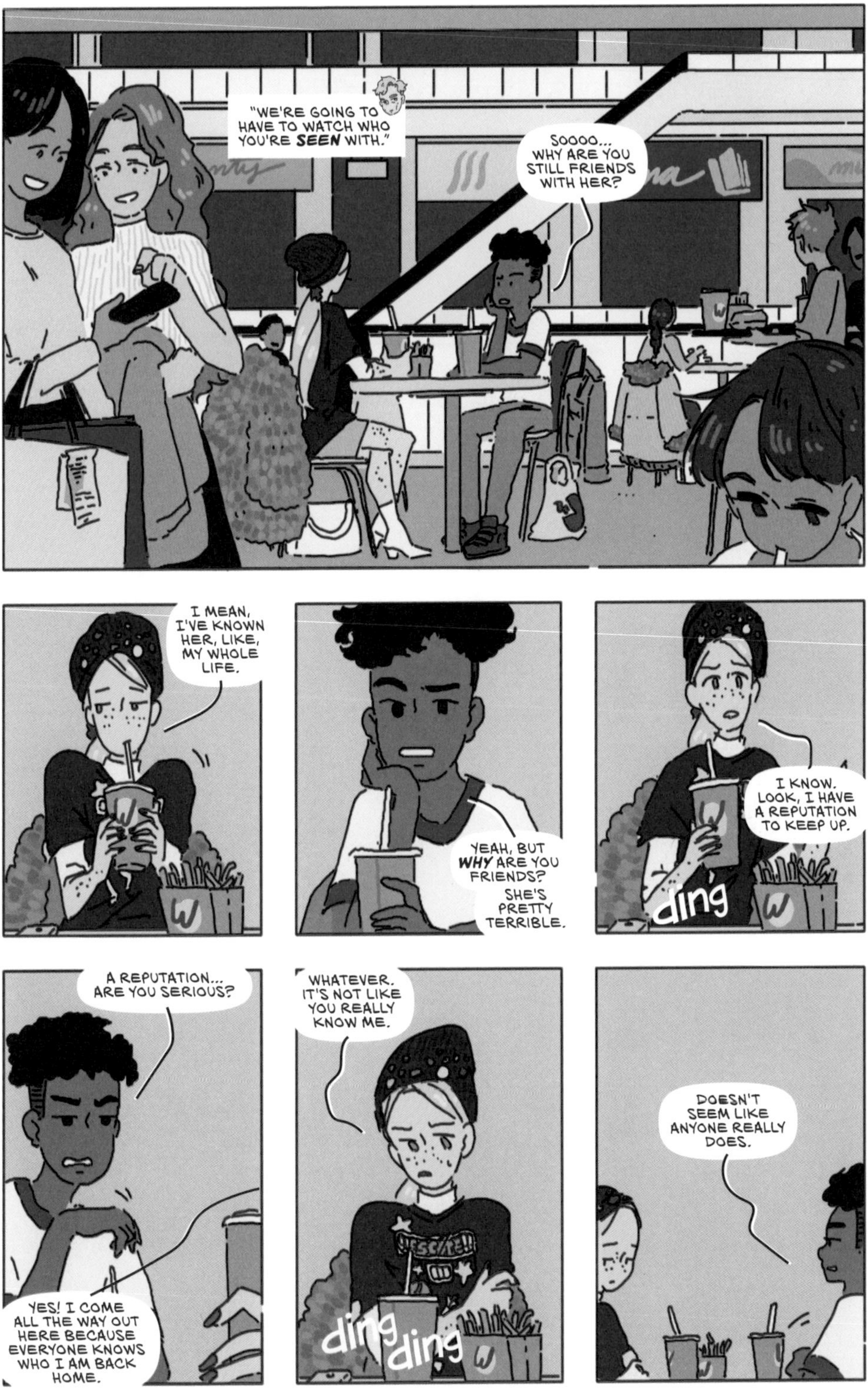
"WE'RE GOING TO HAVE TO WATCH WHO YOU'RE **SEEN** WITH."
SOOOO... WHY ARE YOU STILL FRIENDS WITH HER?
I MEAN, I'VE KNOWN HER, LIKE, MY WHOLE LIFE.
YEAH, BUT **WHY** ARE YOU FRIENDS?
SHE'S PRETTY TERRIBLE.
I KNOW. LOOK, I HAVE A REPUTATION TO KEEP UP.
ding
A REPUTATION... ARE YOU SERIOUS?
YES! I COME ALL THE WAY OUT HERE BECAUSE EVERYONE KNOWS WHO I AM BACK HOME.
WHATEVER. IT'S NOT LIKE YOU REALLY KNOW ME.
ding ding
DOESN'T SEEM LIKE ANYONE REALLY DOES.

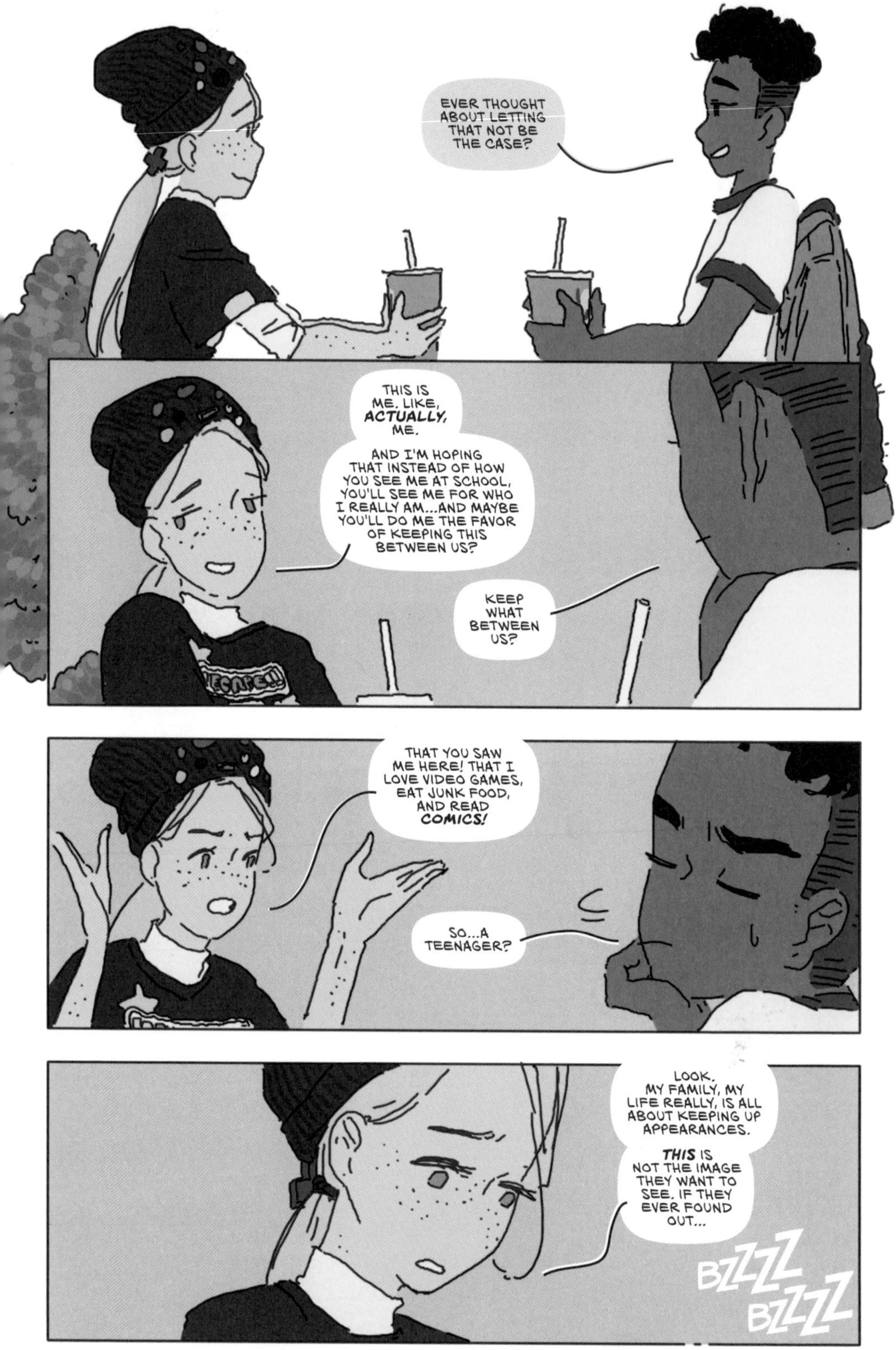
EVER THOUGHT ABOUT LETTING THAT NOT BE THE CASE?
THIS IS ME. LIKE, ACTUALLY, ME.
AND I'M HOPING THAT INSTEAD OF HOW YOU SEE ME AT SCHOOL, YOU'LL SEE ME FOR WHO I REALLY AM...AND MAYBE YOU'LL DO ME THE FAVOR OF KEEPING THIS BETWEEN US?
KEEP WHAT BETWEEN US?
THAT YOU SAW ME HERE! THAT I LOVE VIDEO GAMES, EAT JUNK FOOD, AND READ COMICS!
SO...A TEENAGER?
LOOK. MY FAMILY, MY LIFE REALLY, IS ALL ABOUT KEEPING UP APPEARANCES.
THIS IS NOT THE IMAGE THEY WANT TO SEE. IF THEY EVER FOUND OUT...
BZZZZ
BZZZZ

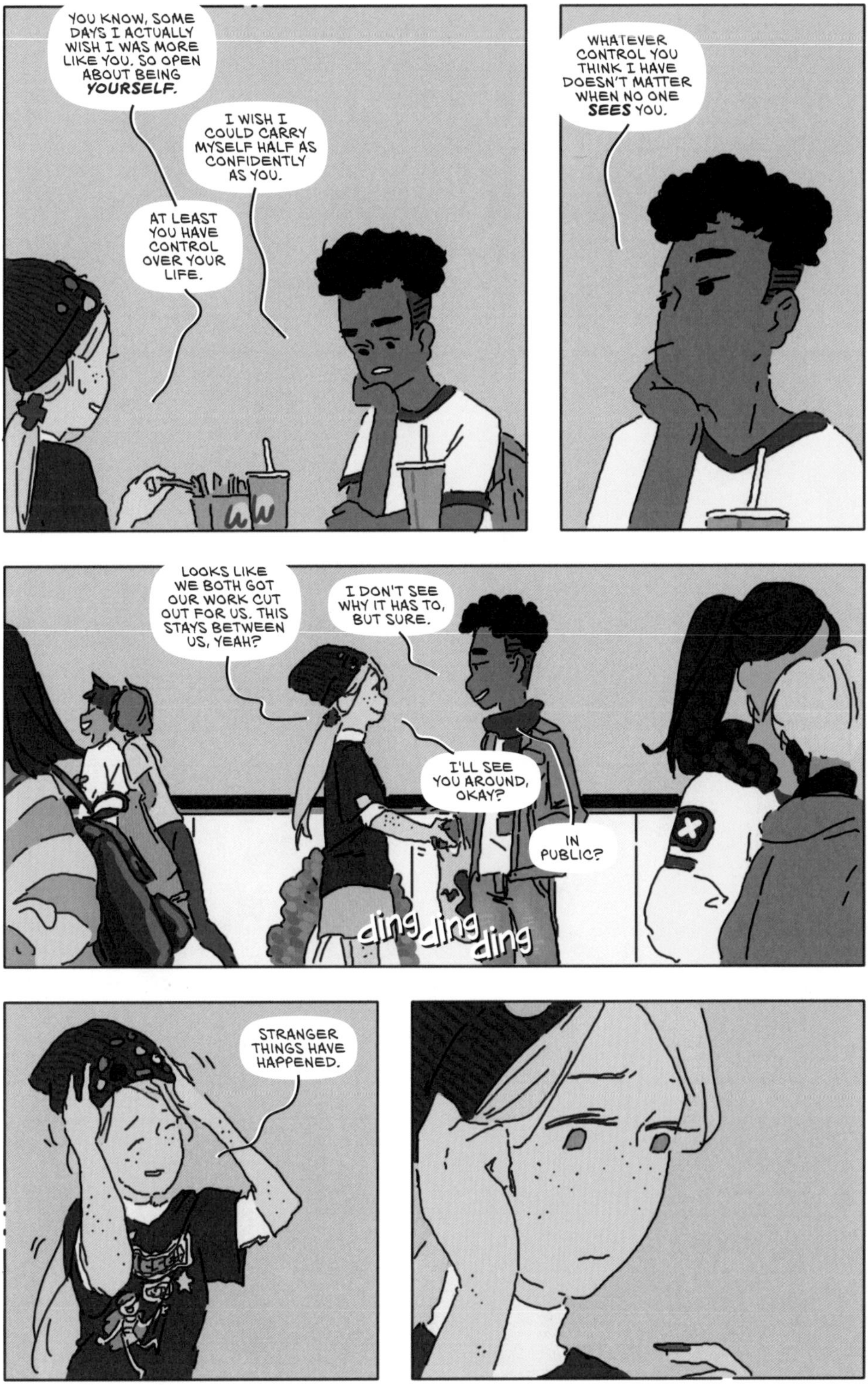
YOU KNOW, SOME DAYS I ACTUALLY WISH I WAS MORE LIKE YOU. SO OPEN ABOUT BEING *YOURSELF.*
AT LEAST YOU HAVE CONTROL OVER YOUR LIFE.
I WISH I COULD CARRY MYSELF HALF AS CONFIDENTLY AS YOU.
WHATEVER CONTROL YOU THINK I HAVE DOESN'T MATTER WHEN NO ONE **SEES** YOU.
LOOKS LIKE WE BOTH GOT OUR WORK CUT OUT FOR US. THIS STAYS BETWEEN US, YEAH?
I DON'T SEE WHY IT HAS TO, BUT SURE.
I'LL SEE YOU AROUND, OKAY?
IN PUBLIC?
ding ding ding
STRANGER THINGS HAVE HAPPENED.

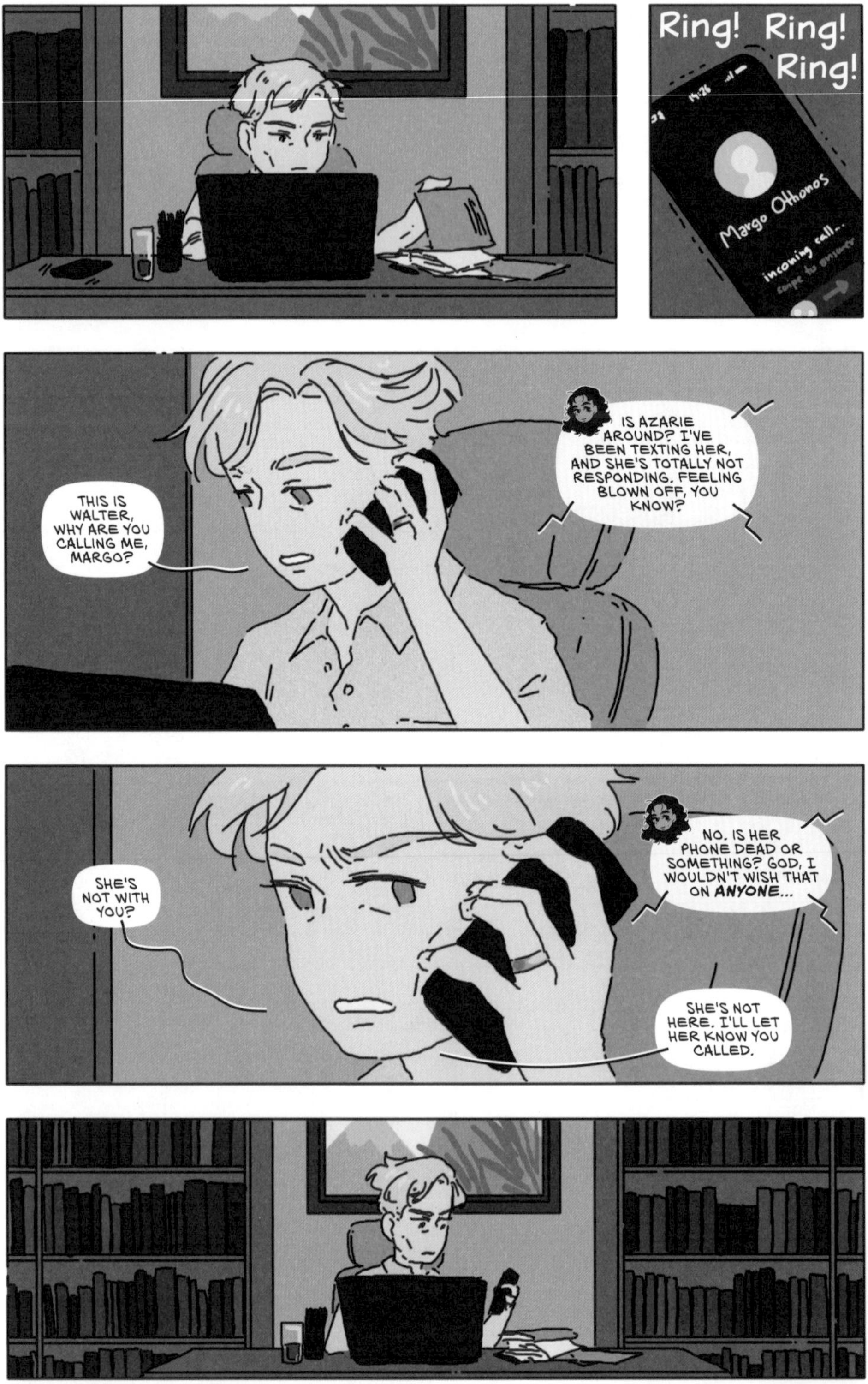
Ring! Ring! Ring!
Margo Othonos
incoming call...
swipe to answer
THIS IS WALTER, WHY ARE YOU CALLING ME, MARGO?
IS AZARIE AROUND? I'VE BEEN TEXTING HER, AND SHE'S TOTALLY NOT RESPONDING. FEELING BLOWN OFF, YOU KNOW?
SHE'S NOT WITH YOU?
NO. IS HER PHONE DEAD OR SOMETHING? GOD, I WOULDN'T WISH THAT ON ANYONE...
SHE'S NOT HERE. I'LL LET HER KNOW YOU CALLED.

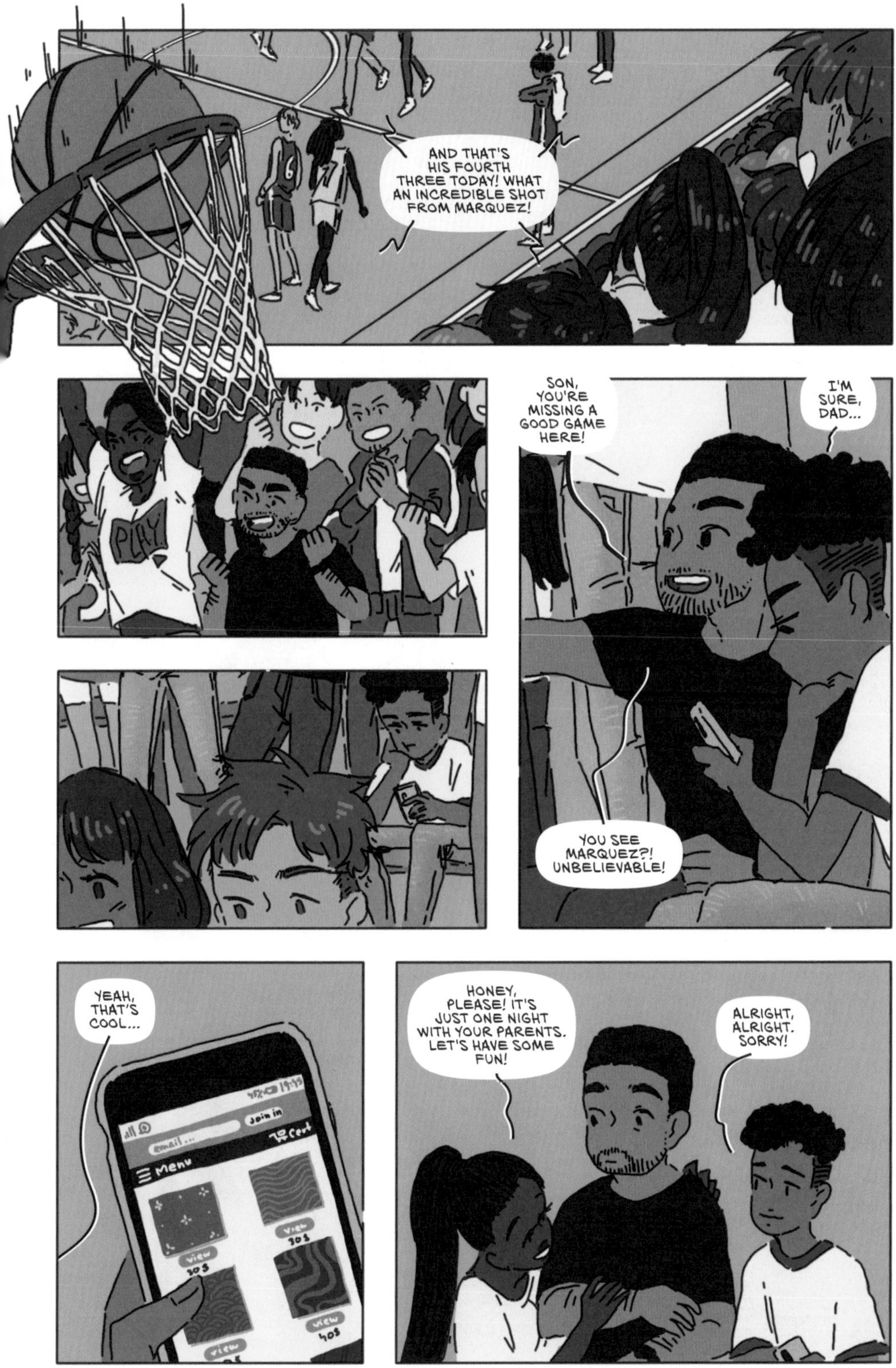
AND THAT'S HIS FOURTH THREE TODAY! WHAT AN INCREDIBLE SHOT FROM MARQUEZ!
PLAY
SON, YOU'RE MISSING A GOOD GAME HERE!
I'M SURE, DAD...
YOU SEE MARQUEZ?! UNBELIEVABLE!
YEAH, THAT'S COOL...
HONEY, PLEASE! IT'S JUST ONE NIGHT WITH YOUR PARENTS. LET'S HAVE SOME FUN!
ALRIGHT, ALRIGHT. SORRY!

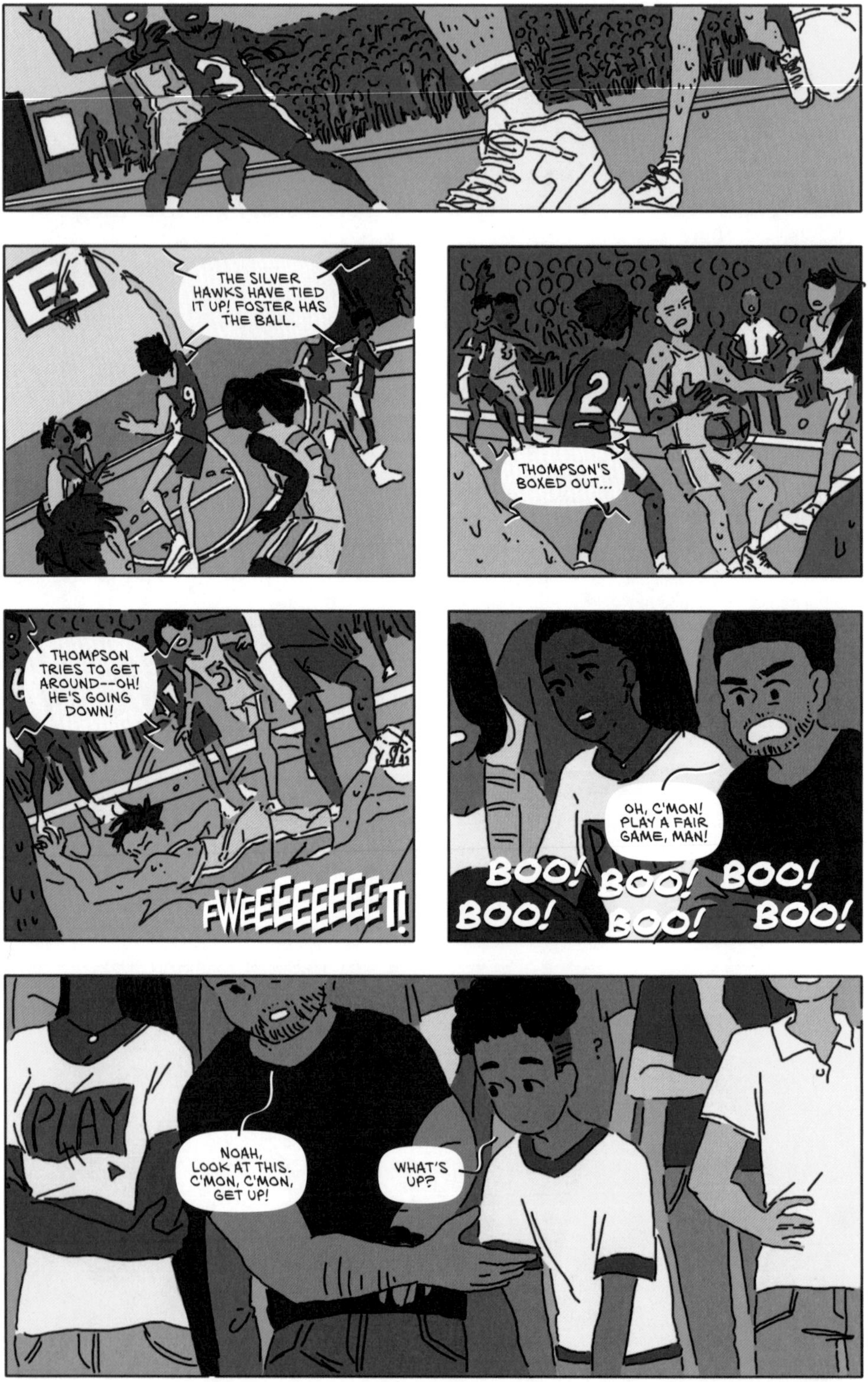

THE SILVER HAWKS HAVE TIED IT UP! FOSTER HAS THE BALL.
THOMPSON'S BOXED OUT...
THOMPSON TRIES TO GET AROUND--OH! HE'S GOING DOWN!
FWEEEEEEEEET!
OH, C'MON! PLAY A FAIR GAME, MAN!
BOO! BOO! BOO! BOO! BOO! BOO!
PLAY
NOAH, LOOK AT THIS. C'MON, C'MON, GET UP!
WHAT'S UP?

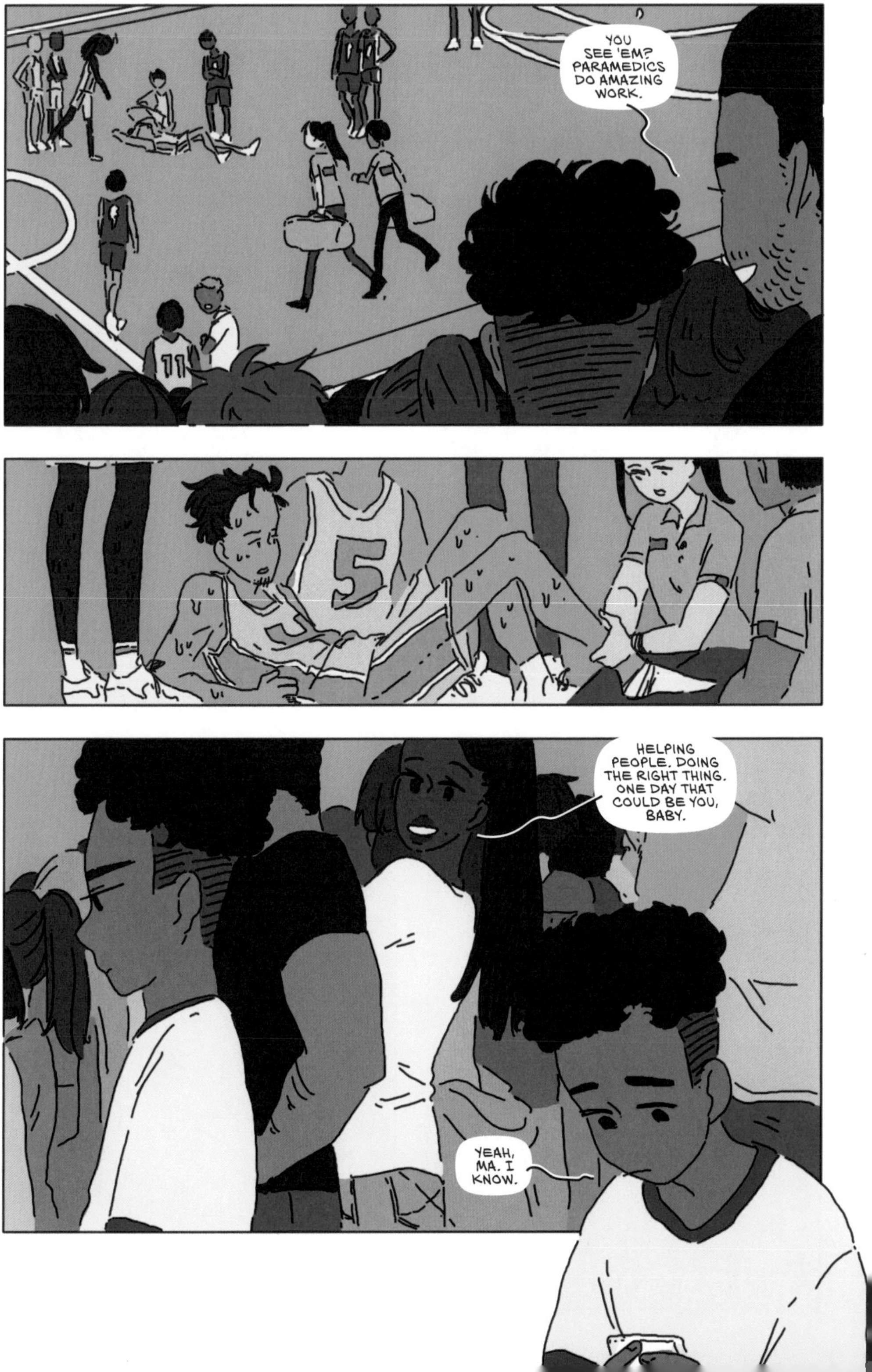
YOU SEE 'EM? PARAMEDICS DO AMAZING WORK.
HELPING PEOPLE. DOING THE RIGHT THING. ONE DAY THAT COULD BE YOU, BABY.
YEAH, MA. I KNOW.

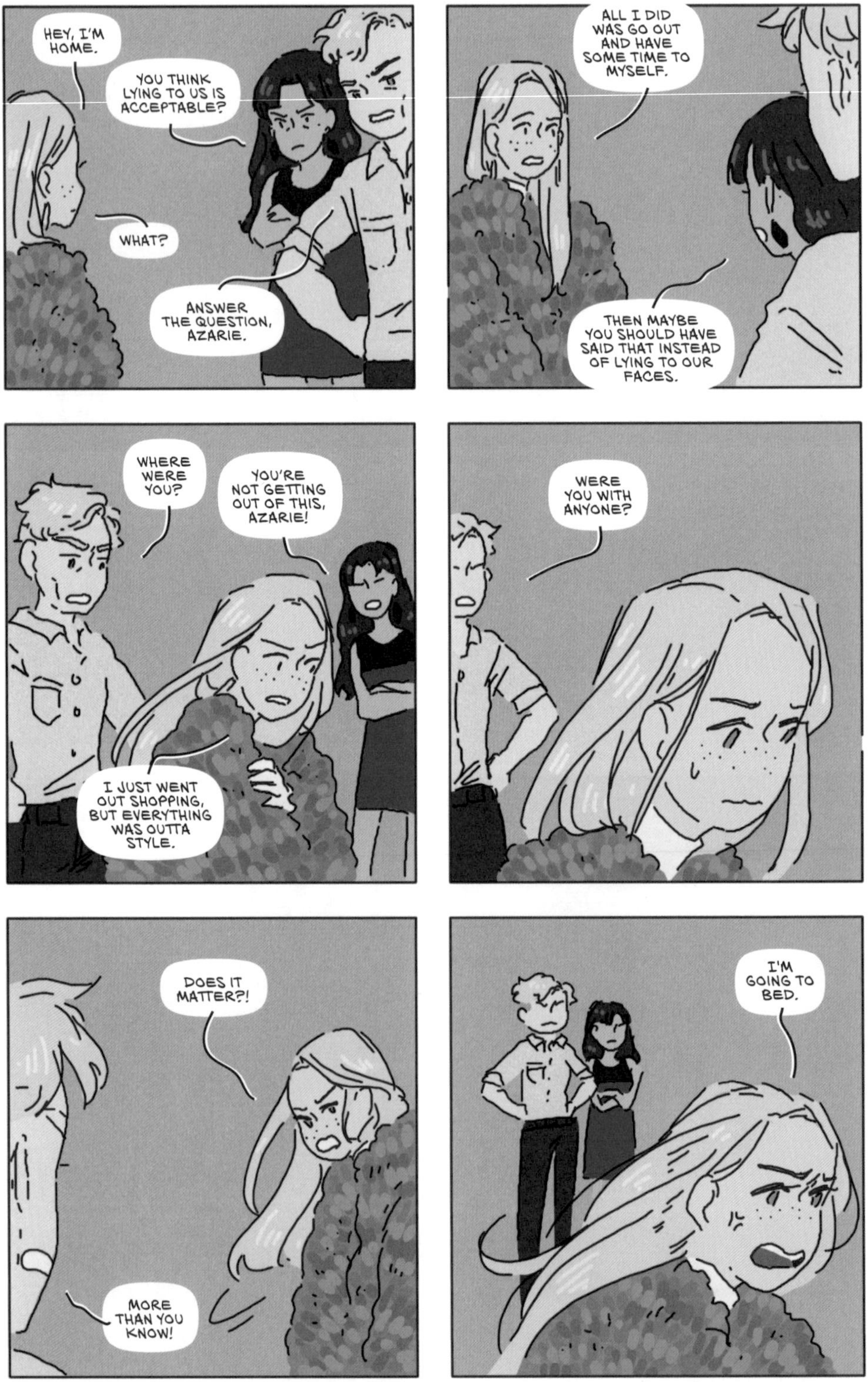
HEY, I'M HOME.
YOU THINK LYING TO US IS ACCEPTABLE?
WHAT?
ANSWER THE QUESTION, AZARIE.
ALL I DID WAS GO OUT AND HAVE SOME TIME TO MYSELF.
THEN MAYBE YOU SHOULD HAVE SAID THAT INSTEAD OF LYING TO OUR FACES.
WHERE WERE YOU?
YOU'RE NOT GETTING OUT OF THIS, AZARIE!
I JUST WENT OUT SHOPPING, BUT EVERYTHING WAS OUTTA STYLE.
WERE YOU WITH ANYONE?
DOES IT MATTER?!
MORE THAN YOU KNOW!
I'M GOING TO BED.

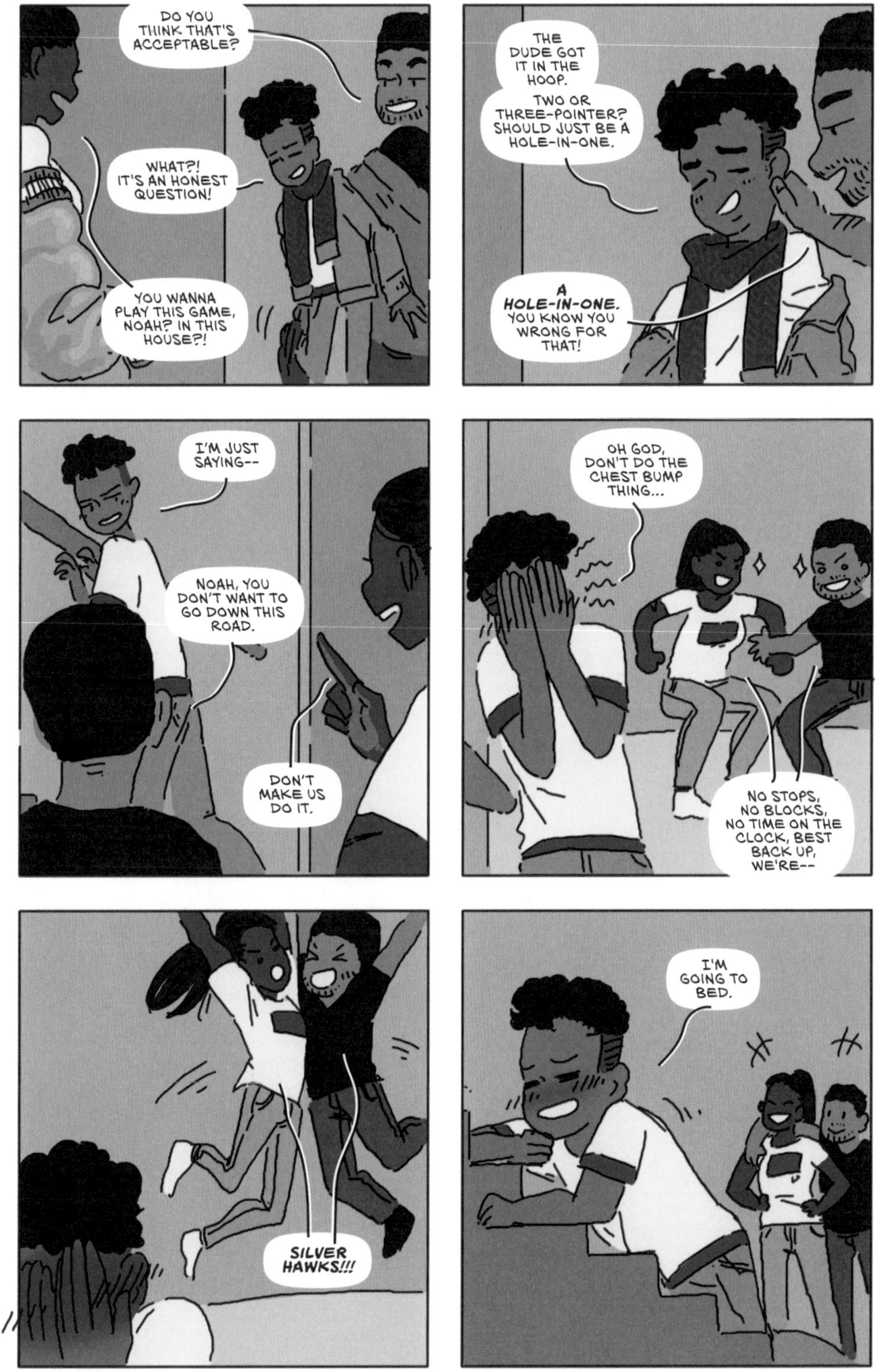
DO YOU THINK THAT'S ACCEPTABLE?
WHAT?! IT'S AN HONEST QUESTION!
YOU WANNA PLAY THIS GAME, NOAH? IN THIS HOUSE?!
THE DUDE GOT IT IN THE HOOP.
TWO OR THREE-POINTER? SHOULD JUST BE A HOLE-IN-ONE.
A HOLE-IN-ONE. YOU KNOW YOU WRONG FOR THAT!
I'M JUST SAYING--
NOAH, YOU DON'T WANT TO GO DOWN THIS ROAD.
DON'T MAKE US DO IT.
OH GOD, DON'T DO THE CHEST BUMP THING...
NO STOPS, NO BLOCKS, NO TIME ON THE CLOCK, BEST BACK UP, WE'RE--
SILVER HAWKS!!!
I'M GOING TO BED.

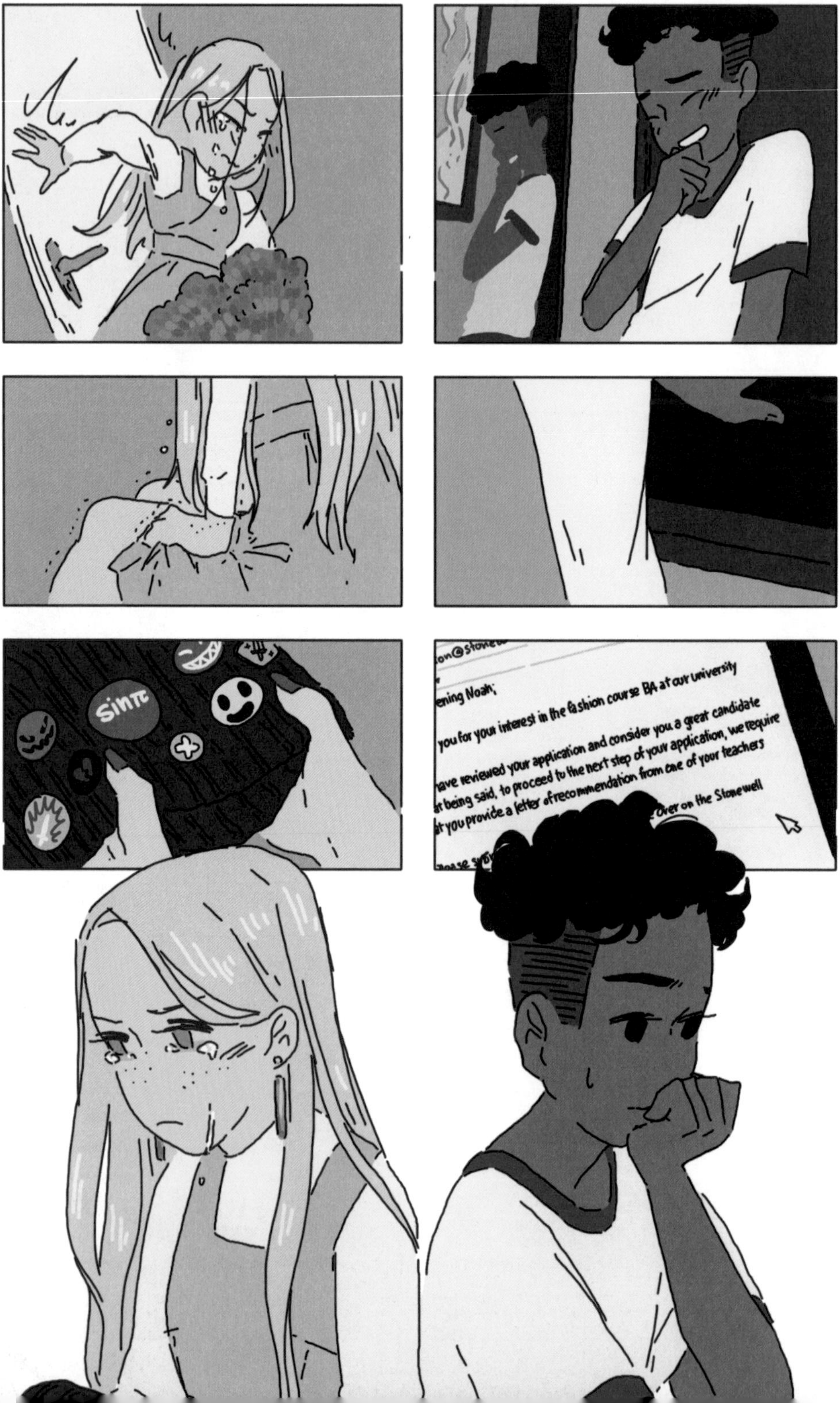
SINTC
ion@stone
ening Noah;
you for your interest in the fashion course BA at our university
have reviewed your application and consider you a great candidate
at being said, to proceed to the next step of your application, we require
at you provide a letter of recommendation from one of your teachers
over on the Stonewell

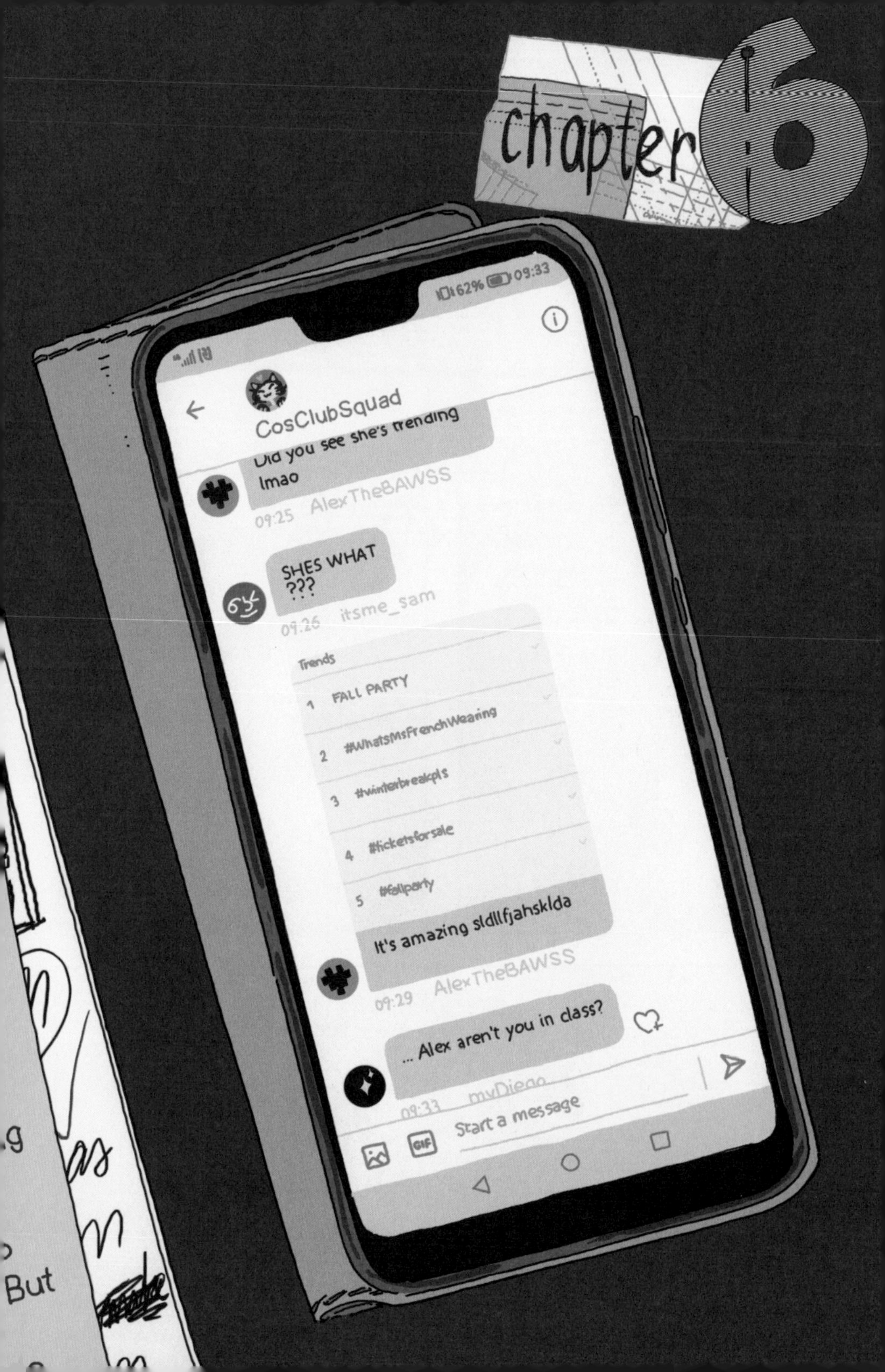
chapter 6
62% 09:33
CosClubSquad
Did you see she's trending lmao
09:25 AlexTheBAWSS
SHES WHAT ???
09:26 itsme_sam
Trends
1 FALL PARTY
2 #WhatsMsFrenchWearing
3 #winterbreakpls
4 #ticketsforsale
5 #fallparty
It's amazing sldllfjahsklda
09:29 AlexTheBAWSS
... Alex aren't you in class?
09:33 myDiego
Start a message

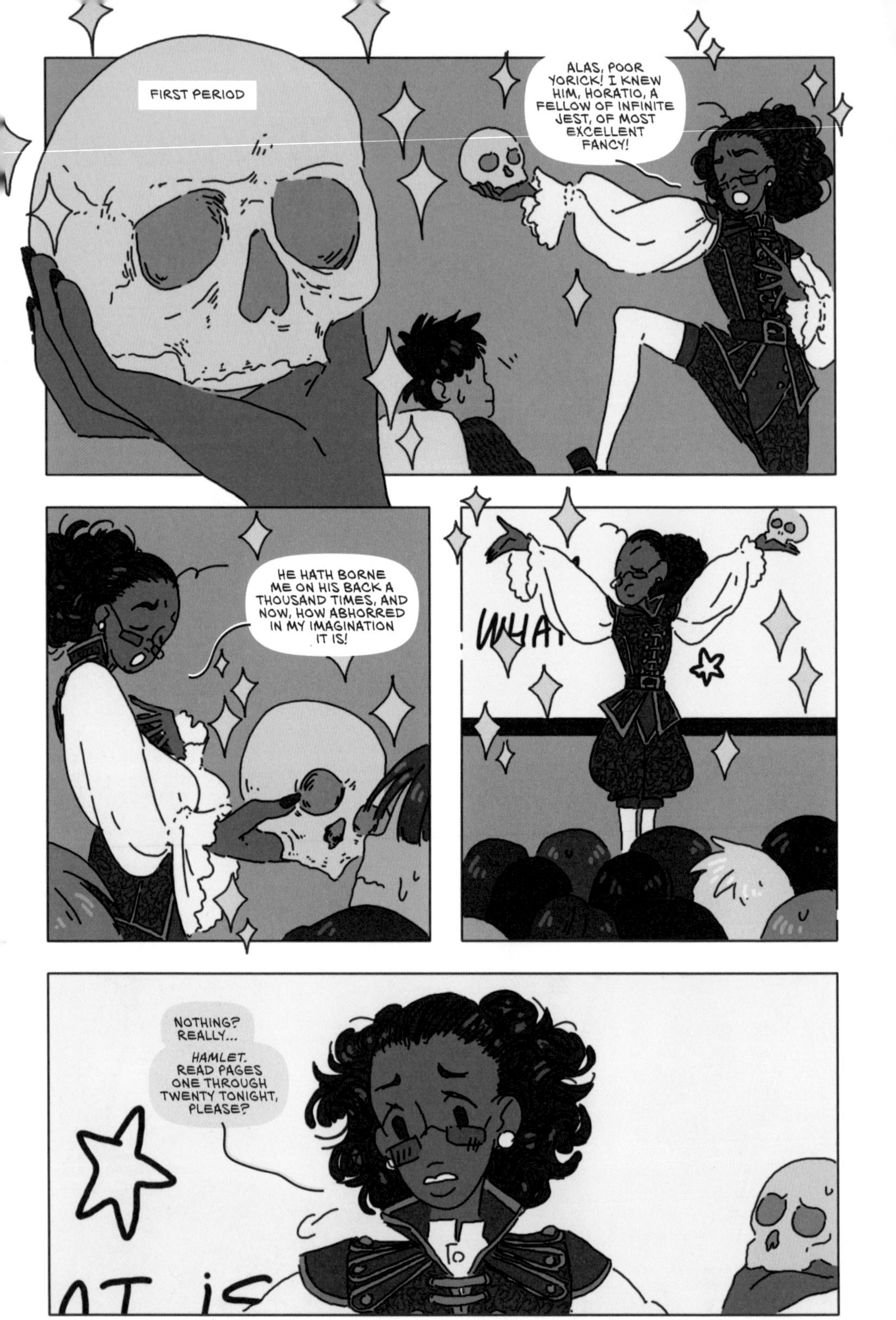
FIRST PERIOD
ALAS, POOR YORICK! I KNEW HIM, HORATIO, A FELLOW OF INFINITE JEST, OF MOST EXCELLENT FANCY!
HE HATH BORNE ME ON HIS BACK A THOUSAND TIMES, AND NOW, HOW ABHORRED IN MY IMAGINATION IT IS!
NOTHING? REALLY...
HAMLET. READ PAGES ONE THROUGH TWENTY TONIGHT, PLEASE?

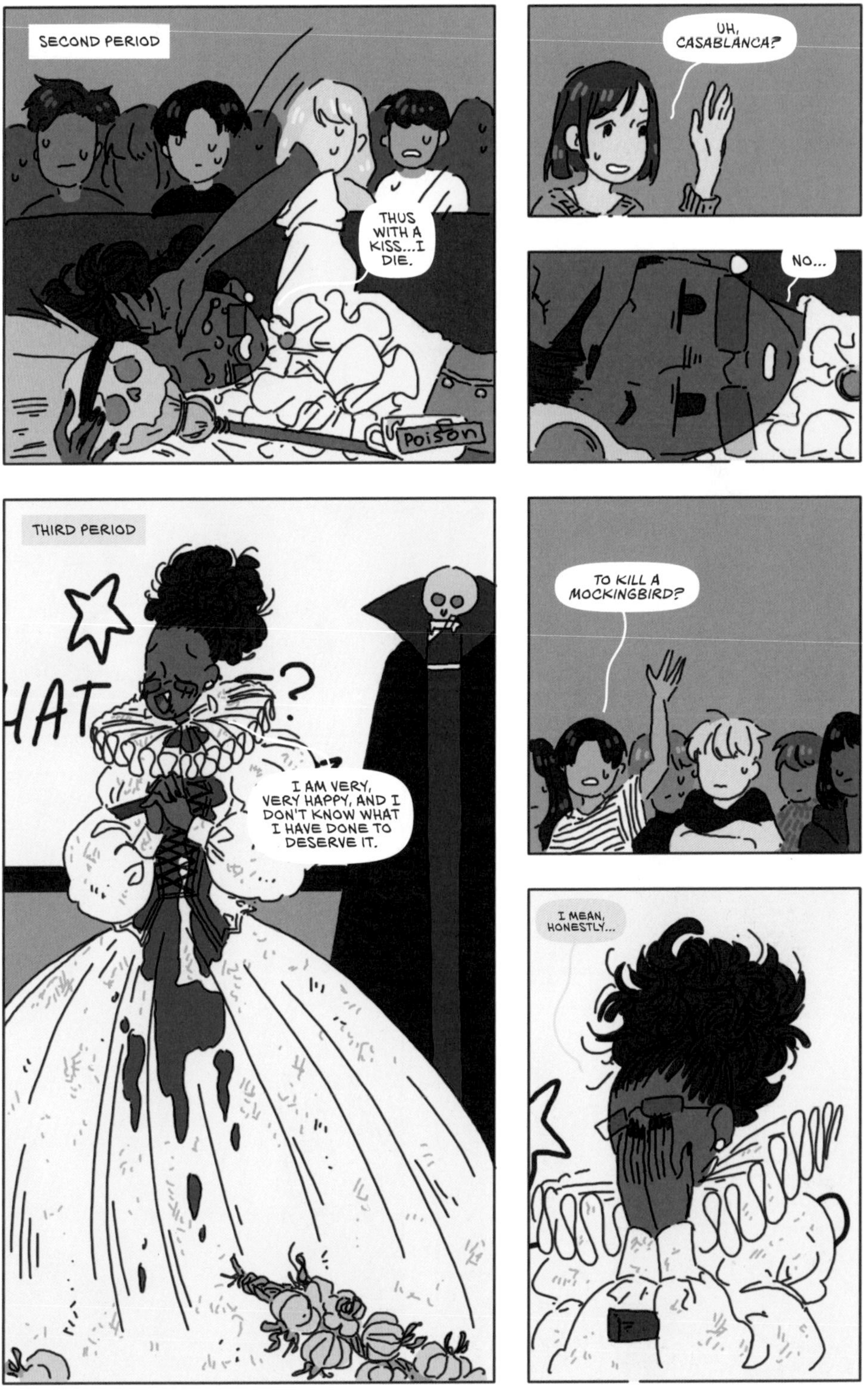
SECOND PERIOD
THUS WITH A KISS...I DIE.
POISON
UH, CASABLANCA?
NO...
THIRD PERIOD
HAT
I AM VERY, VERY HAPPY, AND I DON'T KNOW WHAT I HAVE DONE TO DESERVE IT.
TO KILL A MOCKINGBIRD?
I MEAN, HONESTLY...

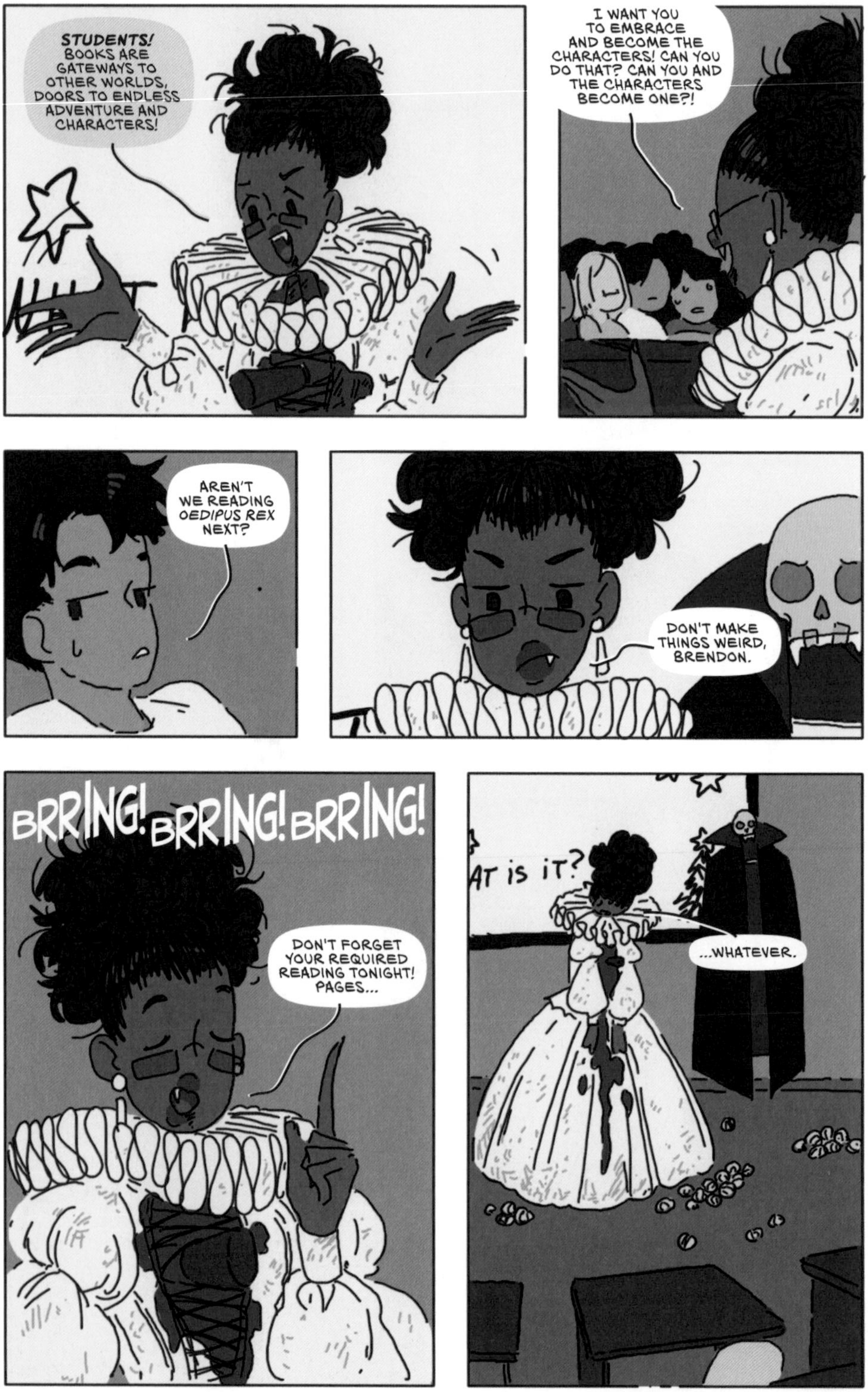

STUDENTS! BOOKS ARE GATEWAYS TO OTHER WORLDS, DOORS TO ENDLESS ADVENTURE AND CHARACTERS!
I WANT YOU TO EMBRACE AND BECOME THE CHARACTERS! CAN YOU DO THAT? CAN YOU AND THE CHARACTERS BECOME ONE?!
AREN'T WE READING OEDIPUS REX NEXT?
DON'T MAKE THINGS WEIRD, BRENDON.
BRRING! BRRING! BRRING!
DON'T FORGET YOUR REQUIRED READING TONIGHT! PAGES...
AT IS IT?
...WHATEVER.

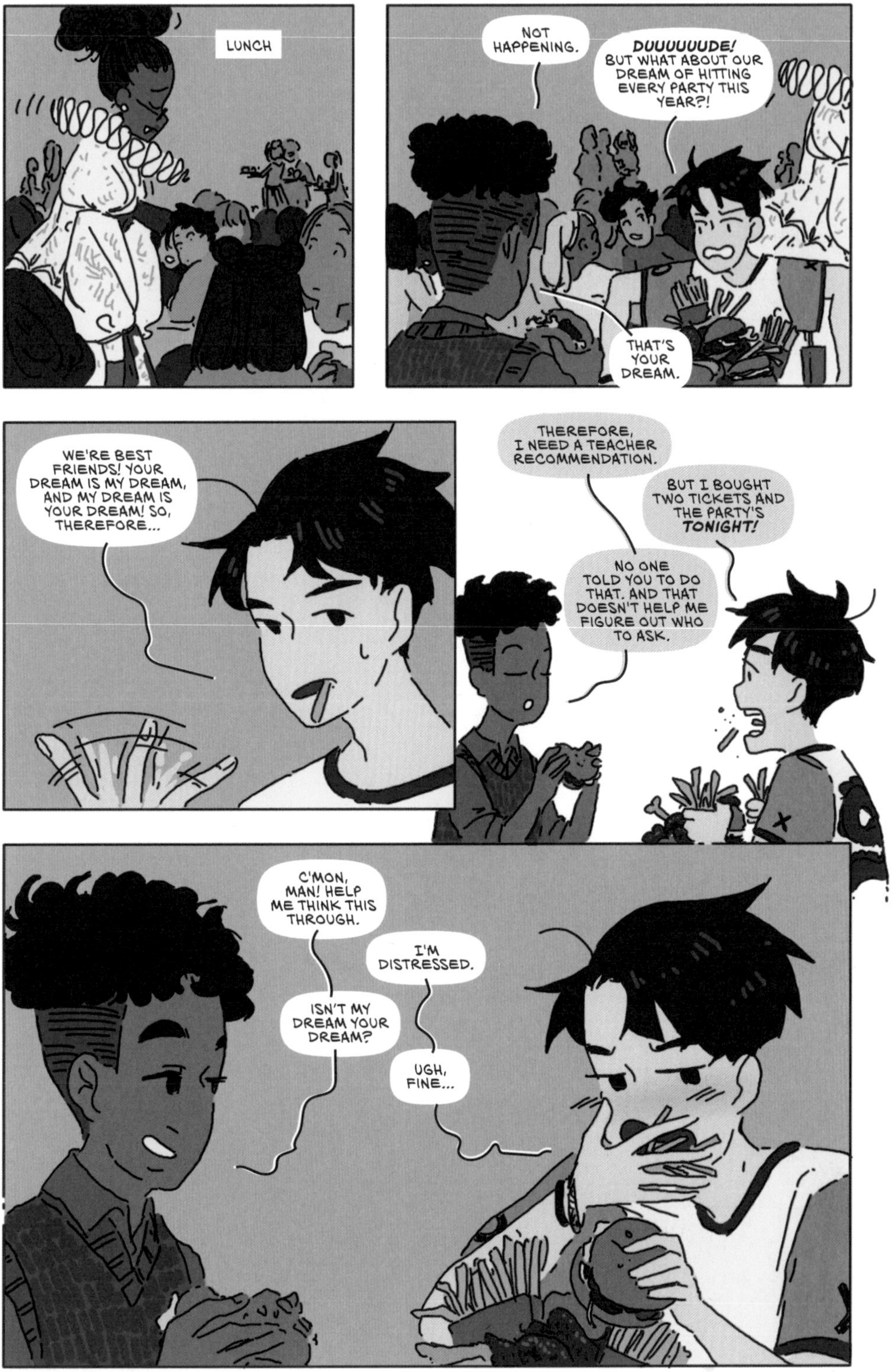
LUNCH
NOT HAPPENING.
DUUUUUUDE! BUT WHAT ABOUT OUR DREAM OF HITTING EVERY PARTY THIS YEAR?!
THAT'S YOUR DREAM.
WE'RE BEST FRIENDS! YOUR DREAM IS MY DREAM, AND MY DREAM IS YOUR DREAM! SO, THEREFORE...
THEREFORE, I NEED A TEACHER RECOMMENDATION.
NO ONE TOLD YOU TO DO THAT. AND THAT DOESN'T HELP ME FIGURE OUT WHO TO ASK.
BUT I BOUGHT TWO TICKETS AND THE PARTY'S TONIGHT!
C'MON, MAN! HELP ME THINK THIS THROUGH.
ISN'T MY DREAM YOUR DREAM?
I'M DISTRESSED.
UGH, FINE...

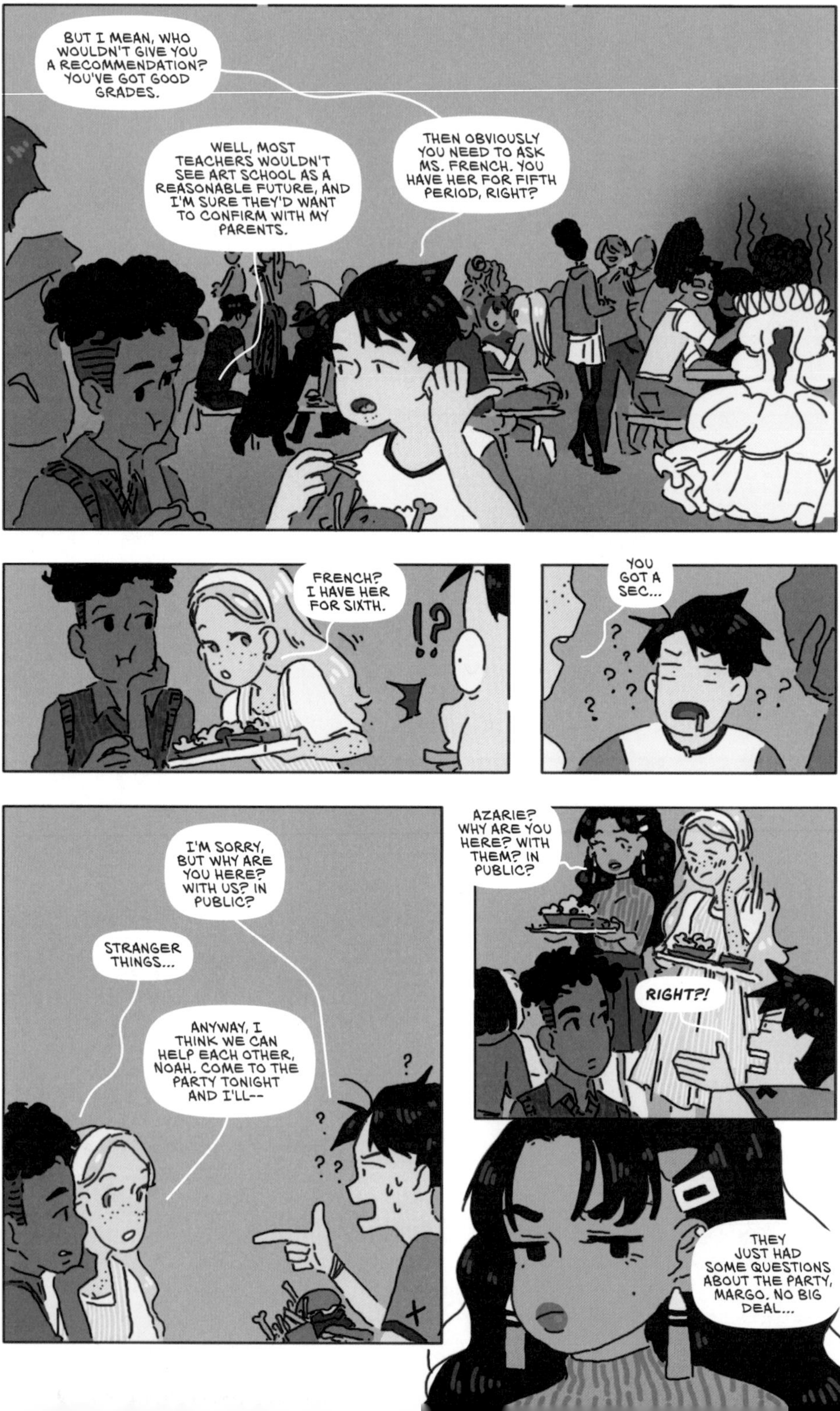
BUT I MEAN, WHO WOULDN'T GIVE YOU A RECOMMENDATION? YOU'VE GOT GOOD GRADES.
WELL, MOST TEACHERS WOULDN'T SEE ART SCHOOL AS A REASONABLE FUTURE, AND I'M SURE THEY'D WANT TO CONFIRM WITH MY PARENTS.
THEN OBVIOUSLY YOU NEED TO ASK MS. FRENCH. YOU HAVE HER FOR FIFTH PERIOD, RIGHT?
FRENCH? I HAVE HER FOR SIXTH.
!?
YOU GOT A SEC...
I'M SORRY, BUT WHY ARE YOU HERE? WITH US? IN PUBLIC?
STRANGER THINGS...
ANYWAY, I THINK WE CAN HELP EACH OTHER, NOAH. COME TO THE PARTY TONIGHT AND I'LL--
AZARIE? WHY ARE YOU HERE? WITH THEM? IN PUBLIC?
RIGHT?!
THEY JUST HAD SOME QUESTIONS ABOUT THE PARTY, MARGO. NO BIG DEAL...

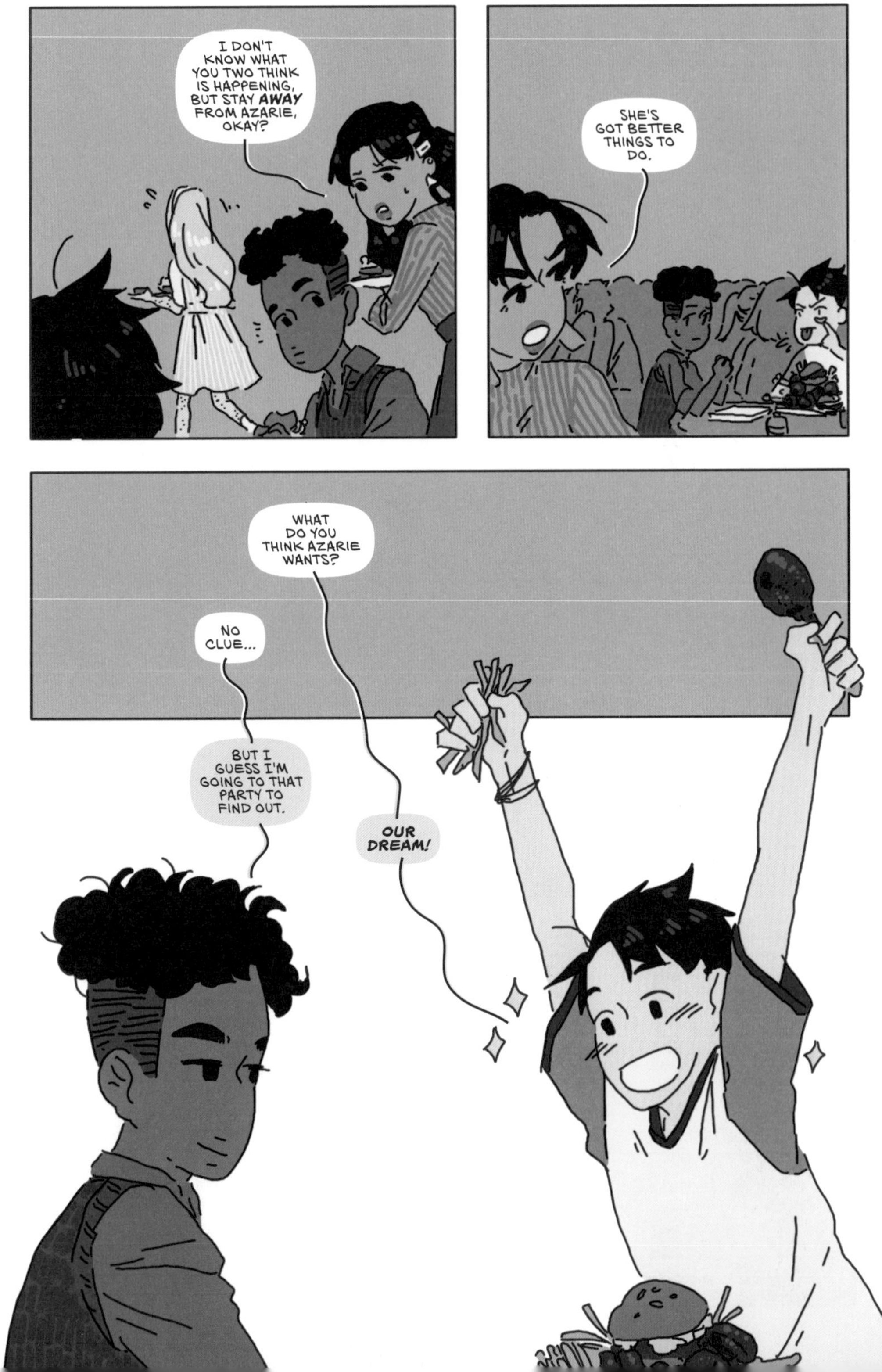
I DON'T KNOW WHAT YOU TWO THINK IS HAPPENING, BUT STAY **AWAY** FROM AZARIE, OKAY?
SHE'S GOT BETTER THINGS TO DO.
WHAT DO YOU THINK AZARIE WANTS?
NO CLUE...
BUT I GUESS I'M GOING TO THAT PARTY TO FIND OUT.
OUR DREAM!

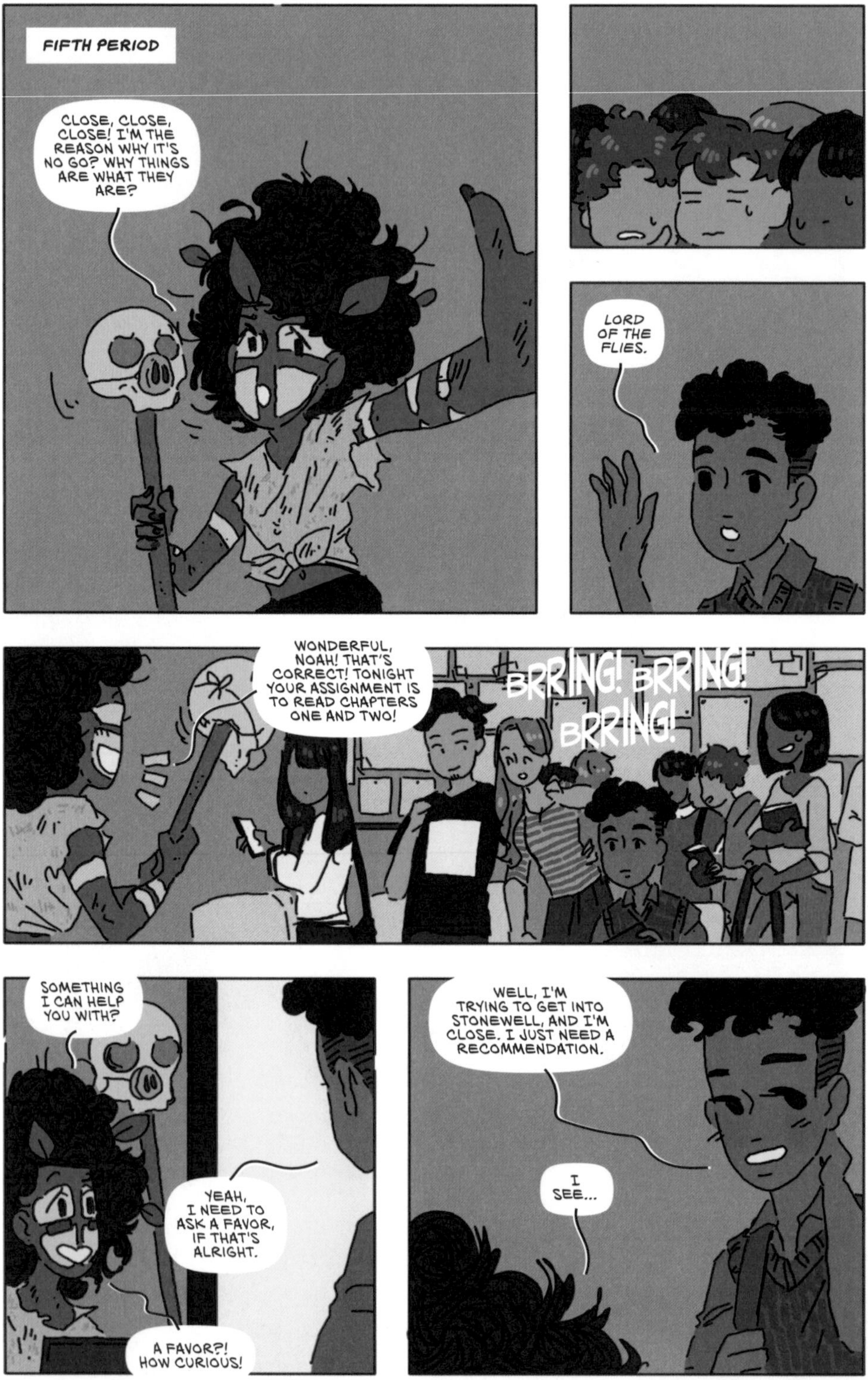
FIFTH PERIOD
CLOSE, CLOSE, CLOSE! I'M THE REASON WHY IT'S NO GO? WHY THINGS ARE WHAT THEY ARE?
LORD OF THE FLIES.
WONDERFUL, NOAH! THAT'S CORRECT! TONIGHT YOUR ASSIGNMENT IS TO READ CHAPTERS ONE AND TWO!
BRRING! BRRING! BRRING!
SOMETHING I CAN HELP YOU WITH?
YEAH, I NEED TO ASK A FAVOR, IF THAT'S ALRIGHT.
A FAVOR?! HOW CURIOUS!
WELL, I'M TRYING TO GET INTO STONEWELL, AND I'M CLOSE. I JUST NEED A RECOMMENDATION.
I SEE...

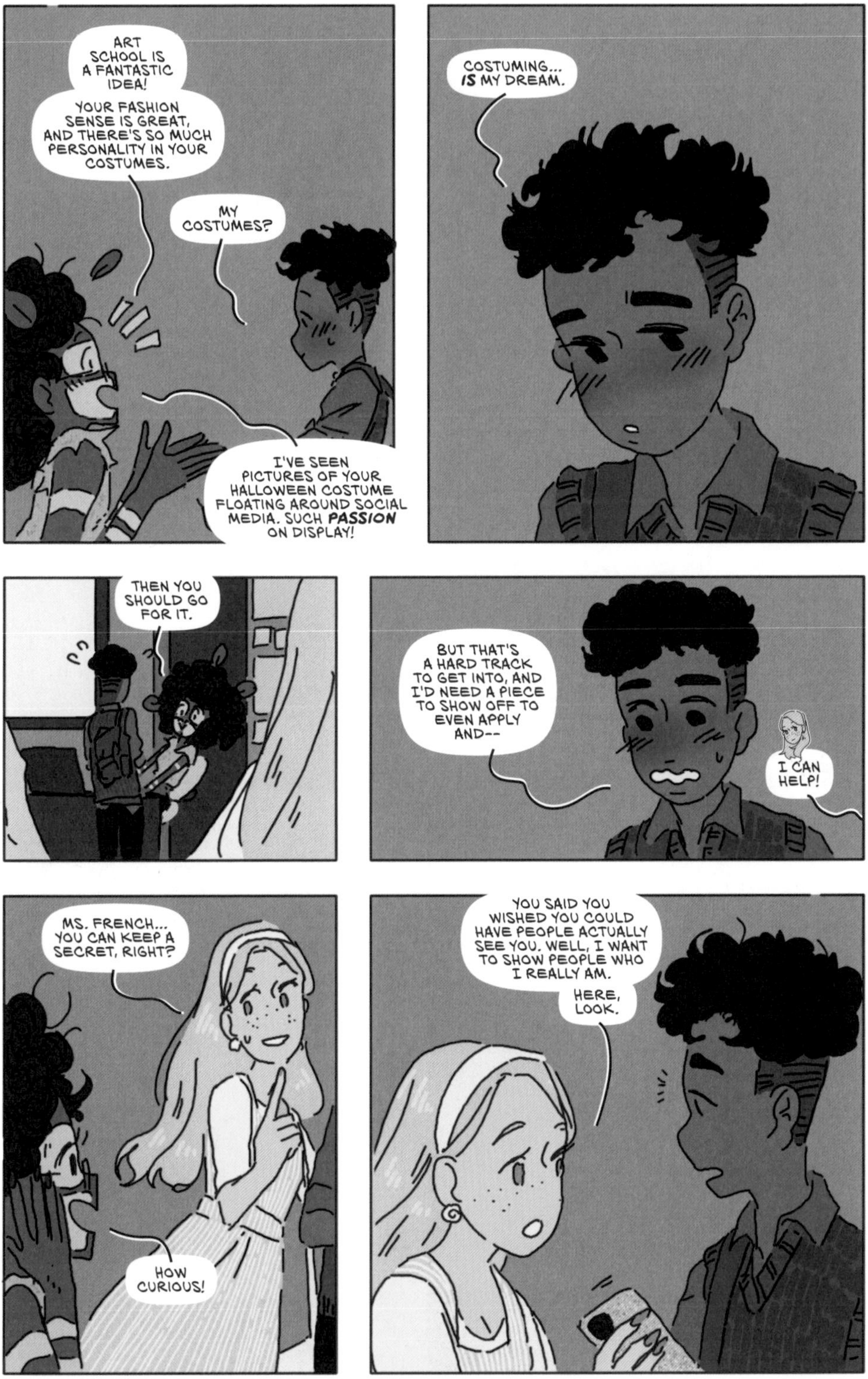
ART SCHOOL IS A FANTASTIC IDEA!
YOUR FASHION SENSE IS GREAT, AND THERE'S SO MUCH PERSONALITY IN YOUR COSTUMES.
MY COSTUMES?
I'VE SEEN PICTURES OF YOUR HALLOWEEN COSTUME FLOATING AROUND SOCIAL MEDIA. SUCH PASSION ON DISPLAY!
COSTUMING... IS MY DREAM.
THEN YOU SHOULD GO FOR IT.
BUT THAT'S A HARD TRACK TO GET INTO, AND I'D NEED A PIECE TO SHOW OFF TO EVEN APPLY AND--
I CAN HELP!
MS. FRENCH... YOU CAN KEEP A SECRET, RIGHT?
HOW CURIOUS!
YOU SAID YOU WISHED YOU COULD HAVE PEOPLE ACTUALLY SEE YOU. WELL, I WANT TO SHOW PEOPLE WHO I REALLY AM.
HERE, LOOK.

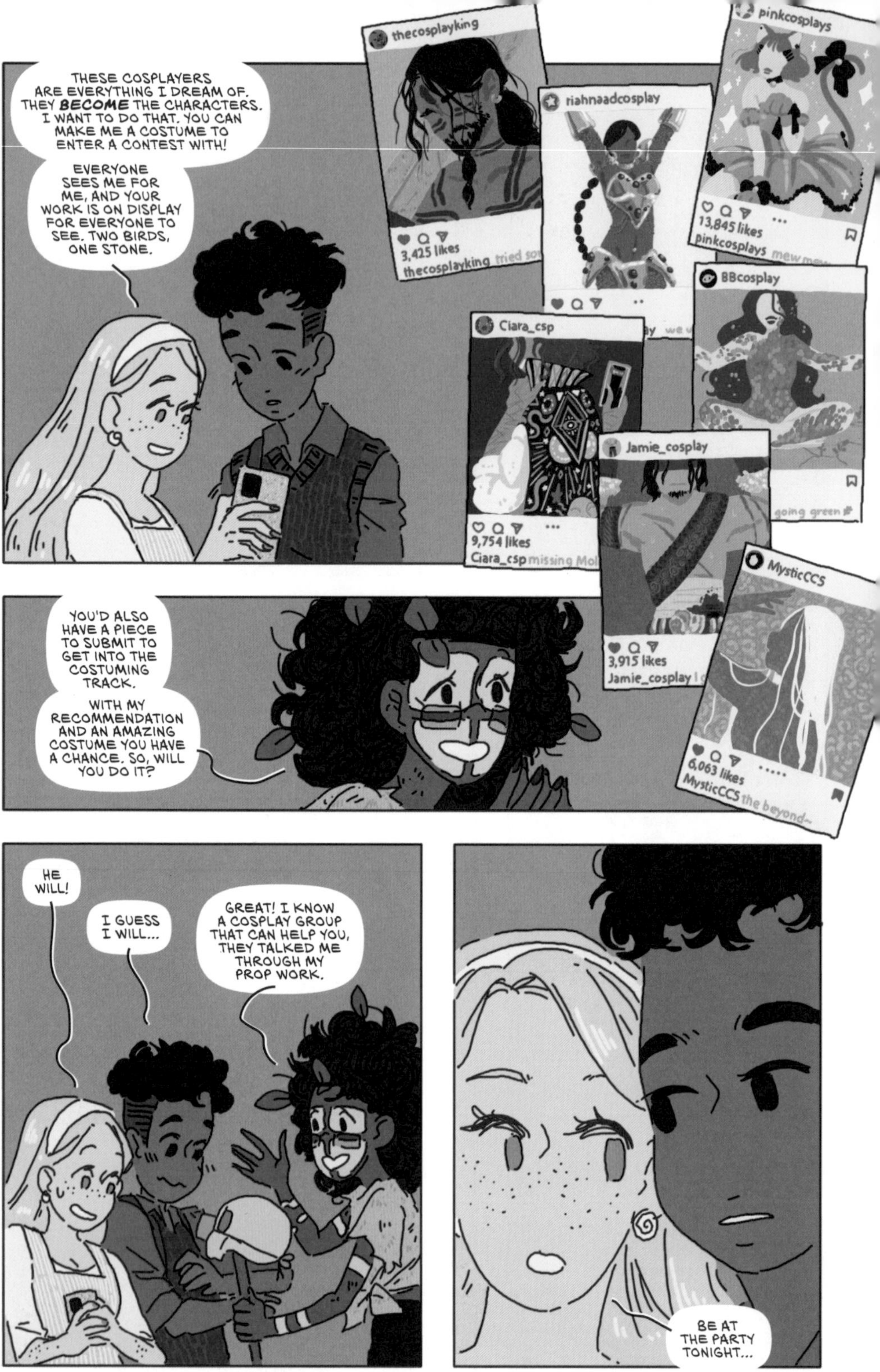
THESE COSPLAYERS ARE EVERYTHING I DREAM OF. THEY **BECOME** THE CHARACTERS. I WANT TO DO THAT. YOU CAN MAKE ME A COSTUME TO ENTER A CONTEST WITH!
EVERYONE SEES ME FOR ME, AND YOUR WORK IS ON DISPLAY FOR EVERYONE TO SEE. TWO BIRDS, ONE STONE.
thecosplayking
3,425 likes
riahnaadcosplay
pinkcosplays
13,845 likes
BBcosplay
going green
Ciara_csp
9,754 likes
Jamie_cosplay
3,915 likes
MysticCCS
6,063 likes
MysticCCS the beyond~
YOU'D ALSO HAVE A PIECE TO SUBMIT TO GET INTO THE COSTUMING TRACK.
WITH MY RECOMMENDATION AND AN AMAZING COSTUME YOU HAVE A CHANCE. SO, WILL YOU DO IT?
HE WILL!
I GUESS I WILL...
GREAT! I KNOW A COSPLAY GROUP THAT CAN HELP YOU, THEY TALKED ME THROUGH MY PROP WORK.
BE AT THE PARTY TONIGHT...

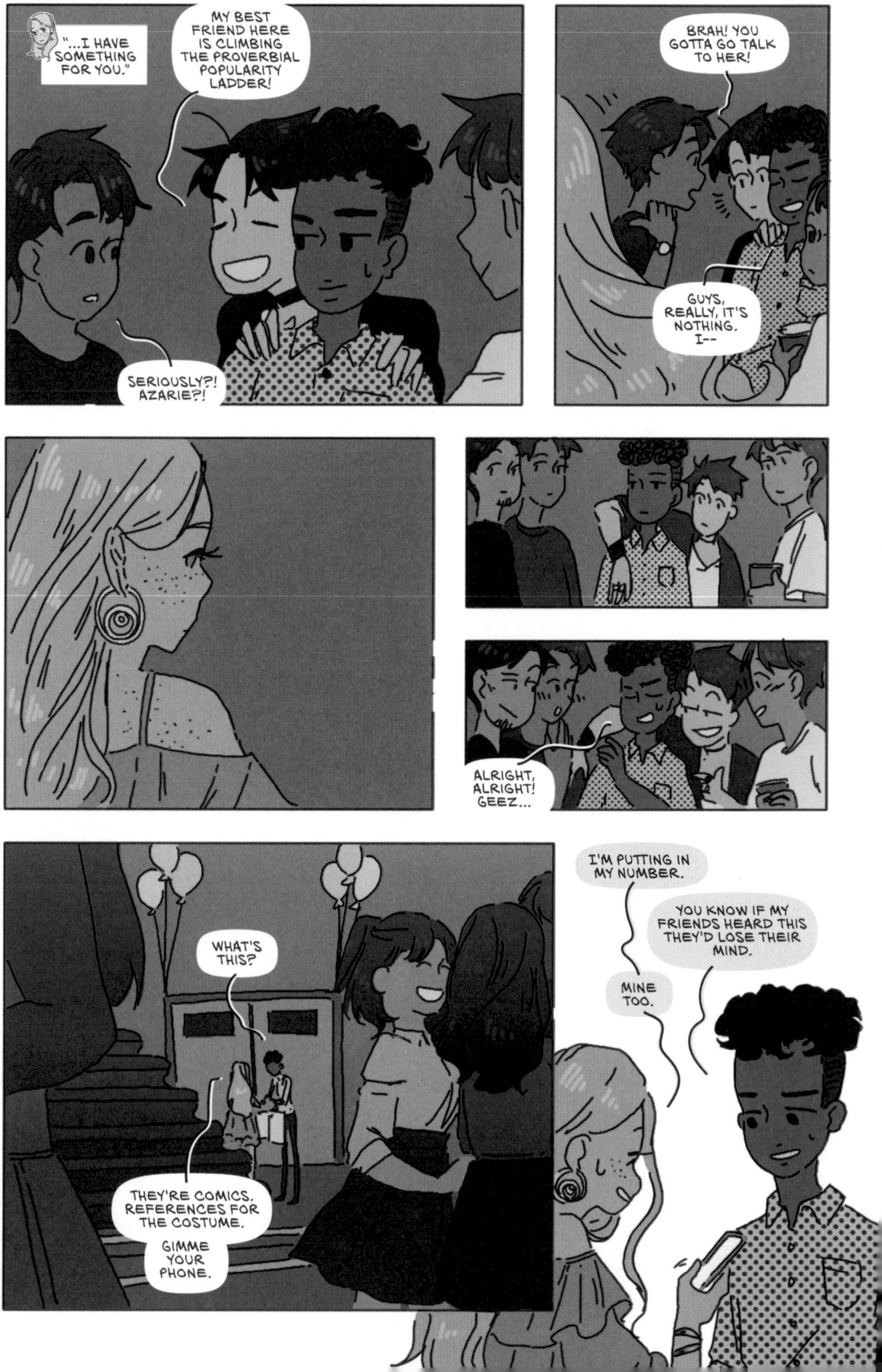
"...I HAVE SOMETHING FOR YOU."
MY BEST FRIEND HERE IS CLIMBING THE PROVERBIAL POPULARITY LADDER!
SERIOUSLY?! AZARIE?!
BRAH! YOU GOTTA GO TALK TO HER!
GUYS, REALLY, IT'S NOTHING. I--
ALRIGHT, ALRIGHT! GEEZ...
WHAT'S THIS?
THEY'RE COMICS. REFERENCES FOR THE COSTUME.
GIMME YOUR PHONE.
I'M PUTTING IN MY NUMBER.
YOU KNOW IF MY FRIENDS HEARD THIS THEY'D LOSE THEIR MIND.
MINE TOO.

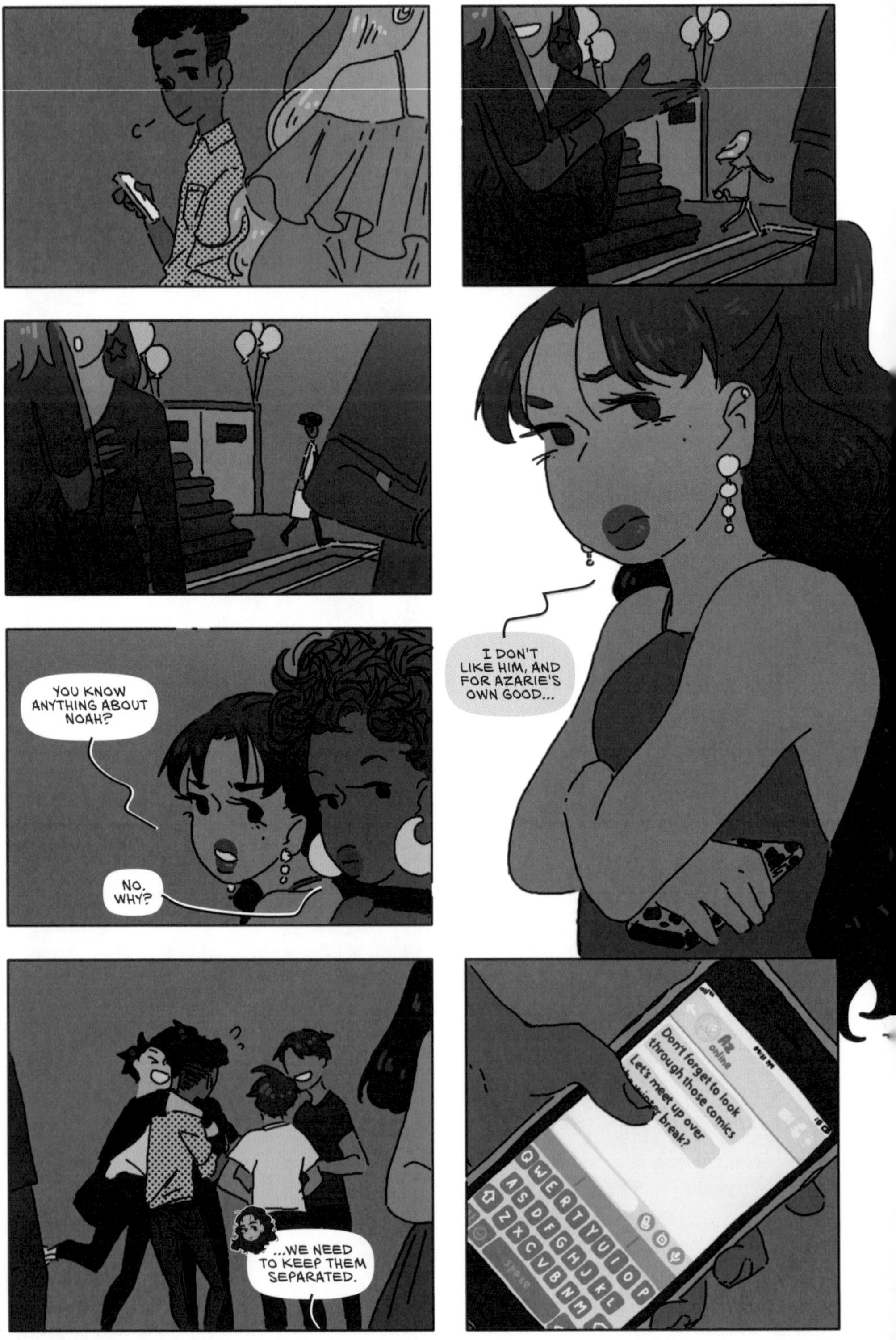
YOU KNOW ANYTHING ABOUT NOAH?
NO. WHY?
I DON'T LIKE HIM, AND FOR AZARIE'S OWN GOOD...
...WE NEED TO KEEP THEM SEPARATED.
Az
online
Don't forget to look through those comics
Let's meet up over

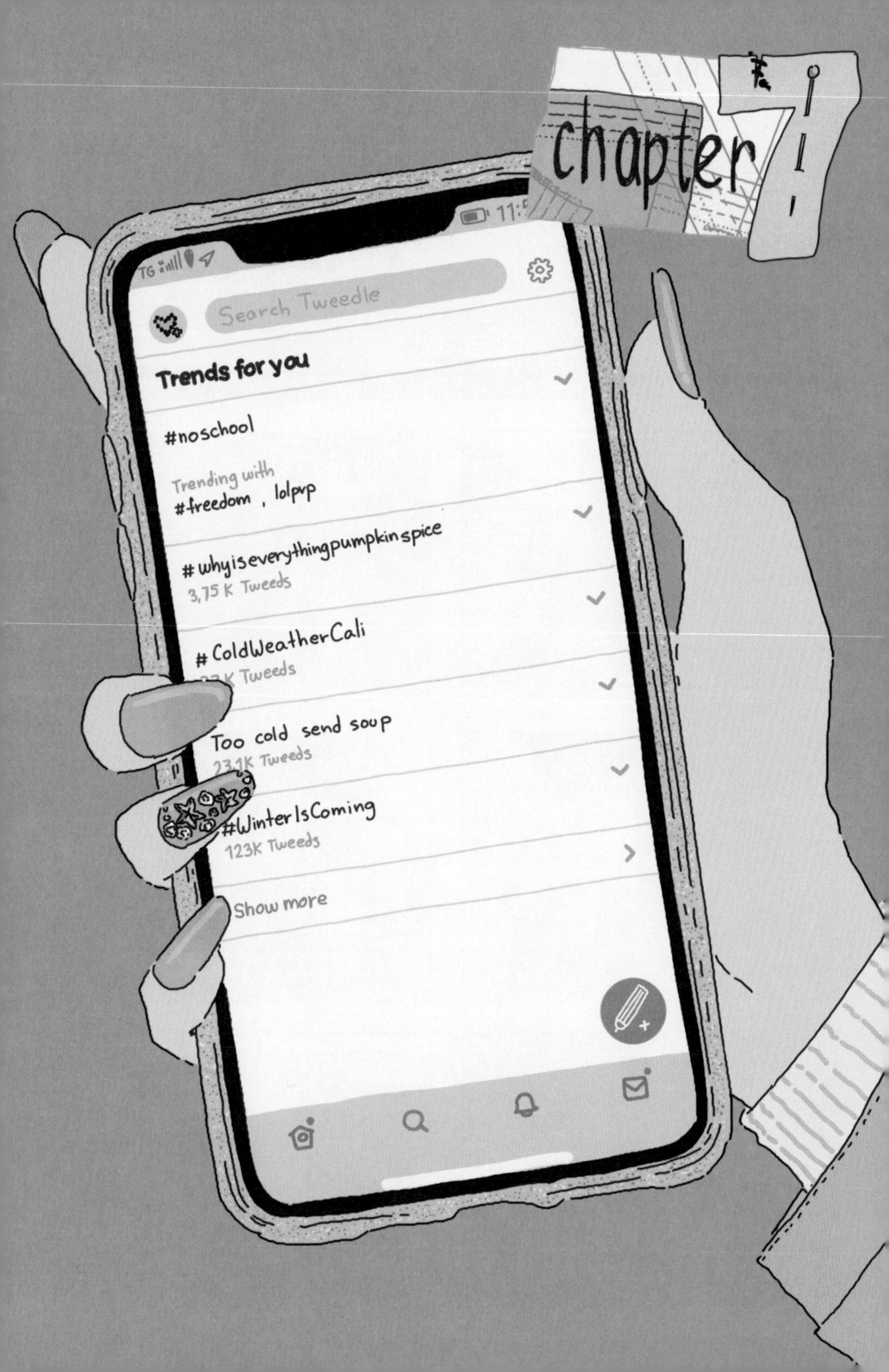
chapter 7
Search Tweedle
Trends for you
#noschool
Trending with
#freedom , lolpvp
#whyiseverythingpumpkinspice
3,75 K Tweeds
#ColdWeatherCali
Too cold send soup
23.1K Tweeds
#WinterIsComing
123K Tweeds
Show more

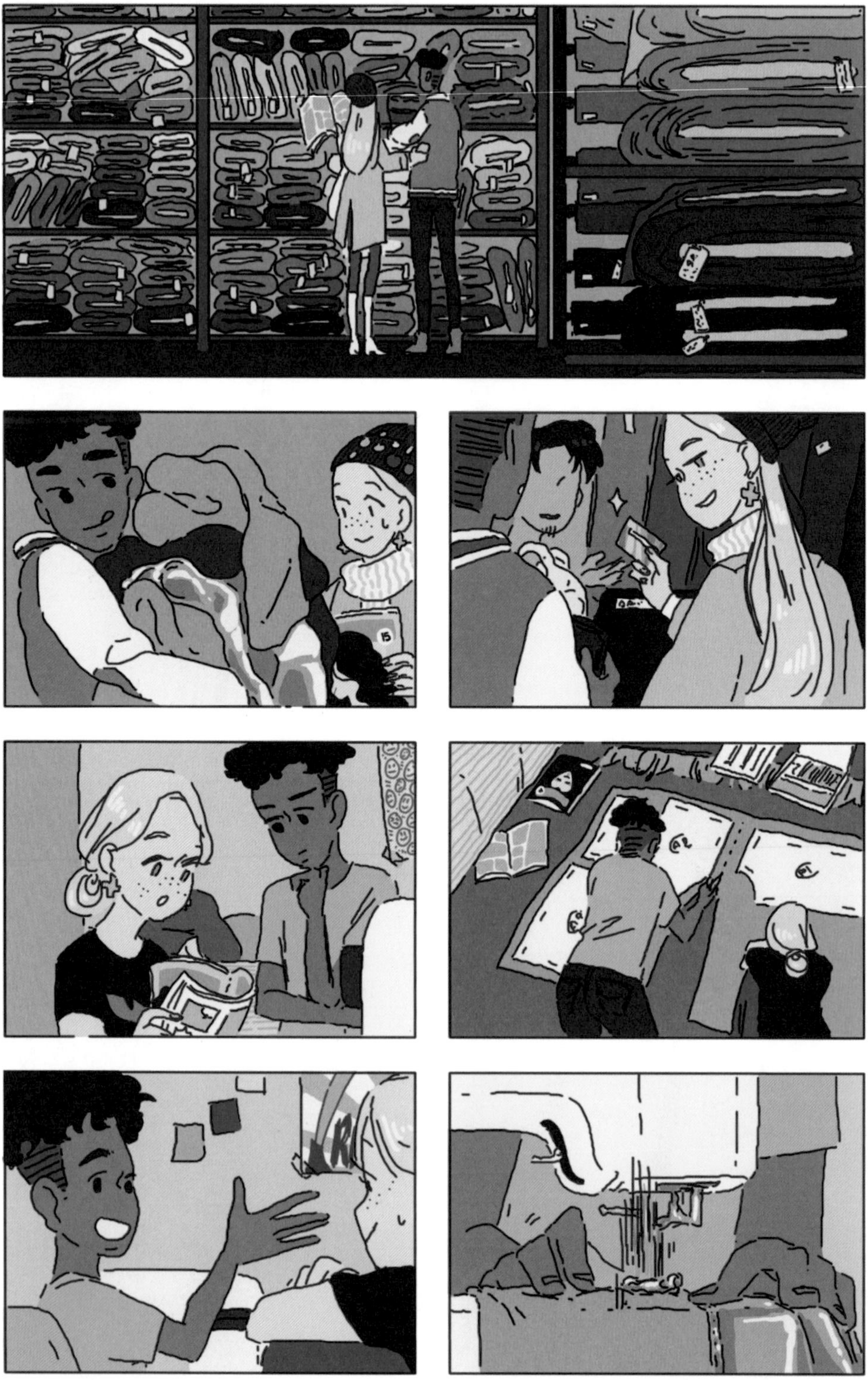

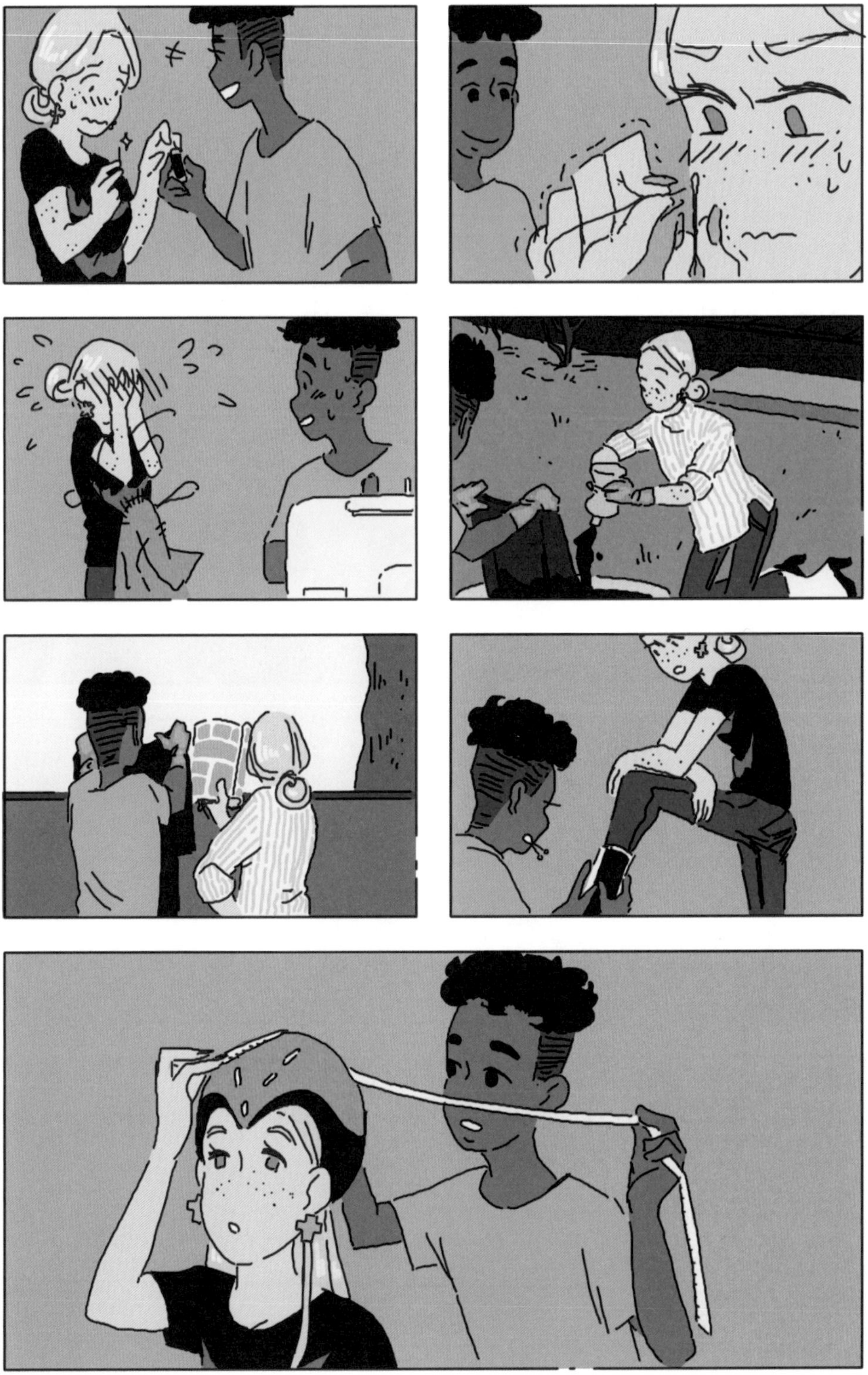

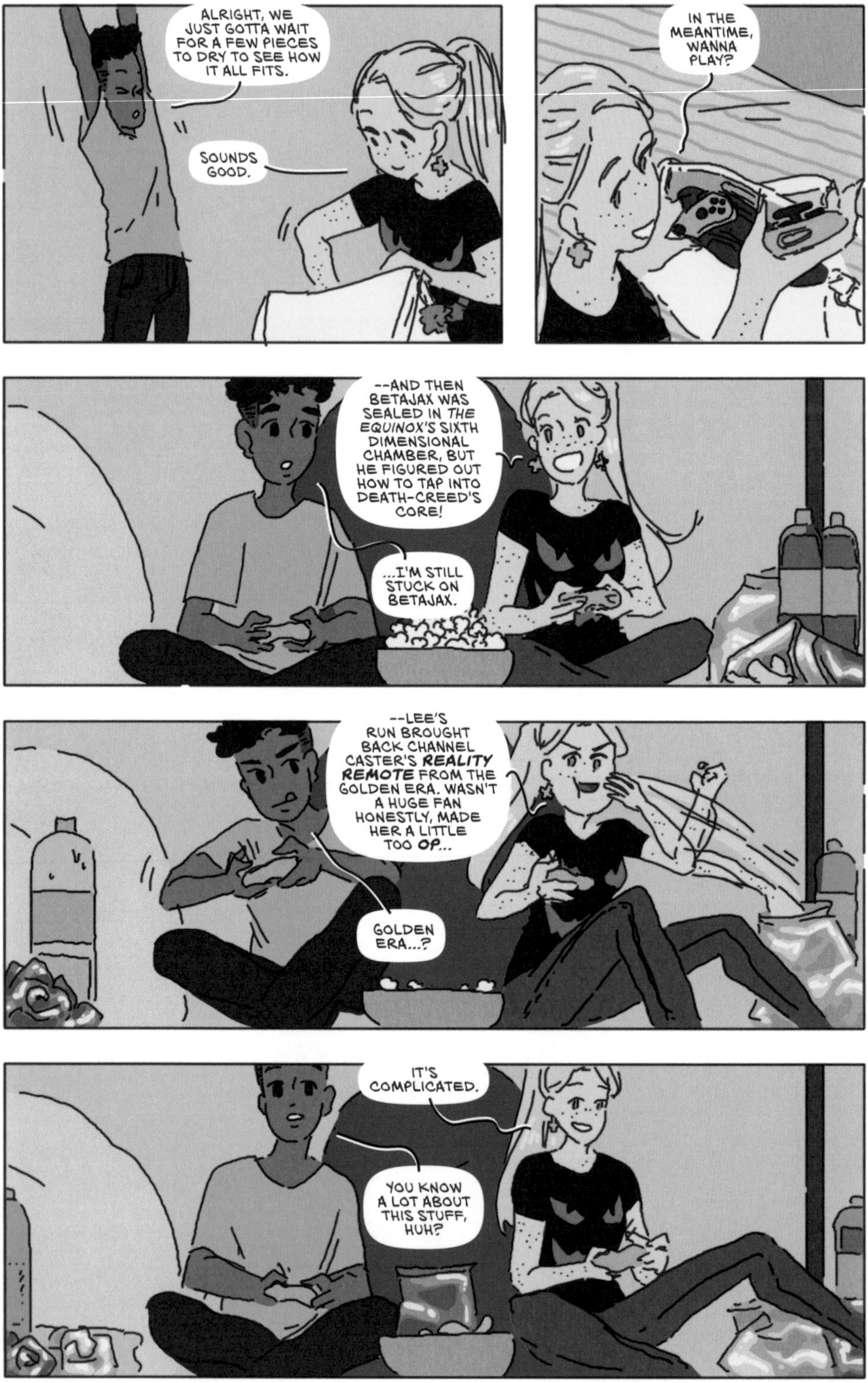
ALRIGHT, WE JUST GOTTA WAIT FOR A FEW PIECES TO DRY TO SEE HOW IT ALL FITS.
SOUNDS GOOD.
IN THE MEANTIME, WANNA PLAY?
--AND THEN BETAJAX WAS SEALED IN *THE EQUINOX'S* SIXTH DIMENSIONAL CHAMBER, BUT HE FIGURED OUT HOW TO TAP INTO DEATH-CREED'S CORE!
...I'M STILL STUCK ON BETAJAX.
--LEE'S RUN BROUGHT BACK CHANNEL CASTER'S ***REALITY REMOTE*** FROM THE GOLDEN ERA. WASN'T A HUGE FAN HONESTLY, MADE HER A LITTLE TOO ***OP***...
GOLDEN ERA...?
IT'S COMPLICATED.
YOU KNOW A LOT ABOUT THIS STUFF, HUH?

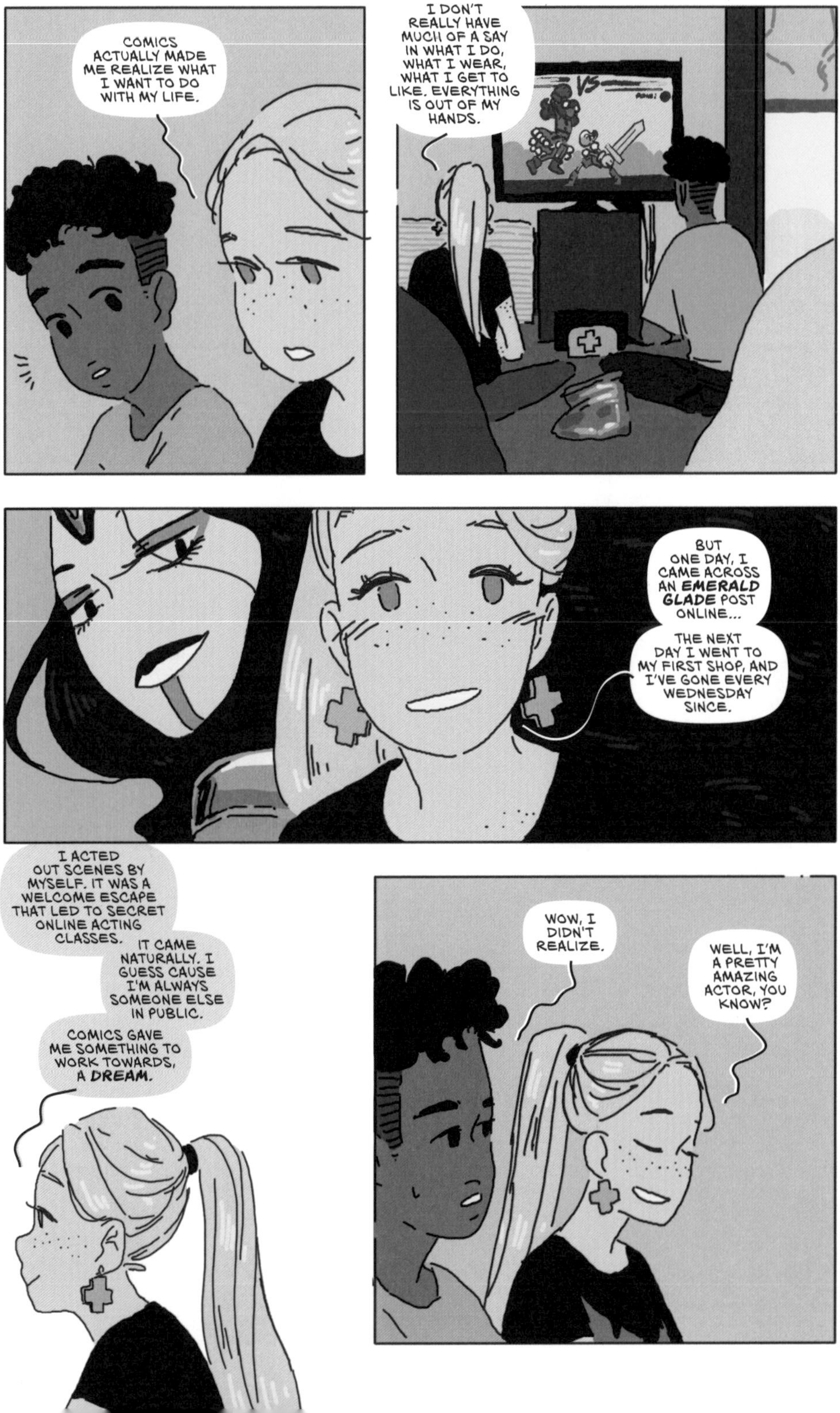
COMICS ACTUALLY MADE ME REALIZE WHAT I WANT TO DO WITH MY LIFE.
I DON'T REALLY HAVE MUCH OF A SAY IN WHAT I DO, WHAT I WEAR, WHAT I GET TO LIKE. EVERYTHING IS OUT OF MY HANDS.
VS
BUT ONE DAY, I CAME ACROSS AN **EMERALD GLADE** POST ONLINE...
THE NEXT DAY I WENT TO MY FIRST SHOP, AND I'VE GONE EVERY WEDNESDAY SINCE.
I ACTED OUT SCENES BY MYSELF. IT WAS A WELCOME ESCAPE THAT LED TO SECRET ONLINE ACTING CLASSES.
IT CAME NATURALLY. I GUESS CAUSE I'M ALWAYS SOMEONE ELSE IN PUBLIC.
COMICS GAVE ME SOMETHING TO WORK TOWARDS, A **DREAM.**
WOW, I DIDN'T REALIZE.
WELL, I'M A PRETTY AMAZING ACTOR, YOU KNOW?

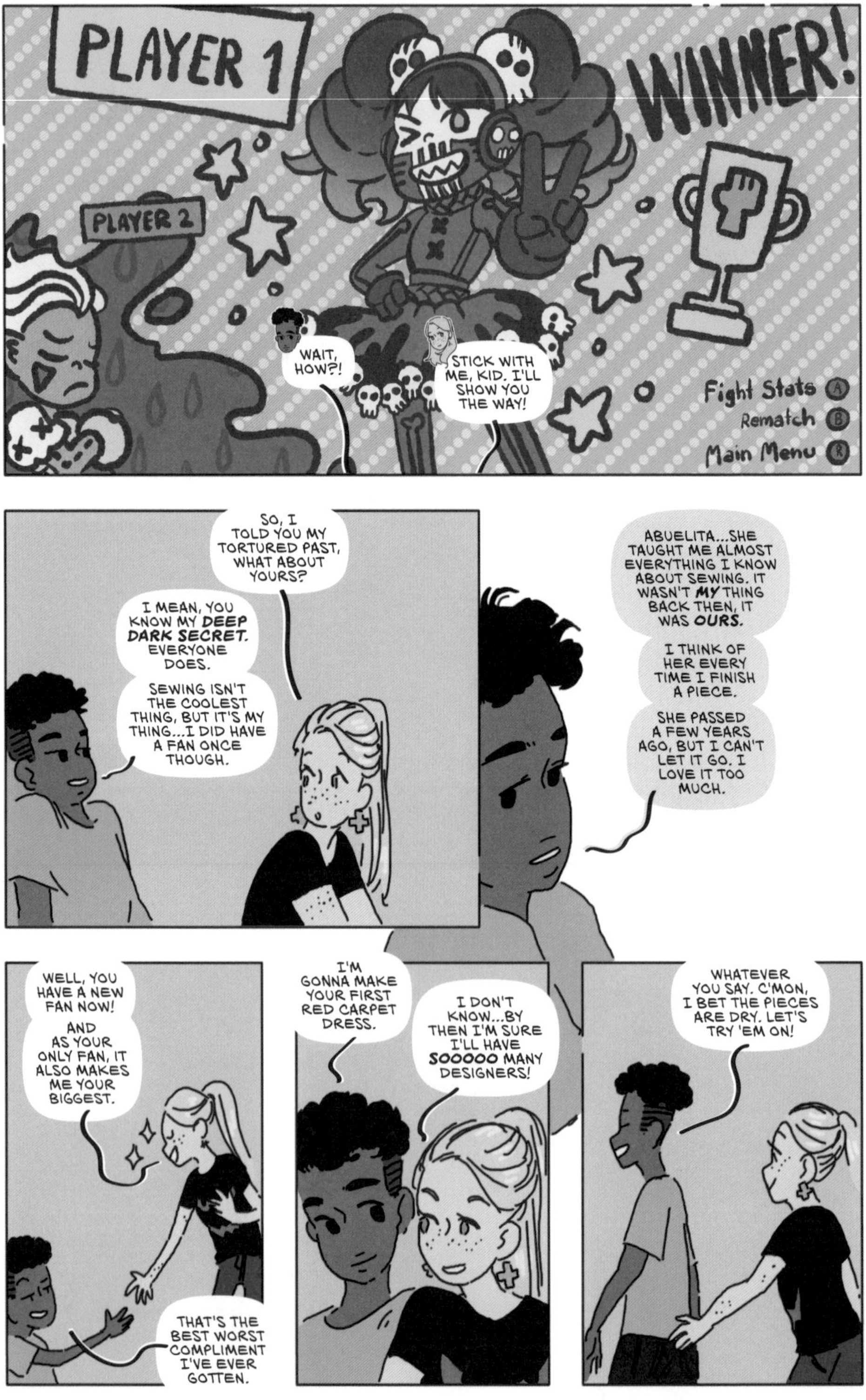
PLAYER 1
WINNER!
PLAYER 2
WAIT, HOW?!
STICK WITH ME, KID. I'LL SHOW YOU THE WAY!
Fight Stats
Rematch
Main Menu
SO, I TOLD YOU MY TORTURED PAST, WHAT ABOUT YOURS?
I MEAN, YOU KNOW MY **DEEP DARK SECRET.** EVERYONE DOES.
SEWING ISN'T THE COOLEST THING, BUT IT'S MY THING...I DID HAVE A FAN ONCE THOUGH.
ABUELITA...SHE TAUGHT ME ALMOST EVERYTHING I KNOW ABOUT SEWING. IT WASN'T ***MY*** THING BACK THEN, IT WAS ***OURS.***
I THINK OF HER EVERY TIME I FINISH A PIECE.
SHE PASSED A FEW YEARS AGO, BUT I CAN'T LET IT GO. I LOVE IT TOO MUCH.
WELL, YOU HAVE A NEW FAN NOW!
AND AS YOUR ONLY FAN, IT ALSO MAKES ME YOUR BIGGEST.
THAT'S THE BEST WORST COMPLIMENT I'VE EVER GOTTEN.
I'M GONNA MAKE YOUR FIRST RED CARPET DRESS.
I DON'T KNOW...BY THEN I'M SURE I'LL HAVE ***SOOOOO*** MANY DESIGNERS!
WHATEVER YOU SAY. C'MON, I BET THE PIECES ARE DRY. LET'S TRY 'EM ON!

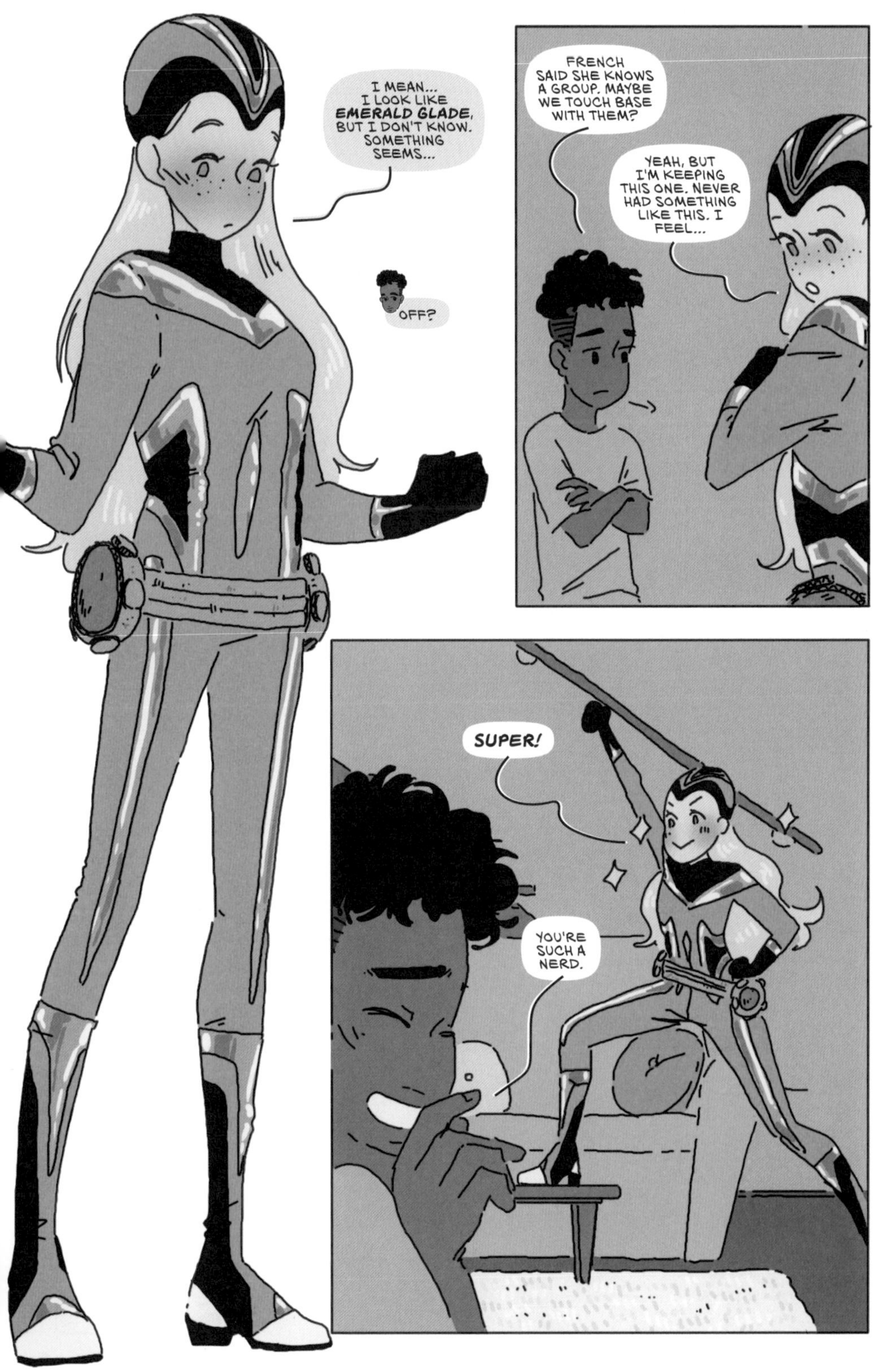
I MEAN... I LOOK LIKE EMERALD GLADE, BUT I DON'T KNOW. SOMETHING SEEMS...
OFF?
FRENCH SAID SHE KNOWS A GROUP. MAYBE WE TOUCH BASE WITH THEM?
YEAH, BUT I'M KEEPING THIS ONE. NEVER HAD SOMETHING LIKE THIS. I FEEL...
SUPER!
YOU'RE SUCH A NERD.

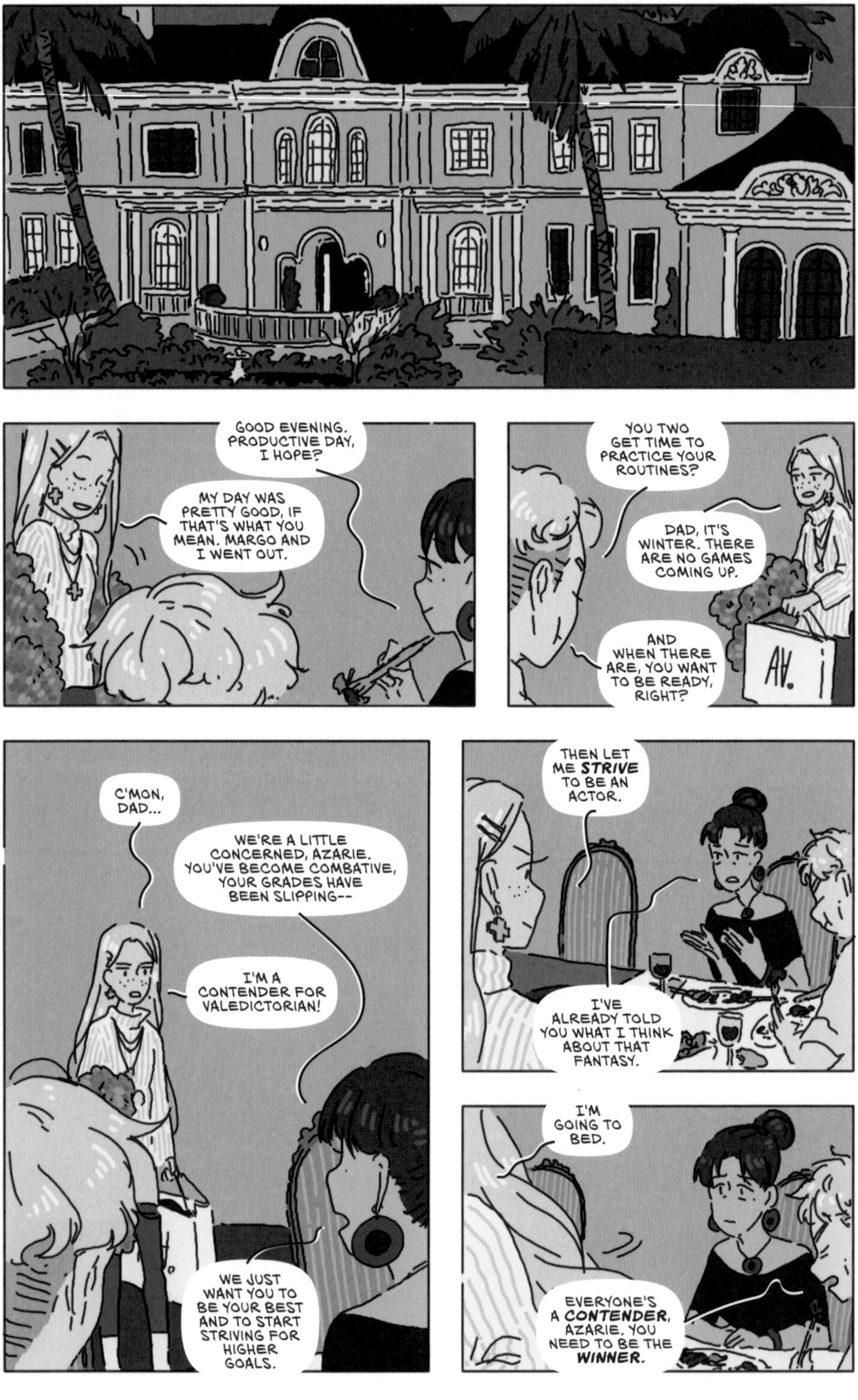
GOOD EVENING. PRODUCTIVE DAY, I HOPE?
MY DAY WAS PRETTY GOOD, IF THAT'S WHAT YOU MEAN. MARGO AND I WENT OUT.
YOU TWO GET TIME TO PRACTICE YOUR ROUTINES?
DAD, IT'S WINTER. THERE ARE NO GAMES COMING UP.
AND WHEN THERE ARE, YOU WANT TO BE READY, RIGHT?
AV.
C'MON, DAD...
WE'RE A LITTLE CONCERNED, AZARIE. YOU'VE BECOME COMBATIVE, YOUR GRADES HAVE BEEN SLIPPING--
I'M A CONTENDER FOR VALEDICTORIAN!
WE JUST WANT YOU TO BE YOUR BEST AND TO START STRIVING FOR HIGHER GOALS.
THEN LET ME **STRIVE** TO BE AN ACTOR.
I'VE ALREADY TOLD YOU WHAT I THINK ABOUT THAT FANTASY.
I'M GOING TO BED.
EVERYONE'S A **CONTENDER**, AZARIE. YOU NEED TO BE THE **WINNER**.

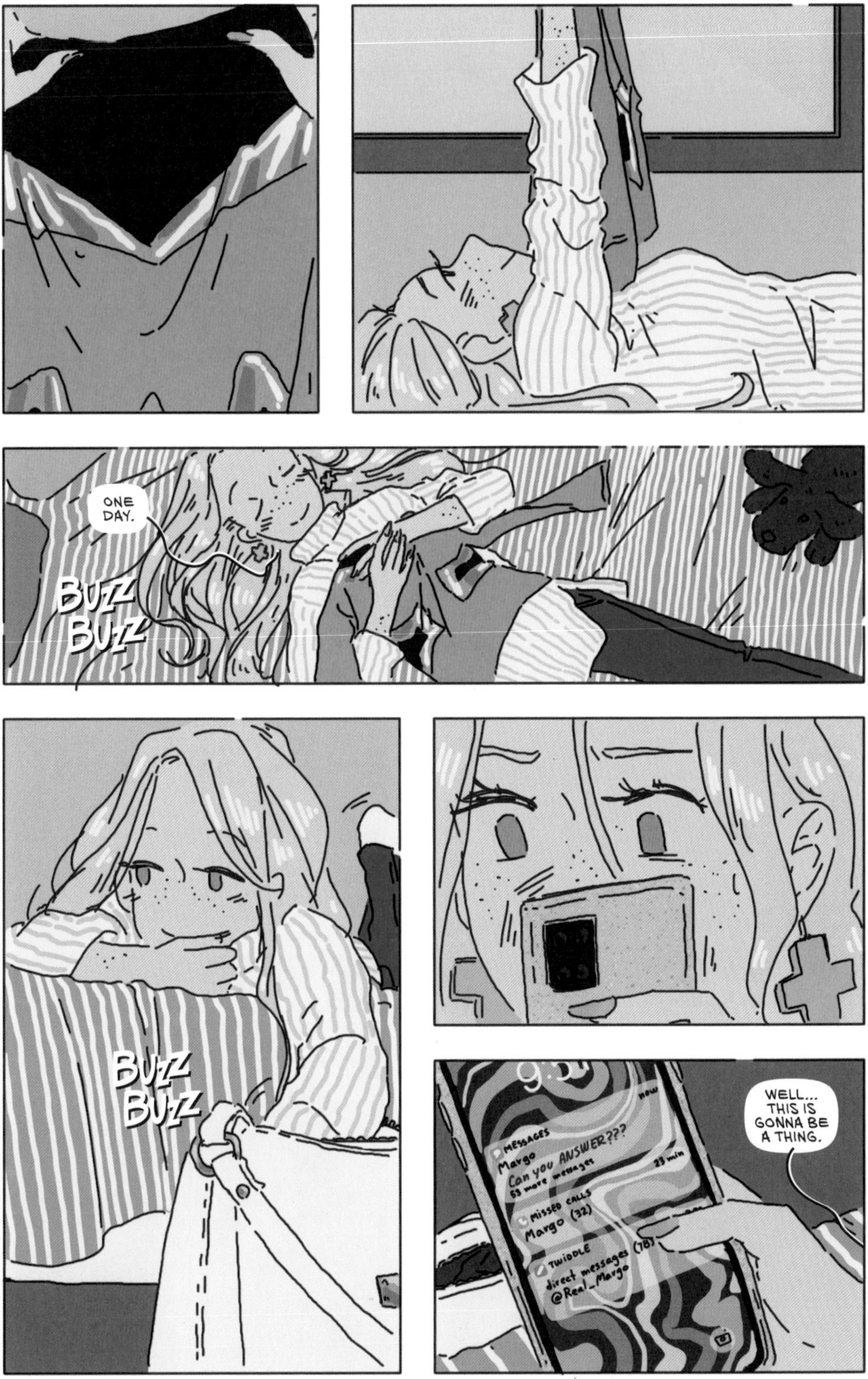
ONE DAY.
BUZZ BUZZ
BUZZ BUZZ
MESSAGES
now
Margo
Can you ANSWER???
53 more messages
23 min
MISSED CALLS
Margo (32)
TWIDDLE
direct messages (78)
@Real_Margo
WELL... THIS IS GONNA BE A THING.

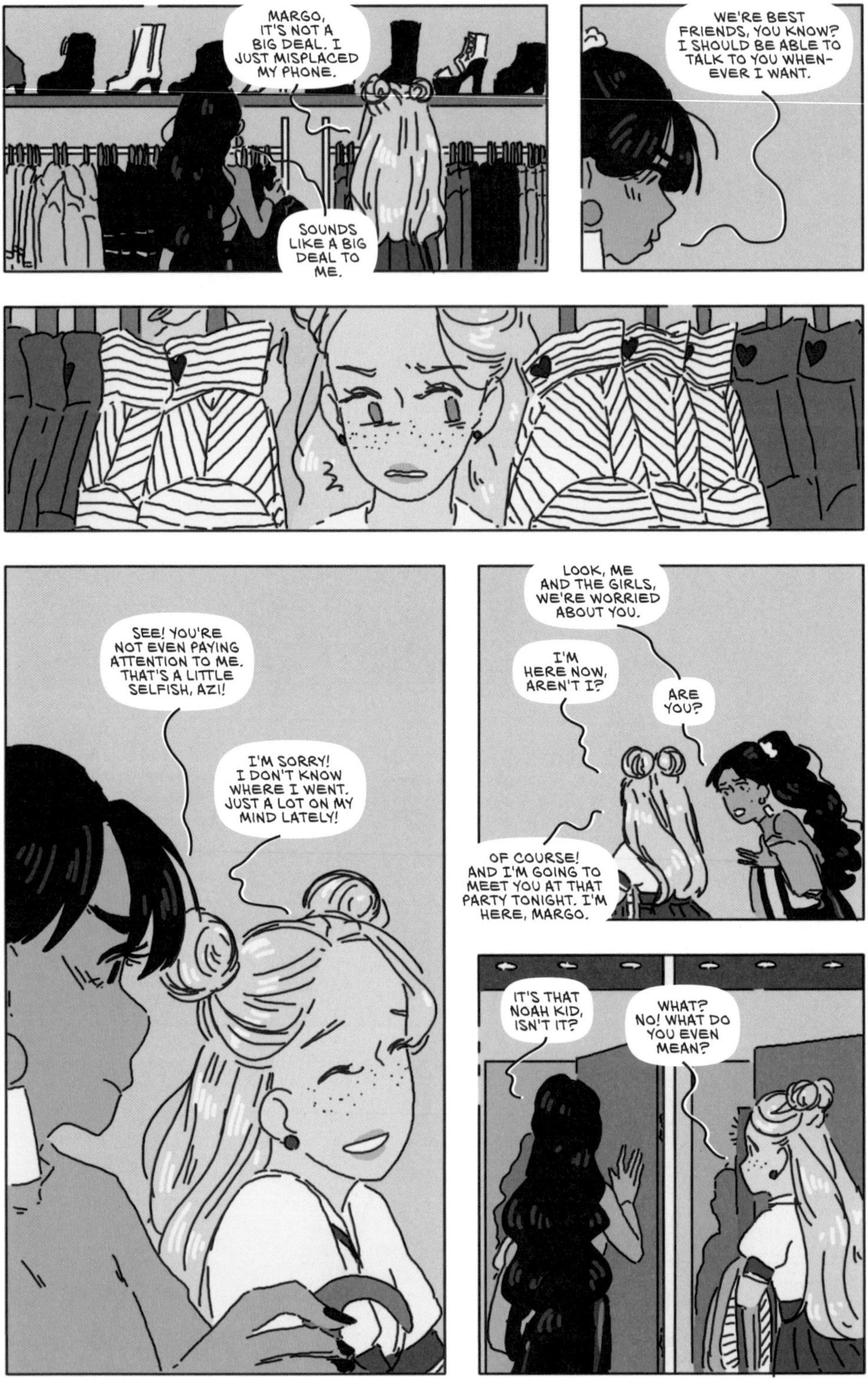
MARGO, IT'S NOT A BIG DEAL. I JUST MISPLACED MY PHONE.
SOUNDS LIKE A BIG DEAL TO ME.
WE'RE BEST FRIENDS, YOU KNOW? I SHOULD BE ABLE TO TALK TO YOU WHEN-EVER I WANT.
SEE! YOU'RE NOT EVEN PAYING ATTENTION TO ME. THAT'S A LITTLE SELFISH, AZI!
I'M SORRY! I DON'T KNOW WHERE I WENT. JUST A LOT ON MY MIND LATELY!
LOOK, ME AND THE GIRLS, WE'RE WORRIED ABOUT YOU.
I'M HERE NOW, AREN'T I?
ARE YOU?
OF COURSE! AND I'M GOING TO MEET YOU AT THAT PARTY TONIGHT. I'M HERE, MARGO.
IT'S THAT NOAH KID, ISN'T IT?
WHAT? NO! WHAT DO YOU EVEN MEAN?

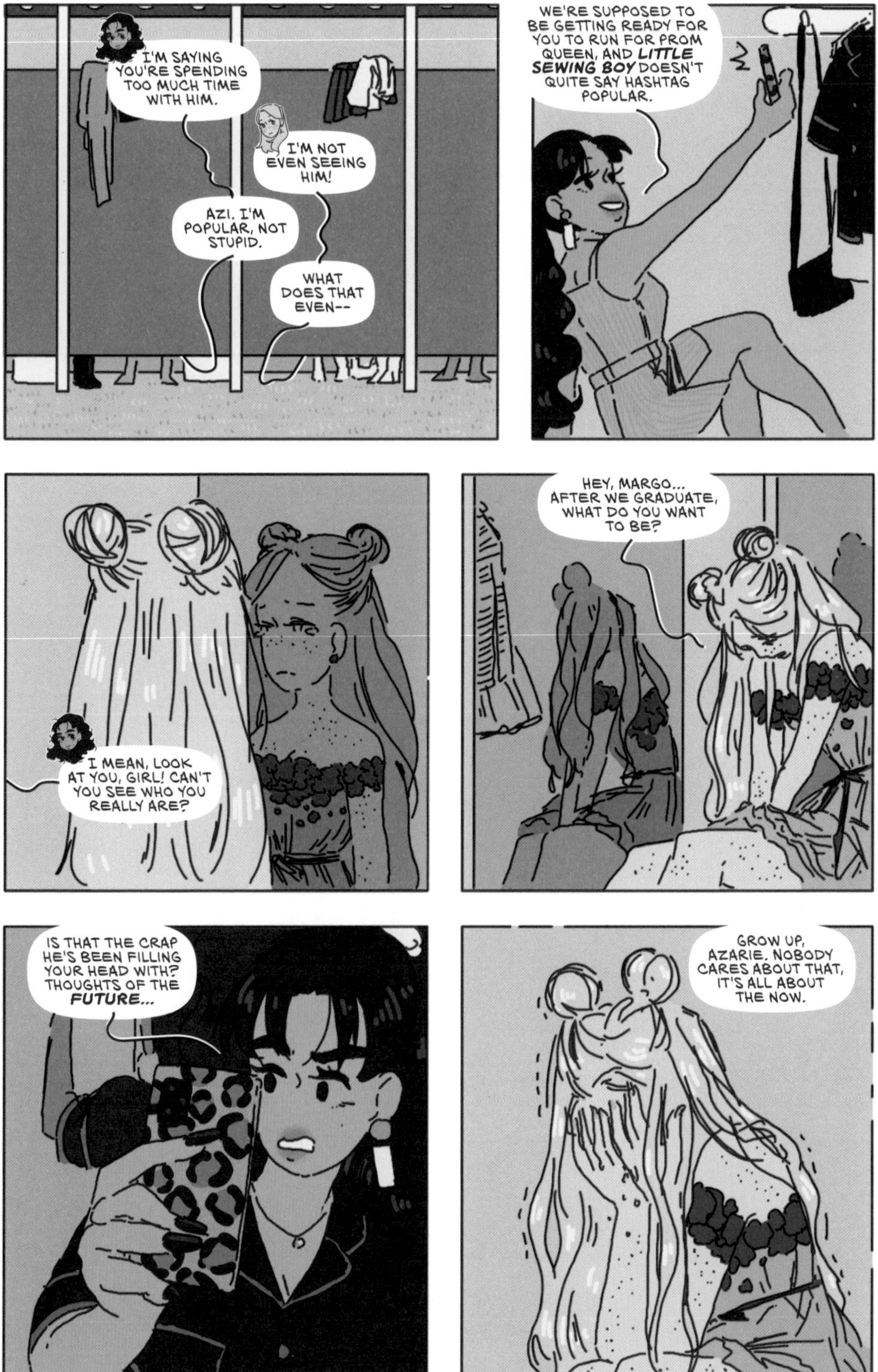
I'M SAYING YOU'RE SPENDING TOO MUCH TIME WITH HIM.
I'M NOT EVEN SEEING HIM!
AZI. I'M POPULAR, NOT STUPID.
WHAT DOES THAT EVEN--
WE'RE SUPPOSED TO BE GETTING READY FOR YOU TO RUN FOR PROM QUEEN, AND **LITTLE SEWING BOY** DOESN'T QUITE SAY HASHTAG POPULAR.
I MEAN, LOOK AT YOU, GIRL! CAN'T YOU SEE WHO YOU REALLY ARE?
HEY, MARGO... AFTER WE GRADUATE, WHAT DO YOU WANT TO BE?
IS THAT THE CRAP HE'S BEEN FILLING YOUR HEAD WITH? THOUGHTS OF THE ***FUTURE...***
GROW UP, AZARIE. NOBODY CARES ABOUT THAT, IT'S ALL ABOUT THE NOW.

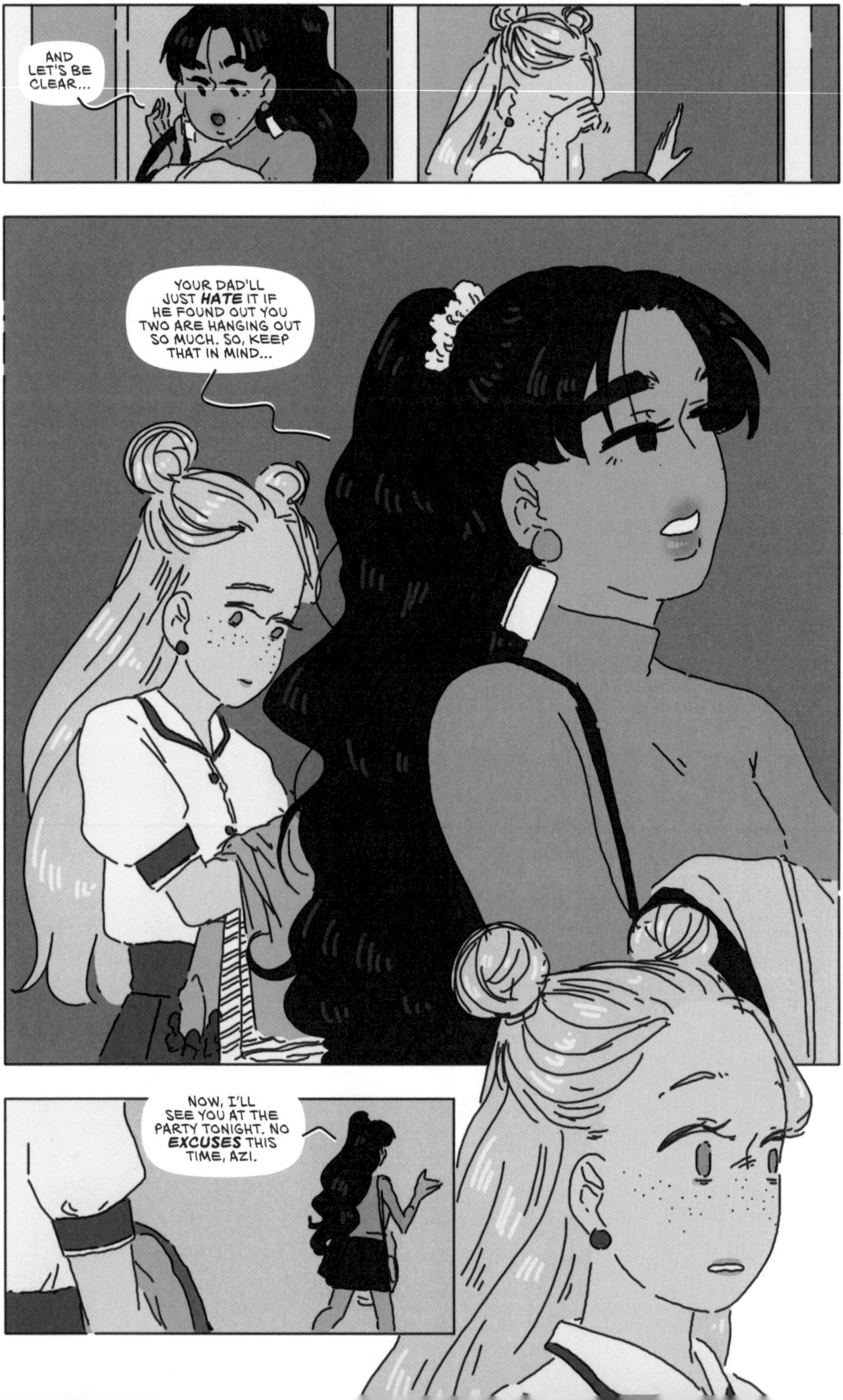
AND LET'S BE CLEAR...
YOUR DAD'LL JUST **HATE** IT IF HE FOUND OUT YOU TWO ARE HANGING OUT SO MUCH. SO, KEEP THAT IN MIND...
NOW, I'LL SEE YOU AT THE PARTY TONIGHT. NO **EXCUSES** THIS TIME, AZI.

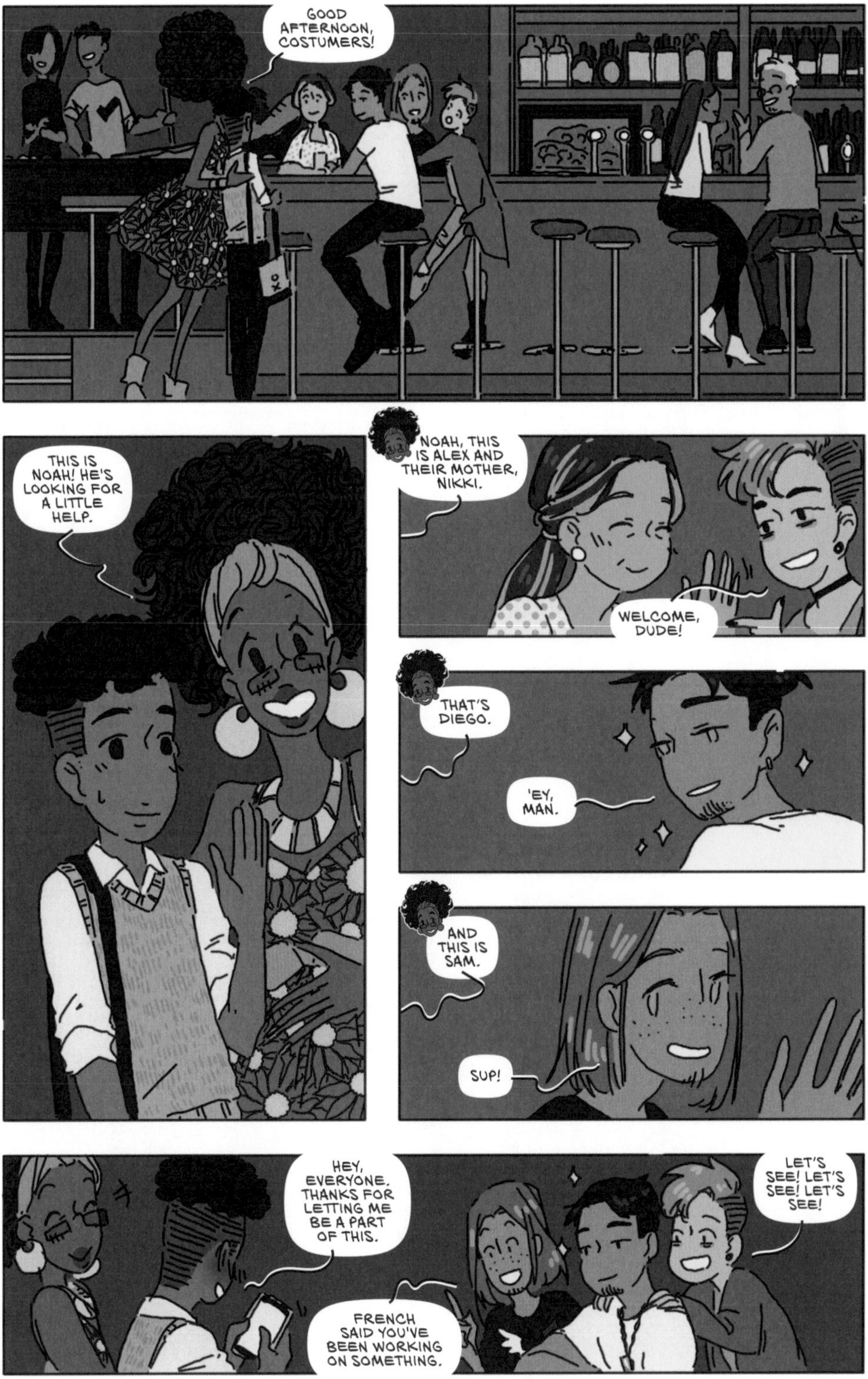
GOOD AFTERNOON, COSTUMERS!
THIS IS NOAH! HE'S LOOKING FOR A LITTLE HELP.
NOAH, THIS IS ALEX AND THEIR MOTHER, NIKKI.
WELCOME, DUDE!
THAT'S DIEGO.
'EY, MAN.
AND THIS IS SAM.
SUP!
HEY, EVERYONE. THANKS FOR LETTING ME BE A PART OF THIS.
FRENCH SAID YOU'VE BEEN WORKING ON SOMETHING.
LET'S SEE! LET'S SEE! LET'S SEE!

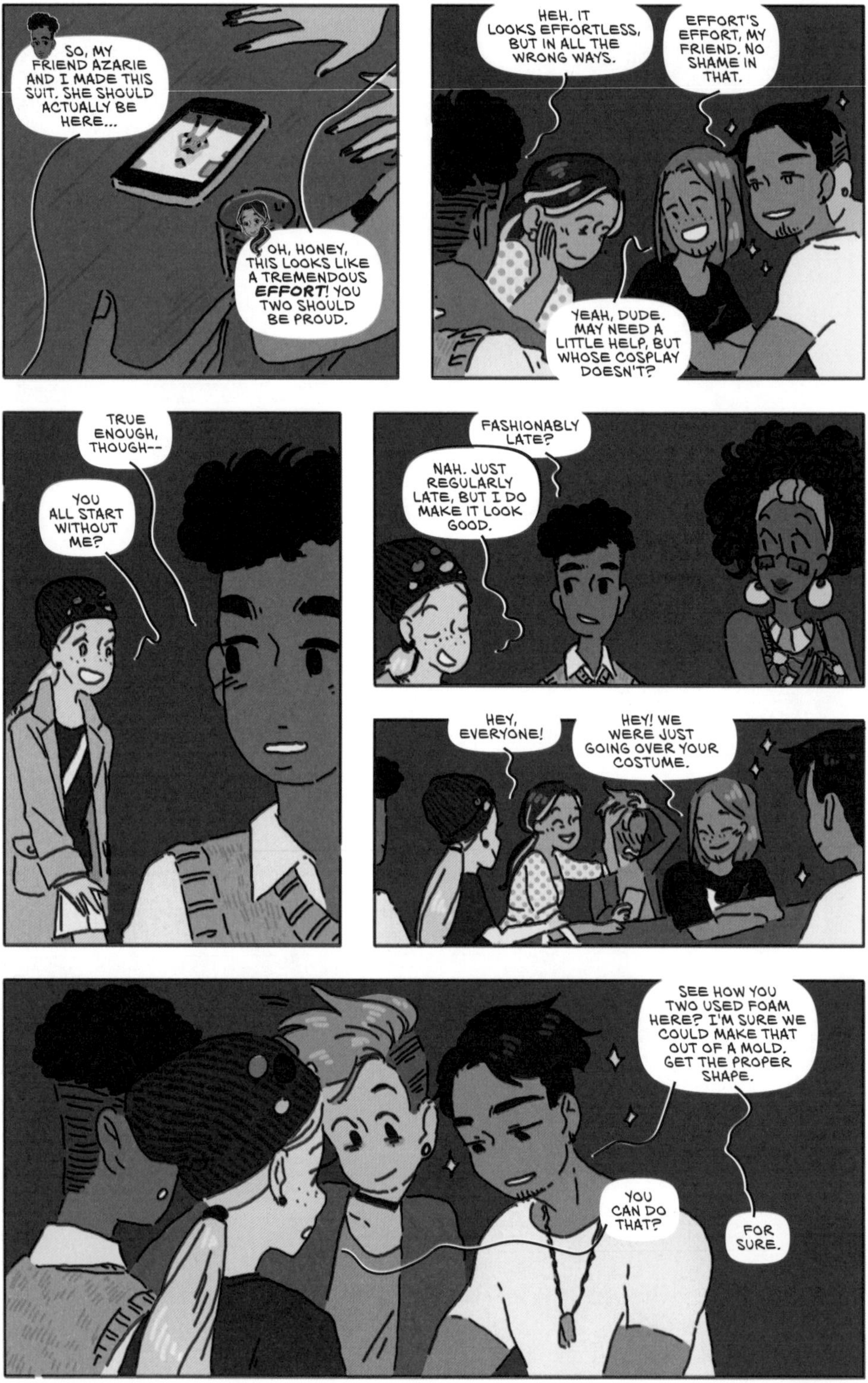
SO, MY FRIEND AZARIE AND I MADE THIS SUIT. SHE SHOULD ACTUALLY BE HERE...
OH, HONEY, THIS LOOKS LIKE A TREMENDOUS EFFORT! YOU TWO SHOULD BE PROUD.
HEH. IT LOOKS EFFORTLESS, BUT IN ALL THE WRONG WAYS.
EFFORT'S EFFORT, MY FRIEND. NO SHAME IN THAT.
YEAH, DUDE. MAY NEED A LITTLE HELP, BUT WHOSE COSPLAY DOESN'T?
TRUE ENOUGH, THOUGH--
YOU ALL START WITHOUT ME?
FASHIONABLY LATE?
NAH. JUST REGULARLY LATE, BUT I DO MAKE IT LOOK GOOD.
HEY, EVERYONE!
HEY! WE WERE JUST GOING OVER YOUR COSTUME.
SEE HOW YOU TWO USED FOAM HERE? I'M SURE WE COULD MAKE THAT OUT OF A MOLD. GET THE PROPER SHAPE.
YOU CAN DO THAT?
FOR SURE.

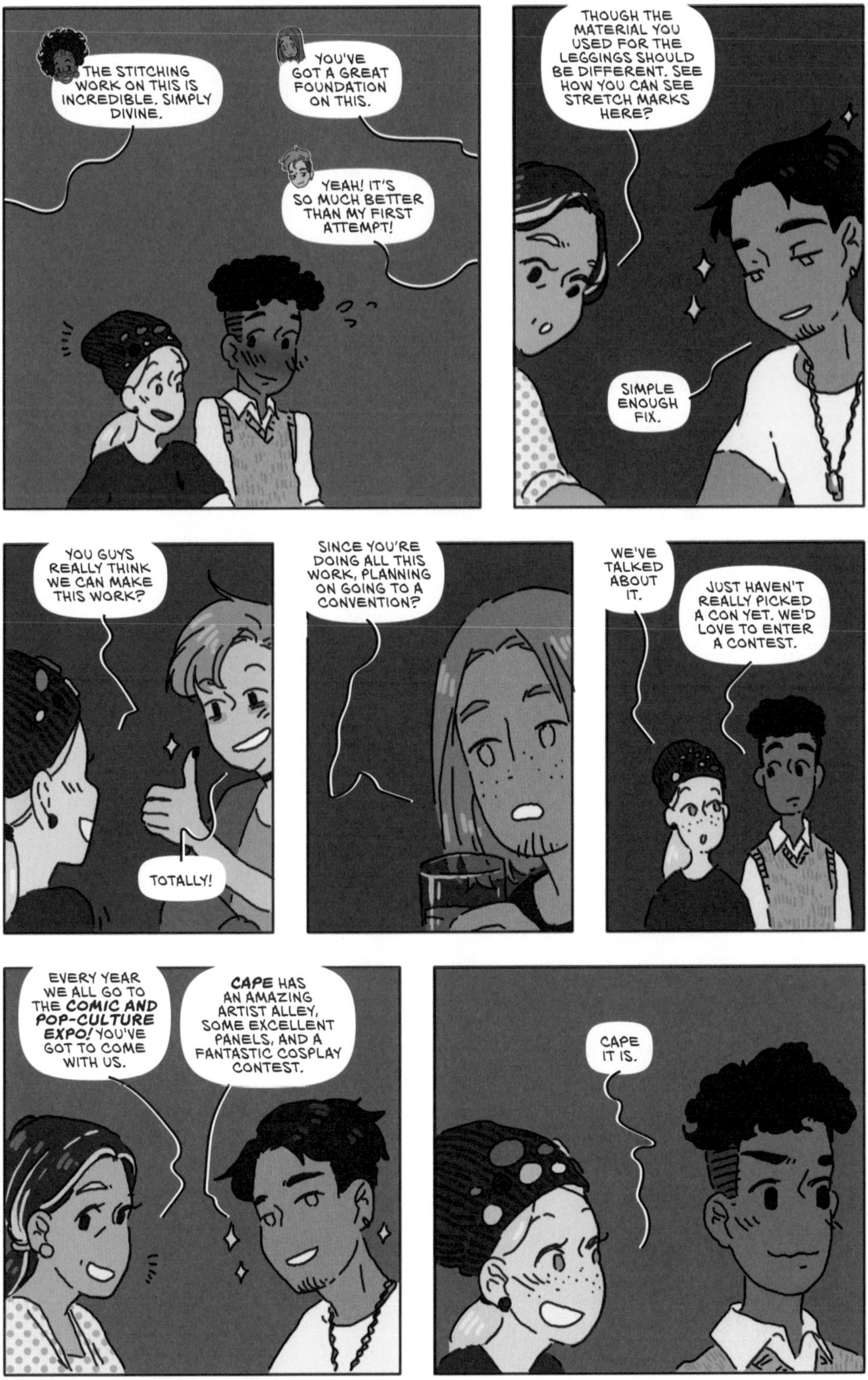
THE STITCHING WORK ON THIS IS INCREDIBLE. SIMPLY DIVINE.
YOU'VE GOT A GREAT FOUNDATION ON THIS.
YEAH! IT'S SO MUCH BETTER THAN MY FIRST ATTEMPT!
THOUGH THE MATERIAL YOU USED FOR THE LEGGINGS SHOULD BE DIFFERENT. SEE HOW YOU CAN SEE STRETCH MARKS HERE?
SIMPLE ENOUGH FIX.
YOU GUYS REALLY THINK WE CAN MAKE THIS WORK?
TOTALLY!
SINCE YOU'RE DOING ALL THIS WORK, PLANNING ON GOING TO A CONVENTION?
WE'VE TALKED ABOUT IT.
JUST HAVEN'T REALLY PICKED A CON YET. WE'D LOVE TO ENTER A CONTEST.
EVERY YEAR WE ALL GO TO THE ***COMIC AND POP-CULTURE EXPO!*** YOU'VE GOT TO COME WITH US.
CAPE HAS AN AMAZING ARTIST ALLEY, SOME EXCELLENT PANELS, AND A FANTASTIC COSPLAY CONTEST.
CAPE IT IS.

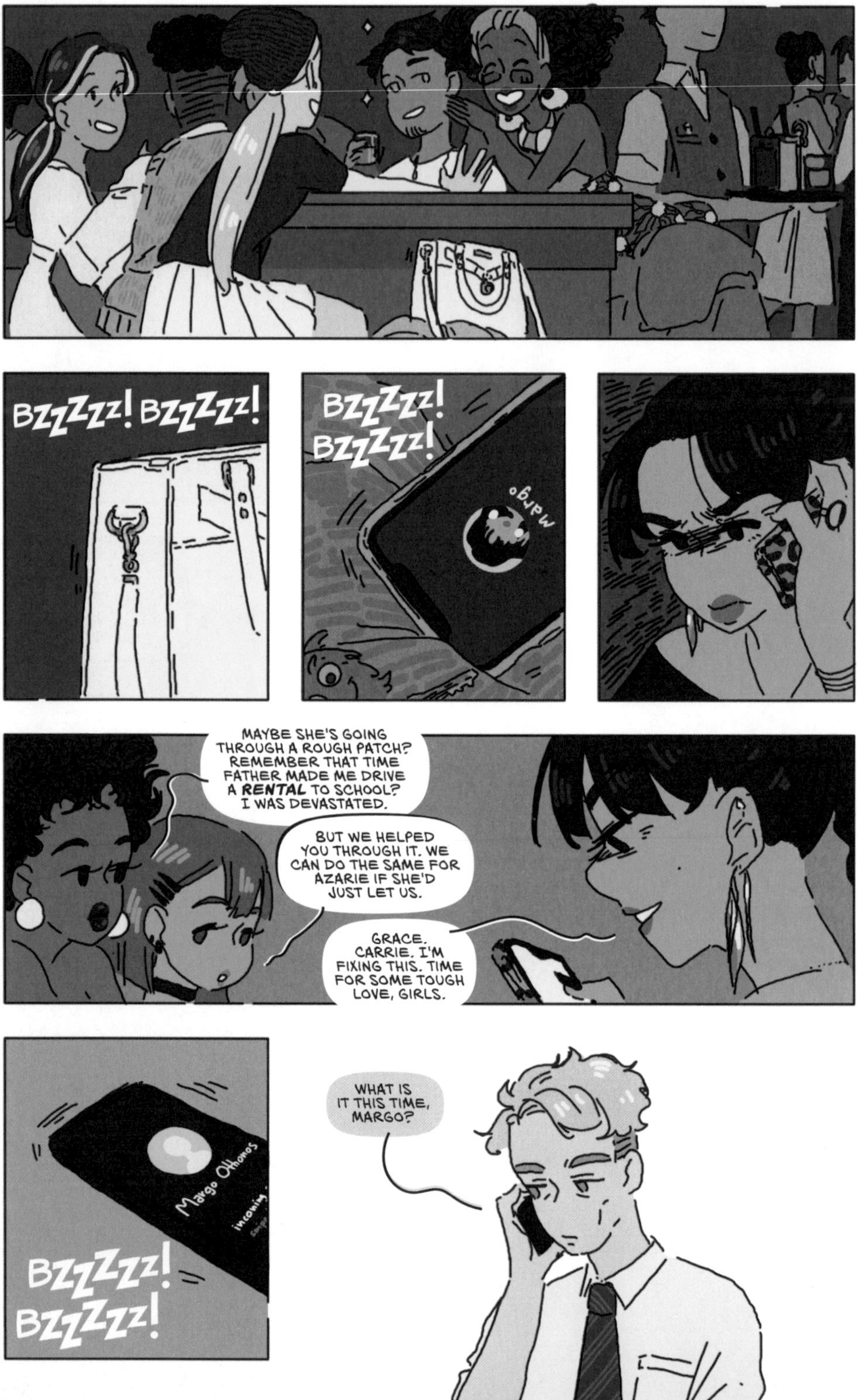
BZZZZZZ! BZZZZZZ!
BZZZZZZ! BZZZZZZ!
margo
MAYBE SHE'S GOING THROUGH A ROUGH PATCH? REMEMBER THAT TIME FATHER MADE ME DRIVE A **RENTAL** TO SCHOOL? I WAS DEVASTATED.
BUT WE HELPED YOU THROUGH IT. WE CAN DO THE SAME FOR AZARIE IF SHE'D JUST LET US.
GRACE. CARRIE. I'M FIXING THIS. TIME FOR SOME TOUGH LOVE, GIRLS.
Margo Othonos
incoming
BZZZZZZ! BZZZZZZ!
WHAT IS IT THIS TIME, MARGO?

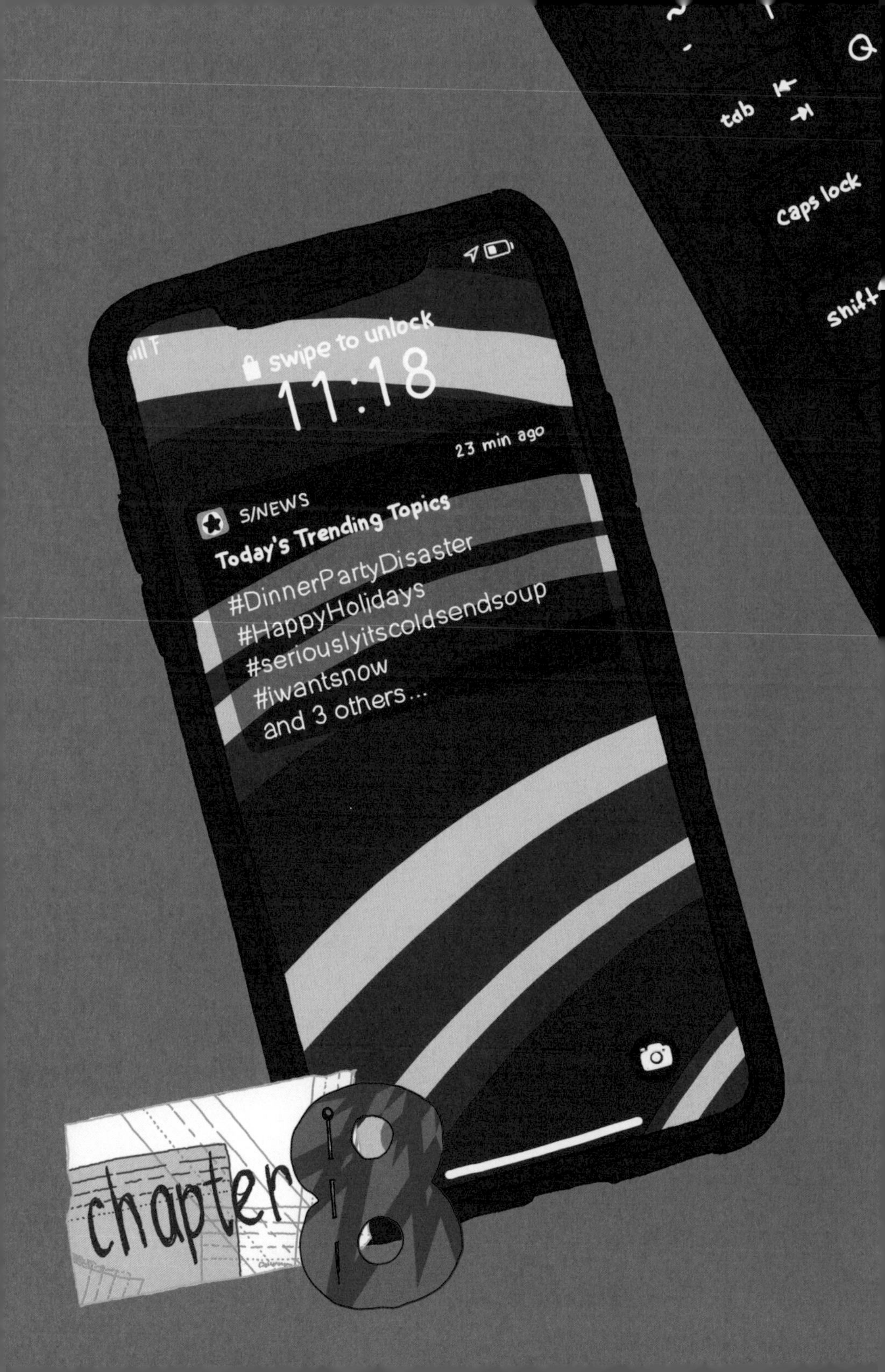
swipe to unlock
11:18
23 min ago
S/NEWS
Today's Trending Topics
#DinnerPartyDisaster
#HappyHolidays
#seriouslyitscoldsendsoup
#iwantsnow
and 3 others...
tab
caps lock
shift
chapter 8

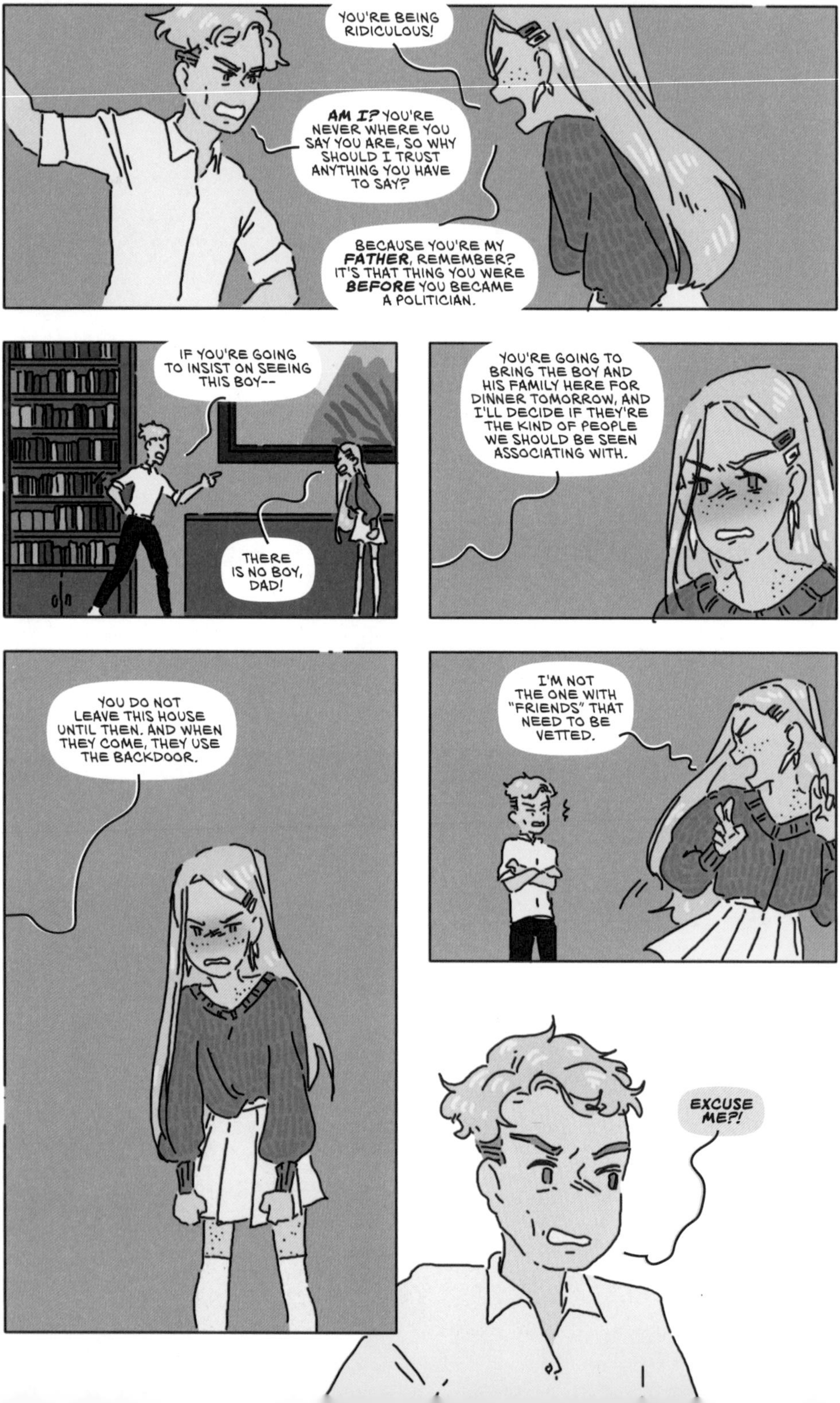

YOU'RE BEING RIDICULOUS!
AM I? YOU'RE NEVER WHERE YOU SAY YOU ARE, SO WHY SHOULD I TRUST ANYTHING YOU HAVE TO SAY?
BECAUSE YOU'RE MY FATHER, REMEMBER? IT'S THAT THING YOU WERE BEFORE YOU BECAME A POLITICIAN.
IF YOU'RE GOING TO INSIST ON SEEING THIS BOY--
THERE IS NO BOY, DAD!
YOU'RE GOING TO BRING THE BOY AND HIS FAMILY HERE FOR DINNER TOMORROW, AND I'LL DECIDE IF THEY'RE THE KIND OF PEOPLE WE SHOULD BE SEEN ASSOCIATING WITH.
YOU DO NOT LEAVE THIS HOUSE UNTIL THEN. AND WHEN THEY COME, THEY USE THE BACKDOOR.
I'M NOT THE ONE WITH "FRIENDS" THAT NEED TO BE VETTED.
EXCUSE ME?!

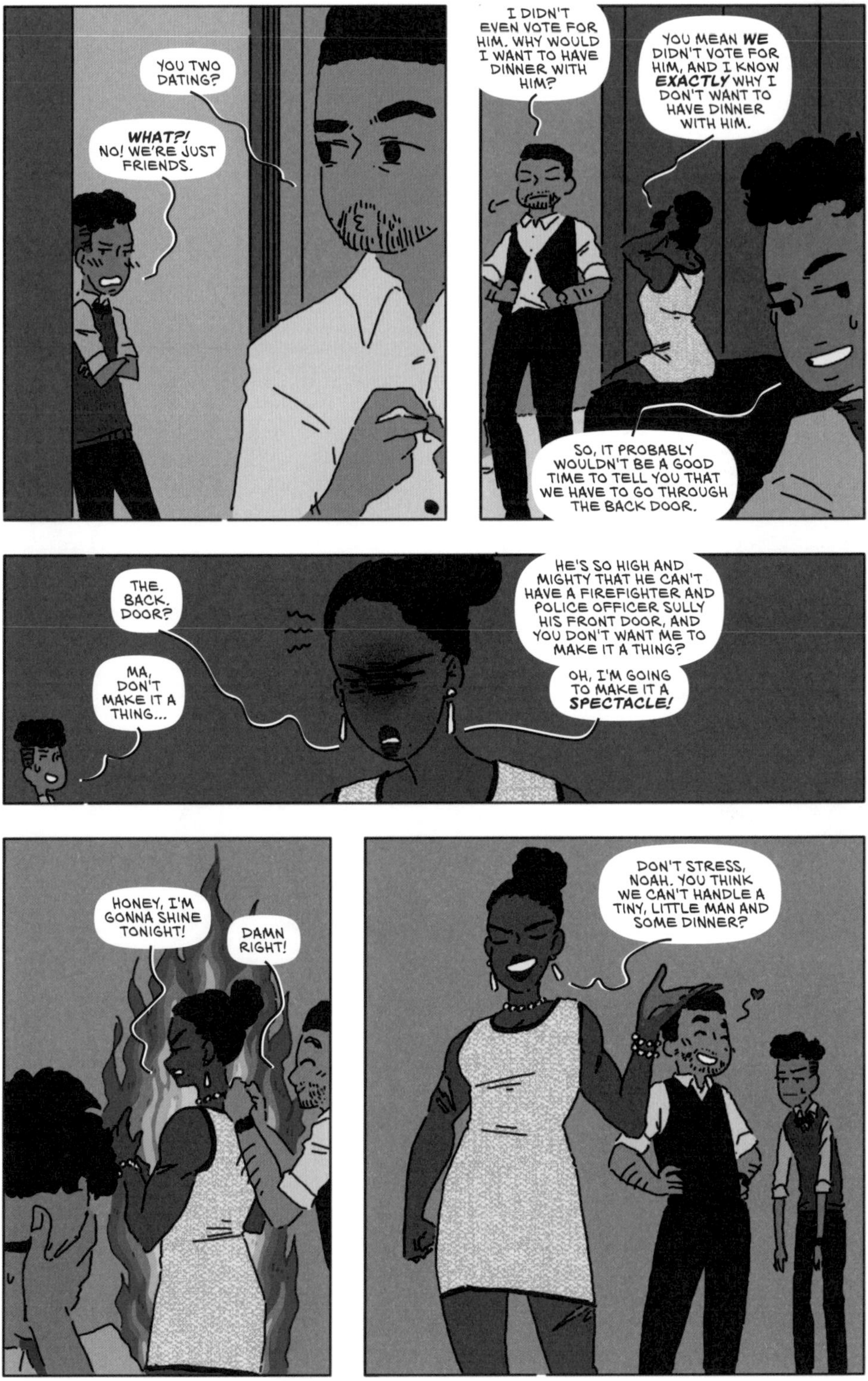
YOU TWO DATING?
WHAT?! NO! WE'RE JUST FRIENDS.
I DIDN'T EVEN VOTE FOR HIM. WHY WOULD I WANT TO HAVE DINNER WITH HIM?
YOU MEAN **WE** DIDN'T VOTE FOR HIM, AND I KNOW ***EXACTLY*** WHY I DON'T WANT TO HAVE DINNER WITH HIM.
SO, IT PROBABLY WOULDN'T BE A GOOD TIME TO TELL YOU THAT WE HAVE TO GO THROUGH THE BACK DOOR.
THE. BACK. DOOR?
MA, DON'T MAKE IT A THING...
HE'S SO HIGH AND MIGHTY THAT HE CAN'T HAVE A FIREFIGHTER AND POLICE OFFICER SULLY HIS FRONT DOOR, AND YOU DON'T WANT ME TO MAKE IT A THING?
OH, I'M GOING TO MAKE IT A ***SPECTACLE!***
HONEY, I'M GONNA SHINE TONIGHT!
DAMN RIGHT!
DON'T STRESS, NOAH. YOU THINK WE CAN'T HANDLE A TINY, LITTLE MAN AND SOME DINNER?

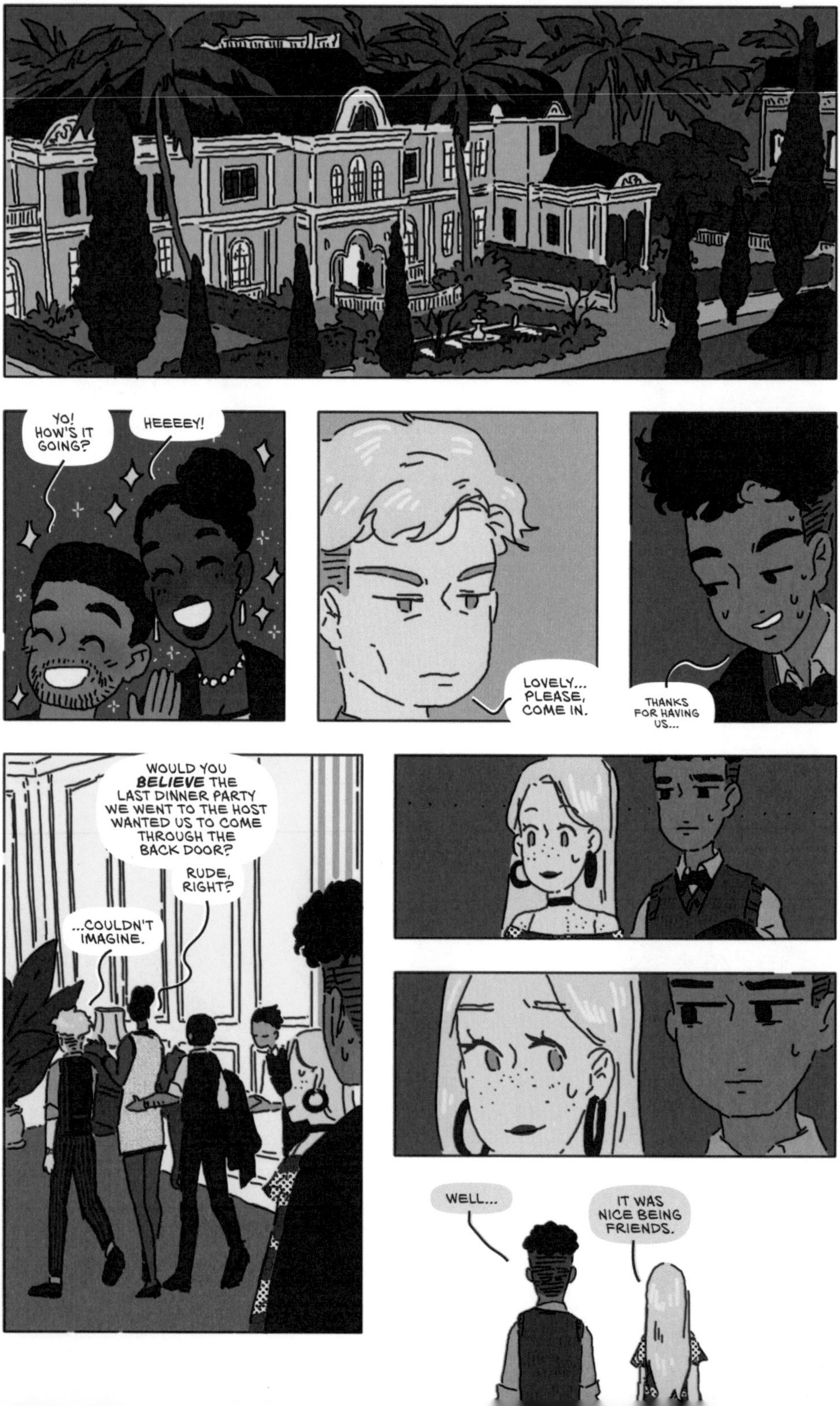
YO! HOW'S IT GOING?
HEEEEY!
LOVELY... PLEASE, COME IN.
THANKS FOR HAVING US...
WOULD YOU **BELIEVE** THE LAST DINNER PARTY WE WENT TO THE HOST WANTED US TO COME THROUGH THE BACK DOOR?
RUDE, RIGHT?
...COULDN'T IMAGINE.
WELL...
IT WAS NICE BEING FRIENDS.

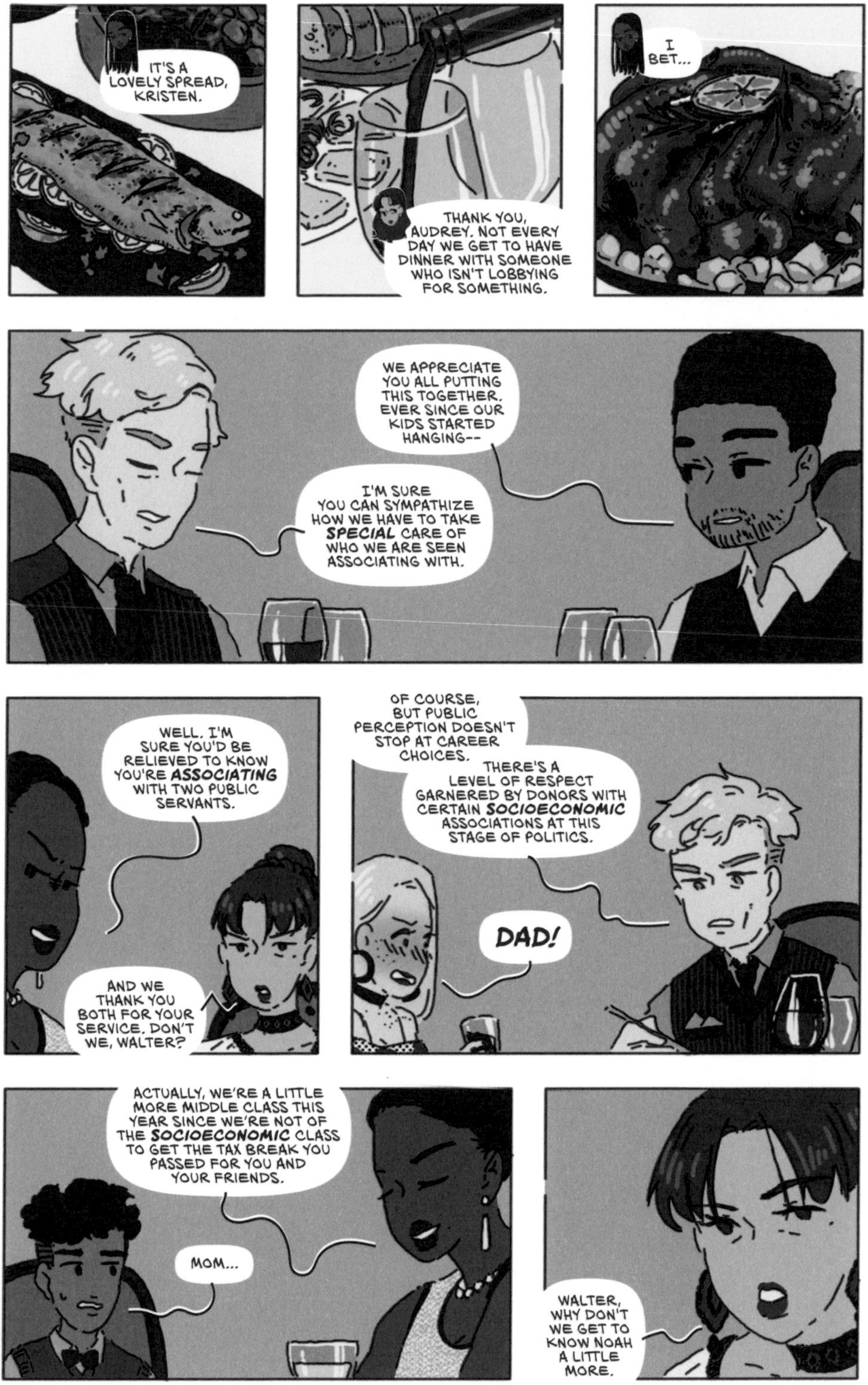
IT'S A LOVELY SPREAD, KRISTEN.
THANK YOU, AUDREY. NOT EVERY DAY WE GET TO HAVE DINNER WITH SOMEONE WHO ISN'T LOBBYING FOR SOMETHING.
I BET...
WE APPRECIATE YOU ALL PUTTING THIS TOGETHER. EVER SINCE OUR KIDS STARTED HANGING--
I'M SURE YOU CAN SYMPATHIZE HOW WE HAVE TO TAKE SPECIAL CARE OF WHO WE ARE SEEN ASSOCIATING WITH.
WELL. I'M SURE YOU'D BE RELIEVED TO KNOW YOU'RE ASSOCIATING WITH TWO PUBLIC SERVANTS.
AND WE THANK YOU BOTH FOR YOUR SERVICE. DON'T WE, WALTER?
OF COURSE, BUT PUBLIC PERCEPTION DOESN'T STOP AT CAREER CHOICES.
THERE'S A LEVEL OF RESPECT GARNERED BY DONORS WITH CERTAIN SOCIOECONOMIC ASSOCIATIONS AT THIS STAGE OF POLITICS.
DAD!
ACTUALLY, WE'RE A LITTLE MORE MIDDLE CLASS THIS YEAR SINCE WE'RE NOT OF THE SOCIOECONOMIC CLASS TO GET THE TAX BREAK YOU PASSED FOR YOU AND YOUR FRIENDS.
MOM...
WALTER, WHY DON'T WE GET TO KNOW NOAH A LITTLE MORE.

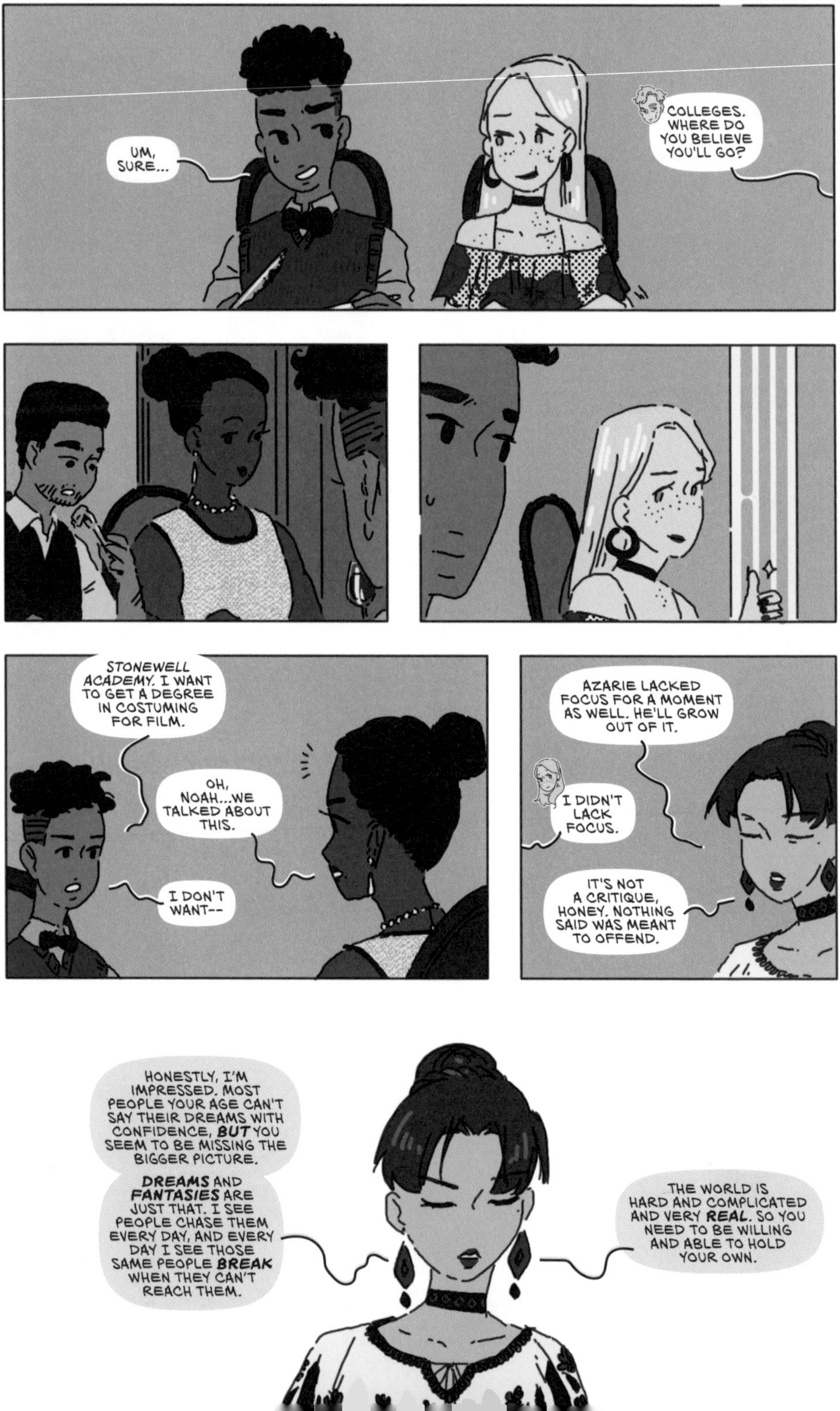
COLLEGES. WHERE DO YOU BELIEVE YOU'LL GO?
UM, SURE...
STONEWELL ACADEMY. I WANT TO GET A DEGREE IN COSTUMING FOR FILM.
OH, NOAH...WE TALKED ABOUT THIS.
I DON'T WANT--
AZARIE LACKED FOCUS FOR A MOMENT AS WELL. HE'LL GROW OUT OF IT.
I DIDN'T LACK FOCUS.
IT'S NOT A CRITIQUE, HONEY. NOTHING SAID WAS MEANT TO OFFEND.
HONESTLY, I'M IMPRESSED. MOST PEOPLE YOUR AGE CAN'T SAY THEIR DREAMS WITH CONFIDENCE, BUT YOU SEEM TO BE MISSING THE BIGGER PICTURE.
DREAMS AND FANTASIES ARE JUST THAT. I SEE PEOPLE CHASE THEM EVERY DAY, AND EVERY DAY I SEE THOSE SAME PEOPLE BREAK WHEN THEY CAN'T REACH THEM.
THE WORLD IS HARD AND COMPLICATED AND VERY REAL. SO YOU NEED TO BE WILLING AND ABLE TO HOLD YOUR OWN.

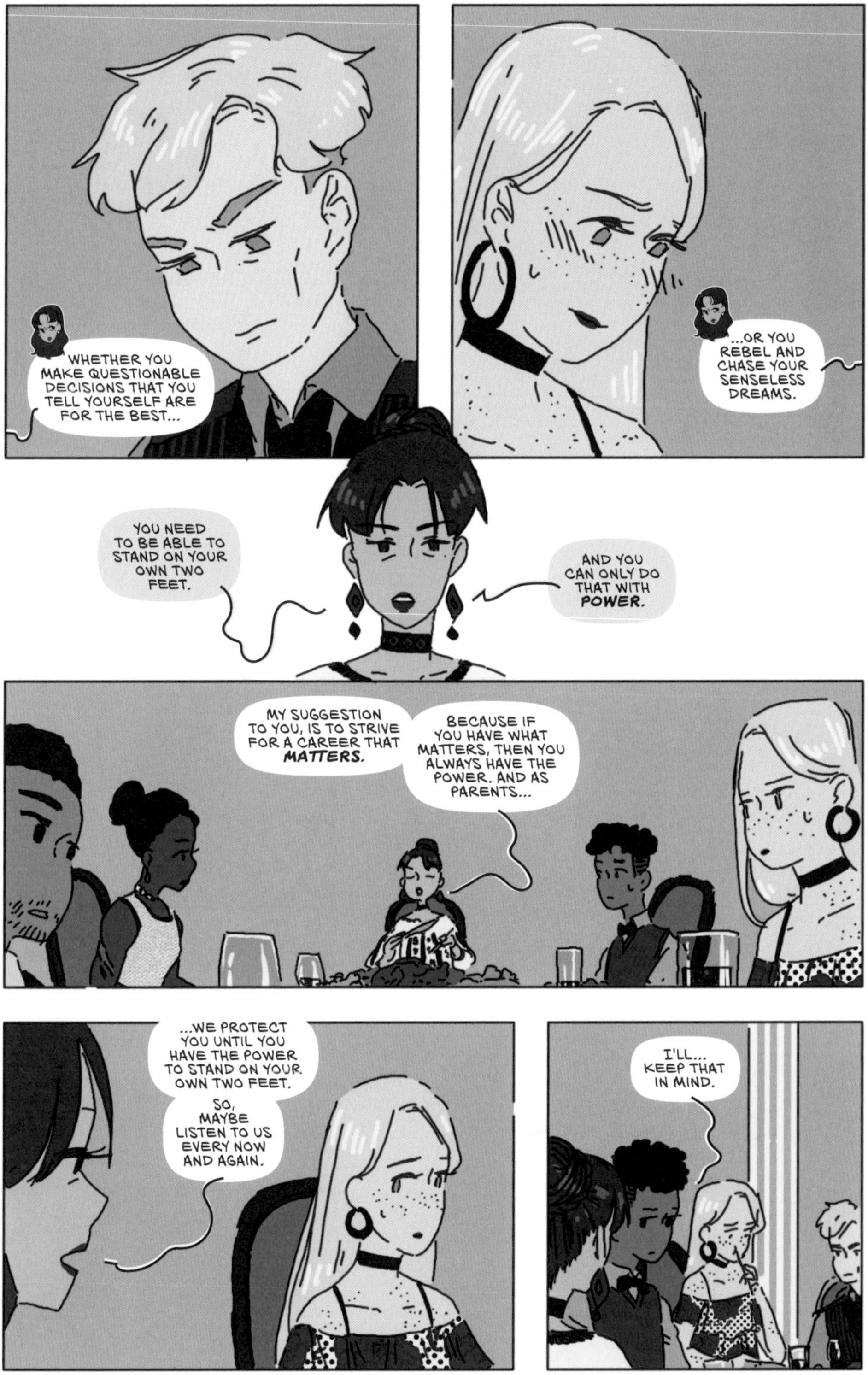
WHETHER YOU MAKE QUESTIONABLE DECISIONS THAT YOU TELL YOURSELF ARE FOR THE BEST...
...OR YOU REBEL AND CHASE YOUR SENSELESS DREAMS.
YOU NEED TO BE ABLE TO STAND ON YOUR OWN TWO FEET.
AND YOU CAN ONLY DO THAT WITH **POWER.**
MY SUGGESTION TO YOU, IS TO STRIVE FOR A CAREER THAT **MATTERS.**
BECAUSE IF YOU HAVE WHAT MATTERS, THEN YOU ALWAYS HAVE THE POWER. AND AS PARENTS...
...WE PROTECT YOU UNTIL YOU HAVE THE POWER TO STAND ON YOUR OWN TWO FEET.
SO, MAYBE LISTEN TO US EVERY NOW AND AGAIN.
I'LL... KEEP THAT IN MIND.

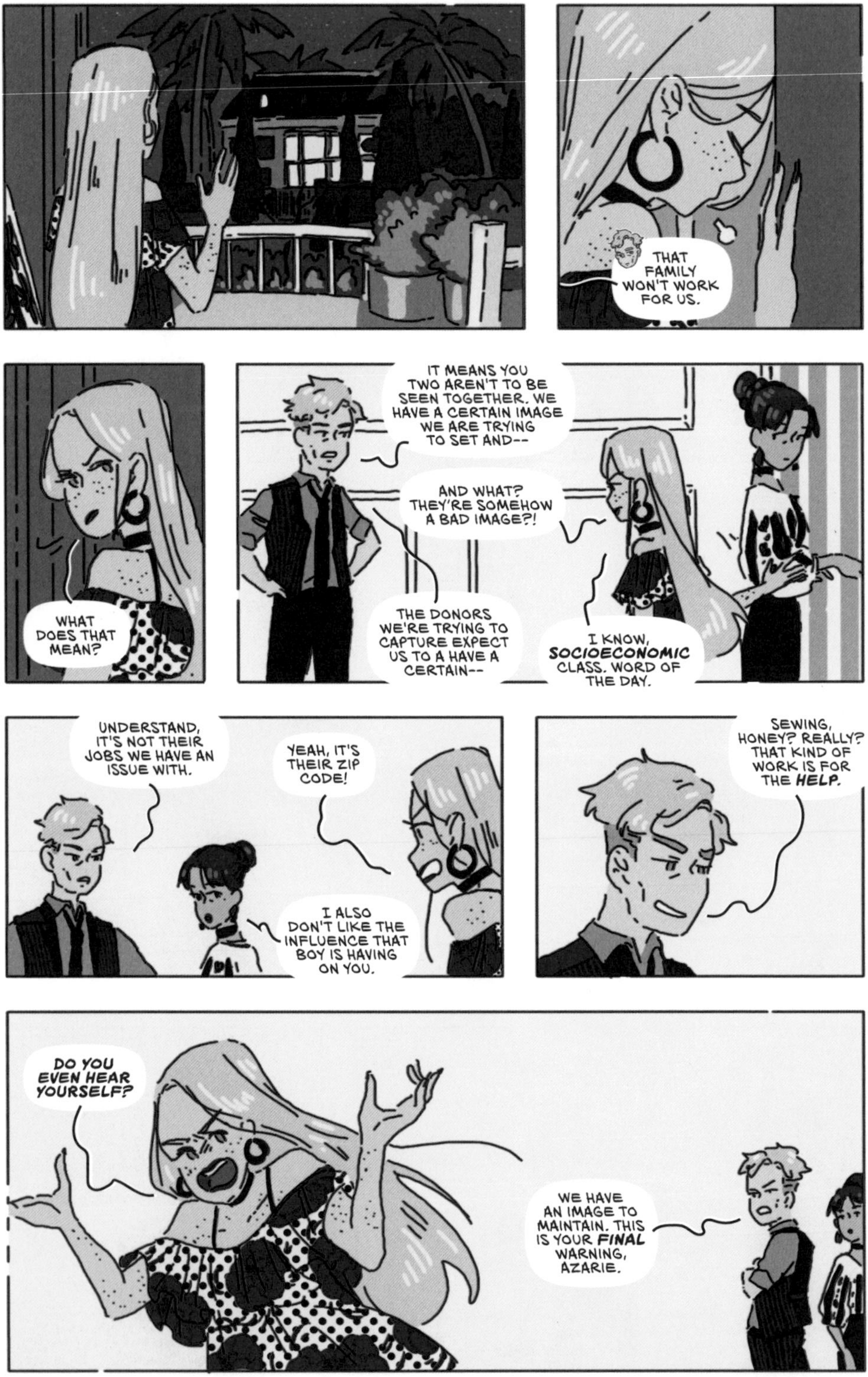
THAT FAMILY WON'T WORK FOR US.
WHAT DOES THAT MEAN?
IT MEANS YOU TWO AREN'T TO BE SEEN TOGETHER. WE HAVE A CERTAIN IMAGE WE ARE TRYING TO SET AND--
AND WHAT? THEY'RE SOMEHOW A BAD IMAGE?!
THE DONORS WE'RE TRYING TO CAPTURE EXPECT US TO A HAVE A CERTAIN--
I KNOW, ***SOCIOECONOMIC*** CLASS. WORD OF THE DAY.
UNDERSTAND, IT'S NOT THEIR JOBS WE HAVE AN ISSUE WITH.
YEAH, IT'S THEIR ZIP CODE!
I ALSO DON'T LIKE THE INFLUENCE THAT BOY IS HAVING ON YOU.
SEWING, HONEY? REALLY? THAT KIND OF WORK IS FOR THE ***HELP.***
DO YOU EVEN HEAR YOURSELF?
WE HAVE AN IMAGE TO MAINTAIN. THIS IS YOUR ***FINAL*** WARNING, AZARIE.

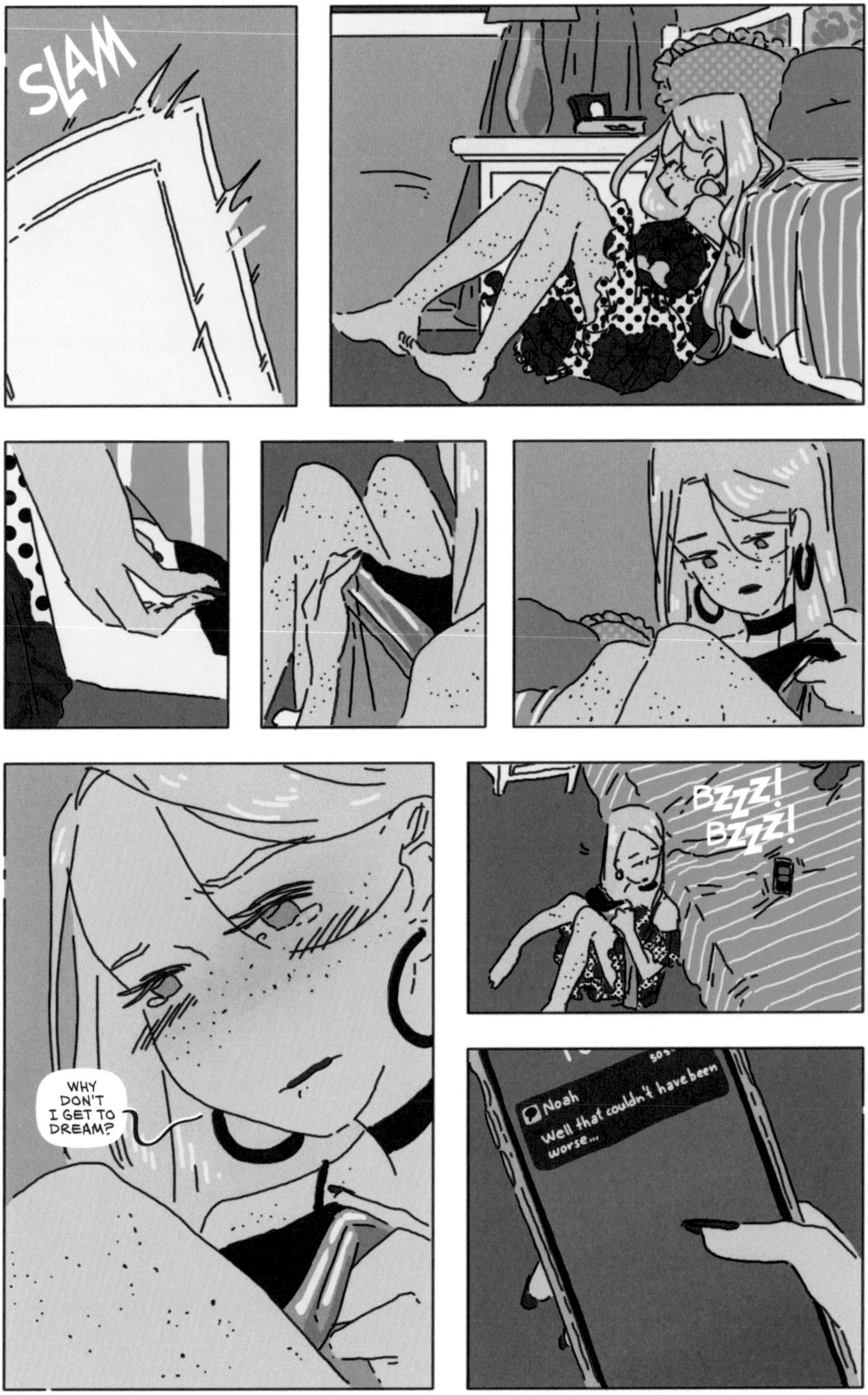
SLAM
BZZZ! BZZZ!
WHY DON'T I GET TO DREAM?
Noah
Well that couldn't have been worse...

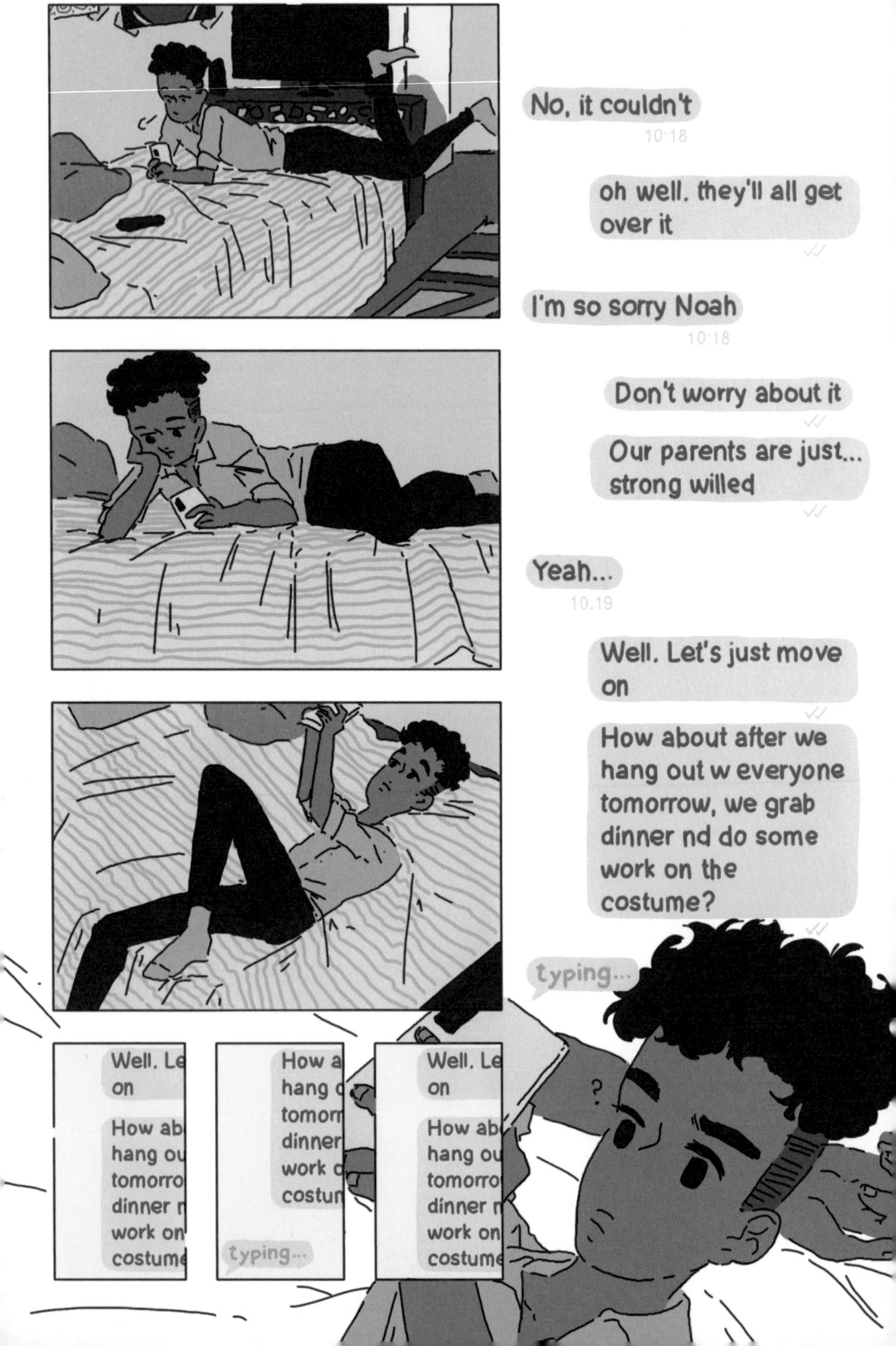
No, it couldn't
10:18
oh well. they'll all get over it
I'm so sorry Noah
10:18
Don't worry about it
Our parents are just... strong willed
Yeah...
10:19
Well. Let's just move on
How about after we hang out w everyone tomorrow, we grab dinner nd do some work on the costume?
typing...
?
typing...

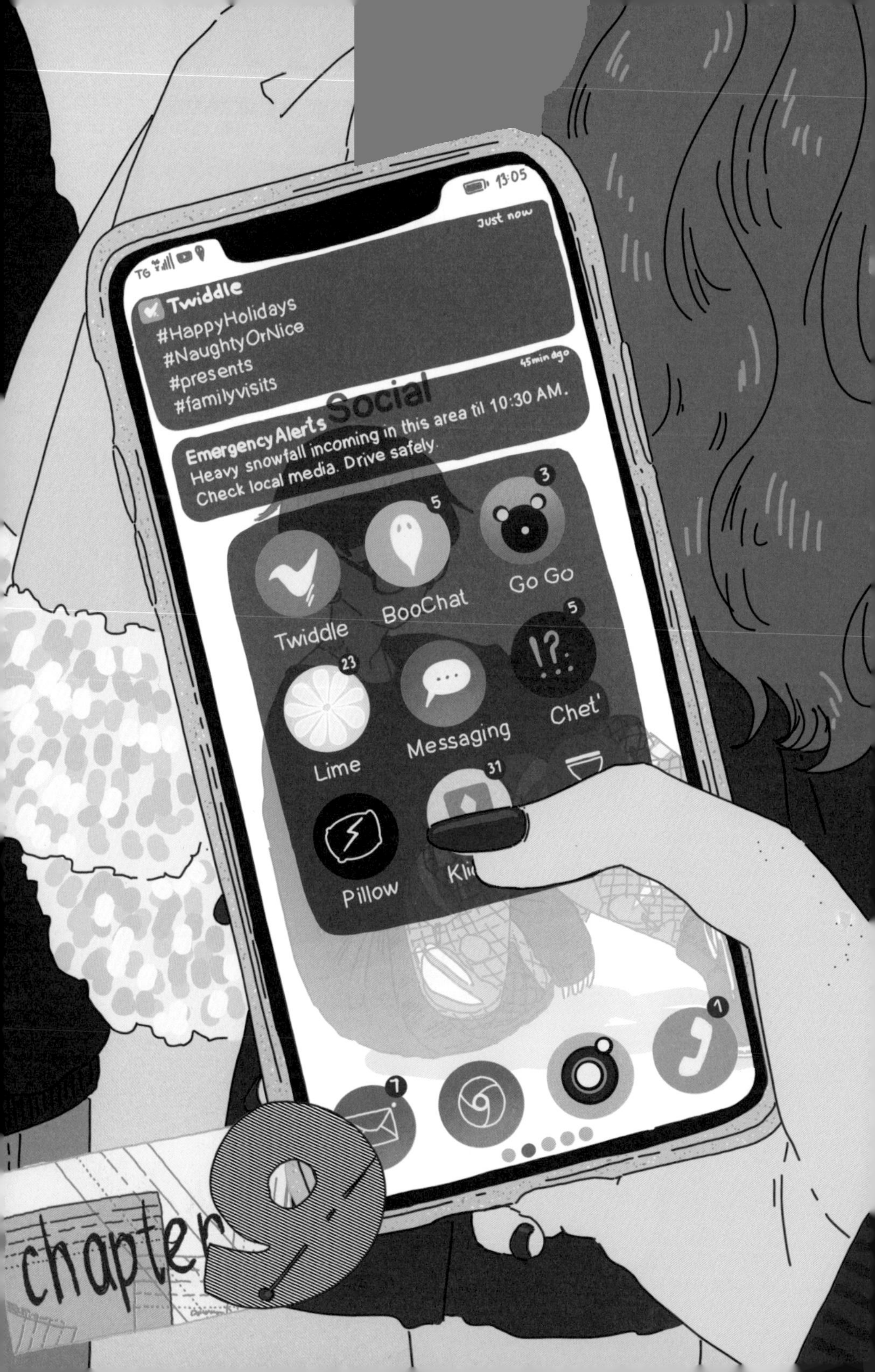
13:05
Just now
Twiddle
#HappyHolidays
#NaughtyOrNice
#presents
#familyvisits
45min ago
Social
Emergency Alerts
Heavy snowfall incoming in this area til 10:30 AM.
Check local media. Drive safely.
Twiddle
BooChat
Go Go
Lime
Messaging
Chet'
Pillow
chapter 9

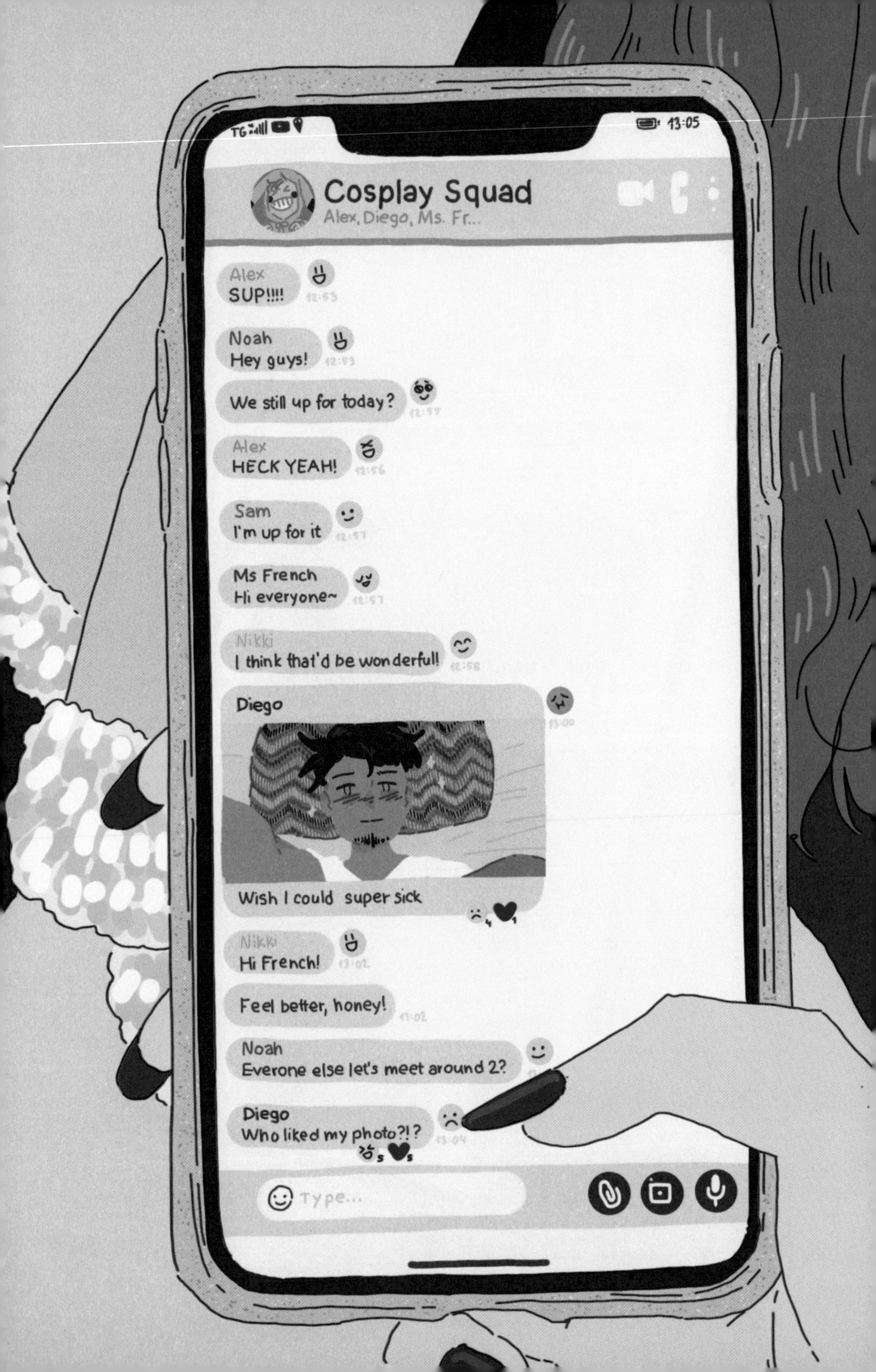

13:05
Cosplay Squad
Alex, Diego, Ms. Fr...
Alex
SUP!!!!
Noah
Hey guys!
We still up for today?
Alex
HECK YEAH!
Sam
I'm up for it
Ms French
Hi everyone~
Nikki
I think that'd be wonderful!
Diego
Wish I could super sick
Nikki
Hi French!
Feel better, honey!
Noah
Everone else let's meet around 2?
Diego
Who liked my photo?!?
Type...

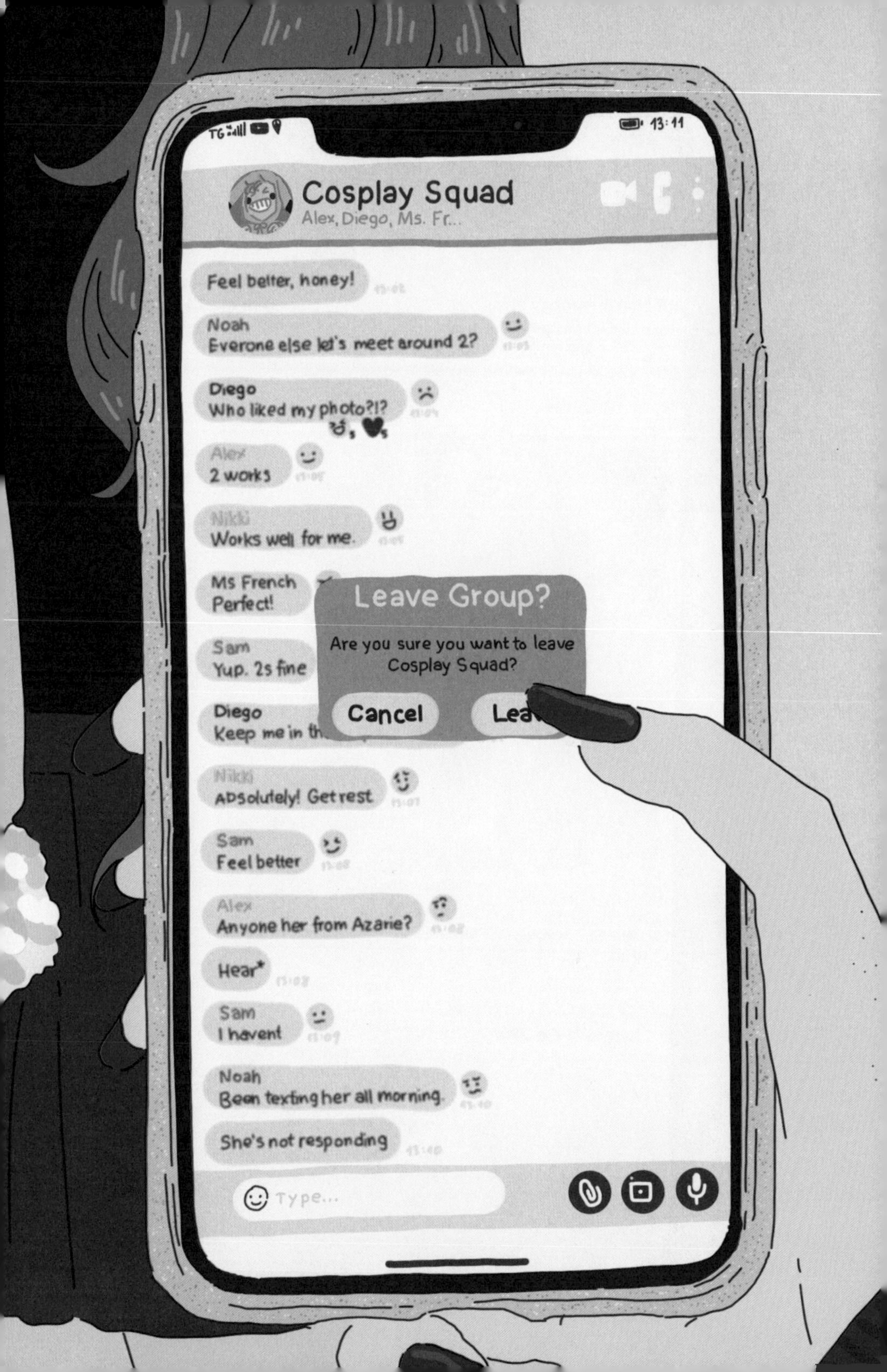
13:11
Cosplay Squad
Alex, Diego, Ms. Fr...
Feel better, honey!
Noah
Everone else let's meet around 2?
Diego
Who liked my photo?!?
Alex
2 works
Nikki
Works well for me.
Ms French
Perfect!
Sam
Yup. 2s fine
Diego
Keep me in th
Nikki
ADsolutely! Get rest
Sam
Feel better
Alex
Anyone her from Azarie?
Hear*
Sam
I havent
Noah
Been texting her all morning.
She's not responding
Type...
Leave Group?
Are you sure you want to leave Cosplay Squad?
Cancel
Lea

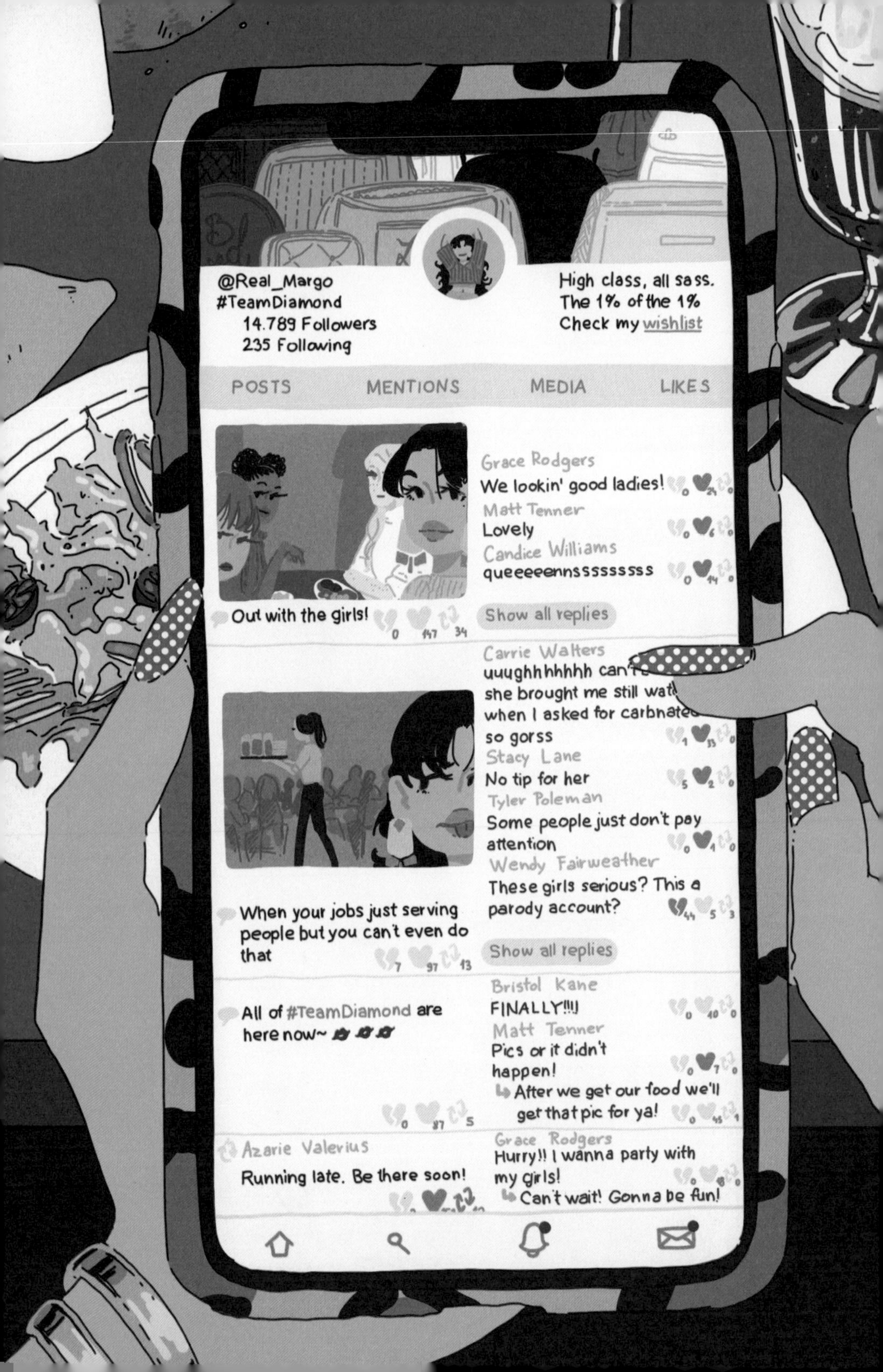

@Real_Margo
#TeamDiamond
14.789 Followers
235 Following
High class, all sass.
The 1% of the 1%
Check my wishlist
POSTS
MENTIONS
MEDIA
LIKES
Out with the girls!
Grace Rodgers
We lookin' good ladies!
Matt Tenner
Lovely
Candice Williams
queeeeennsssssssss
Show all replies
When your jobs just serving people but you can't even do that
Carrie Walters
uuughhhhhh can
she brought me still wat
when I asked for carbnate
so gorss
Stacy Lane
No tip for her
Tyler Poleman
Some people just don't pay attention
Wendy Fairweather
These girls serious? This a parody account?
Show all replies
All of #TeamDiamond are here now~
Bristol Kane
FINALLY!!!!
Matt Tenner
Pics or it didn't happen!
After we get our food we'll get that pic for ya!
Azarie Valerius
Running late. Be there soon!
Grace Rodgers
Hurry!! I wanna party with my girls!
Can't wait! Gonna be fun!

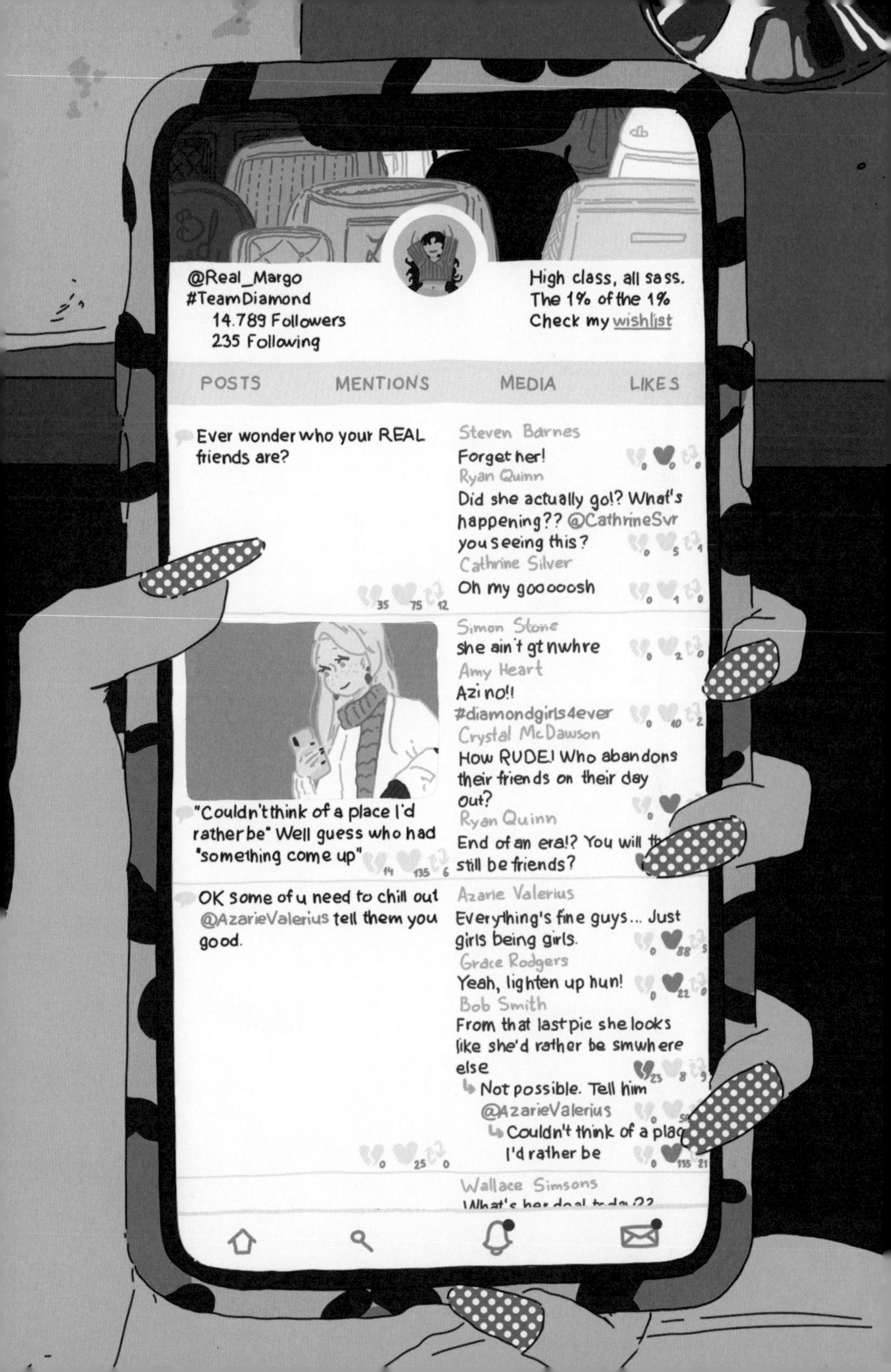

@Real_Margo
#TeamDiamond
14.789 Followers
235 Following
High class, all sass.
The 1% of the 1%
Check my wishlist
POSTS
MENTIONS
MEDIA
LIKES
Ever wonder who your REAL friends are?
Steven Barnes
Forget her!
Ryan Quinn
Did she actually go!? What's happening?? @CathrineSvr you seeing this?
Cathrine Silver
Oh my goooooosh
"Couldn't think of a place I'd rather be" Well guess who had "something come up"
Simon Stone
she ain't gt nwhre
Amy Heart
Azi no!! #diamondgirls4ever
Crystal McDawson
How RUDE! Who abandons their friends on their day out?
Ryan Quinn
End of an era!? You will
still be friends?
OK some of u need to chill out @AzarieValerius tell them you good.
Azarie Valerius
Everything's fine guys... Just girls being girls.
Grace Rodgers
Yeah, lighten up hun!
Bob Smith
From that last pic she looks like she'd rather be smwhere else
Not possible. Tell him @AzarieValerius
Couldn't think of a plac
I'd rather be
Wallace Simsons

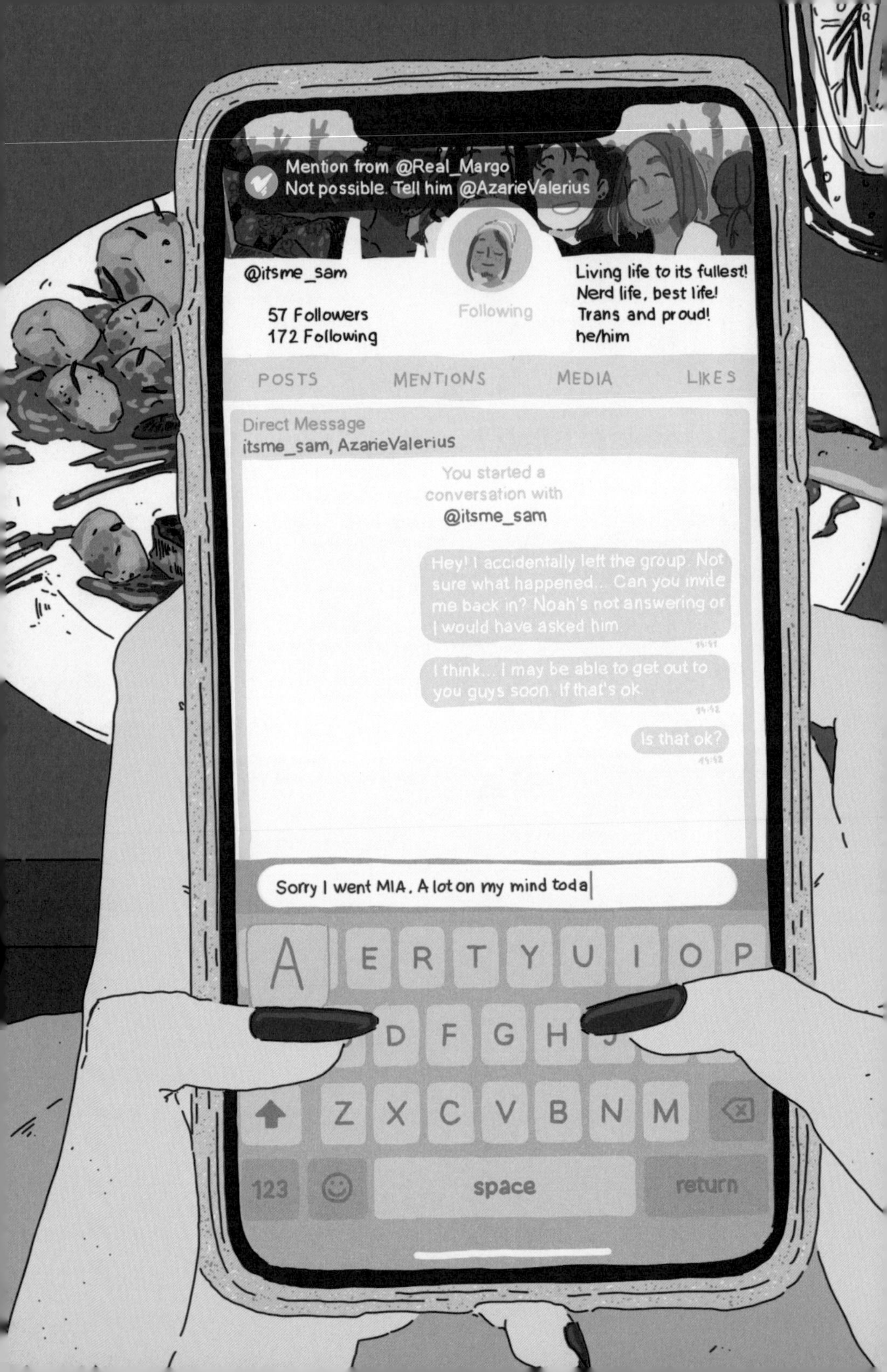
Mention from @Real_Margo
Not possible. Tell him @AzarieValerius
@itsme_sam
57 Followers
172 Following
Following
Living life to its fullest!
Nerd life, best life!
Trans and proud!
he/him
POSTS
MENTIONS
MEDIA
LIKES
Direct Message
itsme_sam, AzarieValerius
You started a conversation with @itsme_sam
Hey! I accidentally left the group. Not sure what happened... Can you invite me back in? Noah's not answering or I would have asked him.
I think... I may be able to get out to you guys soon. If that's ok.
Is that ok?
Sorry I went MIA. A lot on my mind toda
space
return
123

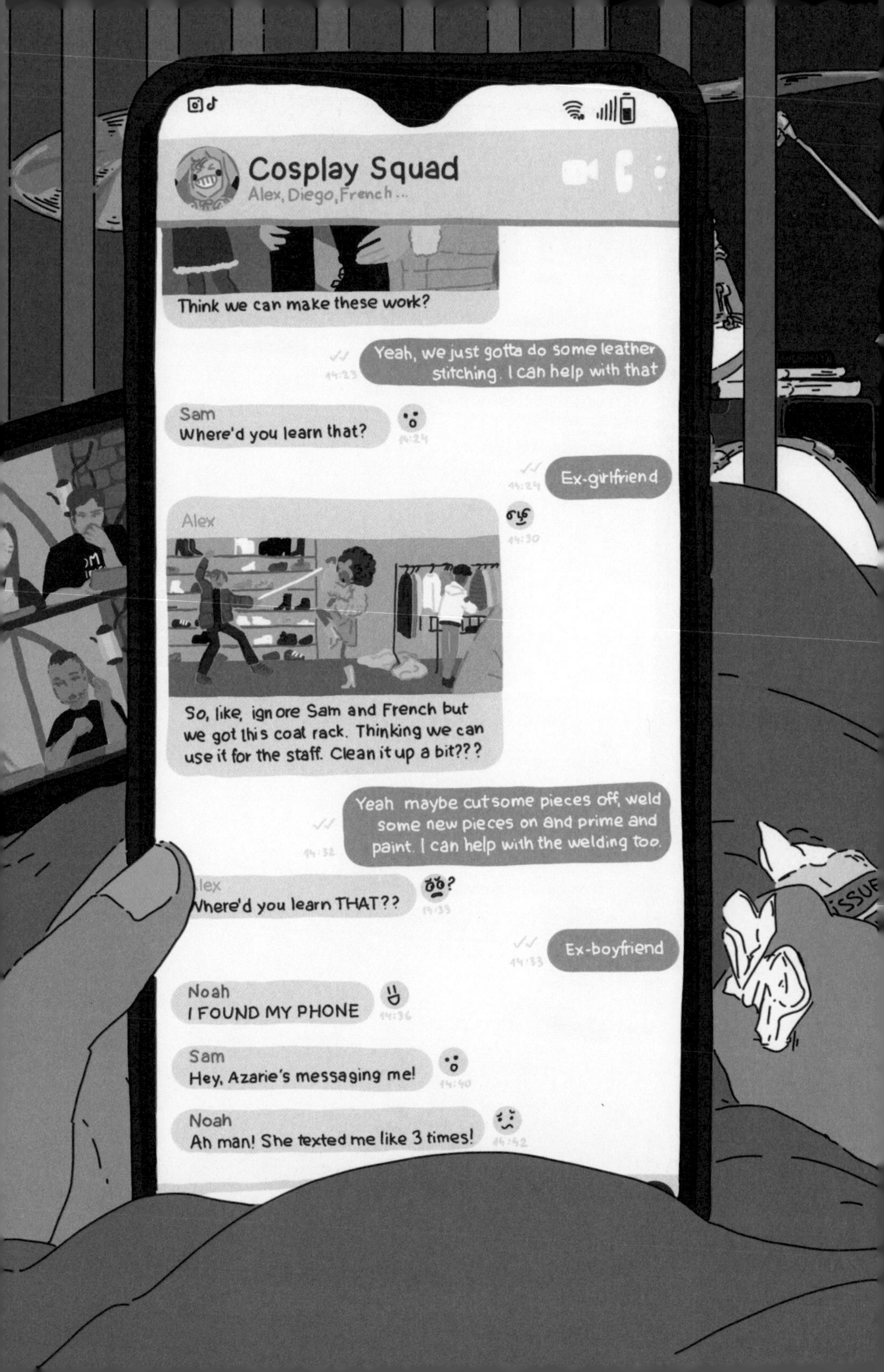

Cosplay Squad
Alex, Diego, French...
Think we can make these work?
Yeah, we just gotta do some leather stitching. I can help with that
14:23
Sam
Where'd you learn that?
14:24
Ex-girlfriend
14:24
Alex
So, like, ignore Sam and French but we got this coat rack. Thinking we can use it for the staff. Clean it up a bit???
14:30
Yeah maybe cut some pieces off, weld some new pieces on and prime and paint. I can help with the welding too.
14:32
Alex
Where'd you learn THAT??
14:33
Ex-boyfriend
14:33
Noah
I FOUND MY PHONE
14:36
Sam
Hey, Azarie's messaging me!
14:40
Noah
Ah man! She texted me like 3 times!
14:42

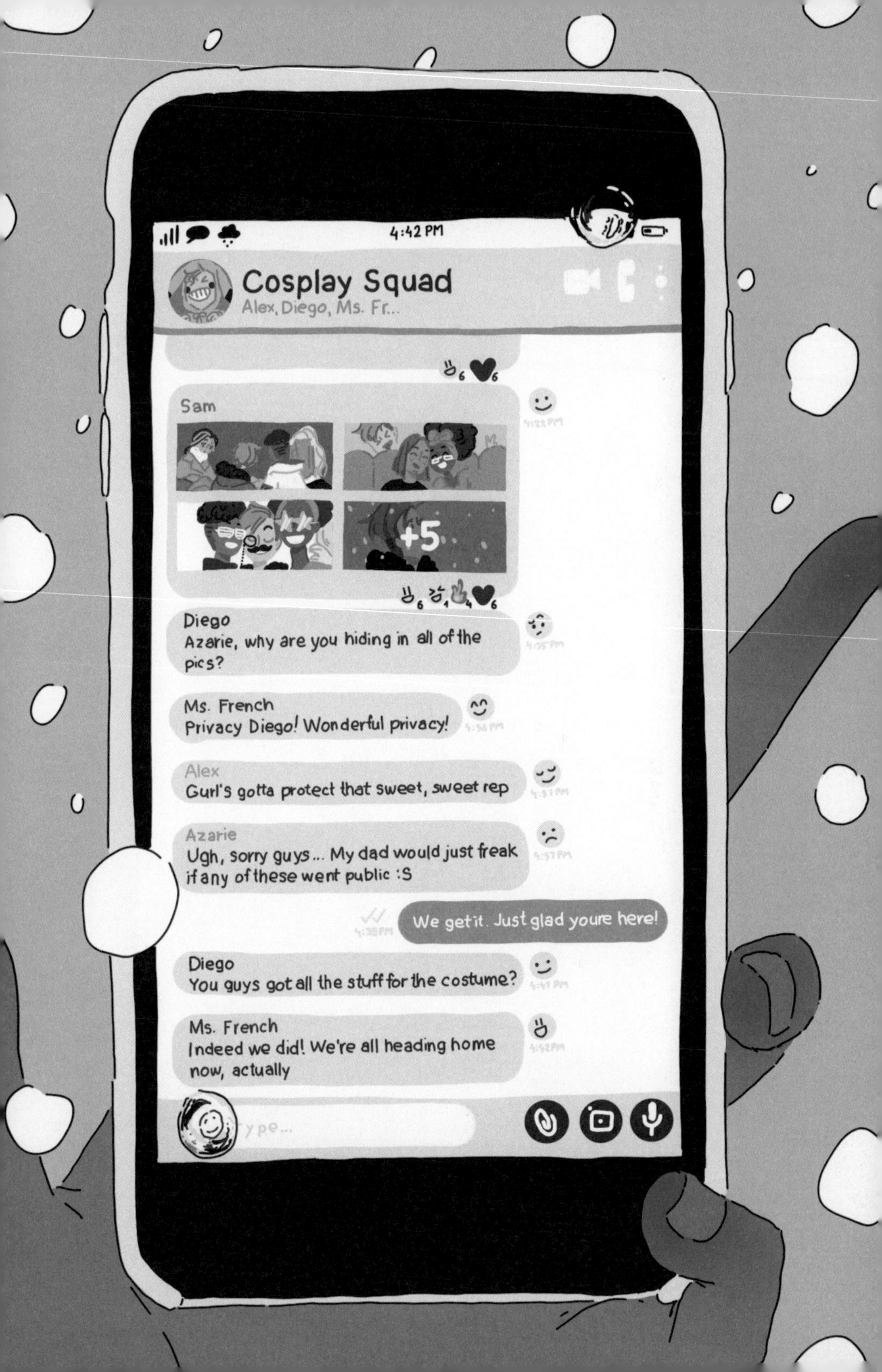
4:42 PM
Cosplay Squad
Alex, Diego, Ms. Fr...
Sam
+5
Diego
Azarie, why are you hiding in all of the pics?
Ms. French
Privacy Diego! Wonderful privacy!
Alex
Gurl's gotta protect that sweet, sweet rep
Azarie
Ugh, sorry guys... My dad would just freak if any of these went public :S
We get it. Just glad youre here!
Diego
You guys got all the stuff for the costume?
Ms. French
Indeed we did! We're all heading home now, actually
Type...

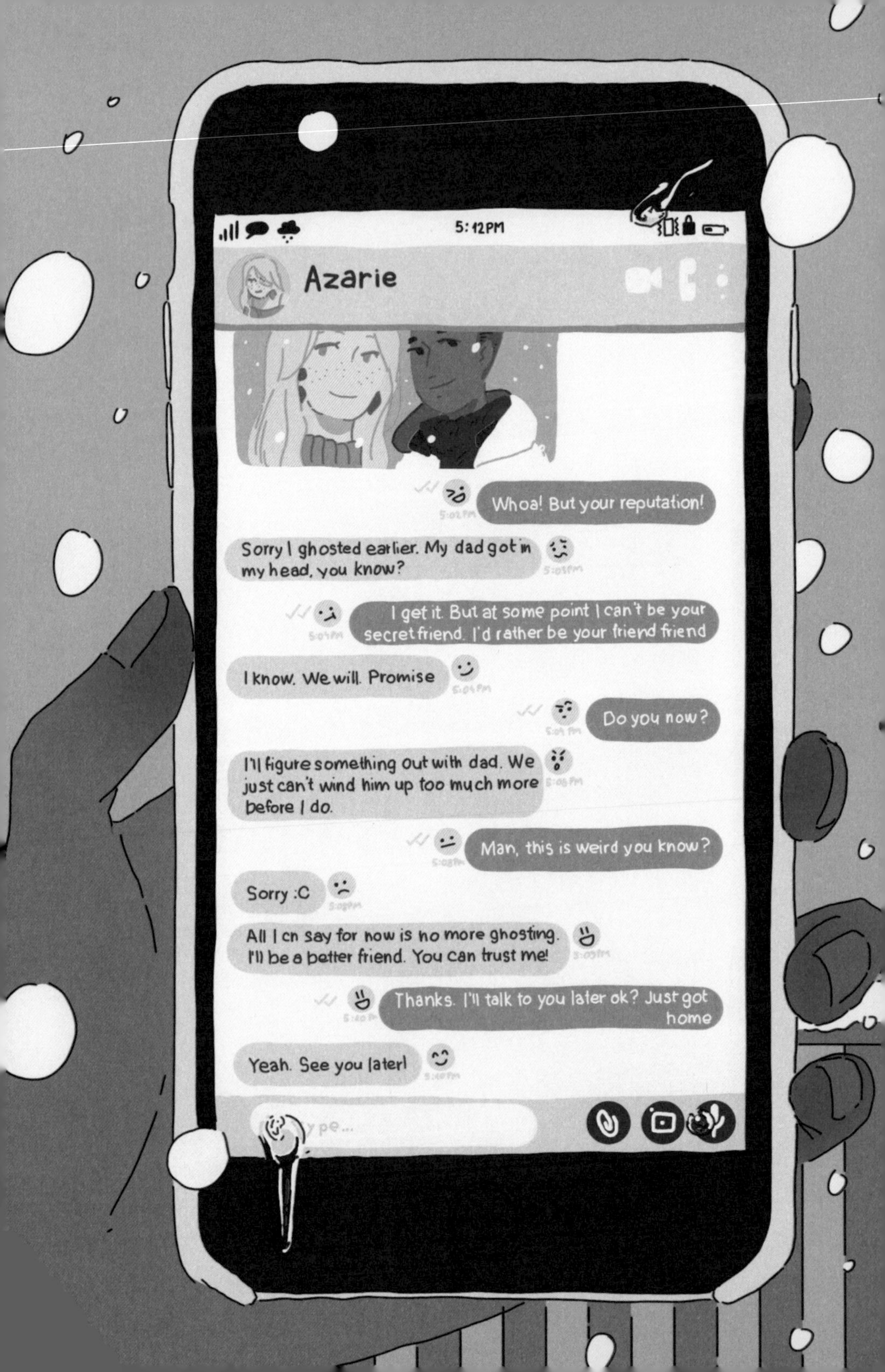
5:12PM
Azarie
Whoa! But your reputation!
Sorry I ghosted earlier. My dad got in my head, you know?
I get it. But at some point I can't be your secret friend. I'd rather be your friend friend
I know. We will. Promise
Do you now?
I'll figure something out with dad. We just can't wind him up too much more before I do.
Man, this is weird you know?
Sorry :C
All I cn say for now is no more ghosting. I'll be a better friend. You can trust me!
Thanks. I'll talk to you later ok? Just got home
Yeah. See you later!

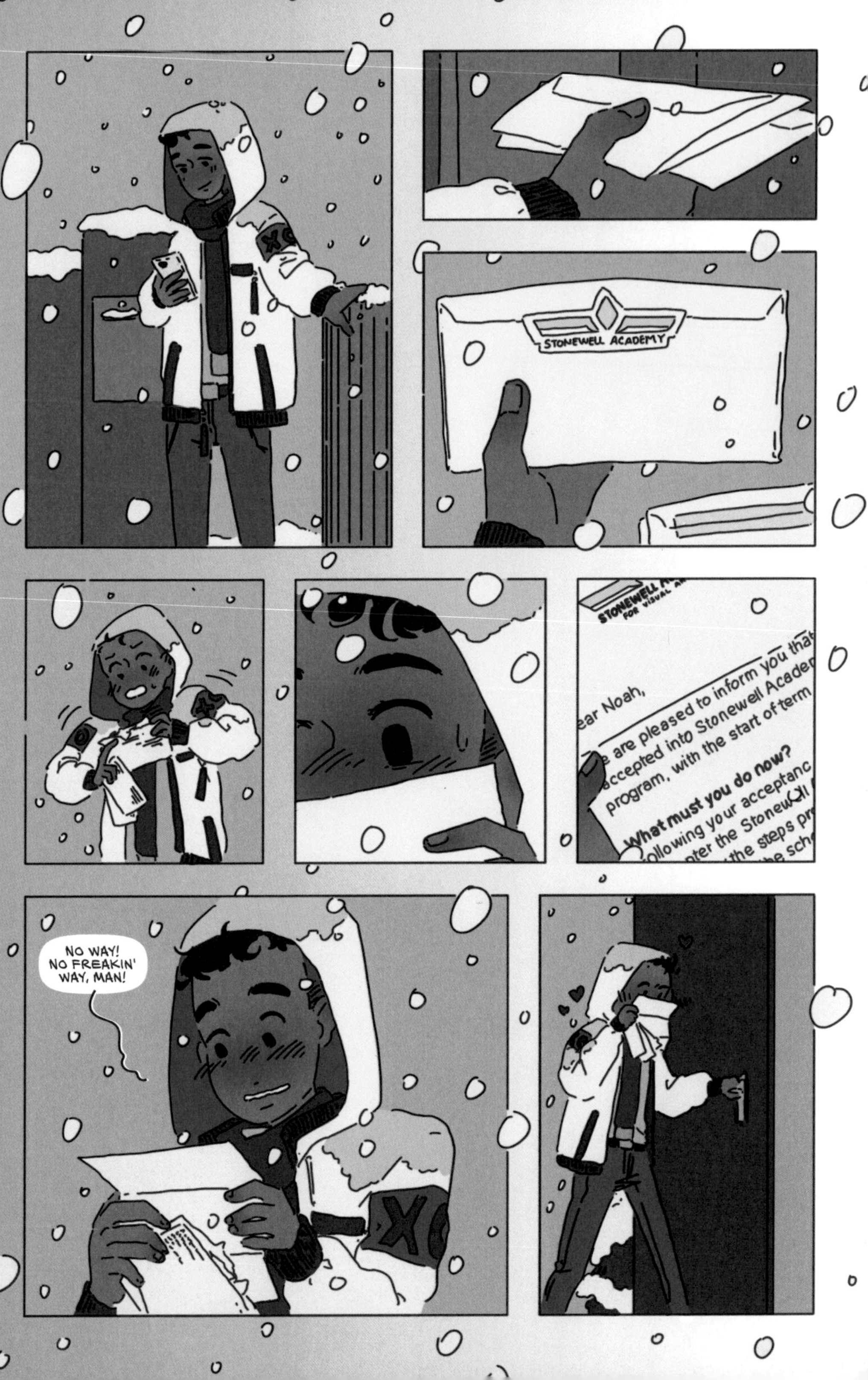
STONEWELL ACADEMY
ear Noah,
e are pleased to inform you tha
accepted into Stonewell Acade
program, with the start of term
What must you do now?
NO WAY! NO FREAKIN' WAY, MAN!

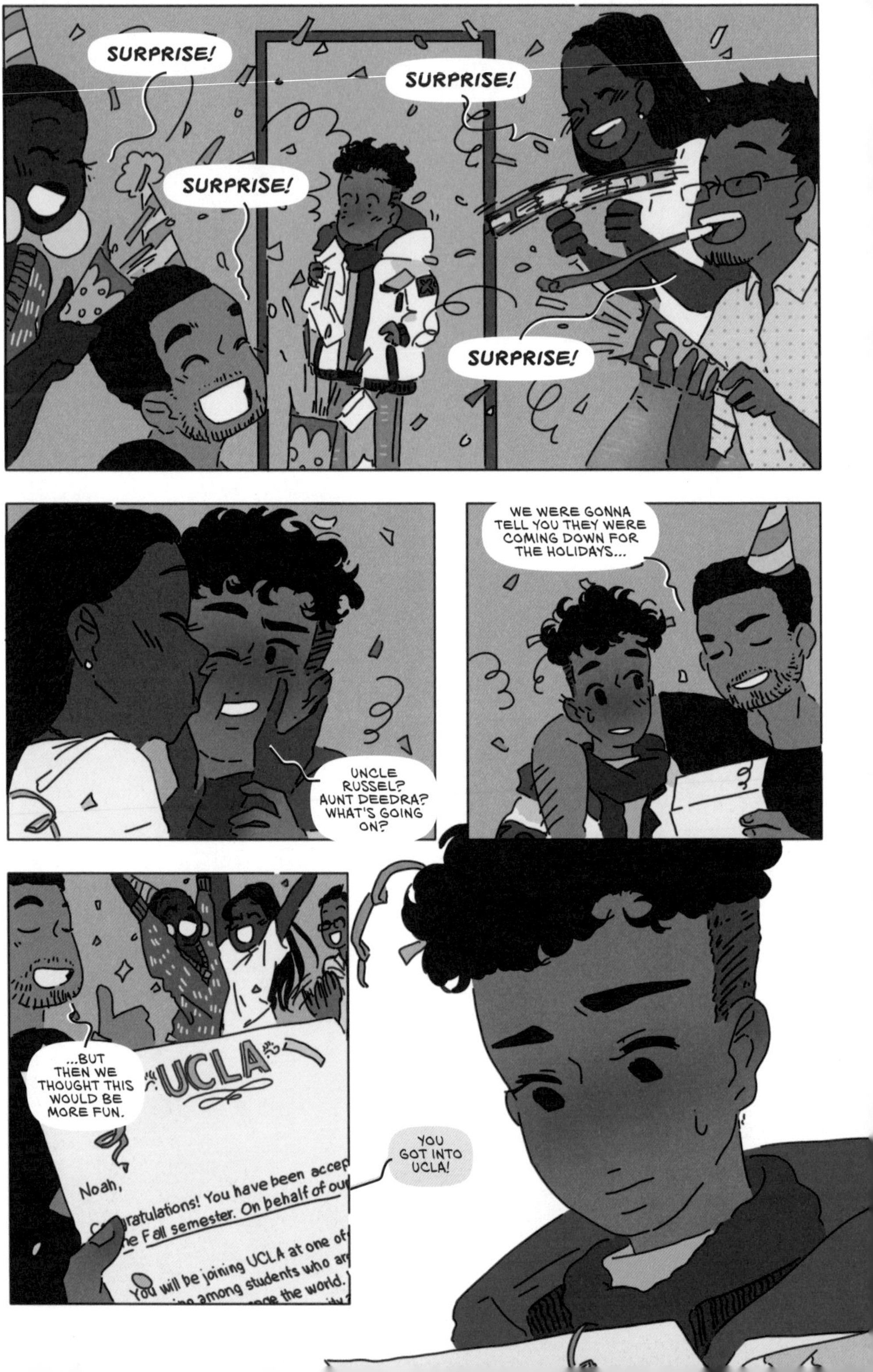
SURPRISE!
SURPRISE!
SURPRISE!
SURPRISE!
UNCLE RUSSEL? AUNT DEEDRA? WHAT'S GOING ON?
WE WERE GONNA TELL YOU THEY WERE COMING DOWN FOR THE HOLIDAYS...
...BUT THEN WE THOUGHT THIS WOULD BE MORE FUN.
UCLA
Noah,
ratulations! You have been accep
he Fall semester. On behalf of ou
You will be joining UCLA at one of
among students who ar
the world.
YOU GOT INTO UCLA!

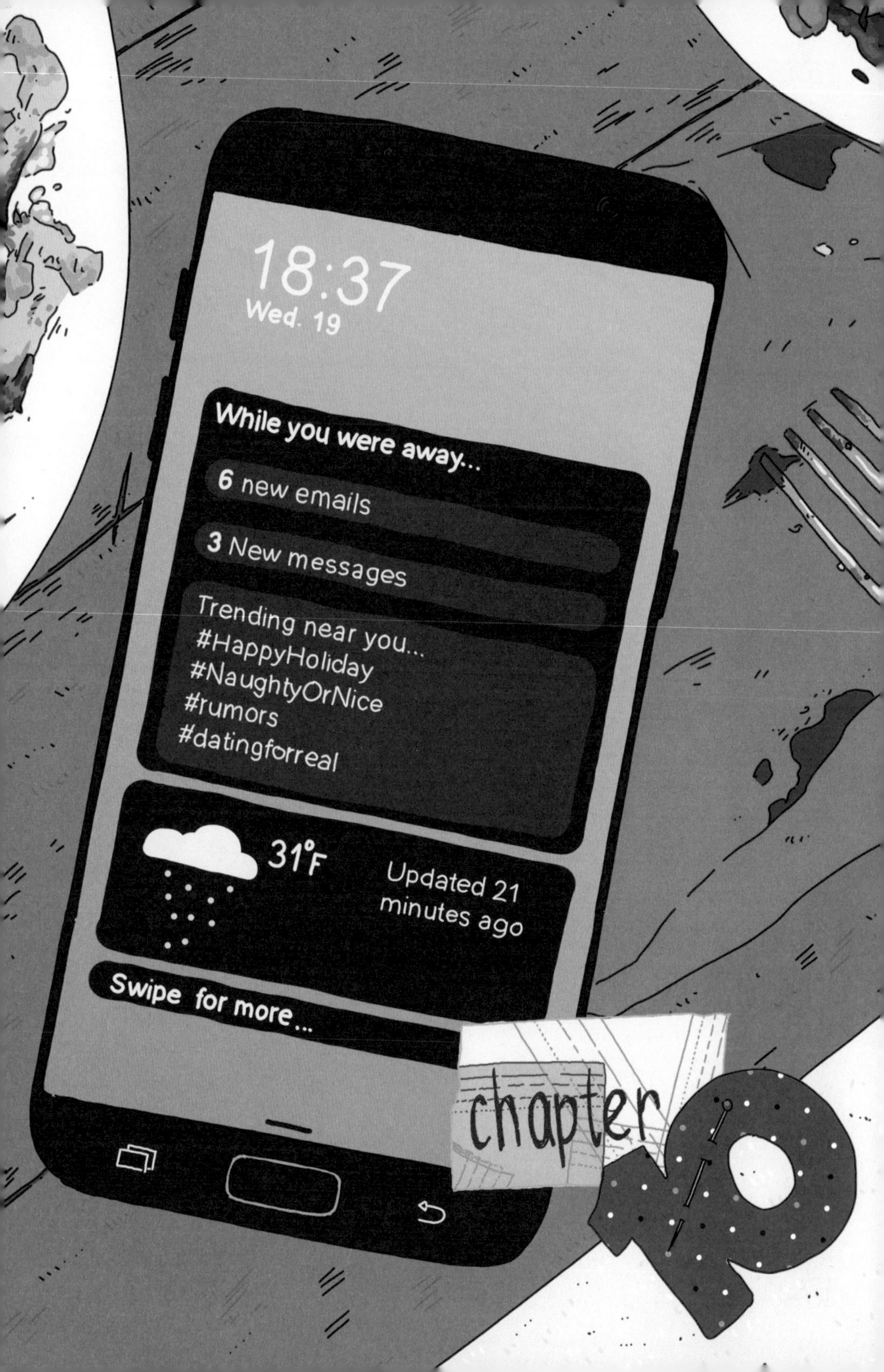
18:37
Wed. 19
While you were away...
6 new emails
3 New messages
Trending near you...
#HappyHoliday
#NaughtyOrNice
#rumors
#datingforreal
31°F
Updated 21 minutes ago
Swipe for more...
chapter 10

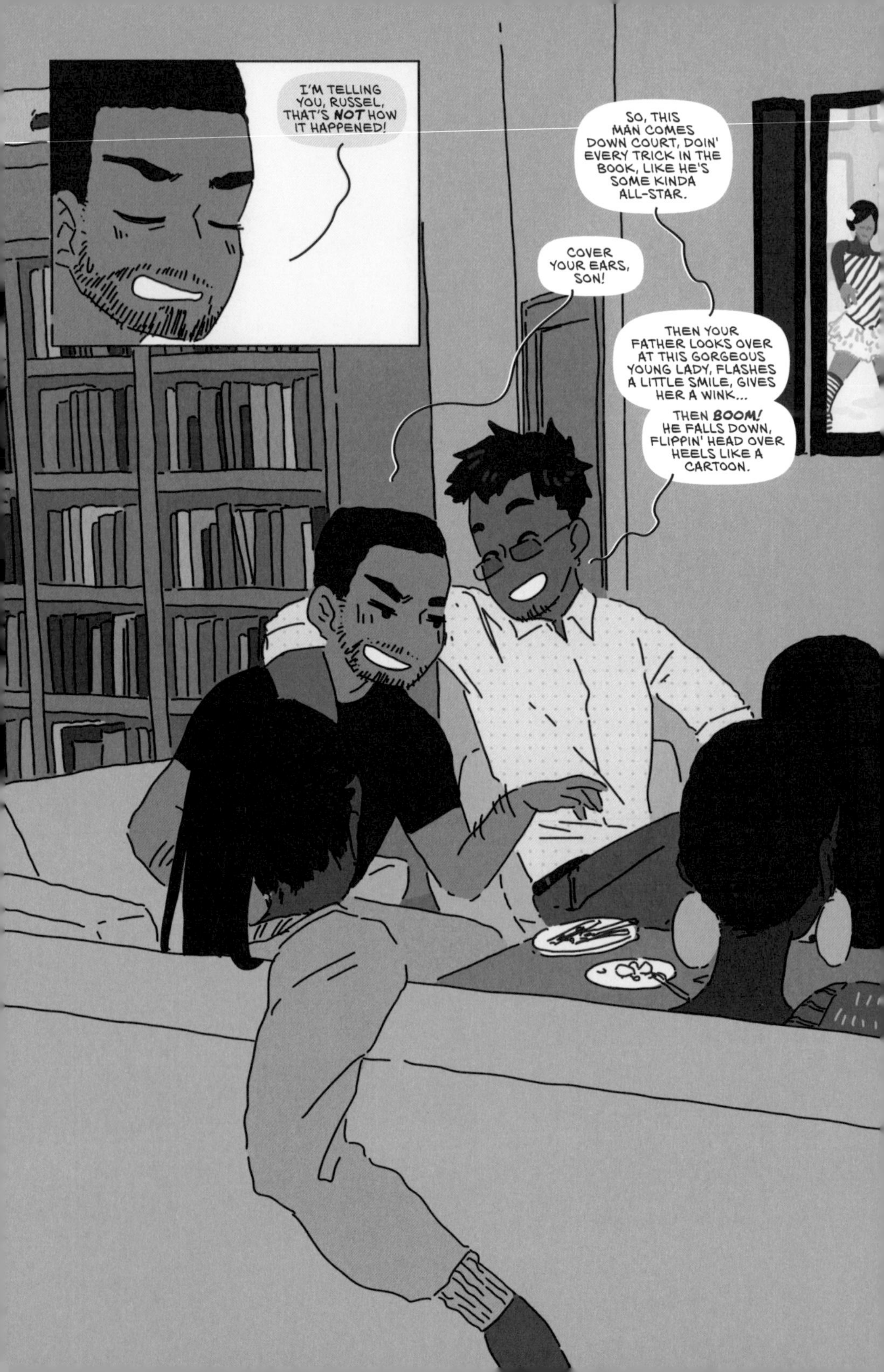
I'M TELLING YOU, RUSSEL, THAT'S **NOT** HOW IT HAPPENED!
SO, THIS MAN COMES DOWN COURT, DOIN' EVERY TRICK IN THE BOOK, LIKE HE'S SOME KINDA ALL-STAR.
COVER YOUR EARS, SON!
THEN YOUR FATHER LOOKS OVER AT THIS GORGEOUS YOUNG LADY, FLASHES A LITTLE SMILE, GIVES HER A WINK...
THEN **BOOM!** HE FALLS DOWN, FLIPPIN' HEAD OVER HEELS LIKE A CARTOON.

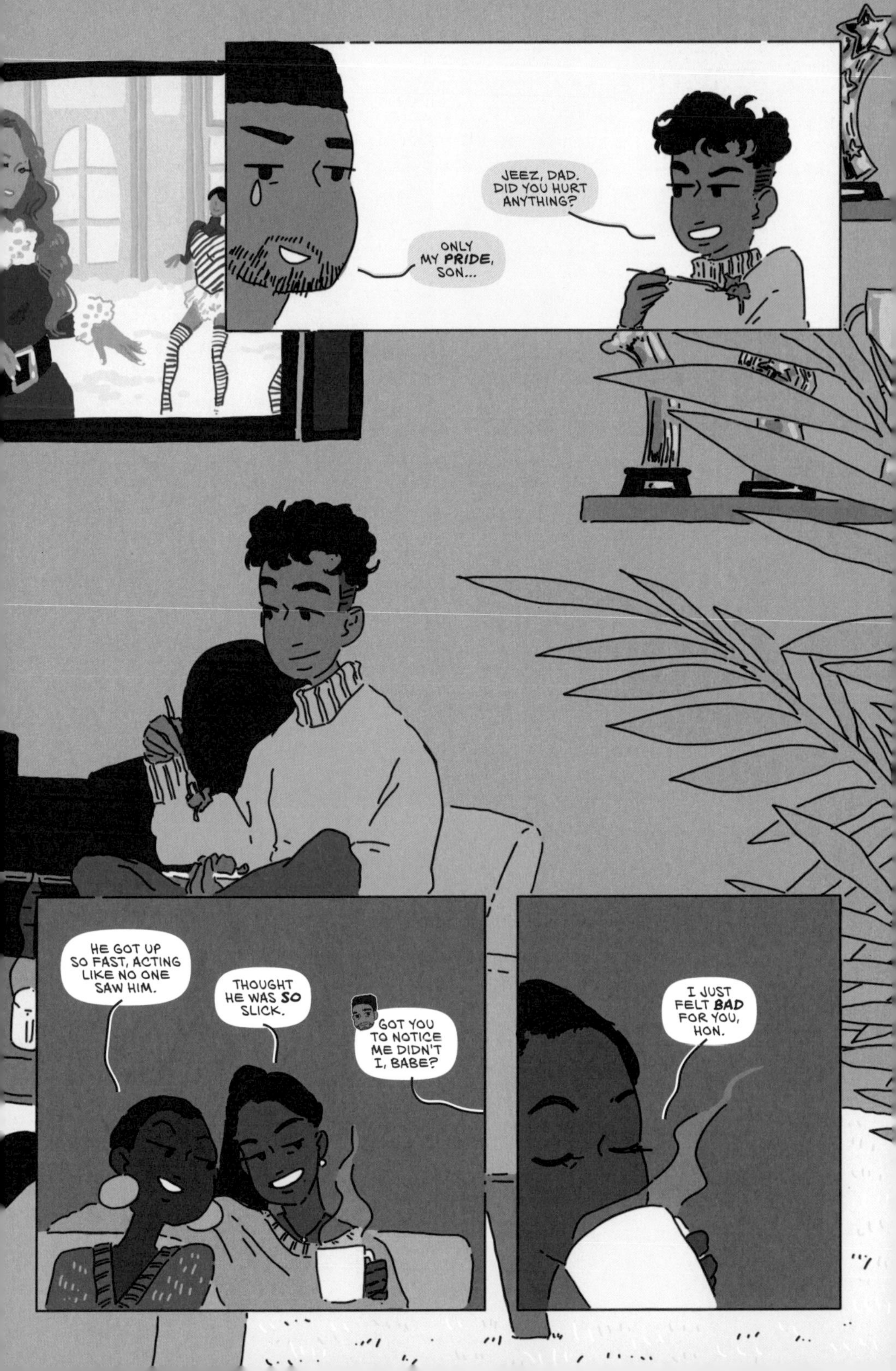
JEEZ, DAD. DID YOU HURT ANYTHING?
ONLY MY **PRIDE**, SON...
HE GOT UP SO FAST, ACTING LIKE NO ONE SAW HIM.
THOUGHT HE WAS **SO** SLICK.
GOT YOU TO NOTICE ME DIDN'T I, BABE?
I JUST FELT **BAD** FOR YOU, HON.

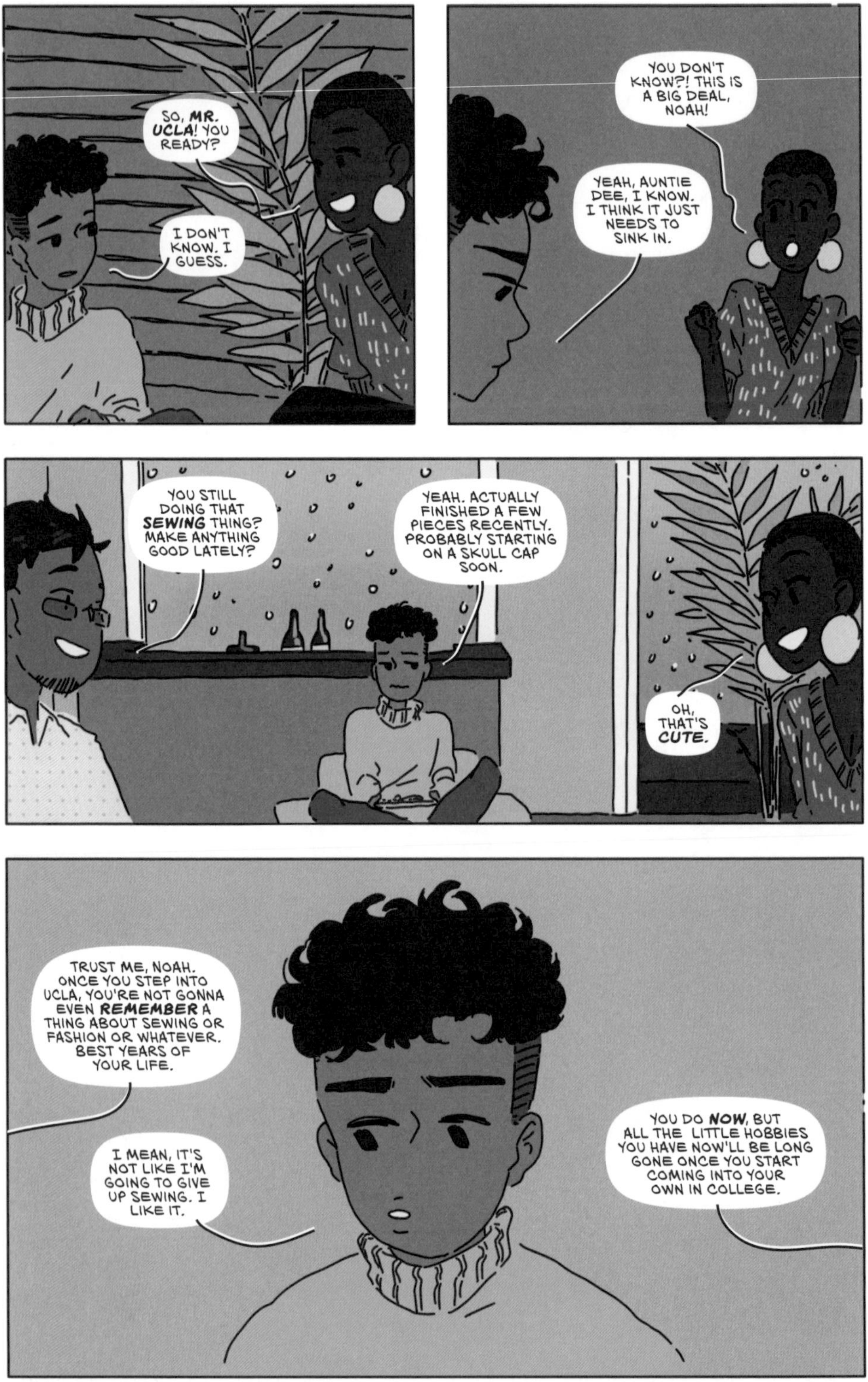
SO, **MR. UCLA**! YOU READY?
I DON'T KNOW. I GUESS.
YOU DON'T KNOW?! THIS IS A BIG DEAL, NOAH!
YEAH, AUNTIE DEE, I KNOW. I THINK IT JUST NEEDS TO SINK IN.
YOU STILL DOING THAT **SEWING** THING? MAKE ANYTHING GOOD LATELY?
YEAH. ACTUALLY FINISHED A FEW PIECES RECENTLY. PROBABLY STARTING ON A SKULL CAP SOON.
OH, THAT'S **CUTE.**
TRUST ME, NOAH. ONCE YOU STEP INTO UCLA, YOU'RE NOT GONNA EVEN **REMEMBER** A THING ABOUT SEWING OR FASHION OR WHATEVER. BEST YEARS OF YOUR LIFE.
I MEAN, IT'S NOT LIKE I'M GOING TO GIVE UP SEWING. I LIKE IT.
YOU DO **NOW**, BUT ALL THE LITTLE HOBBIES YOU HAVE NOW'LL BE LONG GONE ONCE YOU START COMING INTO YOUR OWN IN COLLEGE.

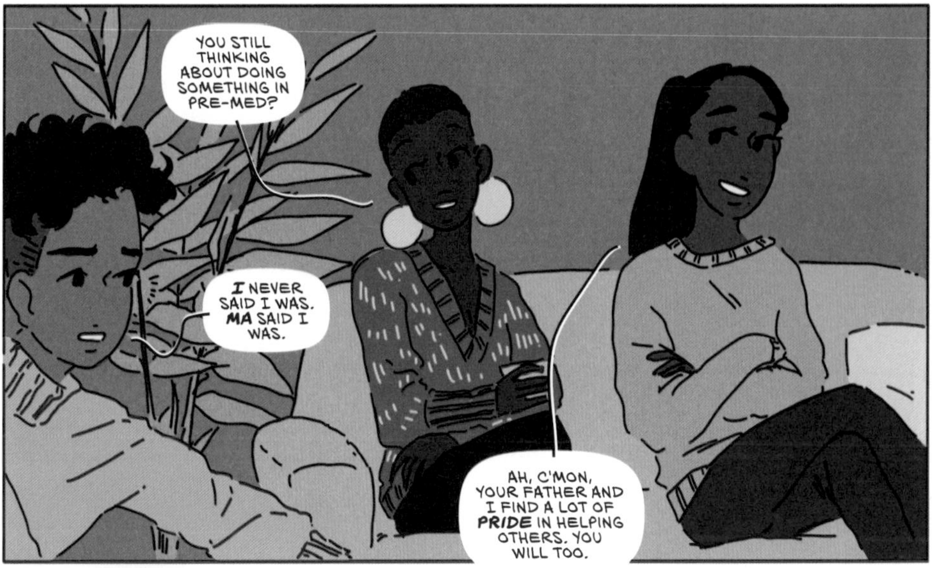
YOU STILL THINKING ABOUT DOING SOMETHING IN PRE-MED?
I NEVER SAID I WAS. MA SAID I WAS.
AH, C'MON, YOUR FATHER AND I FIND A LOT OF PRIDE IN HELPING OTHERS. YOU WILL TOO.

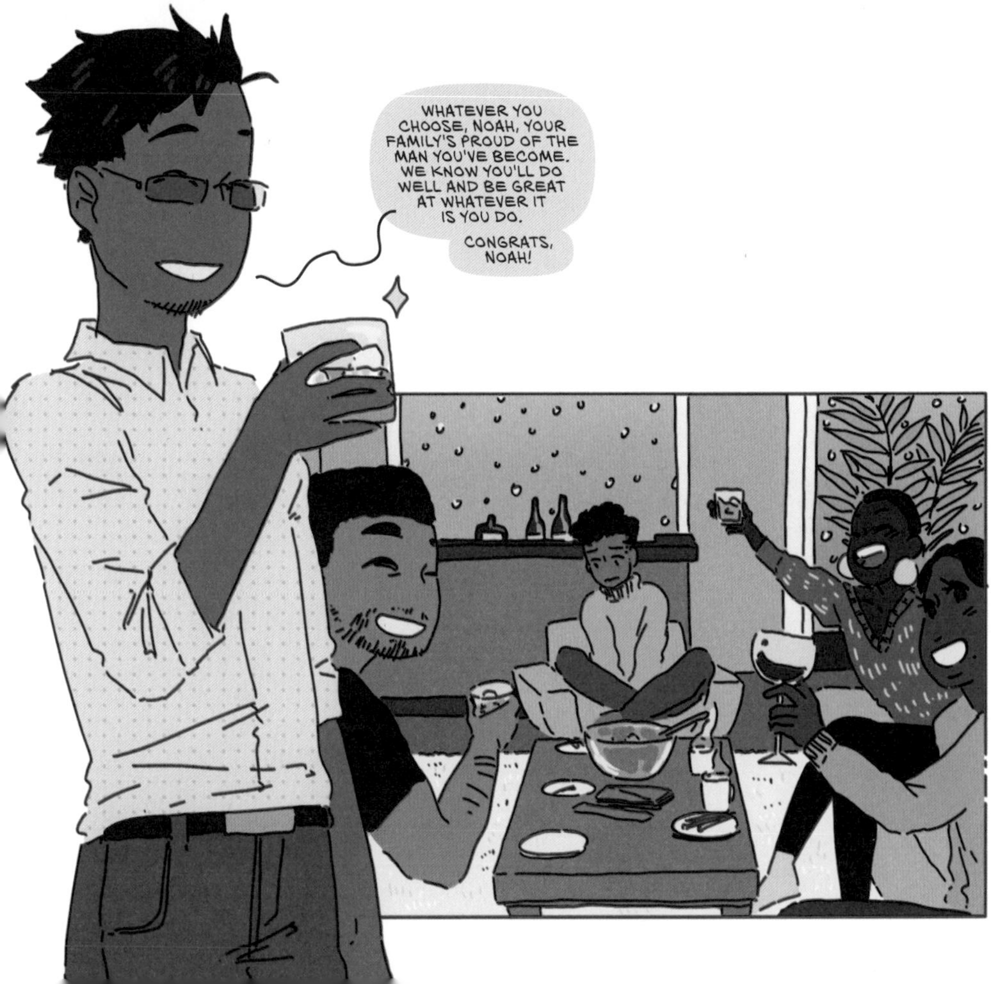
WHATEVER YOU CHOOSE, NOAH, YOUR FAMILY'S PROUD OF THE MAN YOU'VE BECOME. WE KNOW YOU'LL DO WELL AND BE GREAT AT WHATEVER IT IS YOU DO.
CONGRATS, NOAH!

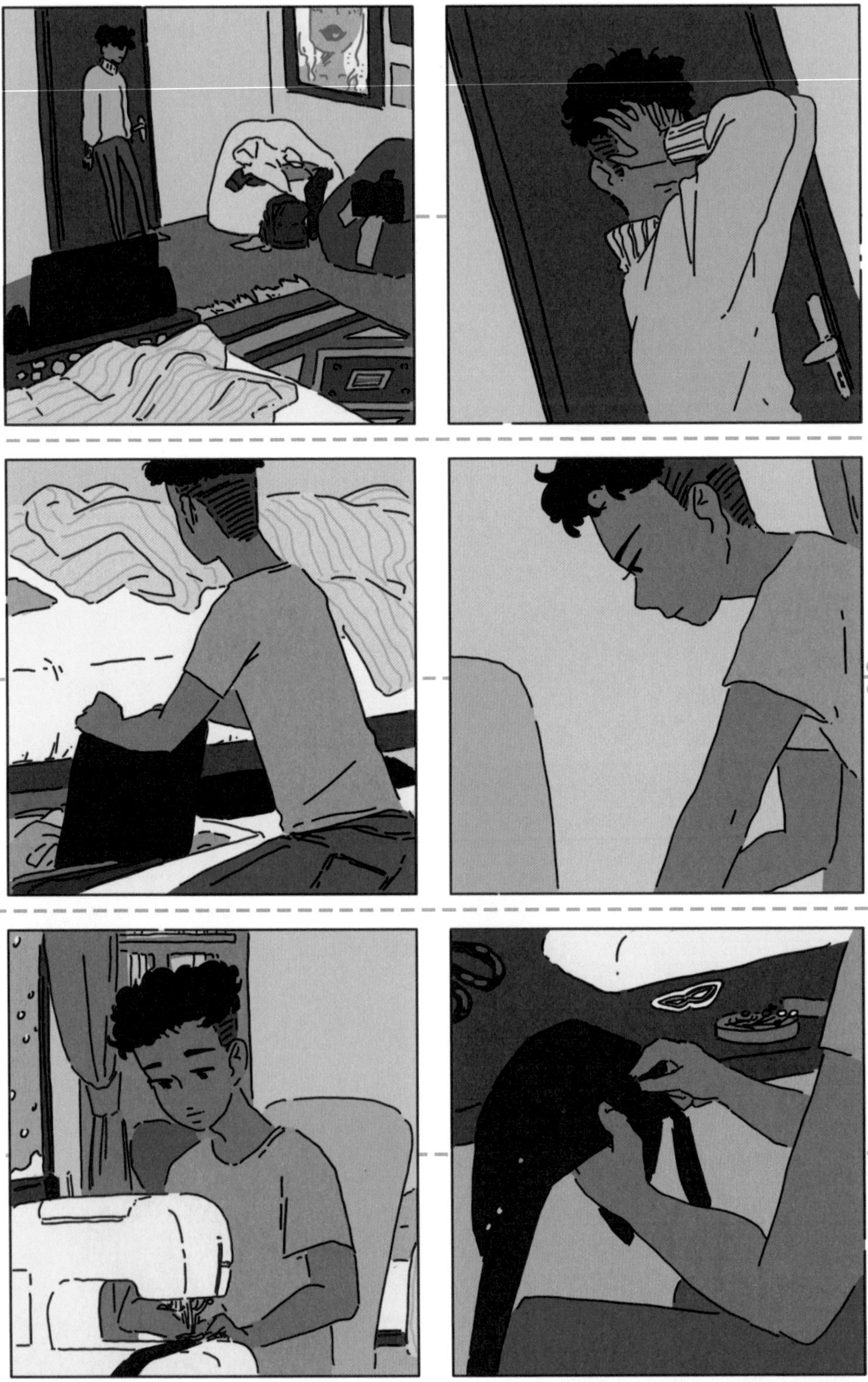

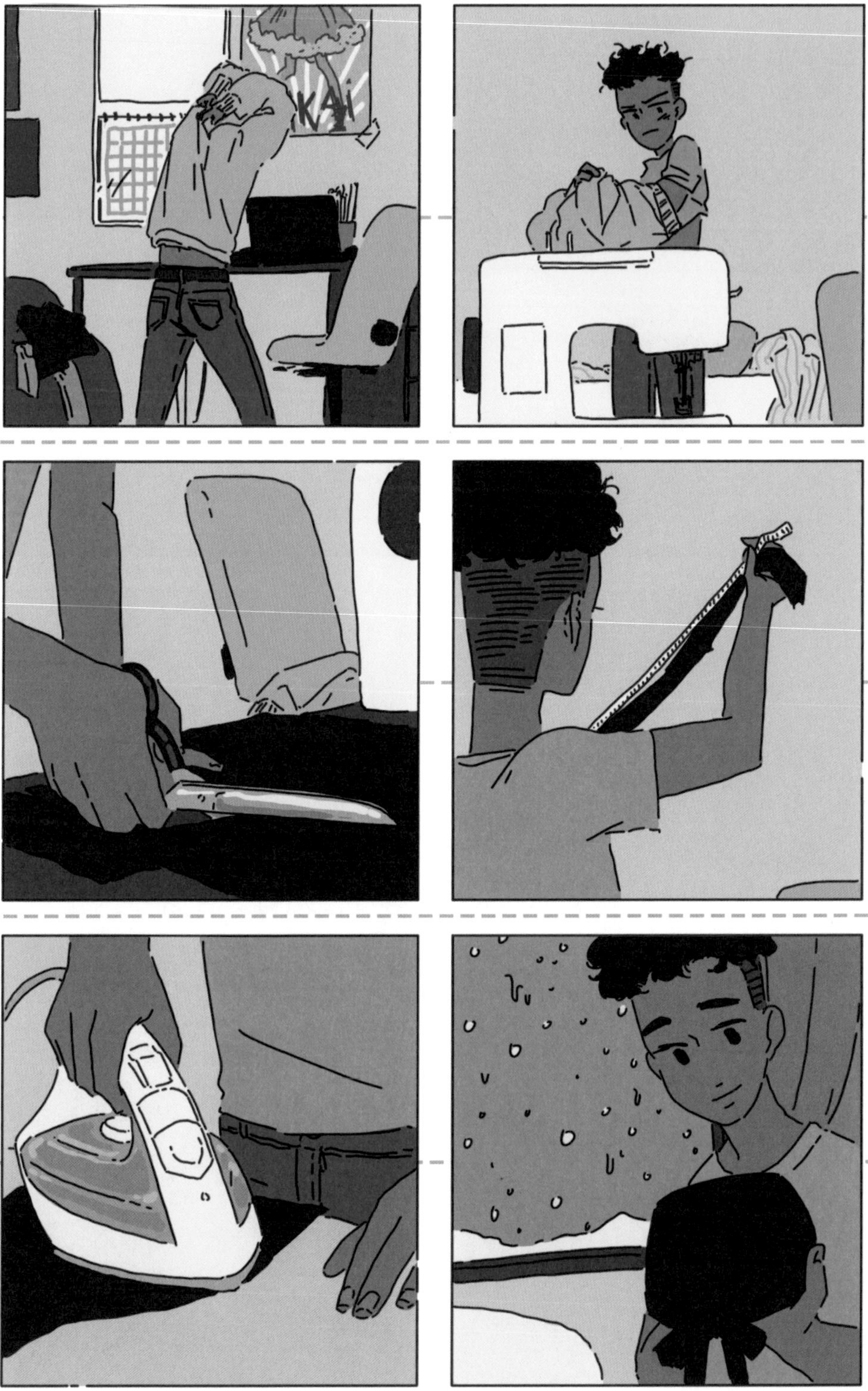
KAi

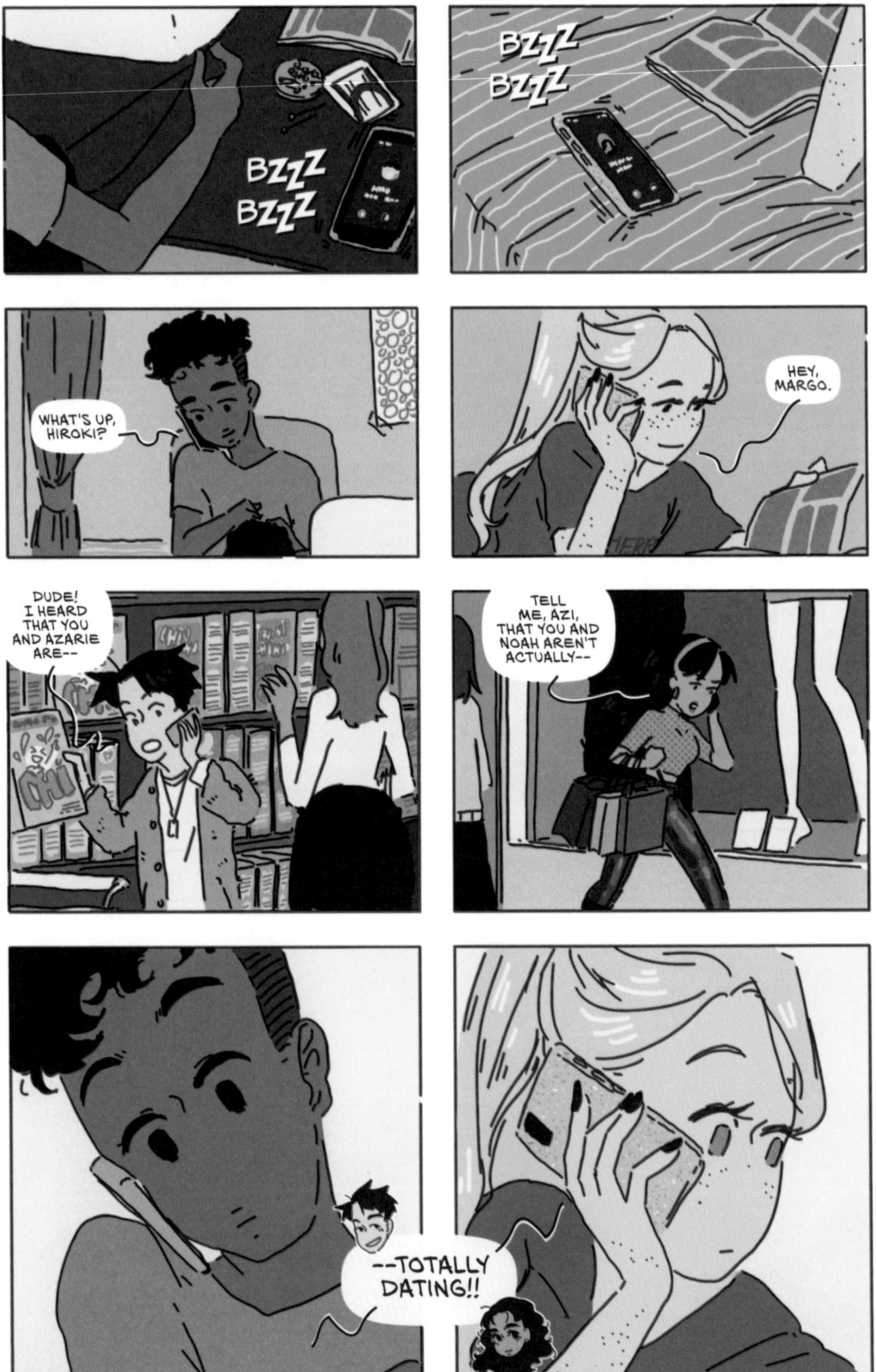
BZZZ
BZZZ
BZZZ
BZZZ
WHAT'S UP, HIROKI?
HEY, MARGO.
DUDE! I HEARD THAT YOU AND AZARIE ARE--
TELL ME, AZI, THAT YOU AND NOAH AREN'T ACTUALLY--
--TOTALLY DATING!!

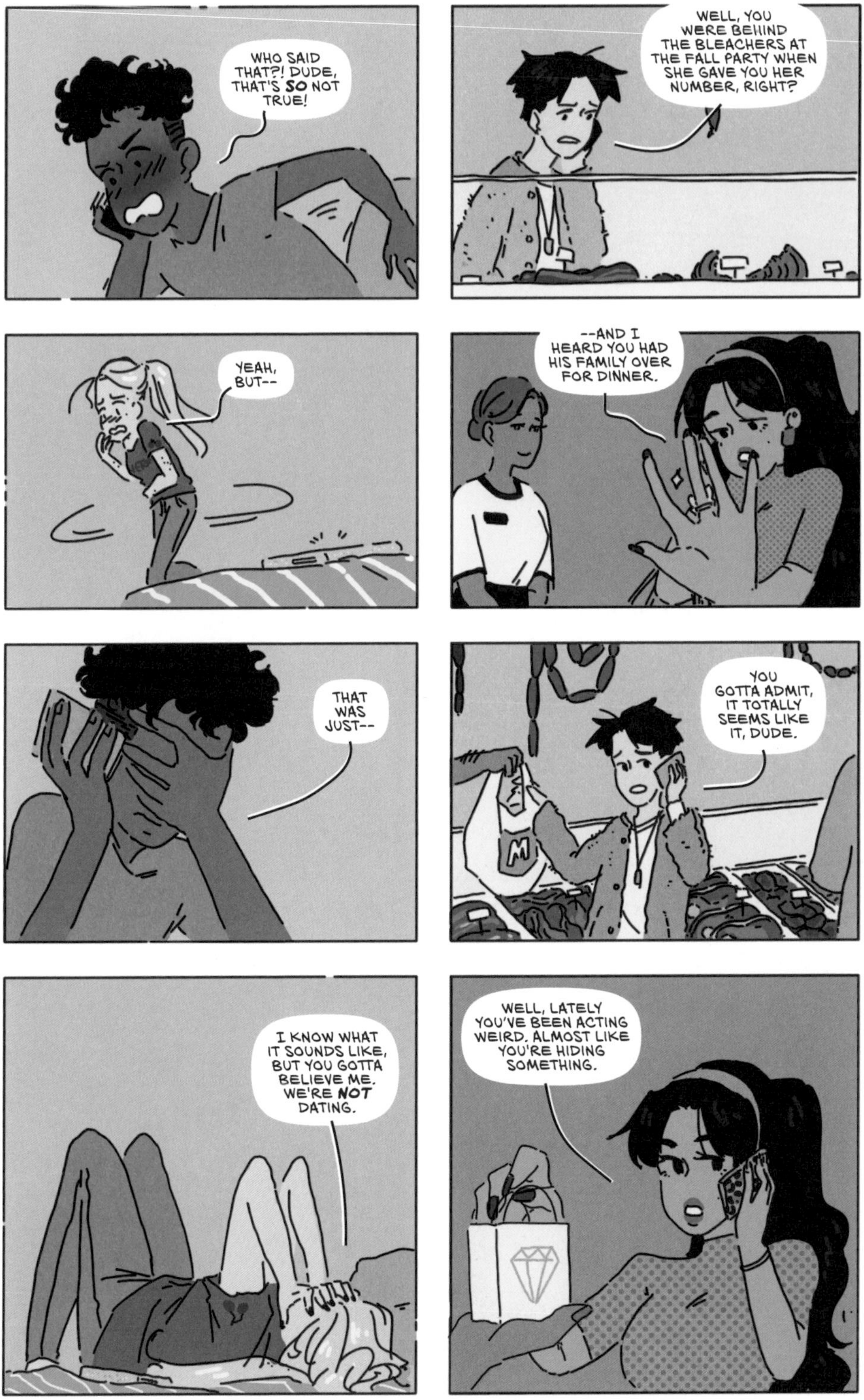
WHO SAID THAT?! DUDE, THAT'S **SO** NOT TRUE!
WELL, YOU WERE BEHIND THE BLEACHERS AT THE FALL PARTY WHEN SHE GAVE YOU HER NUMBER, RIGHT?
YEAH, BUT--
--AND I HEARD YOU HAD HIS FAMILY OVER FOR DINNER.
THAT WAS JUST--
YOU GOTTA ADMIT, IT TOTALLY SEEMS LIKE IT, DUDE.
I KNOW WHAT IT SOUNDS LIKE, BUT YOU GOTTA BELIEVE ME. WE'RE **NOT** DATING.
WELL, LATELY YOU'VE BEEN ACTING WEIRD. ALMOST LIKE YOU'RE HIDING SOMETHING.

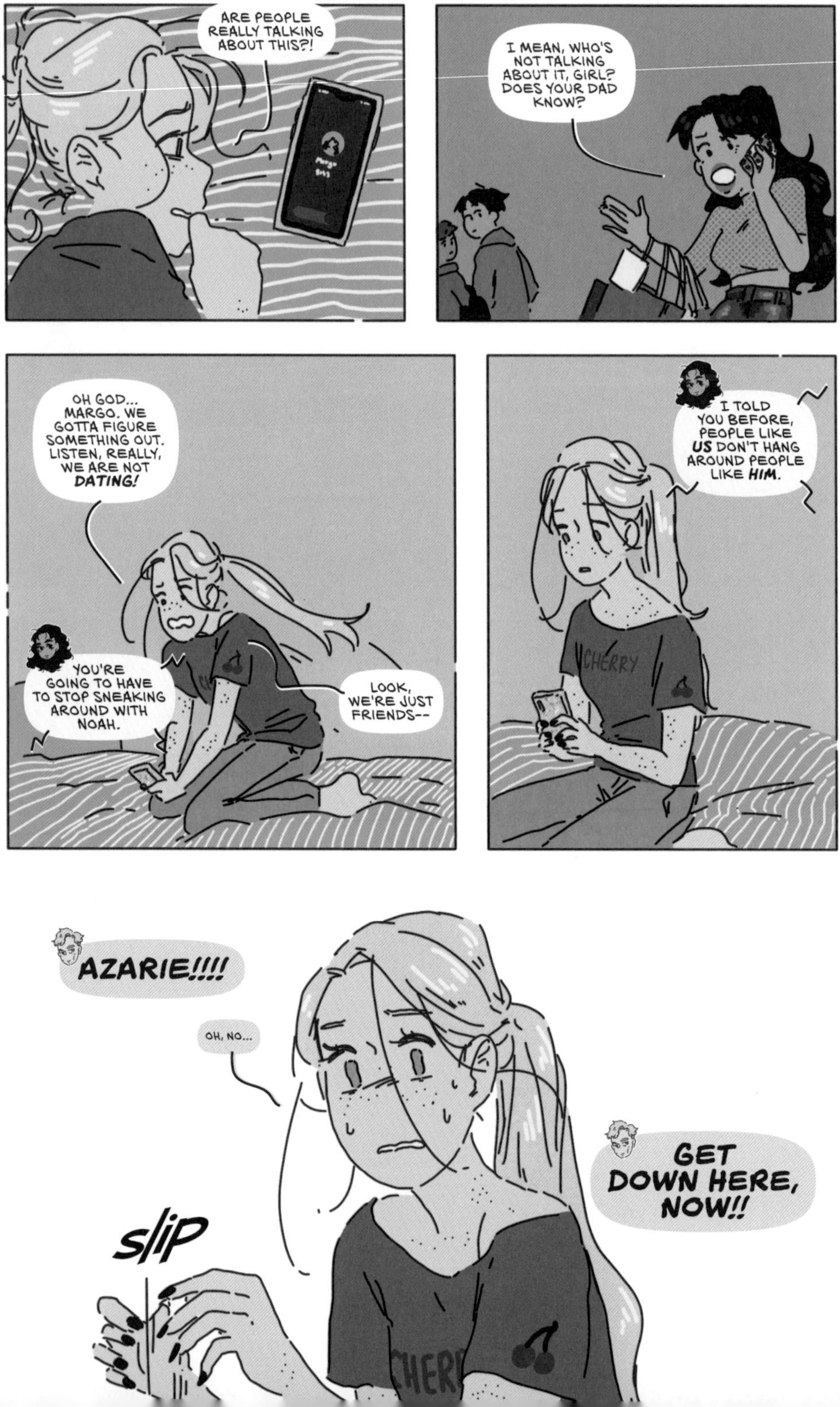
ARE PEOPLE REALLY TALKING ABOUT THIS?!
I MEAN, WHO'S NOT TALKING ABOUT IT, GIRL? DOES YOUR DAD KNOW?
OH GOD... MARGO. WE GOTTA FIGURE SOMETHING OUT. LISTEN, REALLY, WE ARE NOT DATING!
YOU'RE GOING TO HAVE TO STOP SNEAKING AROUND WITH NOAH.
LOOK, WE'RE JUST FRIENDS--
CHERRY
I TOLD YOU BEFORE, PEOPLE LIKE US DON'T HANG AROUND PEOPLE LIKE HIM.
CHERRY
AZARIE!!!!
OH, NO...
GET DOWN HERE, NOW!!
SLIP

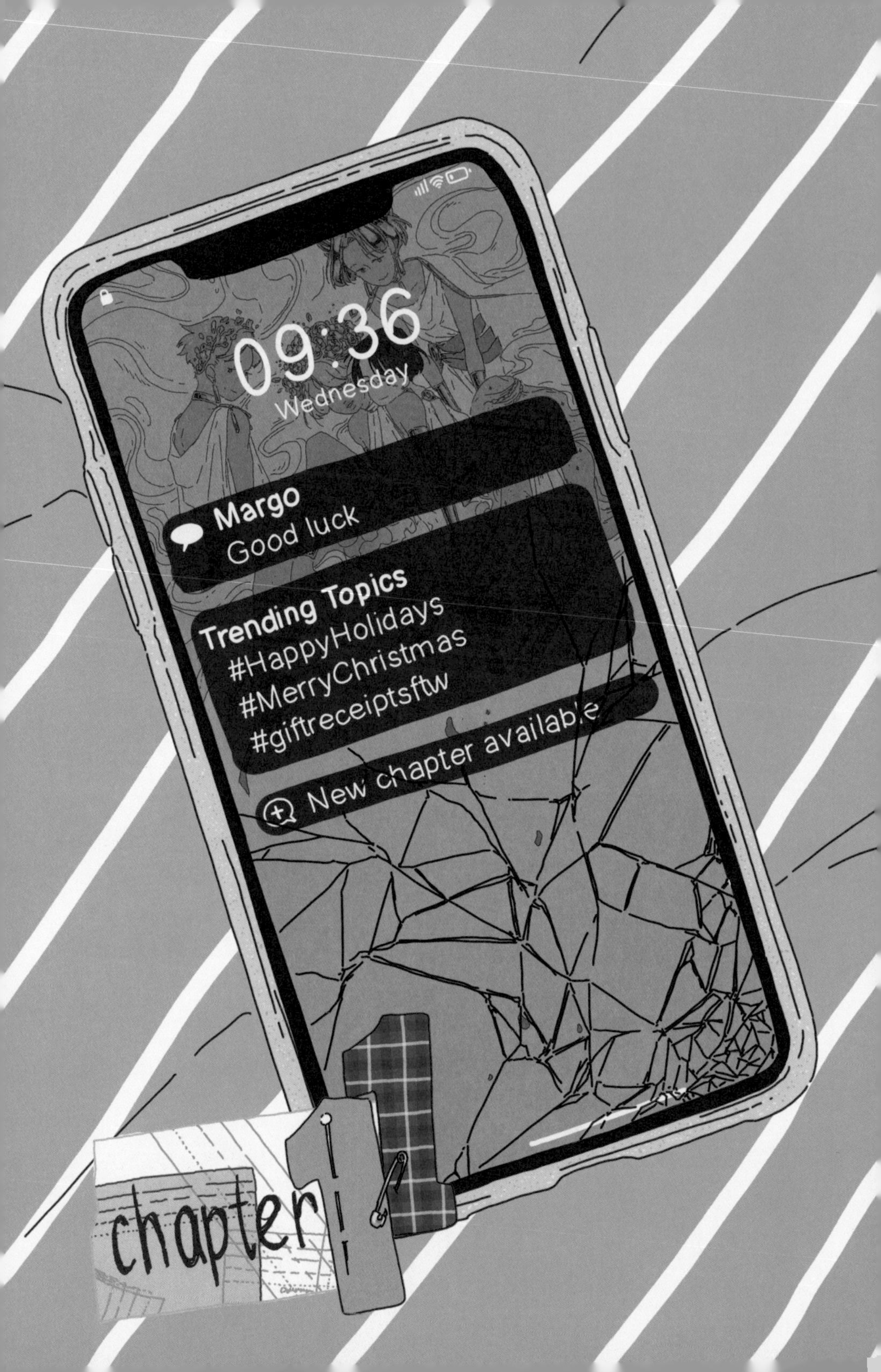
09:36
Wednesday
Margo
Good luck
Trending Topics
#HappyHolidays
#MerryChristmas
#giftreceiptsftw
New chapter available
chapter 1

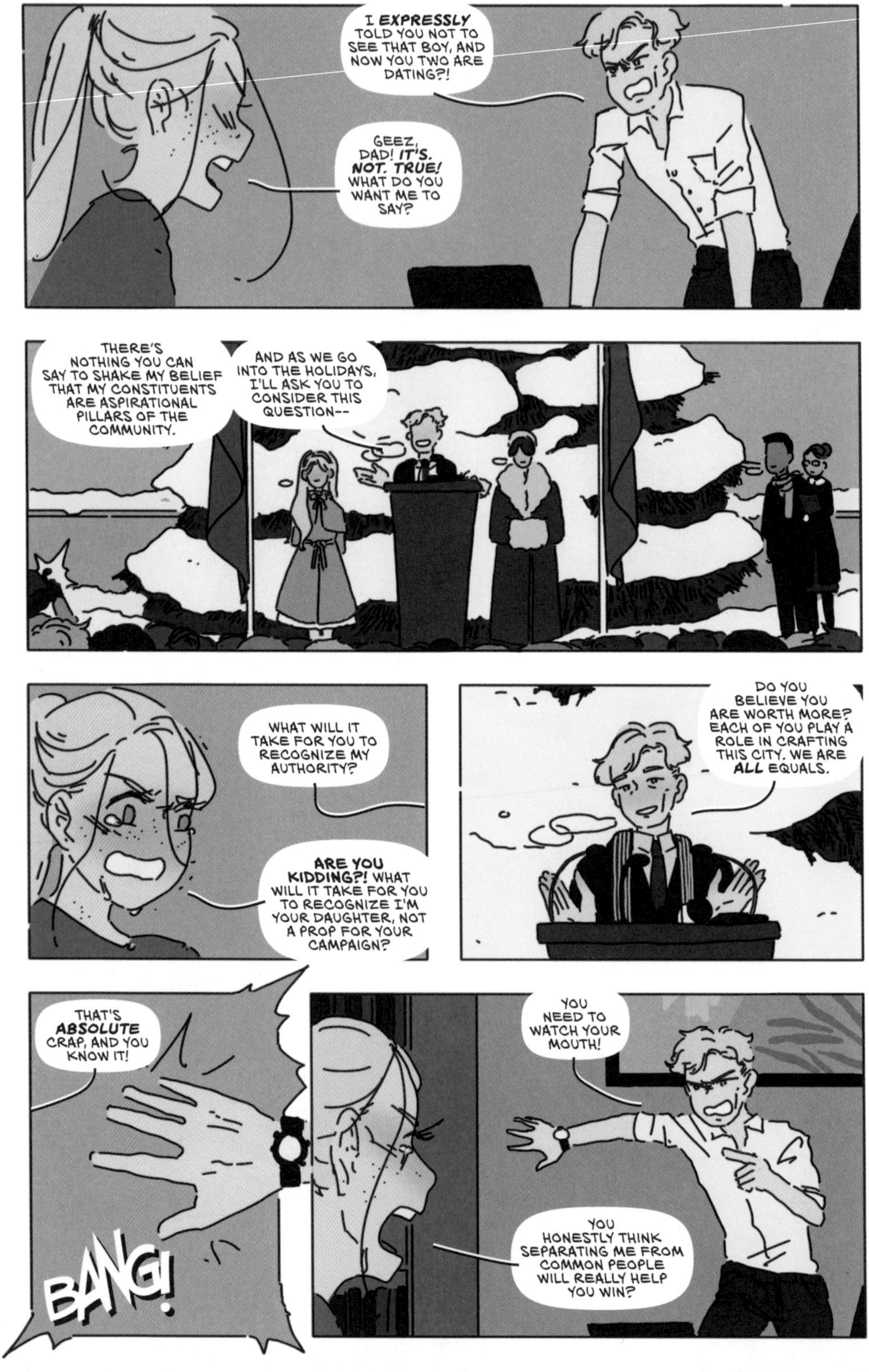
I EXPRESSLY TOLD YOU NOT TO SEE THAT BOY, AND NOW YOU TWO ARE DATING?!
GEEZ, DAD! IT'S. NOT. TRUE! WHAT DO YOU WANT ME TO SAY?
THERE'S NOTHING YOU CAN SAY TO SHAKE MY BELIEF THAT MY CONSTITUENTS ARE ASPIRATIONAL PILLARS OF THE COMMUNITY.
AND AS WE GO INTO THE HOLIDAYS, I'LL ASK YOU TO CONSIDER THIS QUESTION--
WHAT WILL IT TAKE FOR YOU TO RECOGNIZE MY AUTHORITY?
ARE YOU KIDDING?! WHAT WILL IT TAKE FOR YOU TO RECOGNIZE I'M YOUR DAUGHTER, NOT A PROP FOR YOUR CAMPAIGN?
DO YOU BELIEVE YOU ARE WORTH MORE? EACH OF YOU PLAY A ROLE IN CRAFTING THIS CITY. WE ARE ALL EQUALS.
THAT'S ABSOLUTE CRAP, AND YOU KNOW IT!
BANG!
YOU NEED TO WATCH YOUR MOUTH!
YOU HONESTLY THINK SEPARATING ME FROM COMMON PEOPLE WILL REALLY HELP YOU WIN?

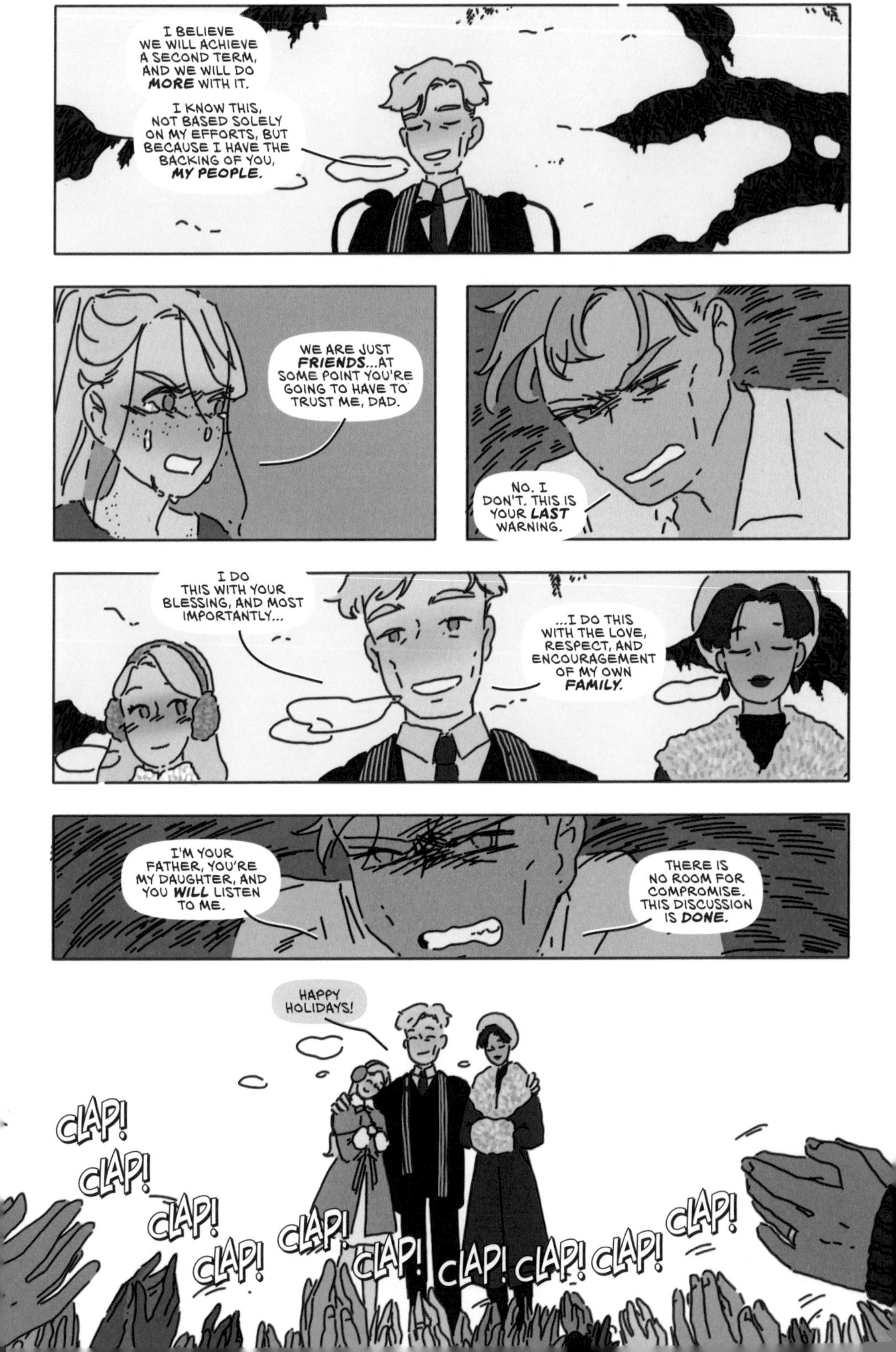
I BELIEVE WE WILL ACHIEVE A SECOND TERM, AND WE WILL DO **MORE** WITH IT.
I KNOW THIS, NOT BASED SOLELY ON MY EFFORTS, BUT BECAUSE I HAVE THE BACKING OF YOU, **MY PEOPLE.**
WE ARE JUST **FRIENDS...**AT SOME POINT YOU'RE GOING TO HAVE TO TRUST ME, DAD.
NO. I DON'T. THIS IS YOUR **LAST** WARNING.
I DO THIS WITH YOUR BLESSING, AND MOST IMPORTANTLY...
...I DO THIS WITH THE LOVE, RESPECT, AND ENCOURAGEMENT OF MY OWN **FAMILY.**
I'M YOUR FATHER, YOU'RE MY DAUGHTER, AND YOU **WILL** LISTEN TO ME.
THERE IS NO ROOM FOR COMPROMISE. THIS DISCUSSION IS **DONE.**
HAPPY HOLIDAYS!
CLAP! CLAP! CLAP! CLAP! CLAP! CLAP! CLAP! CLAP! CLAP! CLAP!

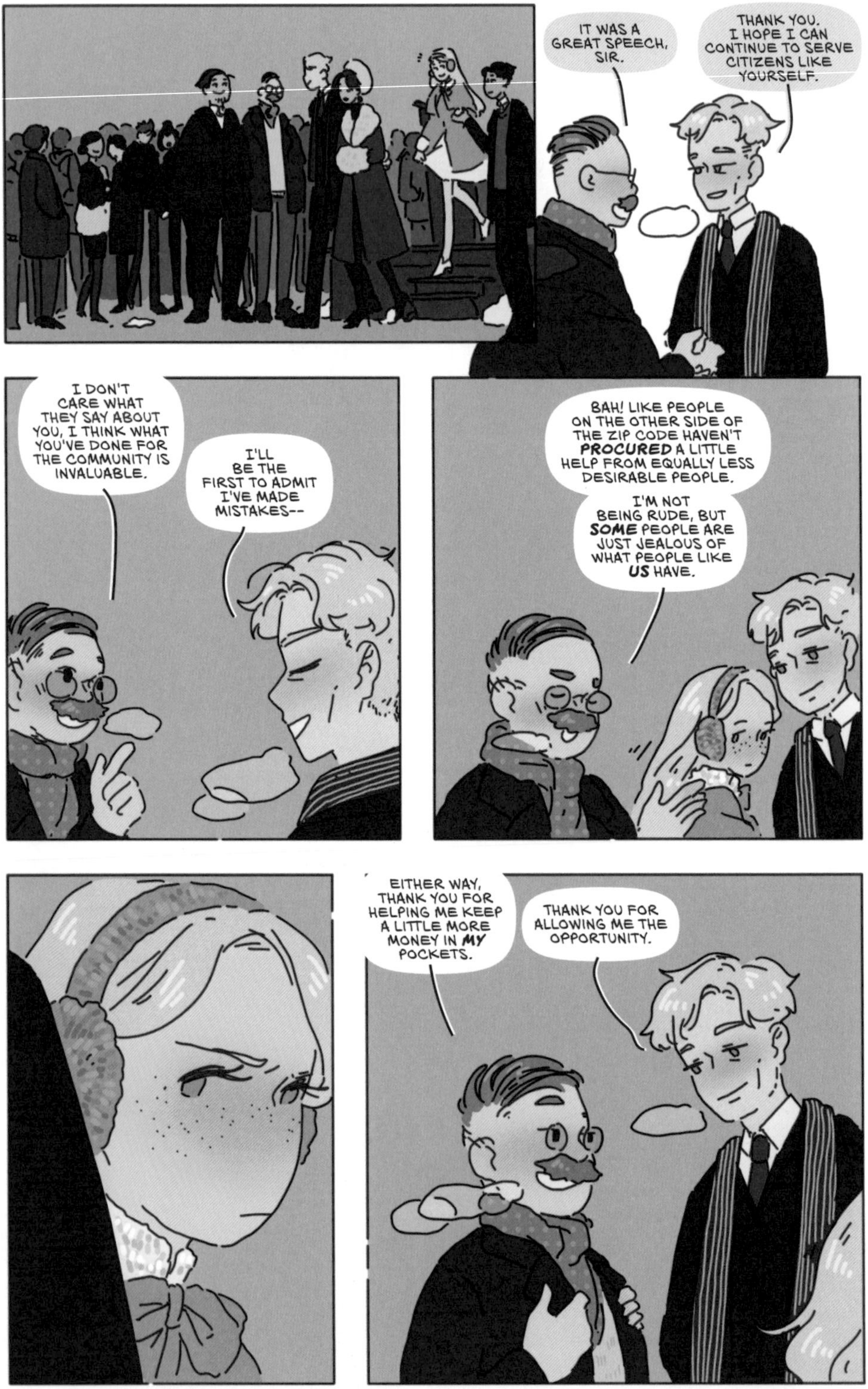
IT WAS A GREAT SPEECH, SIR.
THANK YOU. I HOPE I CAN CONTINUE TO SERVE CITIZENS LIKE YOURSELF.
I DON'T CARE WHAT THEY SAY ABOUT YOU, I THINK WHAT YOU'VE DONE FOR THE COMMUNITY IS INVALUABLE.
I'LL BE THE FIRST TO ADMIT I'VE MADE MISTAKES--
BAH! LIKE PEOPLE ON THE OTHER SIDE OF THE ZIP CODE HAVEN'T **PROCURED** A LITTLE HELP FROM EQUALLY LESS DESIRABLE PEOPLE.
I'M NOT BEING RUDE, BUT **SOME** PEOPLE ARE JUST JEALOUS OF WHAT PEOPLE LIKE **US** HAVE.
EITHER WAY, THANK YOU FOR HELPING ME KEEP A LITTLE MORE MONEY IN **MY** POCKETS.
THANK YOU FOR ALLOWING ME THE OPPORTUNITY.

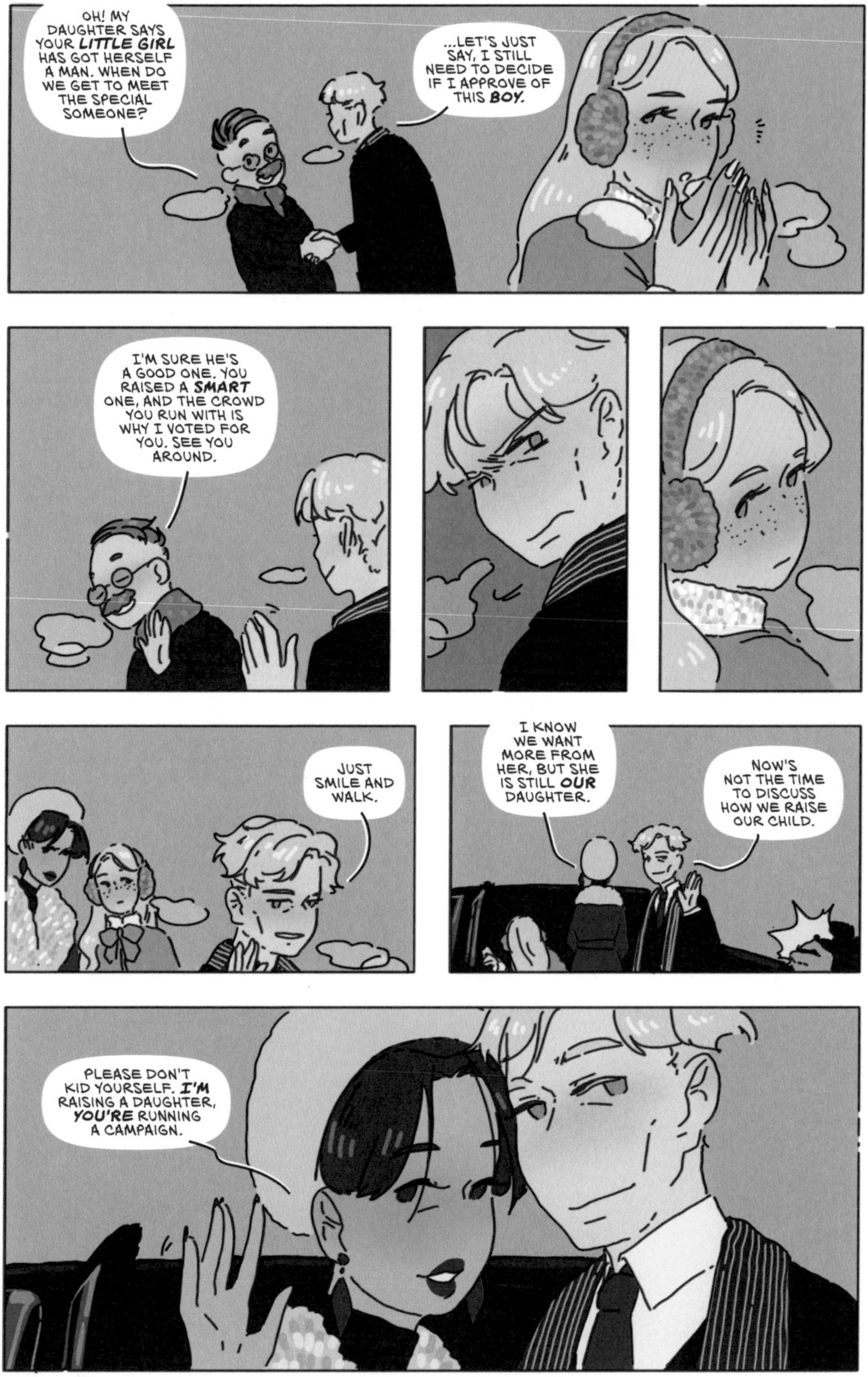
OH! MY DAUGHTER SAYS YOUR LITTLE GIRL HAS GOT HERSELF A MAN. WHEN DO WE GET TO MEET THE SPECIAL SOMEONE?
...LET'S JUST SAY, I STILL NEED TO DECIDE IF I APPROVE OF THIS BOY.
I'M SURE HE'S A GOOD ONE. YOU RAISED A SMART ONE, AND THE CROWD YOU RUN WITH IS WHY I VOTED FOR YOU. SEE YOU AROUND.
JUST SMILE AND WALK.
I KNOW WE WANT MORE FROM HER, BUT SHE IS STILL OUR DAUGHTER.
NOW'S NOT THE TIME TO DISCUSS HOW WE RAISE OUR CHILD.
PLEASE DON'T KID YOURSELF. I'M RAISING A DAUGHTER, YOU'RE RUNNING A CAMPAIGN.

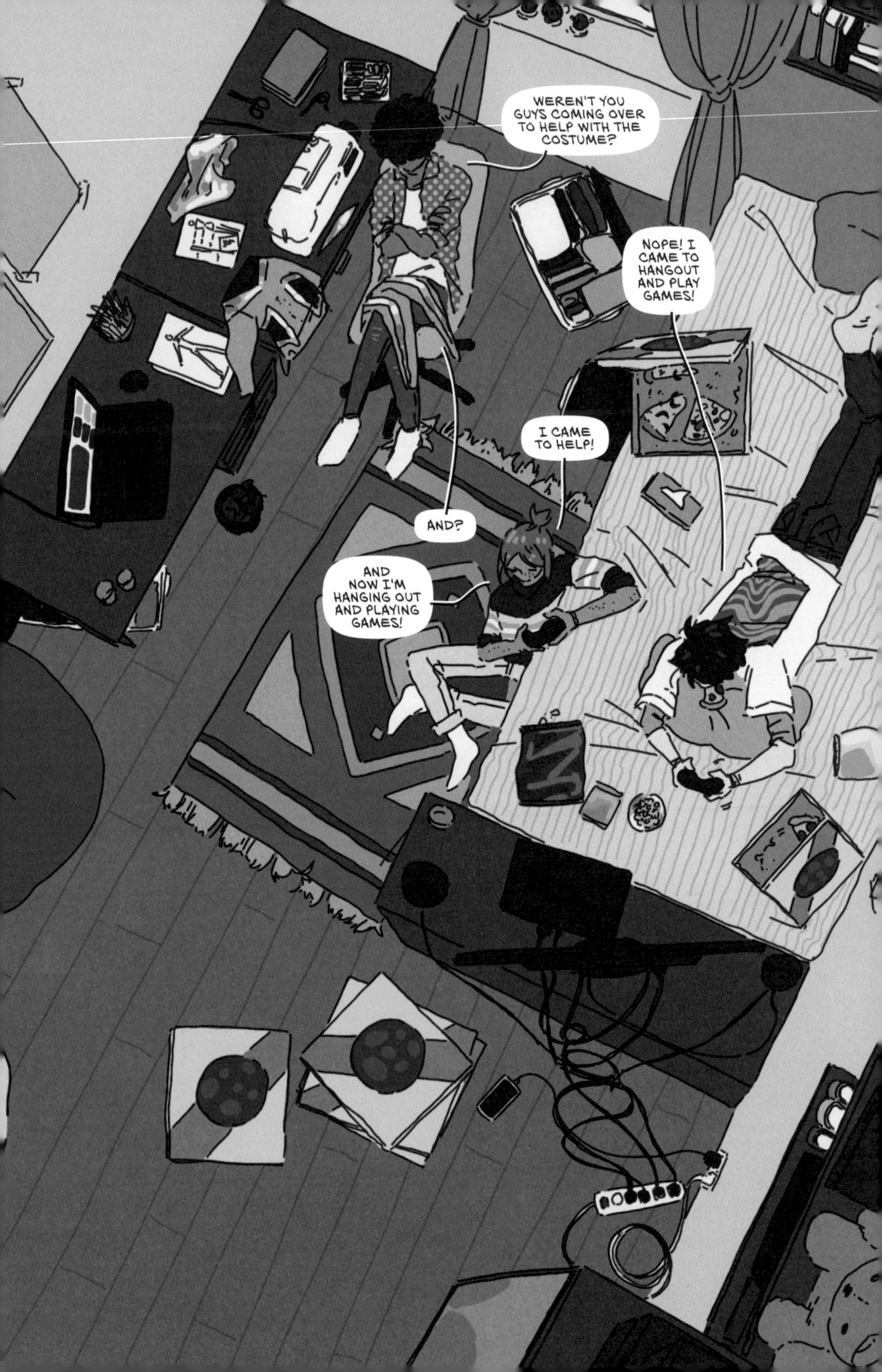
WEREN'T YOU GUYS COMING OVER TO HELP WITH THE COSTUME?
NOPE! I CAME TO HANGOUT AND PLAY GAMES!
I CAME TO HELP!
AND?
AND NOW I'M HANGING OUT AND PLAYING GAMES!

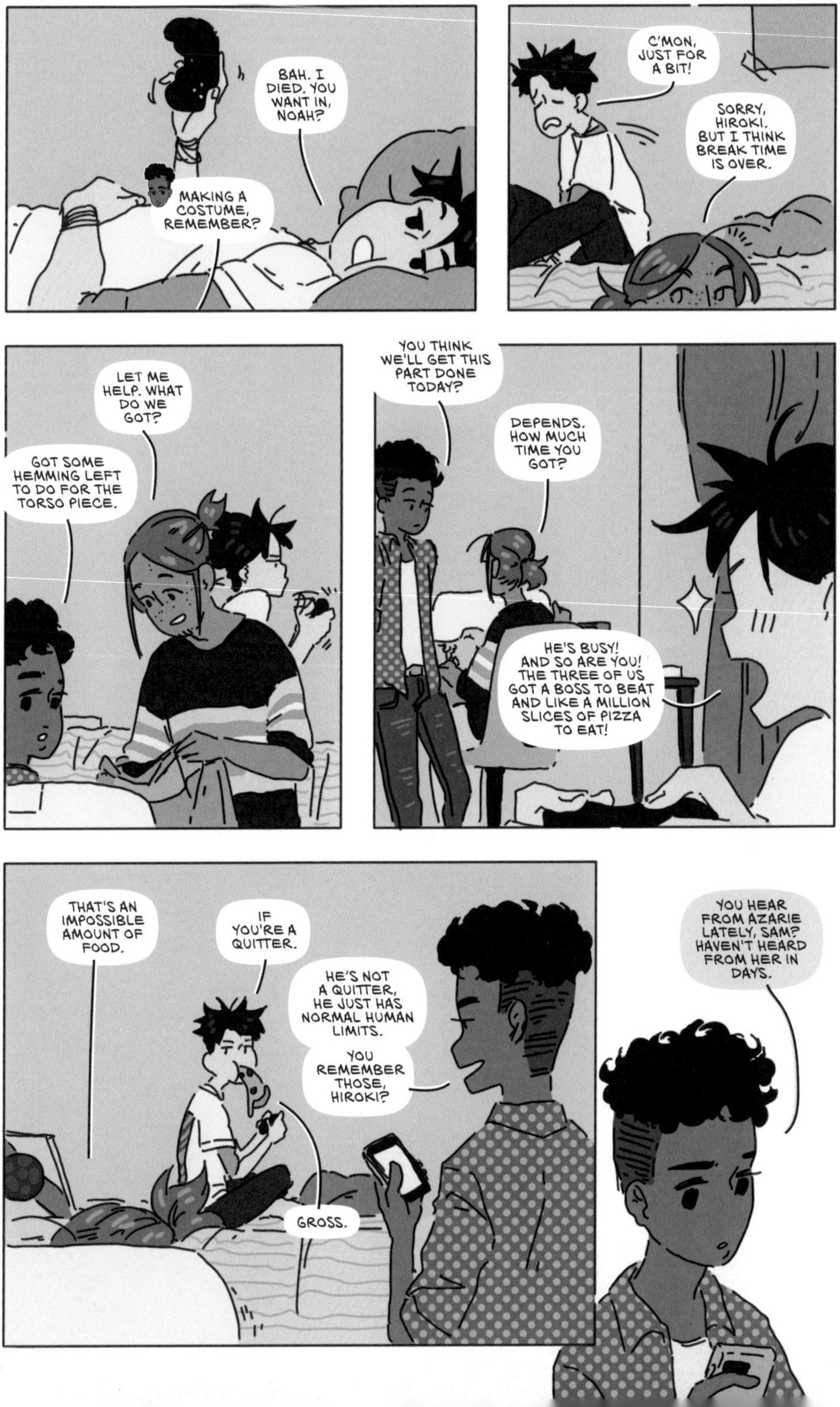
BAH. I DIED. YOU WANT IN, NOAH?
MAKING A COSTUME, REMEMBER?
C'MON, JUST FOR A BIT!
SORRY, HIROKI. BUT I THINK BREAK TIME IS OVER.
LET ME HELP. WHAT DO WE GOT?
GOT SOME HEMMING LEFT TO DO FOR THE TORSO PIECE.
YOU THINK WE'LL GET THIS PART DONE TODAY?
DEPENDS. HOW MUCH TIME YOU GOT?
HE'S BUSY! AND SO ARE YOU! THE THREE OF US GOT A BOSS TO BEAT AND LIKE A MILLION SLICES OF PIZZA TO EAT!
THAT'S AN IMPOSSIBLE AMOUNT OF FOOD.
IF YOU'RE A QUITTER.
HE'S NOT A QUITTER, HE JUST HAS NORMAL HUMAN LIMITS.
YOU REMEMBER THOSE, HIROKI?
GROSS.
YOU HEAR FROM AZARIE LATELY, SAM? HAVEN'T HEARD FROM HER IN DAYS.

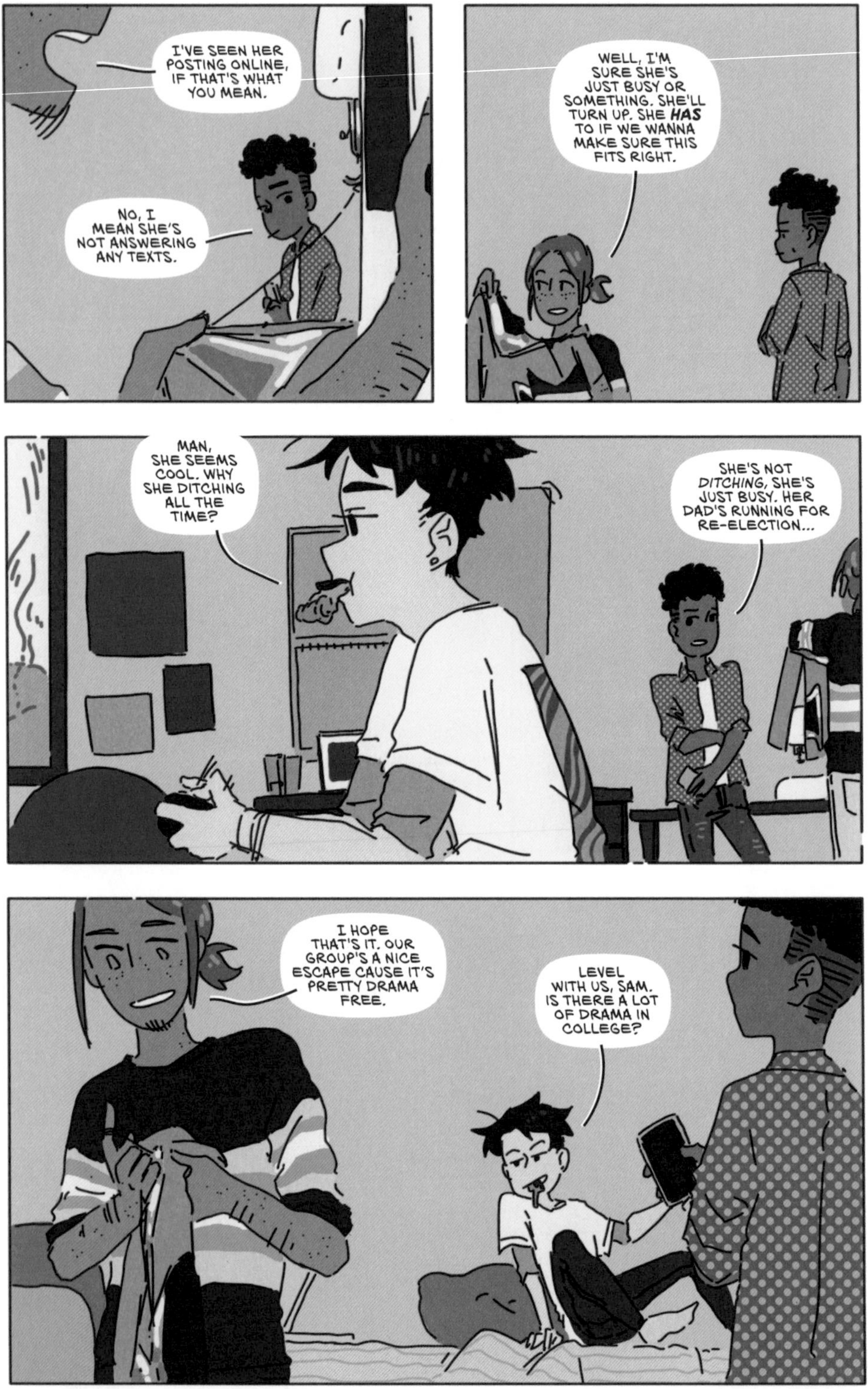
I'VE SEEN HER POSTING ONLINE, IF THAT'S WHAT YOU MEAN.
NO, I MEAN SHE'S NOT ANSWERING ANY TEXTS.
WELL, I'M SURE SHE'S JUST BUSY OR SOMETHING. SHE'LL TURN UP. SHE *HAS* TO IF WE WANNA MAKE SURE THIS FITS RIGHT.
MAN, SHE SEEMS COOL. WHY SHE DITCHING ALL THE TIME?
SHE'S NOT *DITCHING*, SHE'S JUST BUSY. HER DAD'S RUNNING FOR RE-ELECTION...
I HOPE THAT'S IT. OUR GROUP'S A NICE ESCAPE CAUSE IT'S PRETTY DRAMA FREE.
LEVEL WITH US, SAM. IS THERE A LOT OF DRAMA IN COLLEGE?

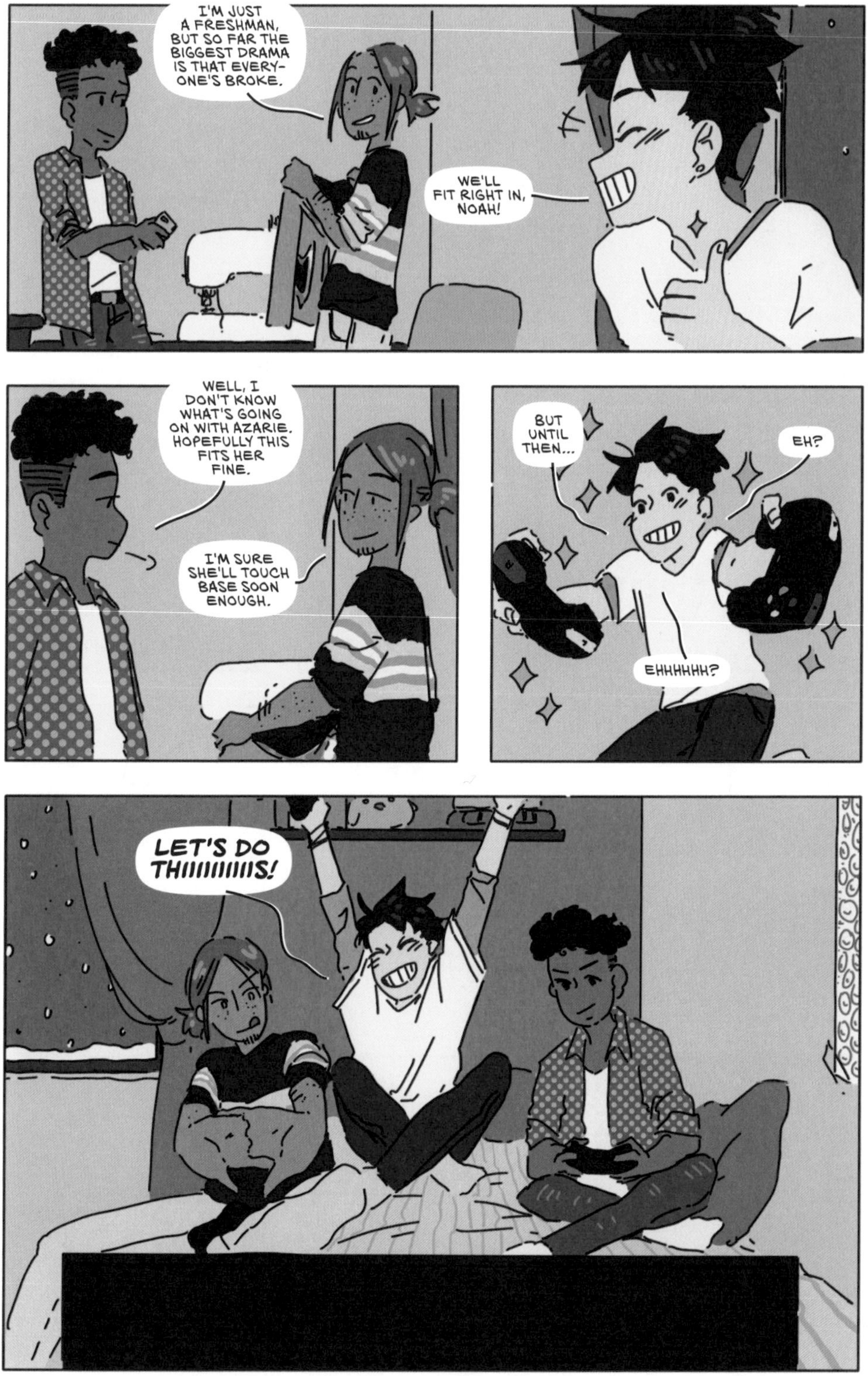
I'M JUST A FRESHMAN, BUT SO FAR THE BIGGEST DRAMA IS THAT EVERY-ONE'S BROKE.
WE'LL FIT RIGHT IN, NOAH!
WELL, I DON'T KNOW WHAT'S GOING ON WITH AZARIE. HOPEFULLY THIS FITS HER FINE.
I'M SURE SHE'LL TOUCH BASE SOON ENOUGH.
BUT UNTIL THEN...
EH?
EHHHHHH?
LET'S DO THIIIIIIIIIS!

Hey, u up for working on the costume or just hanging out or something?

It's been forever since we've talked AND we gotta work on the costume!!!

C'mon, anything?

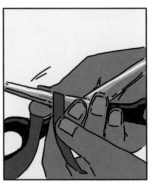

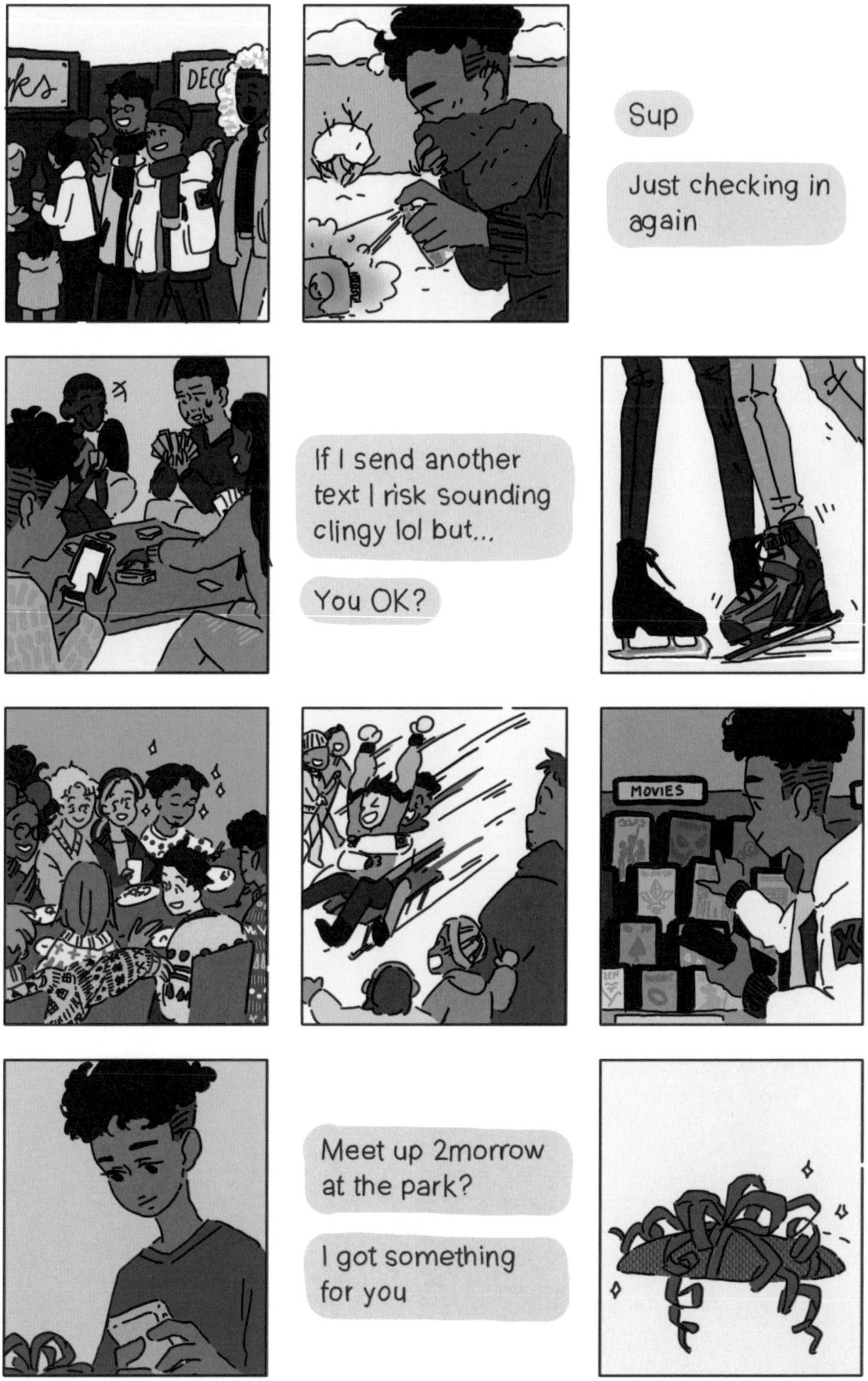

Sup
Just checking in again
If I send another text I risk sounding clingy lol but...
You OK?
MOVIES
Meet up 2morrow at the park?
I got something for you

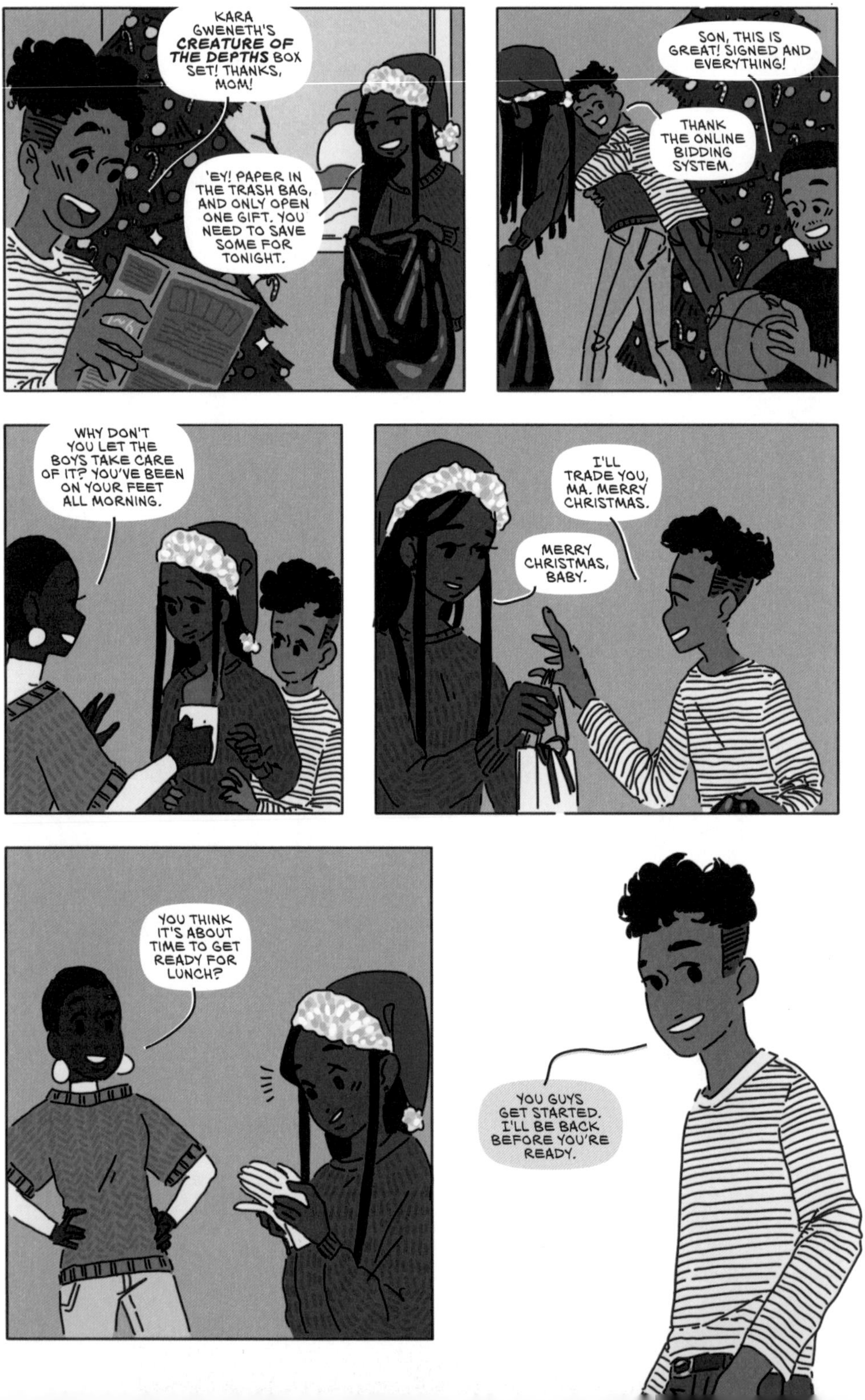
KARA GWENETH'S **CREATURE OF THE DEPTHS** BOX SET! THANKS, MOM!
'EY! PAPER IN THE TRASH BAG, AND ONLY OPEN ONE GIFT. YOU NEED TO SAVE SOME FOR TONIGHT.
SON, THIS IS GREAT! SIGNED AND EVERYTHING!
THANK THE ONLINE BIDDING SYSTEM.
WHY DON'T YOU LET THE BOYS TAKE CARE OF IT? YOU'VE BEEN ON YOUR FEET ALL MORNING.
I'LL TRADE YOU, MA. MERRY CHRISTMAS.
MERRY CHRISTMAS, BABY.
YOU THINK IT'S ABOUT TIME TO GET READY FOR LUNCH?
YOU GUYS GET STARTED. I'LL BE BACK BEFORE YOU'RE READY.

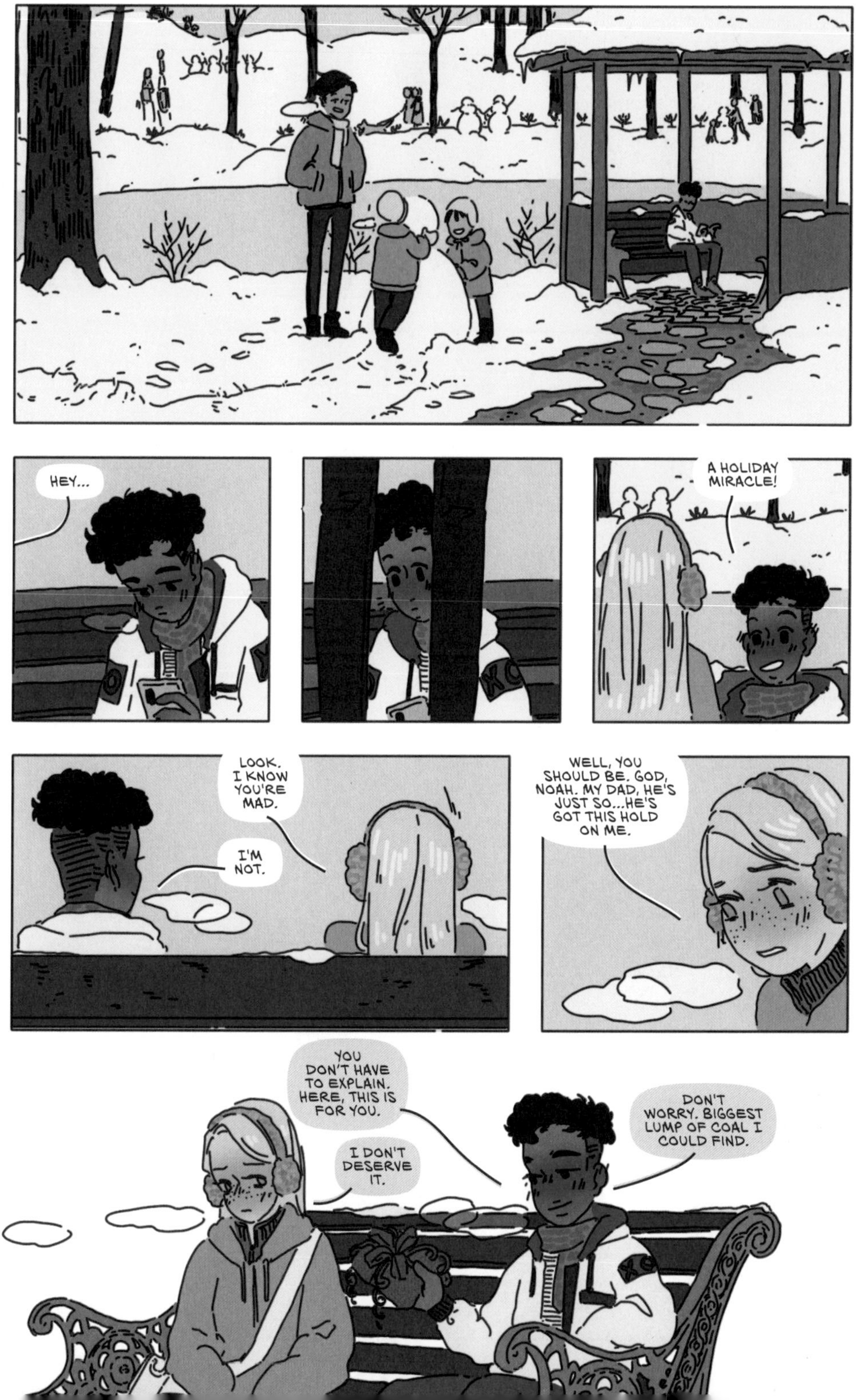
HEY...
A HOLIDAY MIRACLE!
LOOK. I KNOW YOU'RE MAD.
I'M NOT.
WELL, YOU SHOULD BE. GOD, NOAH. MY DAD, HE'S JUST SO...HE'S GOT THIS HOLD ON ME.
YOU DON'T HAVE TO EXPLAIN. HERE, THIS IS FOR YOU.
I DON'T DESERVE IT.
DON'T WORRY. BIGGEST LUMP OF COAL I COULD FIND.

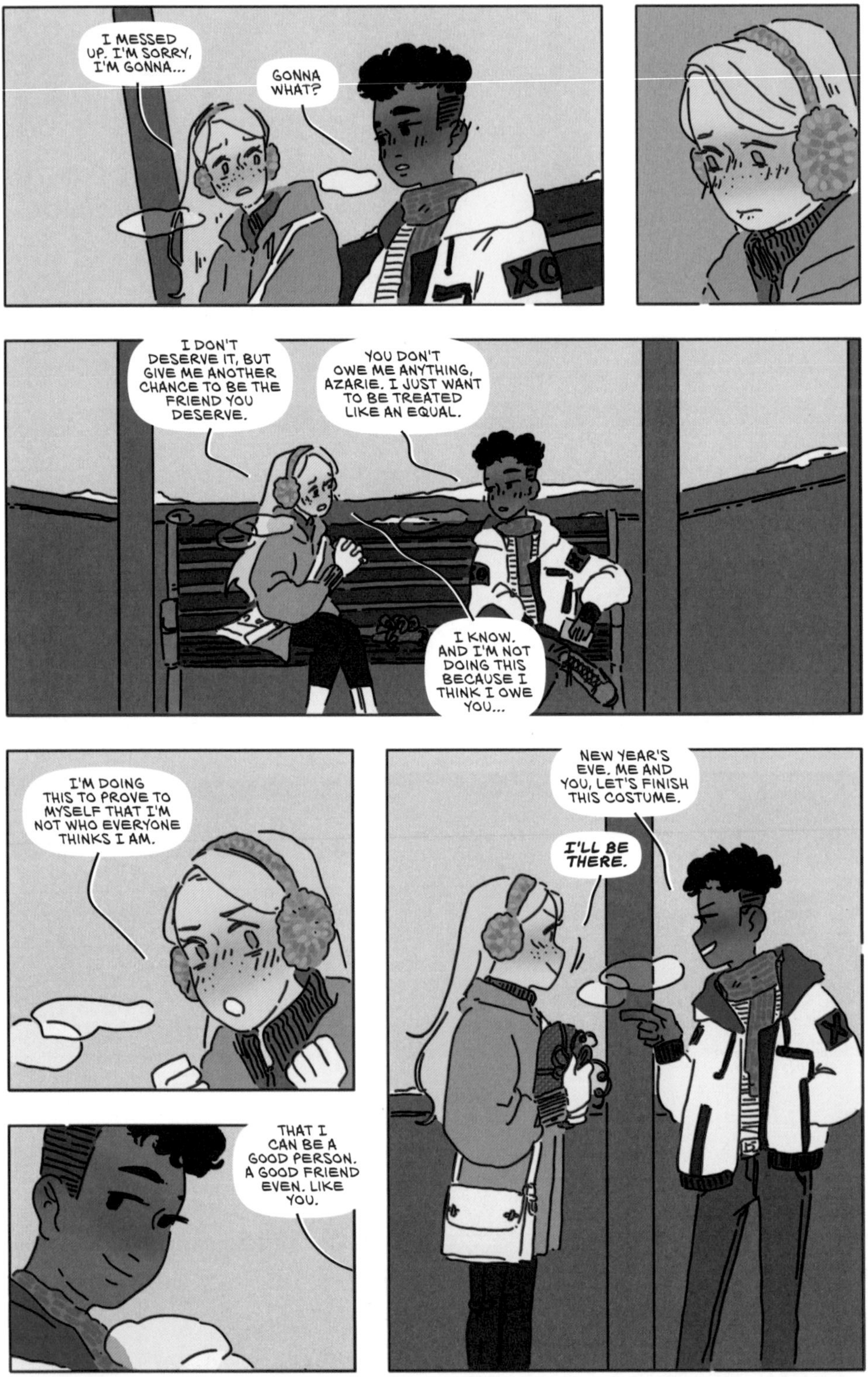
I MESSED UP. I'M SORRY, I'M GONNA...
GONNA WHAT?
I DON'T DESERVE IT, BUT GIVE ME ANOTHER CHANCE TO BE THE FRIEND YOU DESERVE.
YOU DON'T OWE ME ANYTHING, AZARIE. I JUST WANT TO BE TREATED LIKE AN EQUAL.
I KNOW. AND I'M NOT DOING THIS BECAUSE I THINK I OWE YOU...
I'M DOING THIS TO PROVE TO MYSELF THAT I'M NOT WHO EVERYONE THINKS I AM.
THAT I CAN BE A GOOD PERSON. A GOOD FRIEND EVEN. LIKE YOU.
NEW YEAR'S EVE. ME AND YOU, LET'S FINISH THIS COSTUME.
I'LL BE THERE.

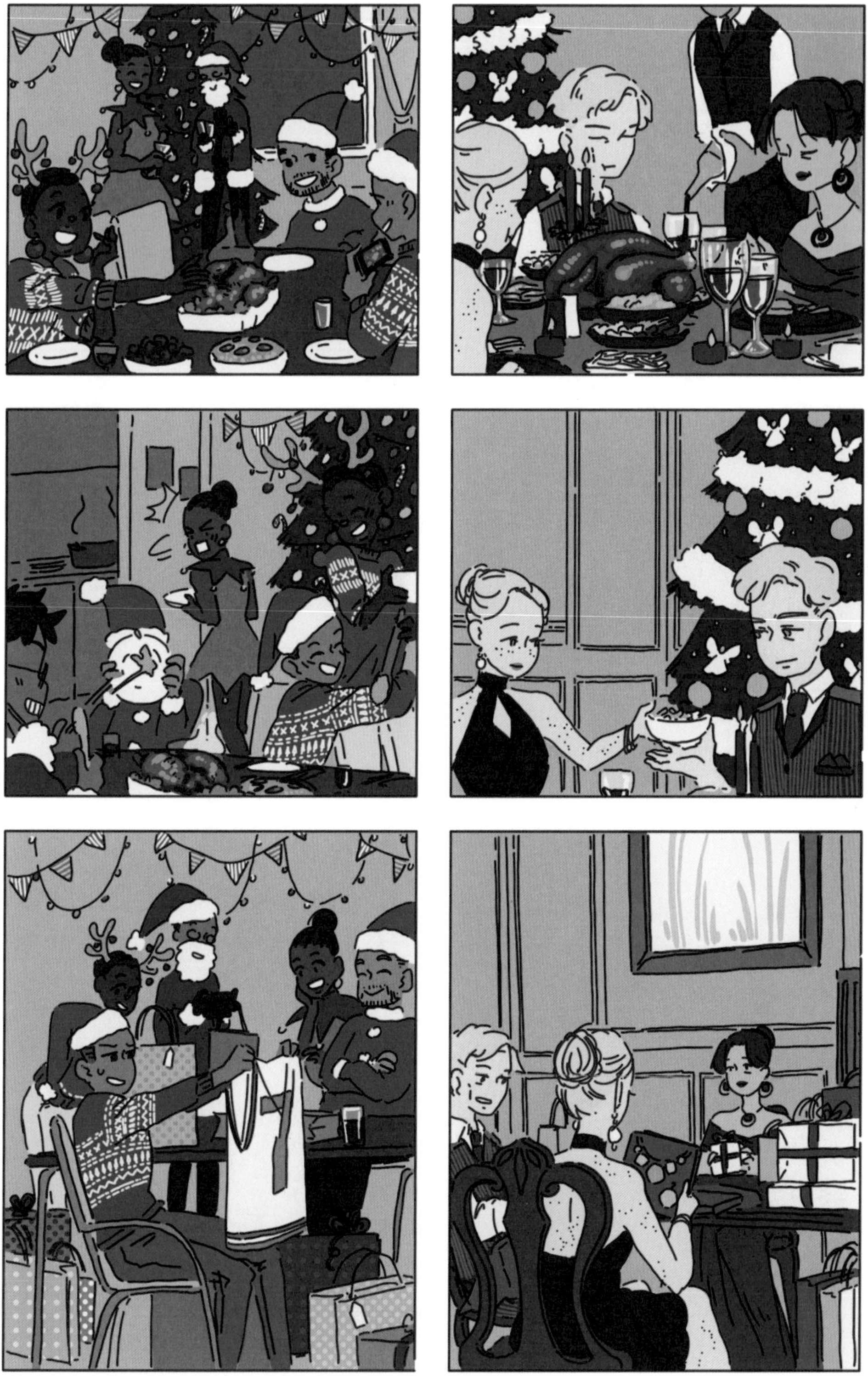

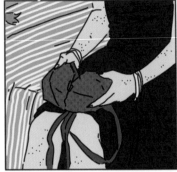

MERRY CHRISTMAS.

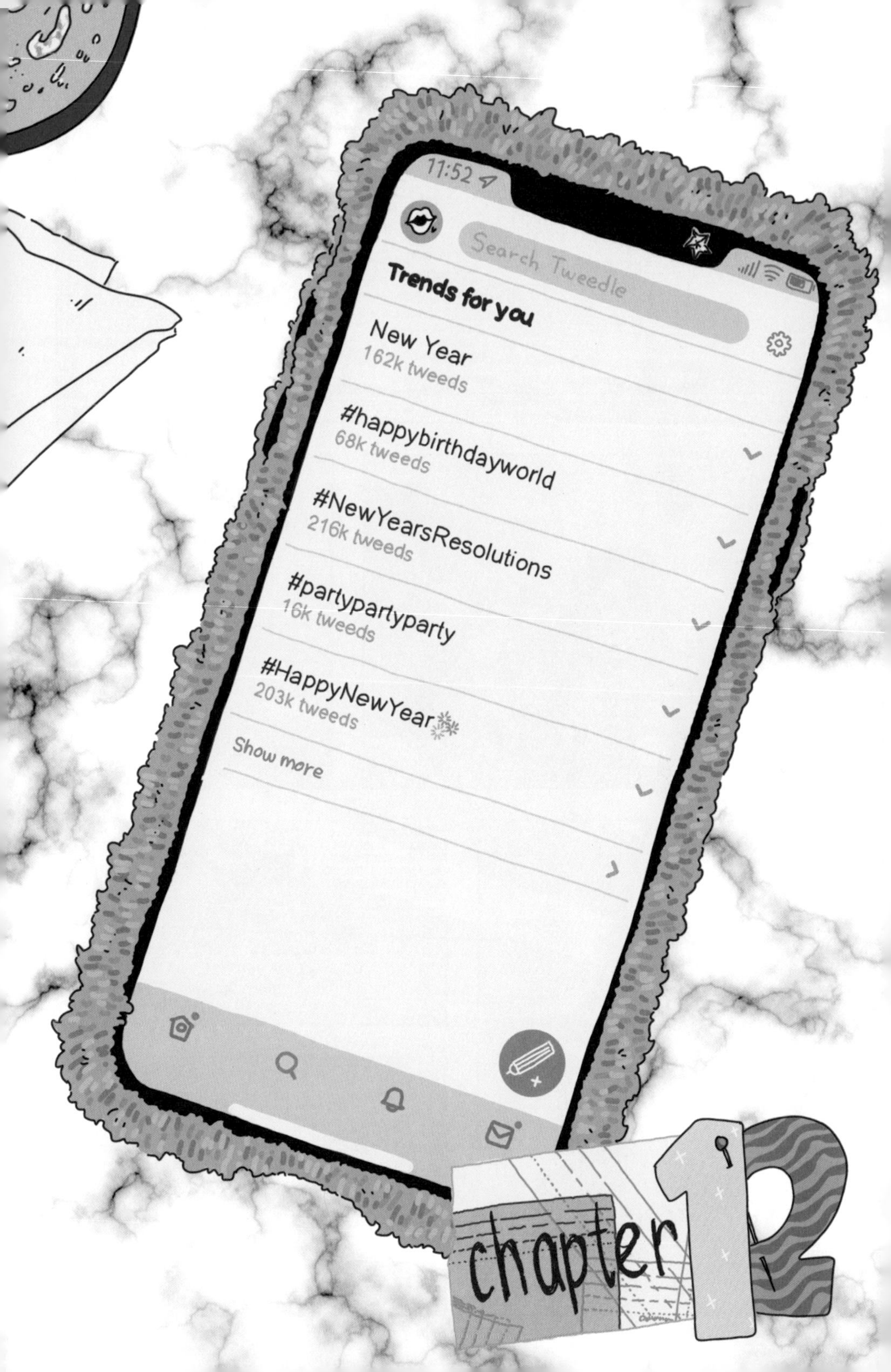
11:52
Search Tweedle
Trends for you
New Year
162k tweeds
#happybirthdayworld
68k tweeds
#NewYearsResolutions
216k tweeds
#partypartyparty
16k tweeds
#HappyNewYear
203k tweeds
Show more
chapter 12

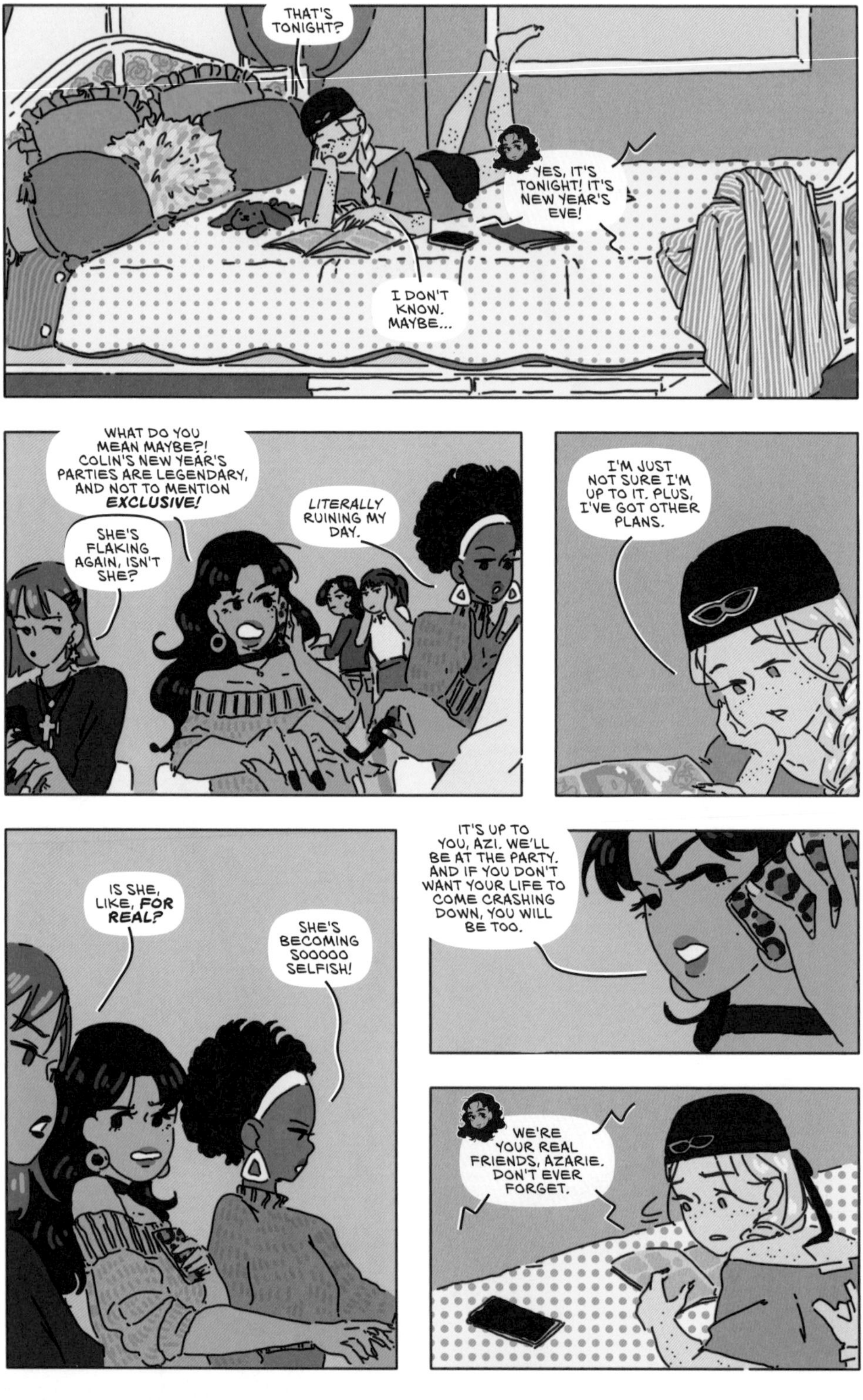
THAT'S TONIGHT?
YES, IT'S TONIGHT! IT'S NEW YEAR'S EVE!
I DON'T KNOW. MAYBE...
WHAT DO YOU MEAN MAYBE?! COLIN'S NEW YEAR'S PARTIES ARE LEGENDARY, AND NOT TO MENTION EXCLUSIVE!
SHE'S FLAKING AGAIN, ISN'T SHE?
LITERALLY RUINING MY DAY.
I'M JUST NOT SURE I'M UP TO IT. PLUS, I'VE GOT OTHER PLANS.
IS SHE, LIKE, FOR REAL?
SHE'S BECOMING SOOOOO SELFISH!
IT'S UP TO YOU, AZI. WE'LL BE AT THE PARTY. AND IF YOU DON'T WANT YOUR LIFE TO COME CRASHING DOWN, YOU WILL BE TOO.
WE'RE YOUR REAL FRIENDS, AZARIE. DON'T EVER FORGET.

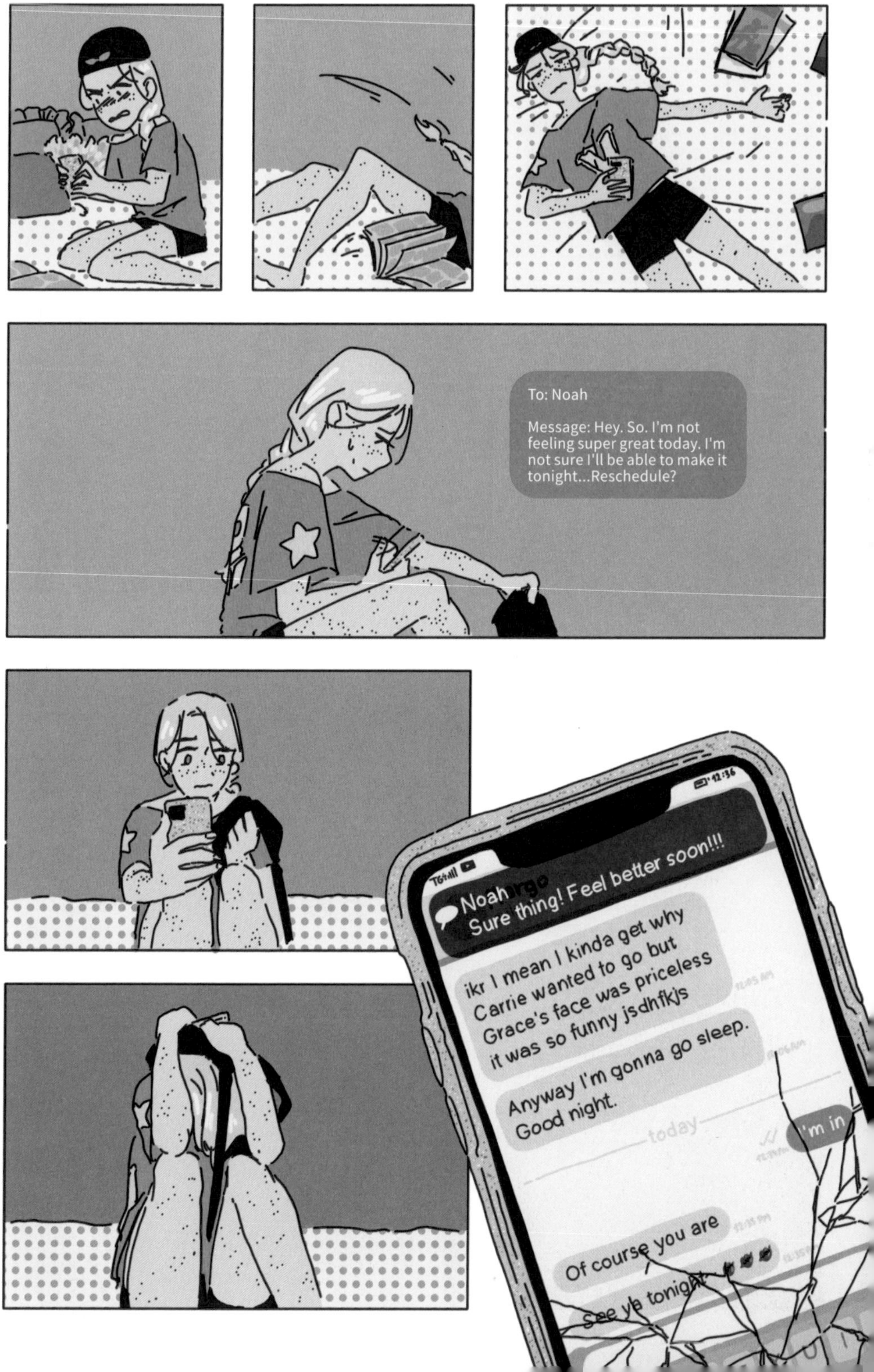
To: Noah
Message: Hey. So. I'm not feeling super great today. I'm not sure I'll be able to make it tonight...Reschedule?
Noah
Sure thing! Feel better soon!!!
ikr I mean I kinda get why Carrie wanted to go but Grace's face was priceless it was so funny jsdhfkjs
Anyway I'm gonna go sleep. Good night.
today
I'm in
Of course you are
See ya tonight

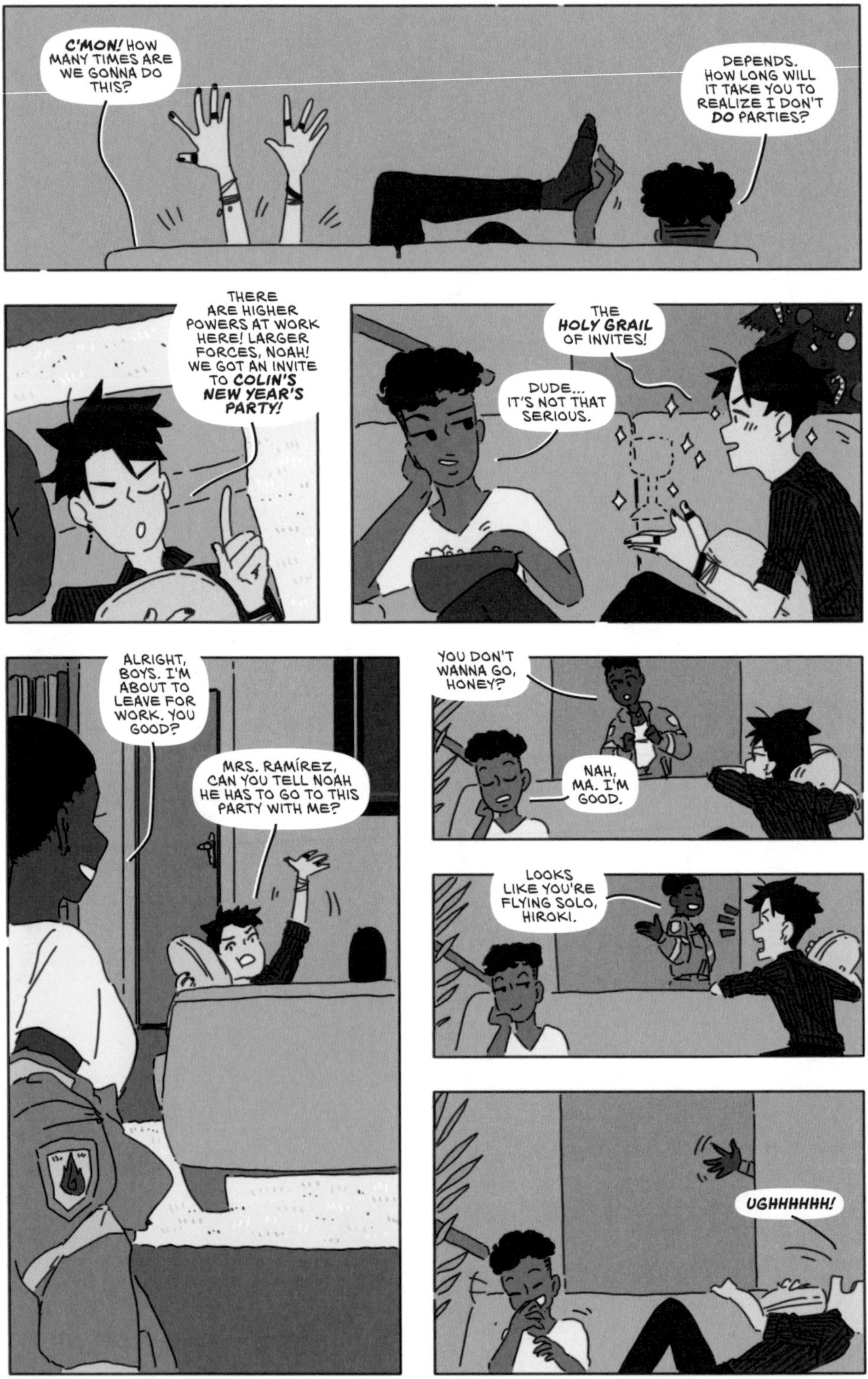
C'MON! HOW MANY TIMES ARE WE GONNA DO THIS?
DEPENDS. HOW LONG WILL IT TAKE YOU TO REALIZE I DON'T DO PARTIES?
THERE ARE HIGHER POWERS AT WORK HERE! LARGER FORCES, NOAH! WE GOT AN INVITE TO COLIN'S NEW YEAR'S PARTY!
THE HOLY GRAIL OF INVITES!
DUDE... IT'S NOT THAT SERIOUS.
ALRIGHT, BOYS. I'M ABOUT TO LEAVE FOR WORK. YOU GOOD?
MRS. RAMÍREZ, CAN YOU TELL NOAH HE HAS TO GO TO THIS PARTY WITH ME?
YOU DON'T WANNA GO, HONEY?
NAH, MA. I'M GOOD.
LOOKS LIKE YOU'RE FLYING SOLO, HIROKI.
UGHHHHHH!

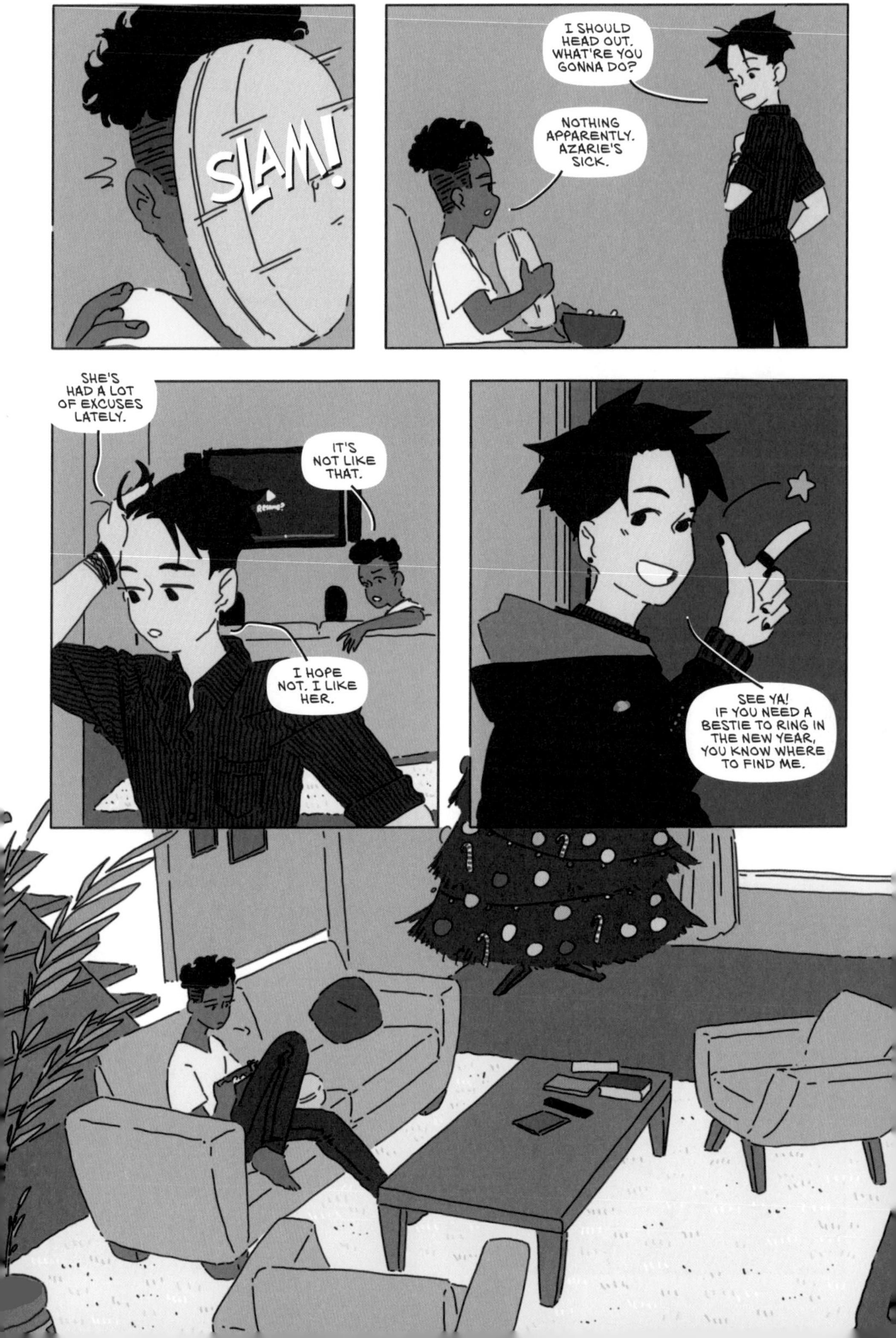
SLAM!
I SHOULD HEAD OUT. WHAT'RE YOU GONNA DO?
NOTHING APPARENTLY. AZARIE'S SICK.
SHE'S HAD A LOT OF EXCUSES LATELY.
IT'S NOT LIKE THAT.
I HOPE NOT. I LIKE HER.
SEE YA! IF YOU NEED A BESTIE TO RING IN THE NEW YEAR, YOU KNOW WHERE TO FIND ME.

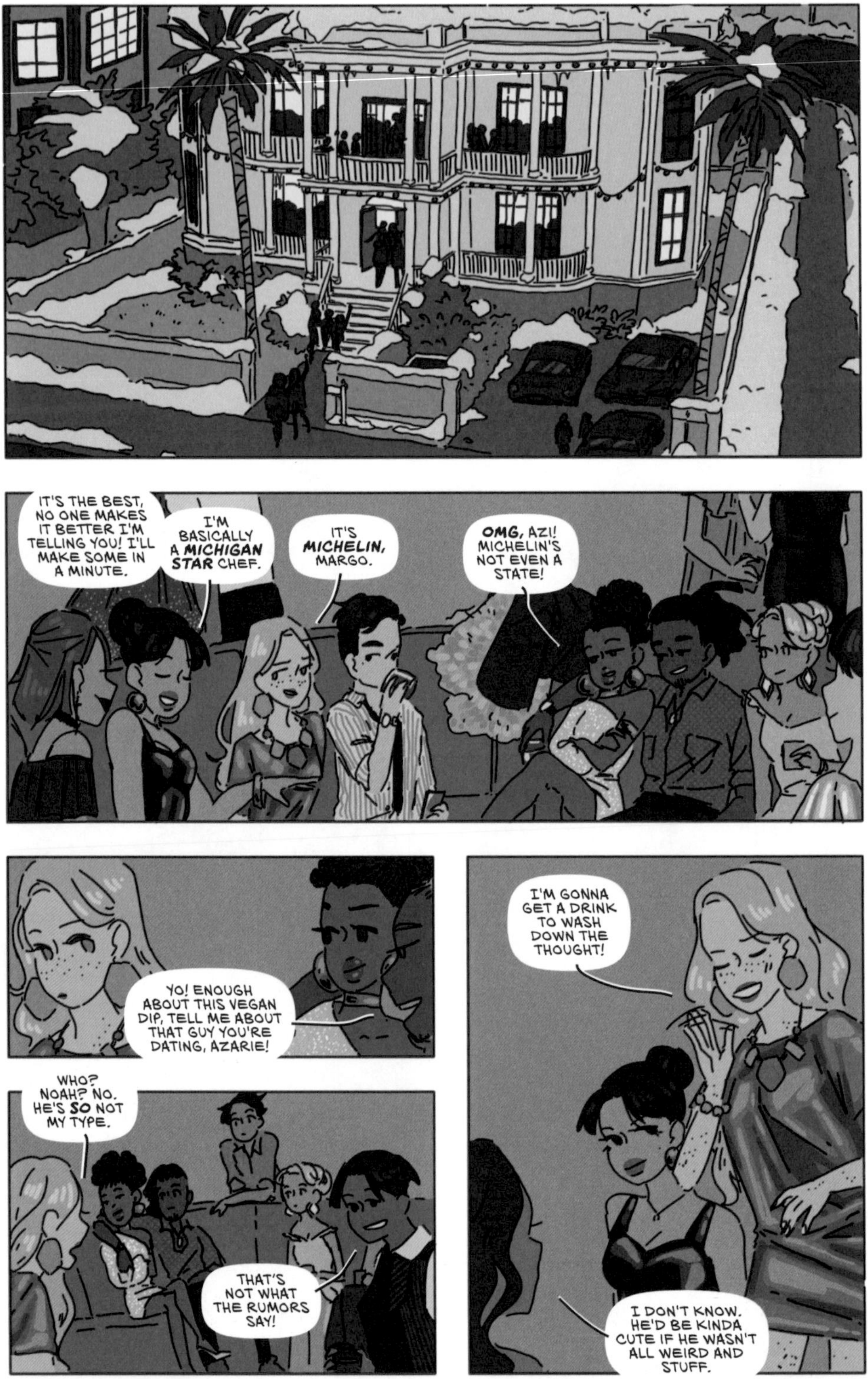
IT'S THE BEST, NO ONE MAKES IT BETTER I'M TELLING YOU! I'LL MAKE SOME IN A MINUTE.
I'M BASICALLY A **MICHIGAN STAR** CHEF.
IT'S **MICHELIN,** MARGO.
OMG, AZI! MICHELIN'S NOT EVEN A STATE!
YO! ENOUGH ABOUT THIS VEGAN DIP, TELL ME ABOUT THAT GUY YOU'RE DATING, AZARIE!
WHO? NOAH? NO. HE'S **SO** NOT MY TYPE.
THAT'S NOT WHAT THE RUMORS SAY!
I'M GONNA GET A DRINK TO WASH DOWN THE THOUGHT!
I DON'T KNOW. HE'D BE KINDA CUTE IF HE WASN'T ALL WEIRD AND STUFF.

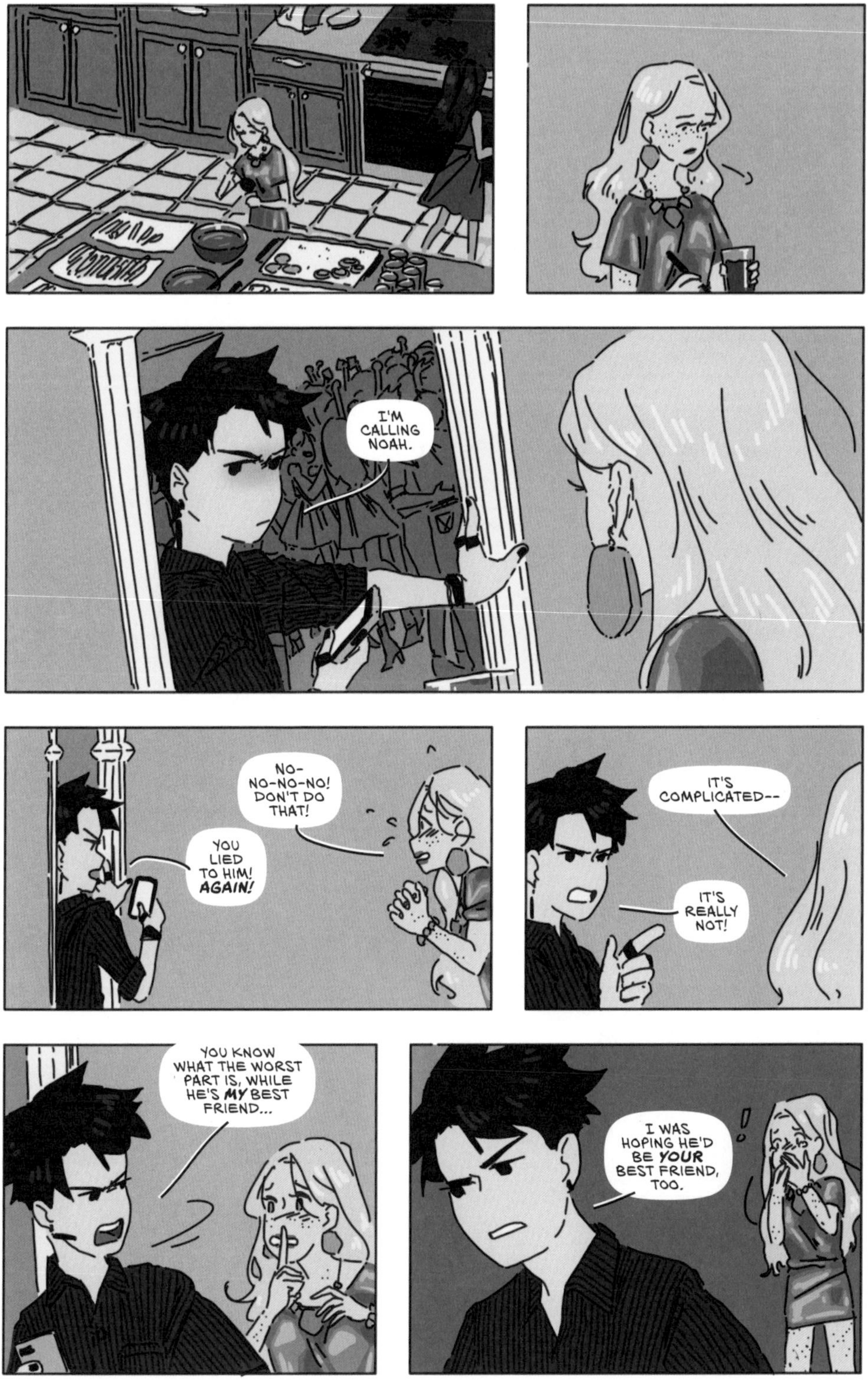
I'M CALLING NOAH.
NO-NO-NO-NO! DON'T DO THAT!
YOU LIED TO HIM! AGAIN!
IT'S COMPLICATED--
IT'S REALLY NOT!
YOU KNOW WHAT THE WORST PART IS, WHILE HE'S MY BEST FRIEND...
I WAS HOPING HE'D BE YOUR BEST FRIEND, TOO.

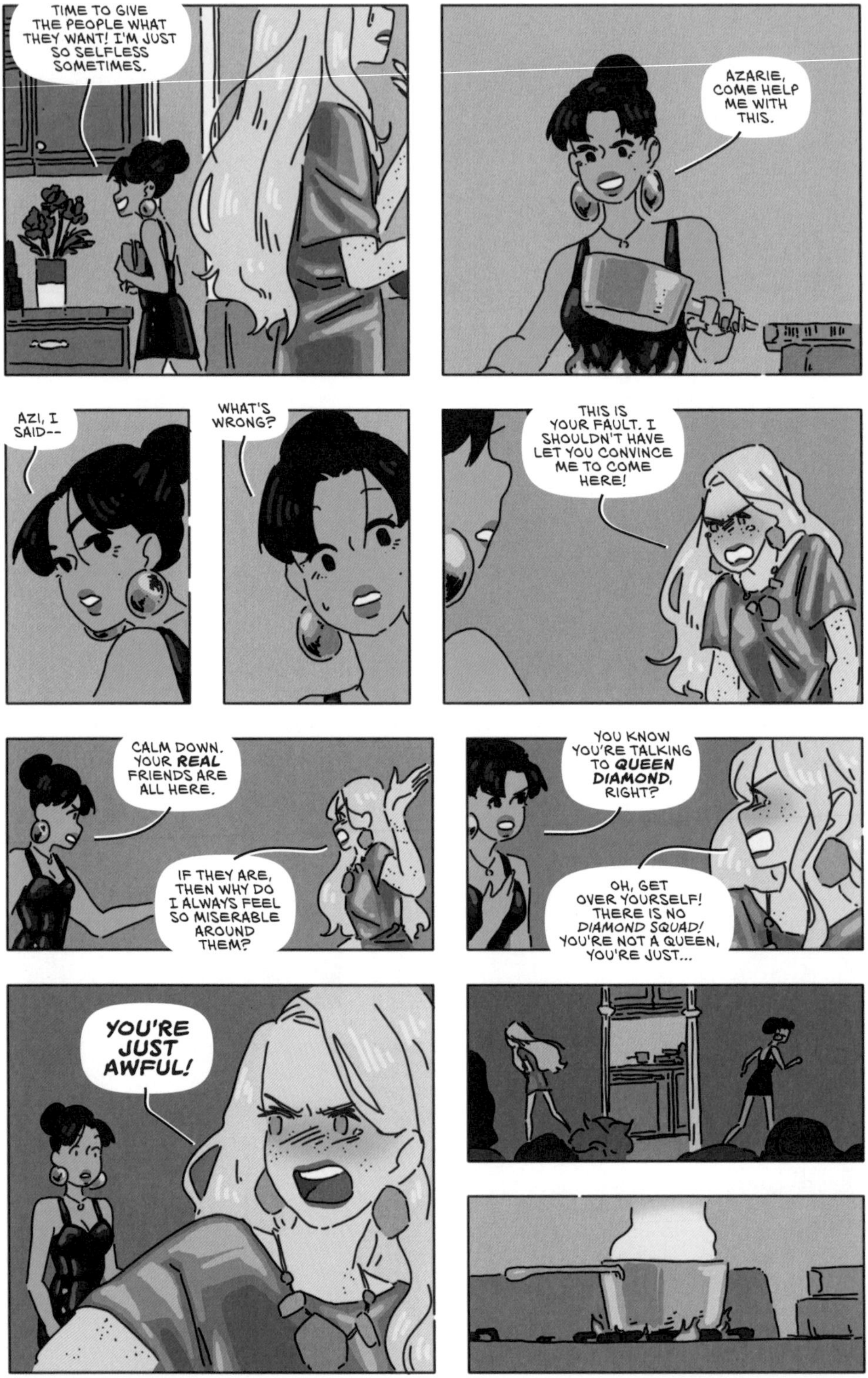
TIME TO GIVE THE PEOPLE WHAT THEY WANT! I'M JUST SO SELFLESS SOMETIMES.
AZARIE, COME HELP ME WITH THIS.
AZI, I SAID--
WHAT'S WRONG?
THIS IS YOUR FAULT. I SHOULDN'T HAVE LET YOU CONVINCE ME TO COME HERE!
CALM DOWN. YOUR **REAL** FRIENDS ARE ALL HERE.
IF THEY ARE, THEN WHY DO I ALWAYS FEEL SO MISERABLE AROUND THEM?
YOU KNOW YOU'RE TALKING TO ***QUEEN DIAMOND***, RIGHT?
OH, GET OVER YOURSELF! THERE IS NO *DIAMOND SQUAD!* YOU'RE NOT A QUEEN, YOU'RE JUST...
YOU'RE JUST AWFUL!

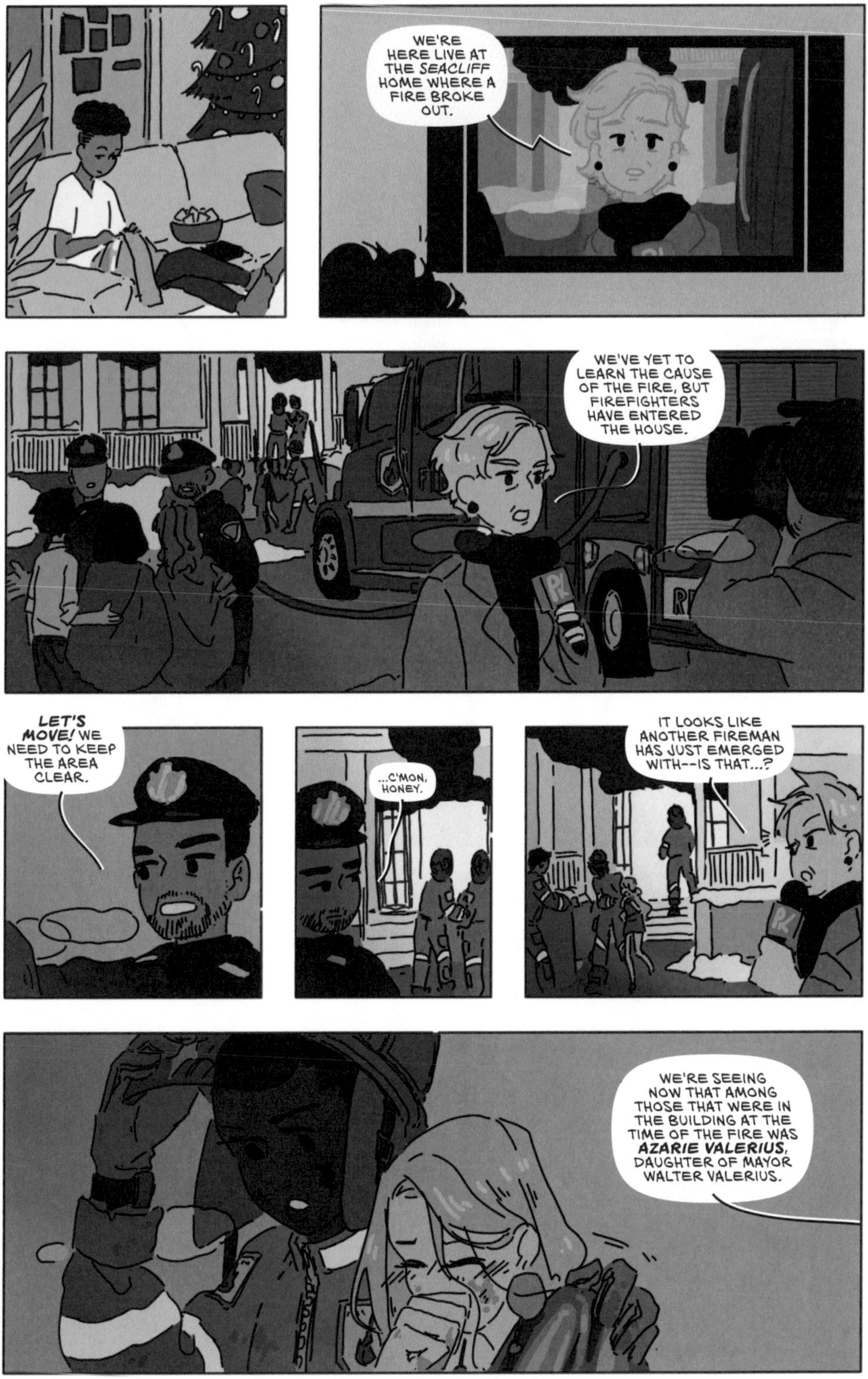
WE'RE HERE LIVE AT THE SEACLIFF HOME WHERE A FIRE BROKE OUT.
WE'VE YET TO LEARN THE CAUSE OF THE FIRE, BUT FIREFIGHTERS HAVE ENTERED THE HOUSE.
LET'S MOVE! WE NEED TO KEEP THE AREA CLEAR.
...C'MON, HONEY.
IT LOOKS LIKE ANOTHER FIREMAN HAS JUST EMERGED WITH--IS THAT...?
WE'RE SEEING NOW THAT AMONG THOSE THAT WERE IN THE BUILDING AT THE TIME OF THE FIRE WAS AZARIE VALERIUS, DAUGHTER OF MAYOR WALTER VALERIUS.

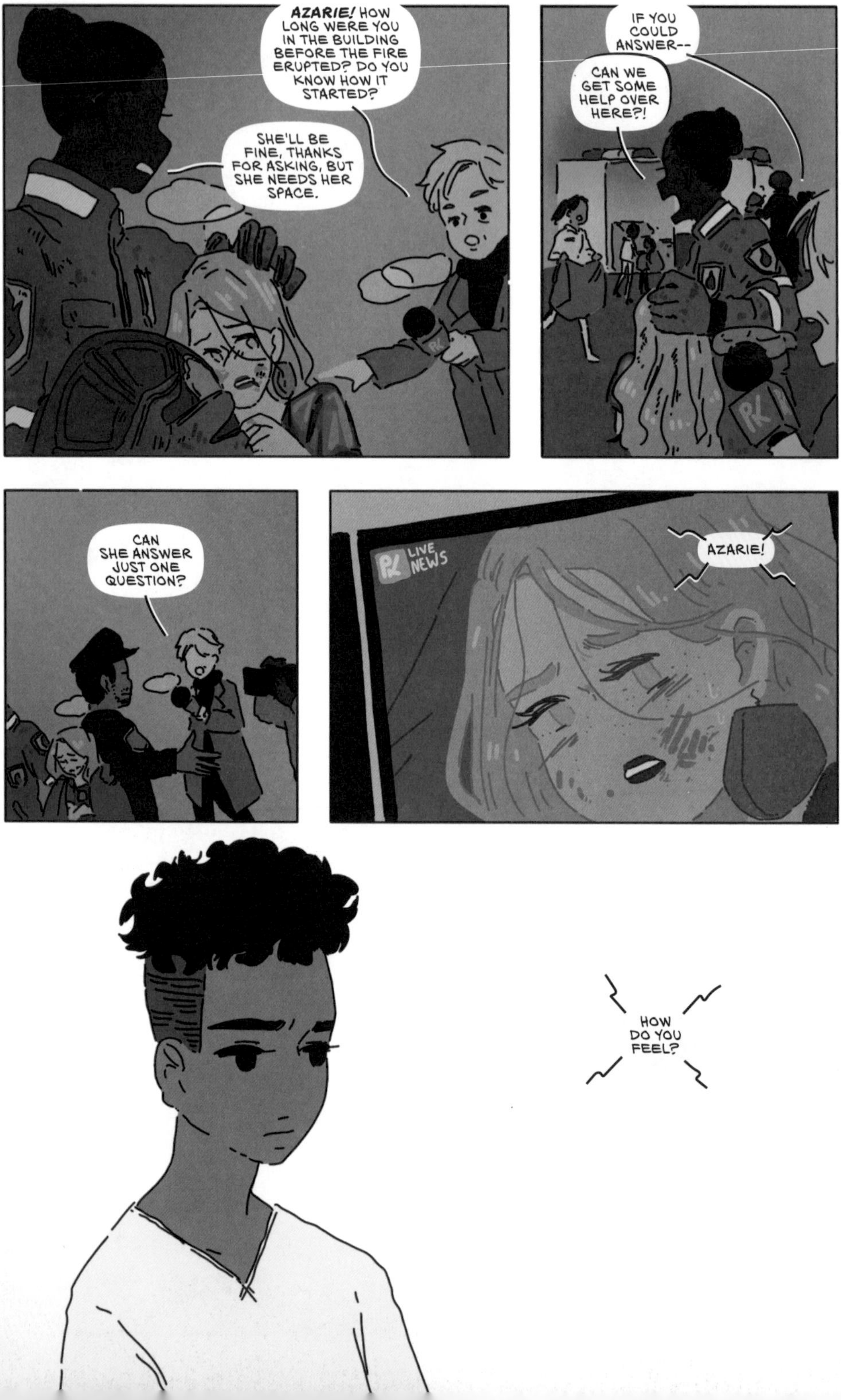
AZARIE! HOW LONG WERE YOU IN THE BUILDING BEFORE THE FIRE ERUPTED? DO YOU KNOW HOW IT STARTED?
SHE'LL BE FINE, THANKS FOR ASKING, BUT SHE NEEDS HER SPACE.
IF YOU COULD ANSWER--
CAN WE GET SOME HELP OVER HERE?!
CAN SHE ANSWER JUST ONE QUESTION?
LIVE NEWS
AZARIE!
HOW DO YOU FEEL?

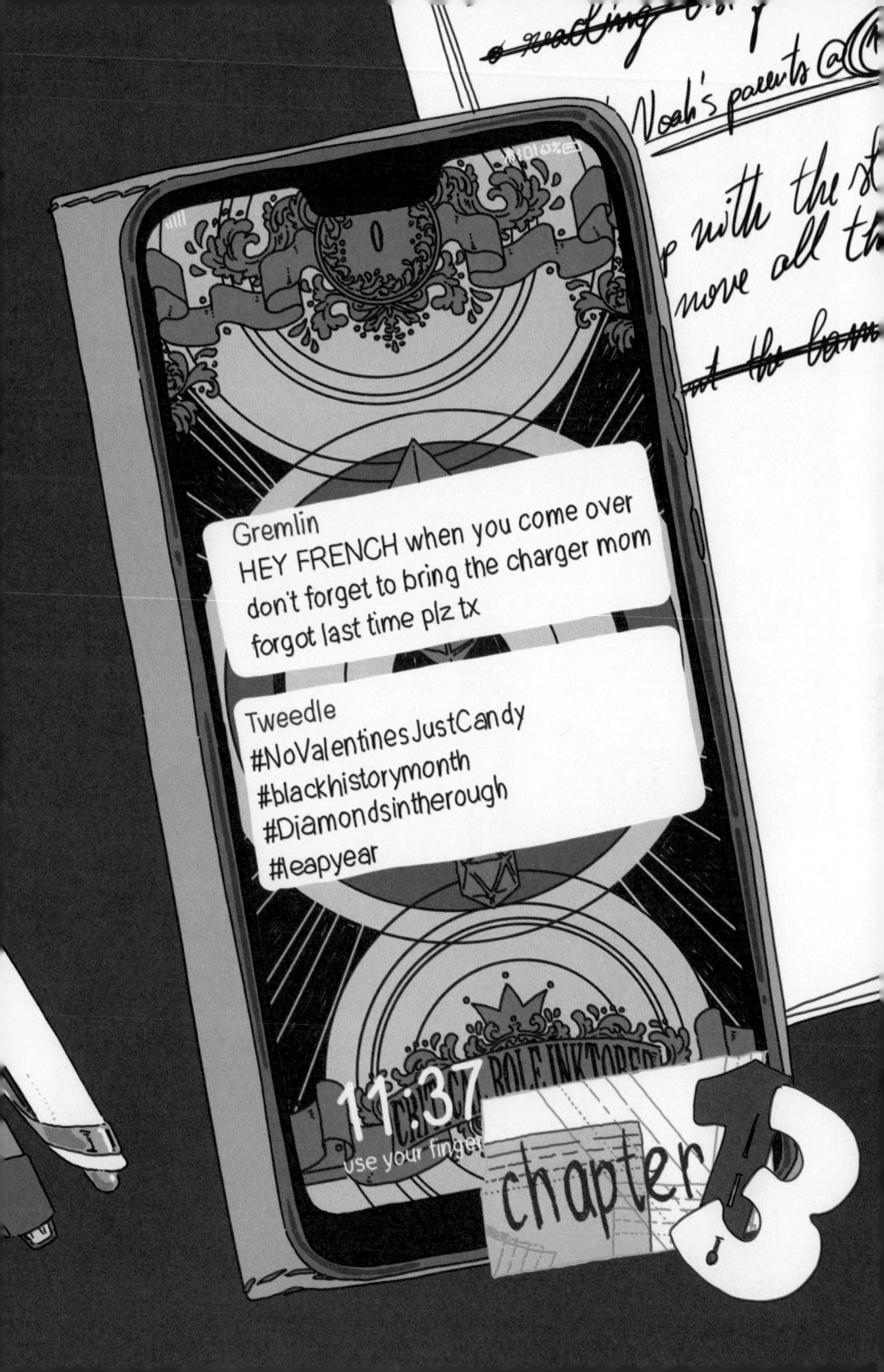
Gremlin
HEY FRENCH when you come over don't forget to bring the charger mom forgot last time plz tx
Tweedle
#NoValentinesJustCandy
#blackhistorymonth
#Diamondsintherough
#leapyear
11:37
chapter 13

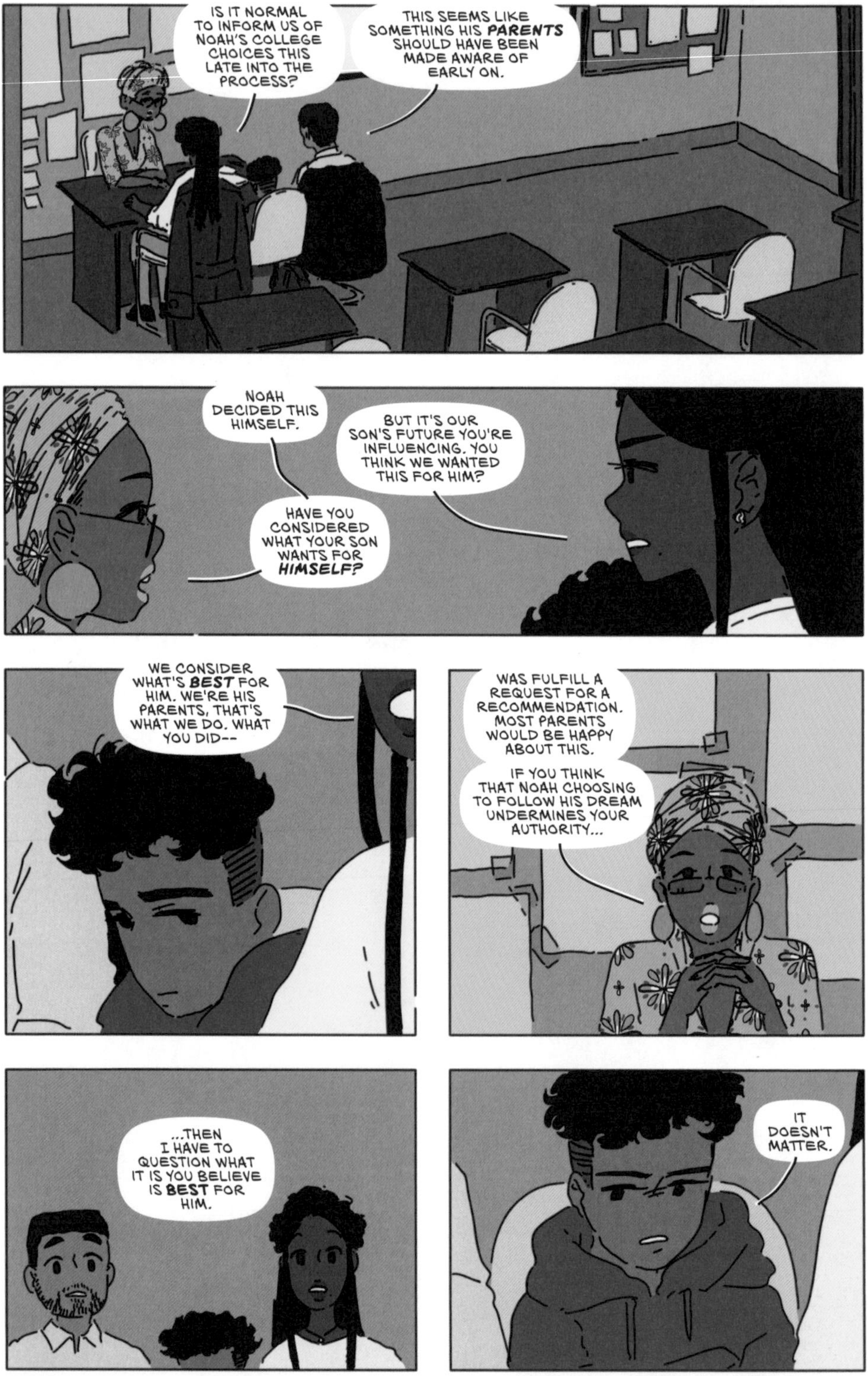
IS IT NORMAL TO INFORM US OF NOAH'S COLLEGE CHOICES THIS LATE INTO THE PROCESS?
THIS SEEMS LIKE SOMETHING HIS **PARENTS** SHOULD HAVE BEEN MADE AWARE OF EARLY ON.
NOAH DECIDED THIS HIMSELF.
BUT IT'S OUR SON'S FUTURE YOU'RE INFLUENCING. YOU THINK WE WANTED THIS FOR HIM?
HAVE YOU CONSIDERED WHAT YOUR SON WANTS FOR **HIMSELF?**
WE CONSIDER WHAT'S **BEST** FOR HIM. WE'RE HIS PARENTS, THAT'S WHAT WE DO. WHAT YOU DID--
WAS FULFILL A REQUEST FOR A RECOMMENDATION. MOST PARENTS WOULD BE HAPPY ABOUT THIS.
IF YOU THINK THAT NOAH CHOOSING TO FOLLOW HIS DREAM UNDERMINES YOUR AUTHORITY...
...THEN I HAVE TO QUESTION WHAT IT IS YOU BELIEVE IS **BEST** FOR HIM.
IT DOESN'T MATTER.

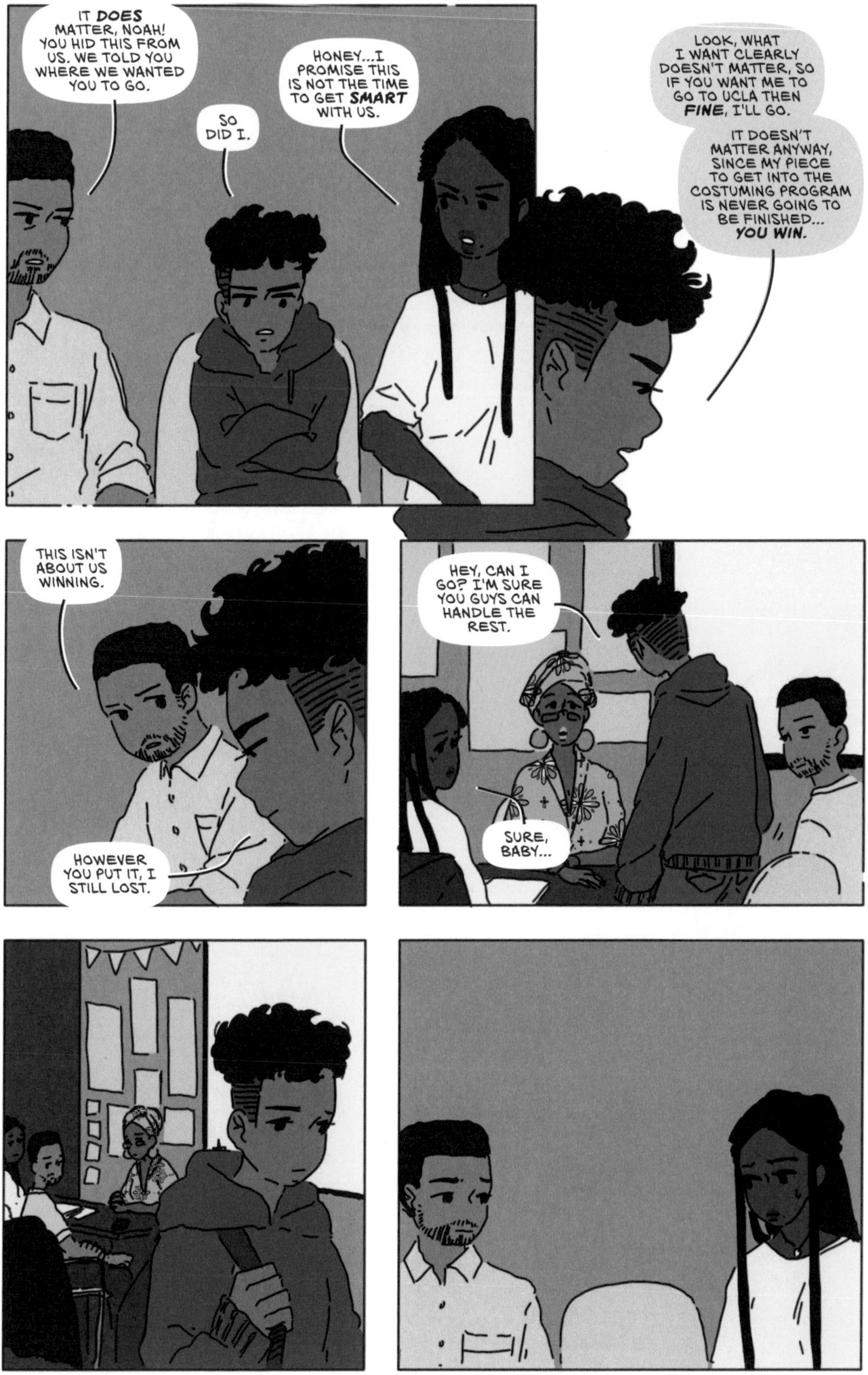
IT **DOES** MATTER, NOAH! YOU HID THIS FROM US. WE TOLD YOU WHERE WE WANTED YOU TO GO.
SO DID I.
HONEY...I PROMISE THIS IS NOT THE TIME TO GET **SMART** WITH US.
LOOK, WHAT I WANT CLEARLY DOESN'T MATTER, SO IF YOU WANT ME TO GO TO UCLA THEN **FINE**, I'LL GO.
IT DOESN'T MATTER ANYWAY, SINCE MY PIECE TO GET INTO THE COSTUMING PROGRAM IS NEVER GOING TO BE FINISHED... ***YOU WIN.***
THIS ISN'T ABOUT US WINNING.
HOWEVER YOU PUT IT, I STILL LOST.
HEY, CAN I GO? I'M SURE YOU GUYS CAN HANDLE THE REST.
SURE, BABY...

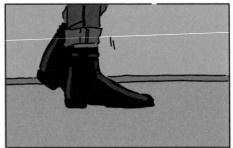

HEY...
IT'S BEEN
A WHILE.

TWO
MONTHS TO
BE EXACT.

YOU JUST
GET OUT OF
CLASS, OR
SOMETHING?

PARENT-TEACHER
CONFERENCE.

OH,
YEAH...
COOL.

...MY DAD
WANTED ME TO
PASS THESE OUT. IT'S
TOTALLY LAME, I KNOW,
BUT HE WOULDN'T
GET OFF MY BACK
ABOUT IT.

I THINK
HE'S GETTING
DESPERATE FOR
VOTES. HAHA...
HEH...

WELL, IF
YOU'RE LOOKING
FOR HELP...WHY
DON'T YOU GO TALK
TO A *FRIEND*
INSTEAD?

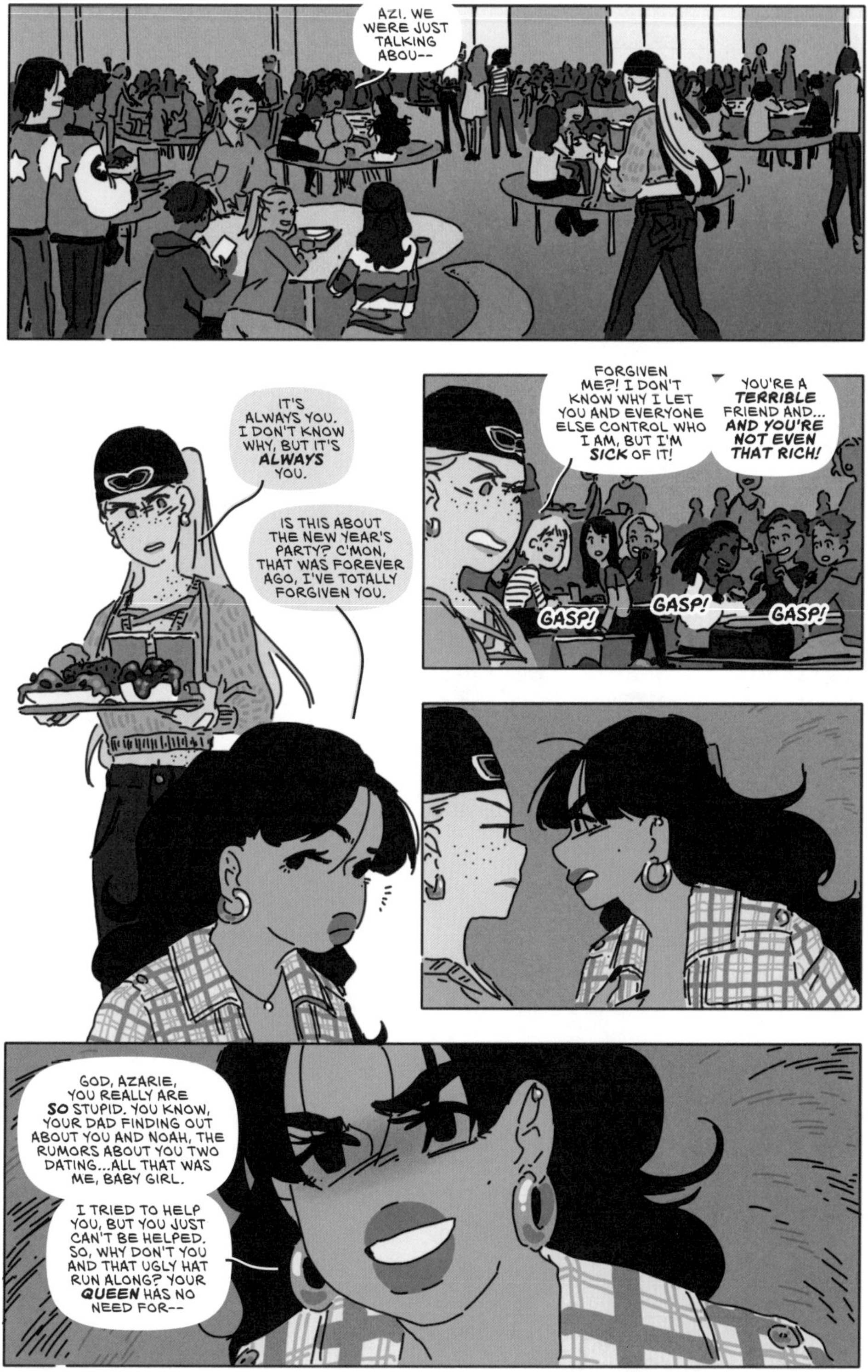
AZI. WE WERE JUST TALKING ABOU--
IT'S ALWAYS YOU. I DON'T KNOW WHY, BUT IT'S **ALWAYS** YOU.
IS THIS ABOUT THE NEW YEAR'S PARTY? C'MON, THAT WAS FOREVER AGO, I'VE TOTALLY FORGIVEN YOU.
FORGIVEN ME?! I DON'T KNOW WHY I LET YOU AND EVERYONE ELSE CONTROL WHO I AM, BUT I'M **SICK** OF IT!
YOU'RE A **TERRIBLE** FRIEND AND... **AND YOU'RE NOT EVEN THAT RICH!**
GASP!
GASP!
GASP!
GOD, AZARIE, YOU REALLY ARE **SO** STUPID. YOU KNOW, YOUR DAD FINDING OUT ABOUT YOU AND NOAH, THE RUMORS ABOUT YOU TWO DATING...ALL THAT WAS ME, BABY GIRL.
I TRIED TO HELP YOU, BUT YOU JUST CAN'T BE HELPED. SO, WHY DON'T YOU AND THAT UGLY HAT RUN ALONG? YOUR **QUEEN** HAS NO NEED FOR--

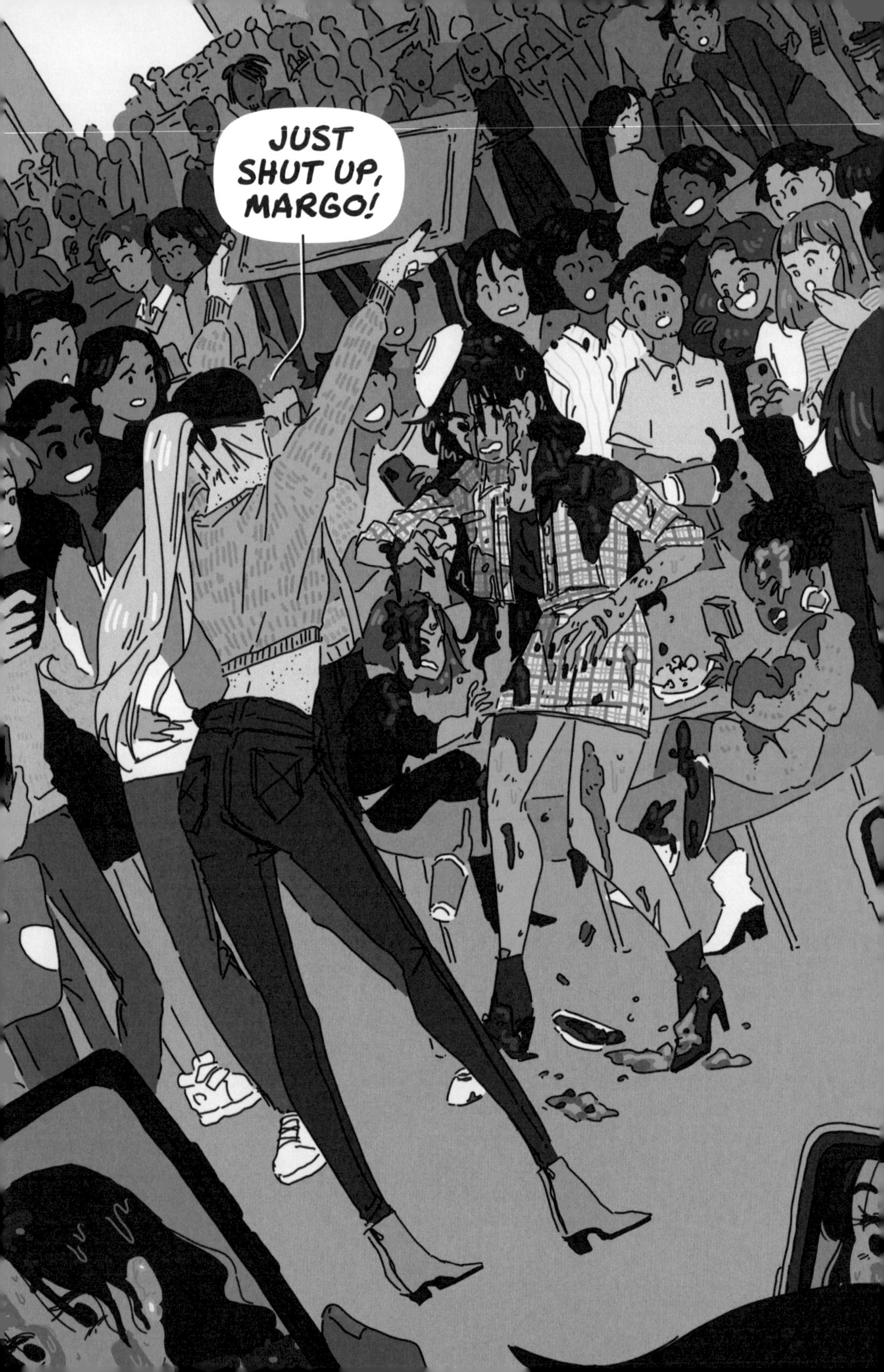
JUST SHUT UP, MARGO!

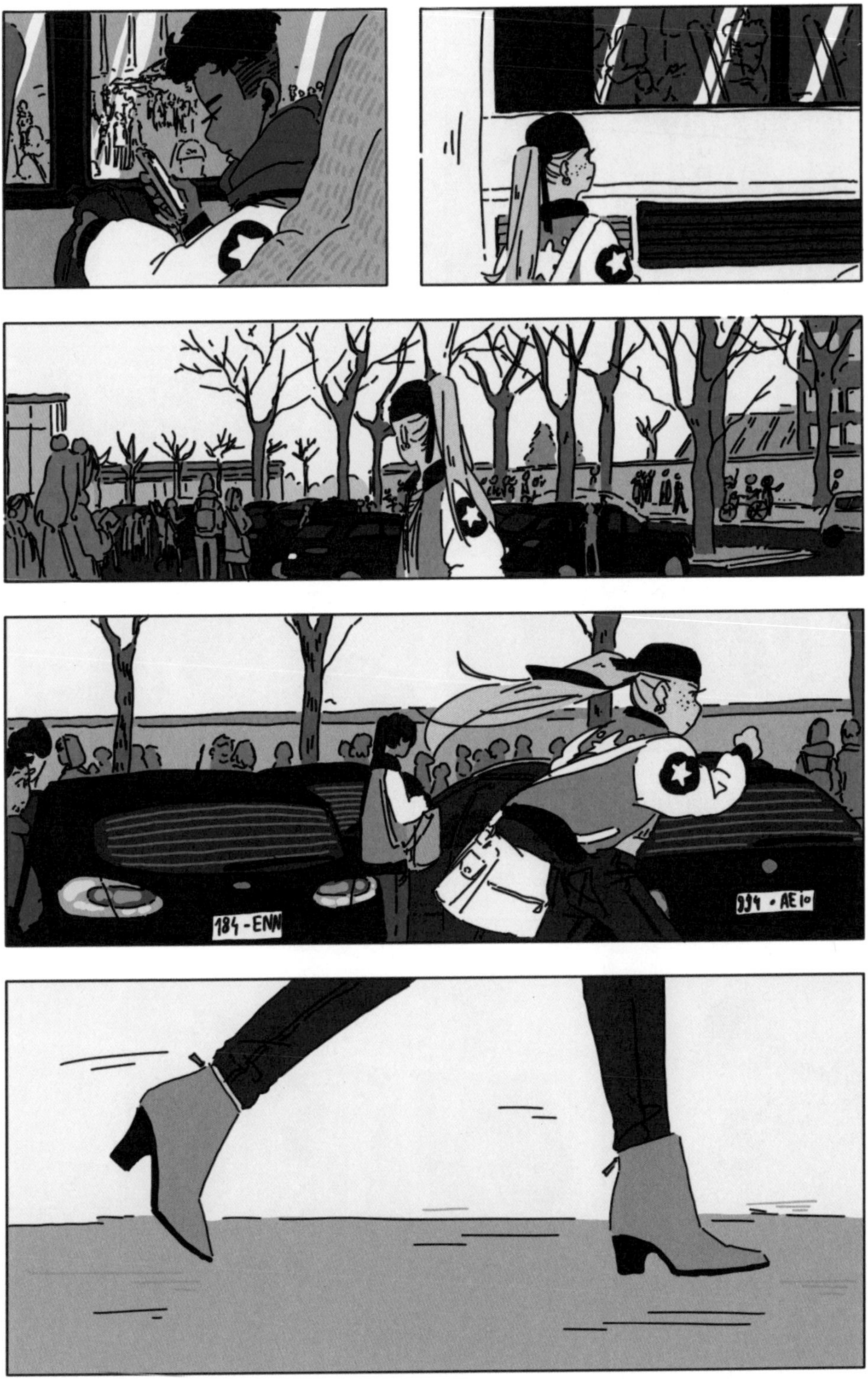
184-ENN

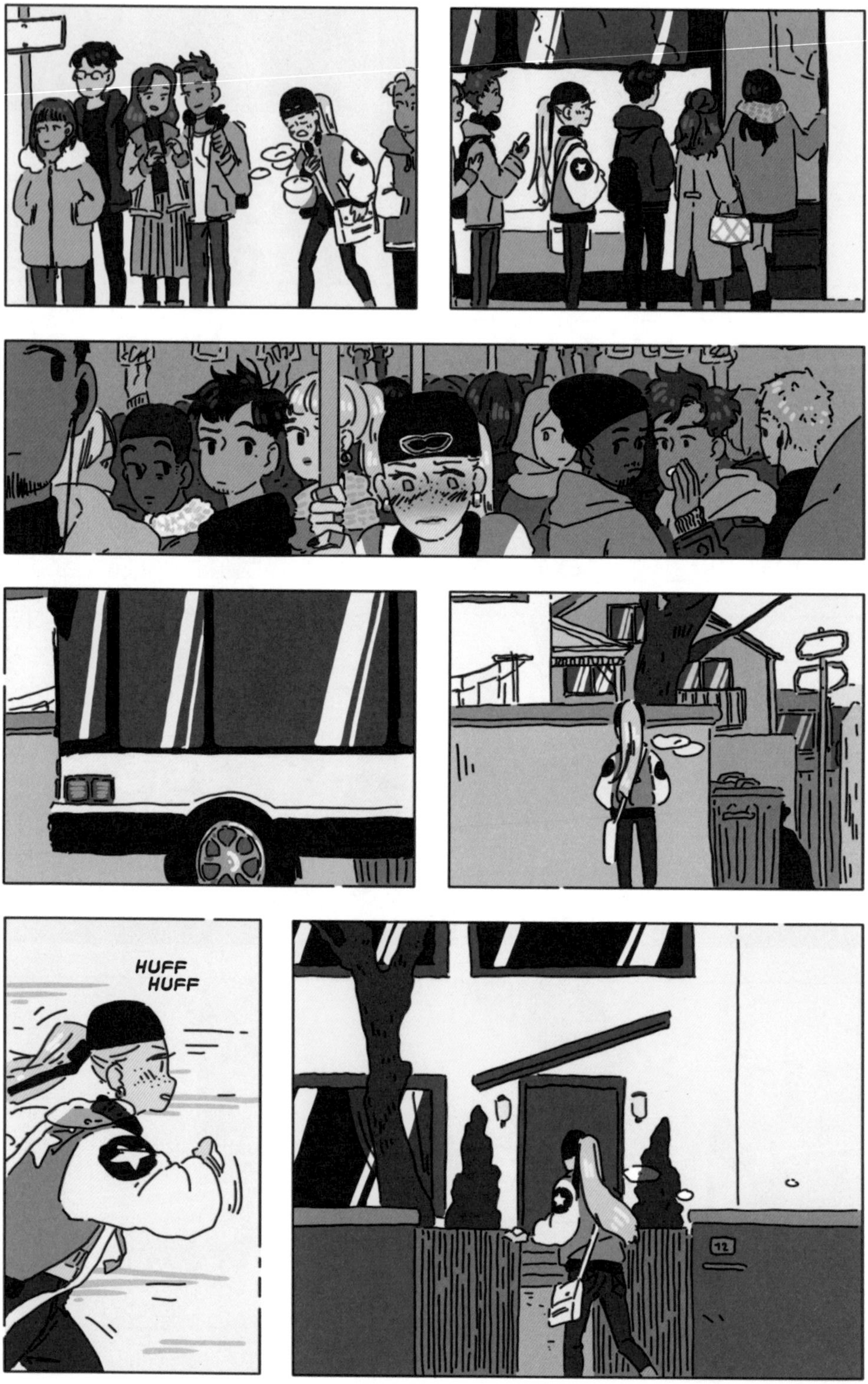
HUFF
HUFF

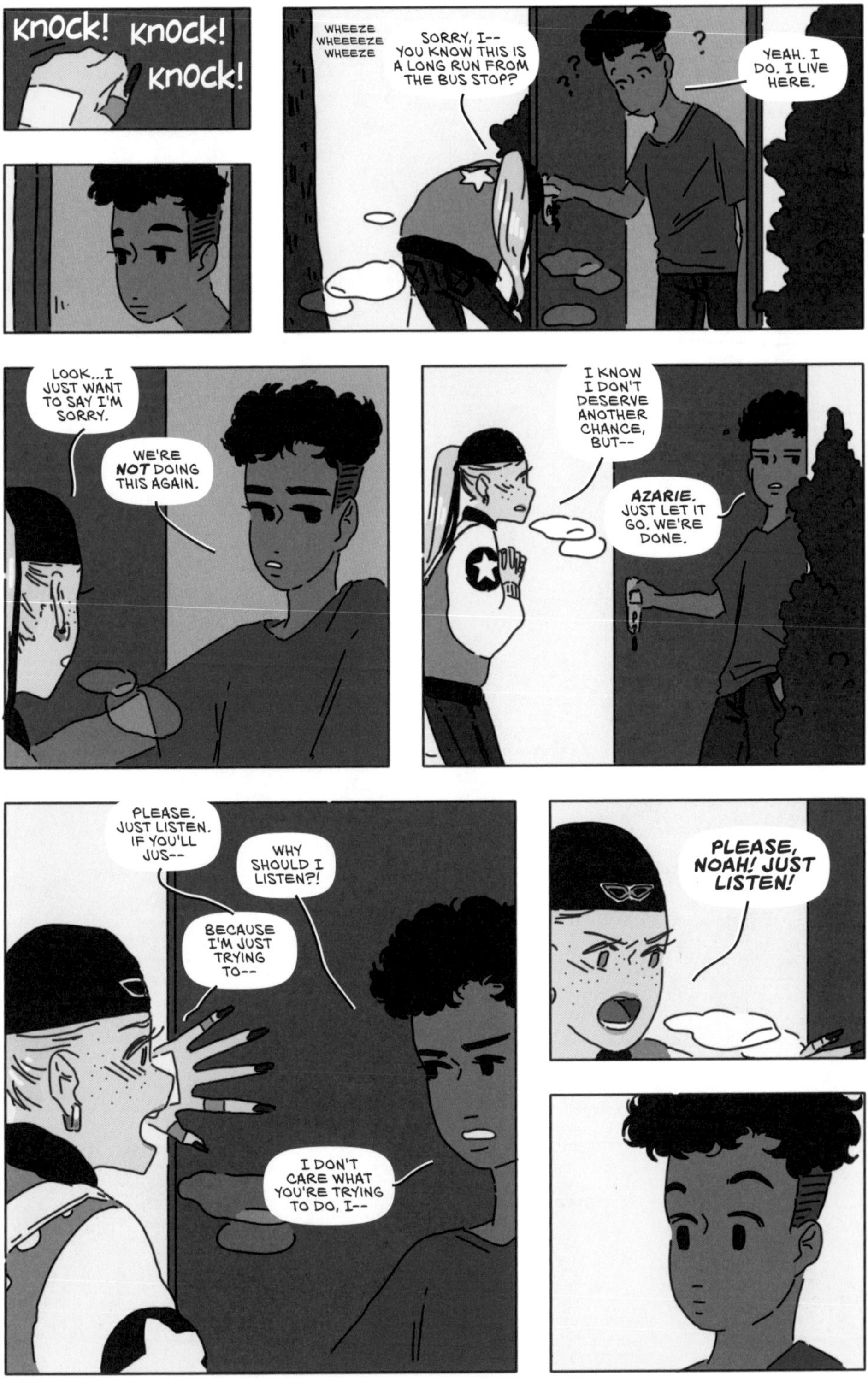
KNOCK! KNOCK! KNOCK!
WHEEZE WHEEEEZE WHEEZE
SORRY, I-- YOU KNOW THIS IS A LONG RUN FROM THE BUS STOP?
YEAH. I DO. I LIVE HERE.
LOOK...I JUST WANT TO SAY I'M SORRY.
WE'RE **NOT** DOING THIS AGAIN.
I KNOW I DON'T DESERVE ANOTHER CHANCE, BUT--
AZARIE. JUST LET IT GO. WE'RE DONE.
PLEASE. JUST LISTEN. IF YOU'LL JUS--
WHY SHOULD I LISTEN?!
BECAUSE I'M JUST TRYING TO--
I DON'T CARE WHAT YOU'RE TRYING TO DO, I--
PLEASE, NOAH! JUST LISTEN!

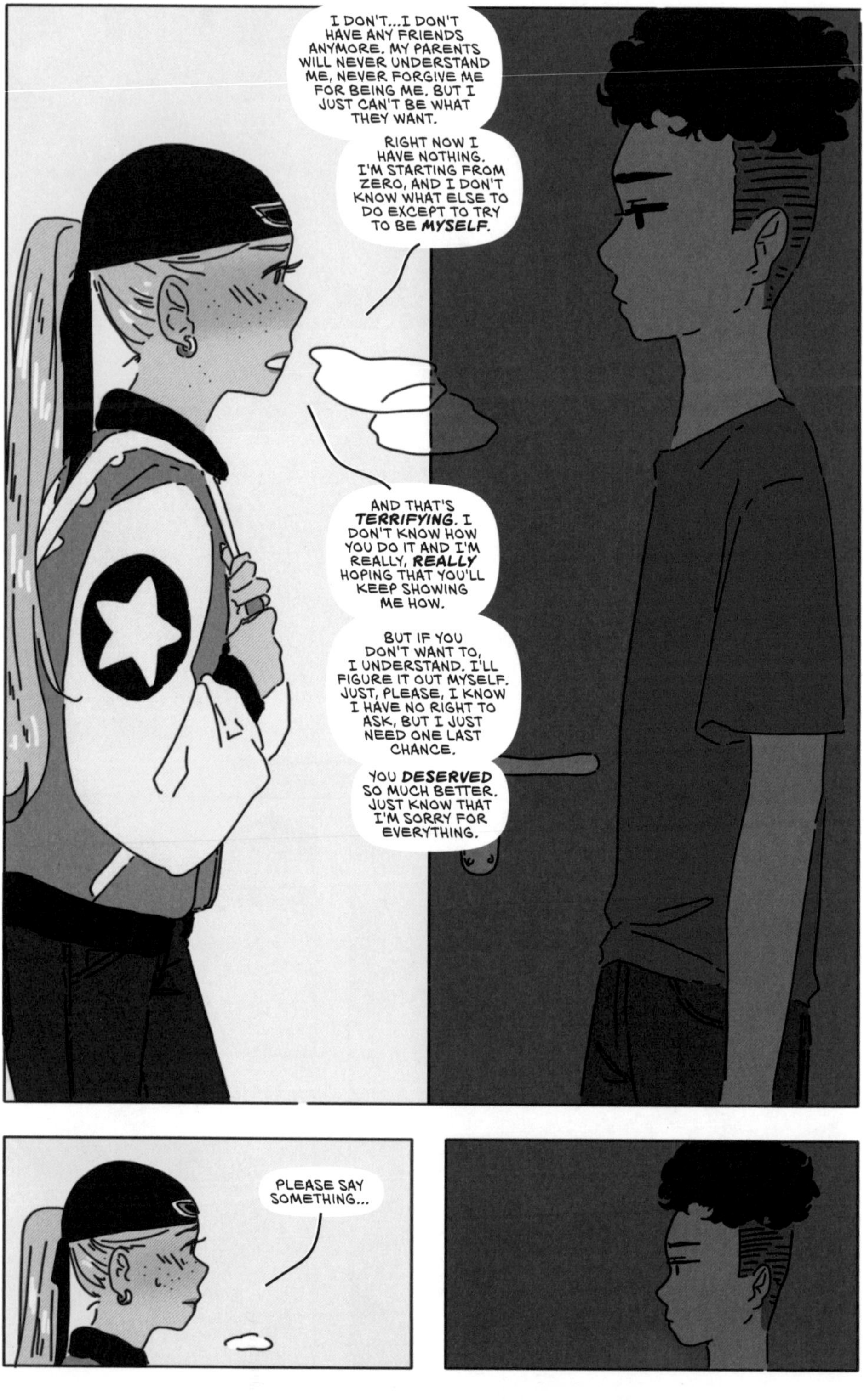
I DON'T...I DON'T HAVE ANY FRIENDS ANYMORE. MY PARENTS WILL NEVER UNDERSTAND ME, NEVER FORGIVE ME FOR BEING ME. BUT I JUST CAN'T BE WHAT THEY WANT.
RIGHT NOW I HAVE NOTHING. I'M STARTING FROM ZERO, AND I DON'T KNOW WHAT ELSE TO DO EXCEPT TO TRY TO BE MYSELF.
AND THAT'S TERRIFYING. I DON'T KNOW HOW YOU DO IT AND I'M REALLY, REALLY HOPING THAT YOU'LL KEEP SHOWING ME HOW.
BUT IF YOU DON'T WANT TO, I UNDERSTAND. I'LL FIGURE IT OUT MYSELF. JUST, PLEASE, I KNOW I HAVE NO RIGHT TO ASK, BUT I JUST NEED ONE LAST CHANCE.
YOU DESERVED SO MUCH BETTER. JUST KNOW THAT I'M SORRY FOR EVERYTHING.
PLEASE SAY SOMETHING...

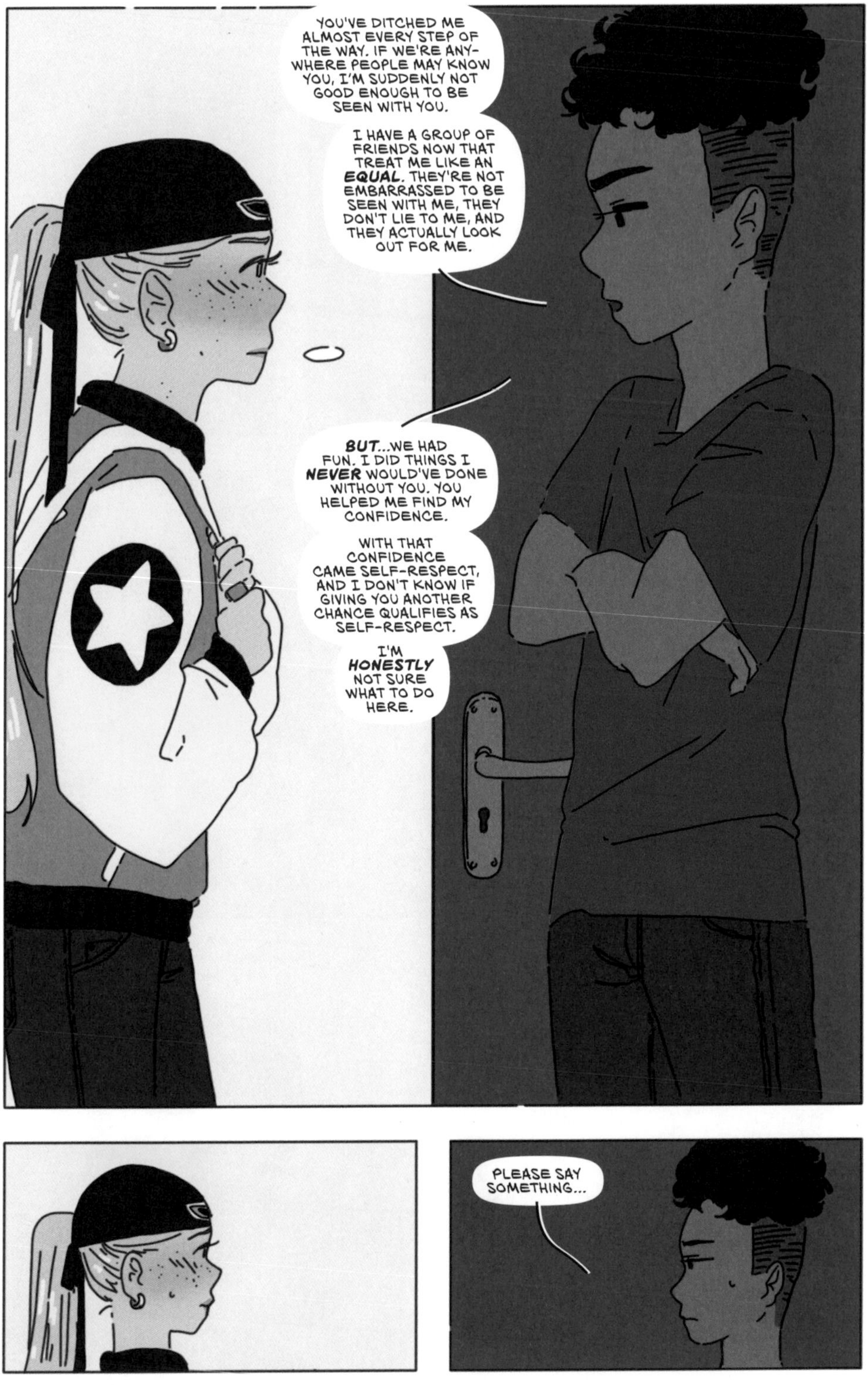
YOU'VE DITCHED ME ALMOST EVERY STEP OF THE WAY. IF WE'RE ANY-WHERE PEOPLE MAY KNOW YOU, I'M SUDDENLY NOT GOOD ENOUGH TO BE SEEN WITH YOU.
I HAVE A GROUP OF FRIENDS NOW THAT TREAT ME LIKE AN **EQUAL.** THEY'RE NOT EMBARRASSED TO BE SEEN WITH ME, THEY DON'T LIE TO ME, AND THEY ACTUALLY LOOK OUT FOR ME.
BUT...WE HAD FUN. I DID THINGS I **NEVER** WOULD'VE DONE WITHOUT YOU. YOU HELPED ME FIND MY CONFIDENCE.
WITH THAT CONFIDENCE CAME SELF-RESPECT, AND I DON'T KNOW IF GIVING YOU ANOTHER CHANCE QUALIFIES AS SELF-RESPECT.
I'M **HONESTLY** NOT SURE WHAT TO DO HERE.
PLEASE SAY SOMETHING...

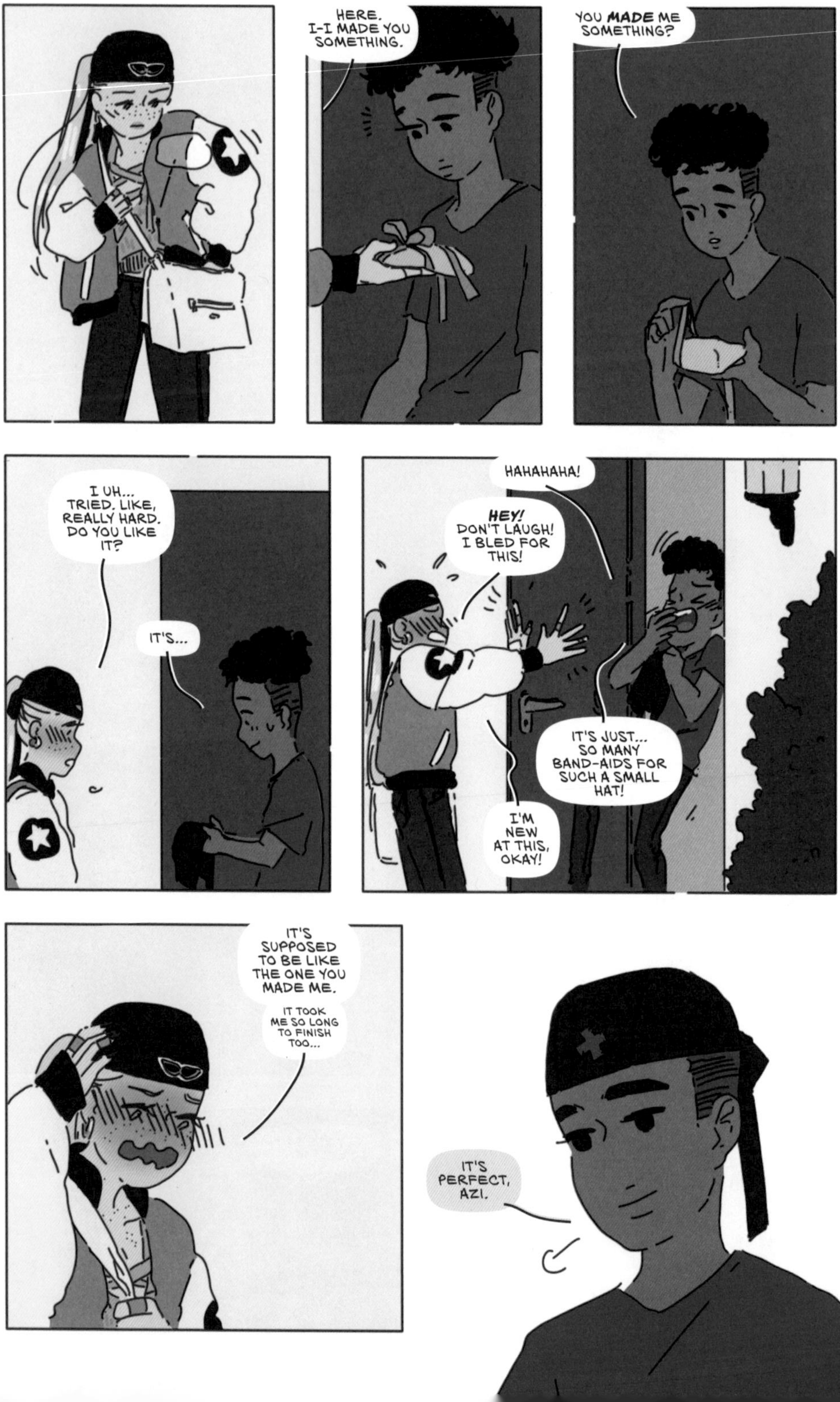
HERE. I-I MADE YOU SOMETHING.
YOU MADE ME SOMETHING?
I UH... TRIED. LIKE, REALLY HARD. DO YOU LIKE IT?
IT'S...
HAHAHAHA!
HEY! DON'T LAUGH! I BLED FOR THIS!
IT'S JUST... SO MANY BAND-AIDS FOR SUCH A SMALL HAT!
I'M NEW AT THIS, OKAY!
IT'S SUPPOSED TO BE LIKE THE ONE YOU MADE ME.
IT TOOK ME SO LONG TO FINISH TOO...
IT'S PERFECT, AZI.

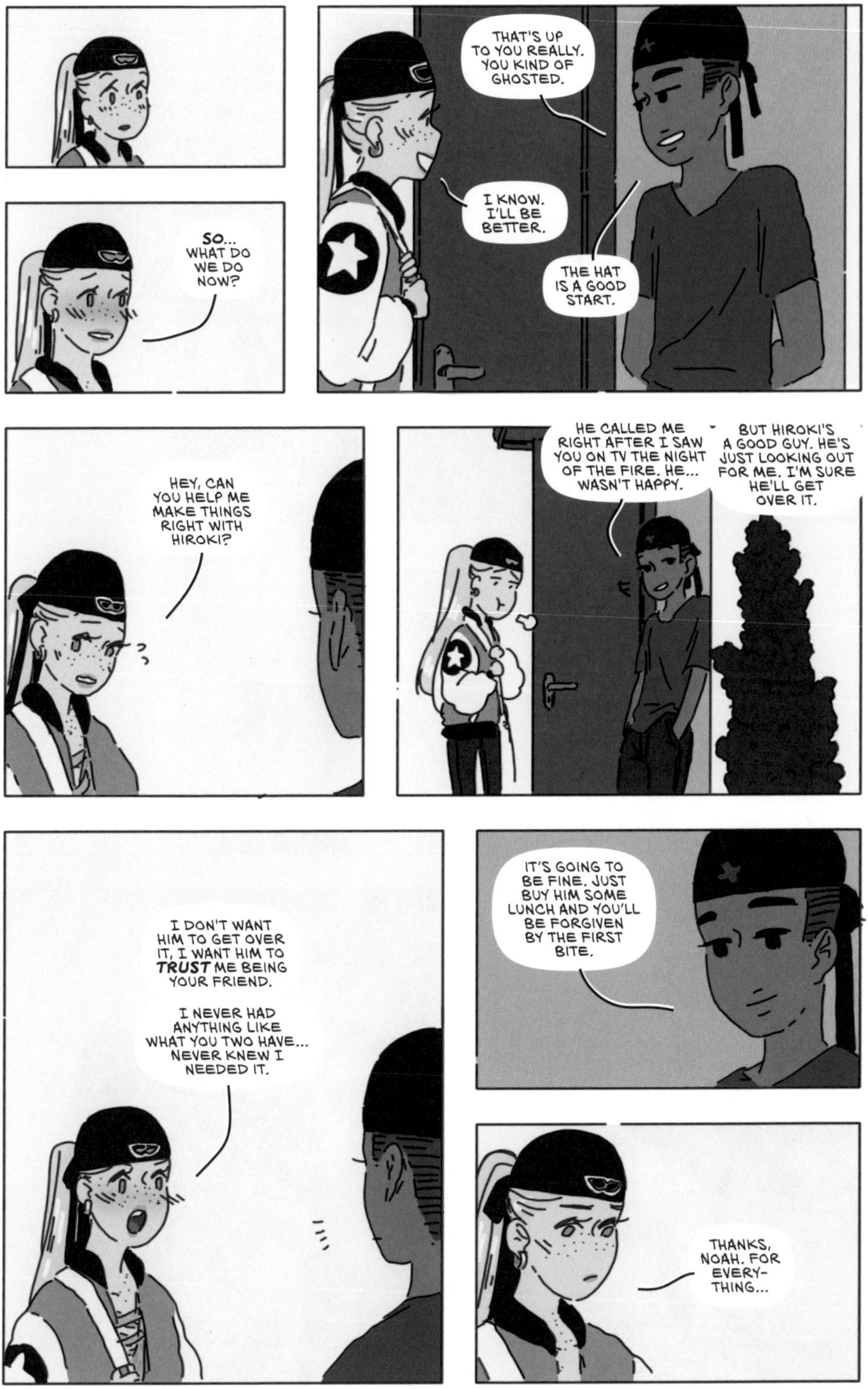

SO... WHAT DO WE DO NOW?
THAT'S UP TO YOU REALLY. YOU KIND OF GHOSTED.
I KNOW. I'LL BE BETTER.
THE HAT IS A GOOD START.
HEY, CAN YOU HELP ME MAKE THINGS RIGHT WITH HIROKI?
HE CALLED ME RIGHT AFTER I SAW YOU ON TV THE NIGHT OF THE FIRE. HE... WASN'T HAPPY.
BUT HIROKI'S A GOOD GUY. HE'S JUST LOOKING OUT FOR ME. I'M SURE HE'LL GET OVER IT.
I DON'T WANT HIM TO GET OVER IT, I WANT HIM TO TRUST ME BEING YOUR FRIEND.
I NEVER HAD ANYTHING LIKE WHAT YOU TWO HAVE... NEVER KNEW I NEEDED IT.
IT'S GOING TO BE FINE. JUST BUY HIM SOME LUNCH AND YOU'LL BE FORGIVEN BY THE FIRST BITE.
THANKS, NOAH. FOR EVERY-THING...

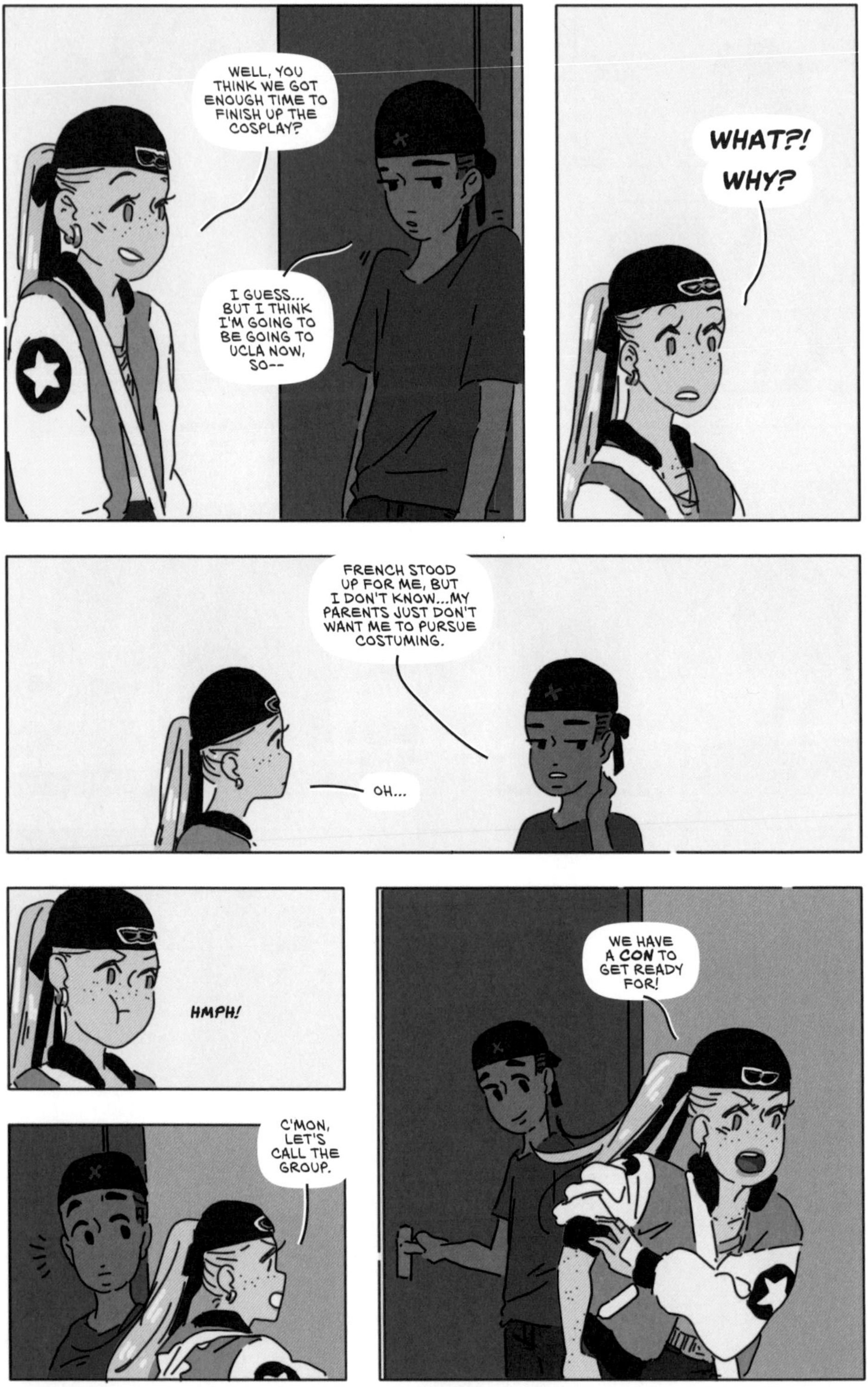
WELL, YOU THINK WE GOT ENOUGH TIME TO FINISH UP THE COSPLAY?
I GUESS... BUT I THINK I'M GOING TO BE GOING TO UCLA NOW, SO--
WHAT?! WHY?
FRENCH STOOD UP FOR ME, BUT I DON'T KNOW...MY PARENTS JUST DON'T WANT ME TO PURSUE COSTUMING.
OH...
HMPH!
C'MON, LET'S CALL THE GROUP.
WE HAVE A CON TO GET READY FOR!

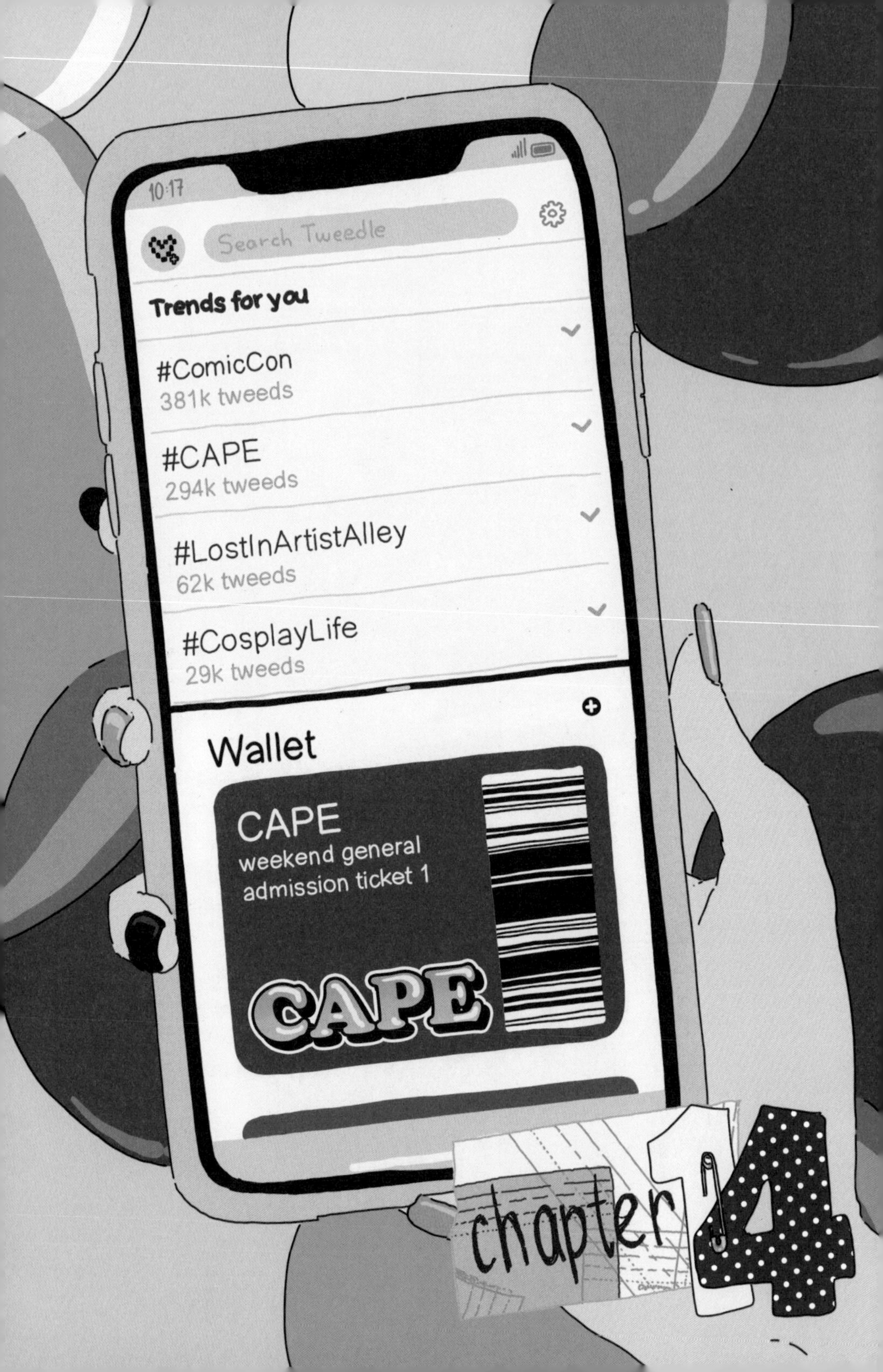
10:17
Search Tweedle
Trends for you
#ComicCon
381k tweeds
#CAPE
294k tweeds
#LostInArtistAlley
62k tweeds
#CosplayLife
29k tweeds
Wallet
CAPE
weekend general
admission ticket 1
CAPE
chapter 14

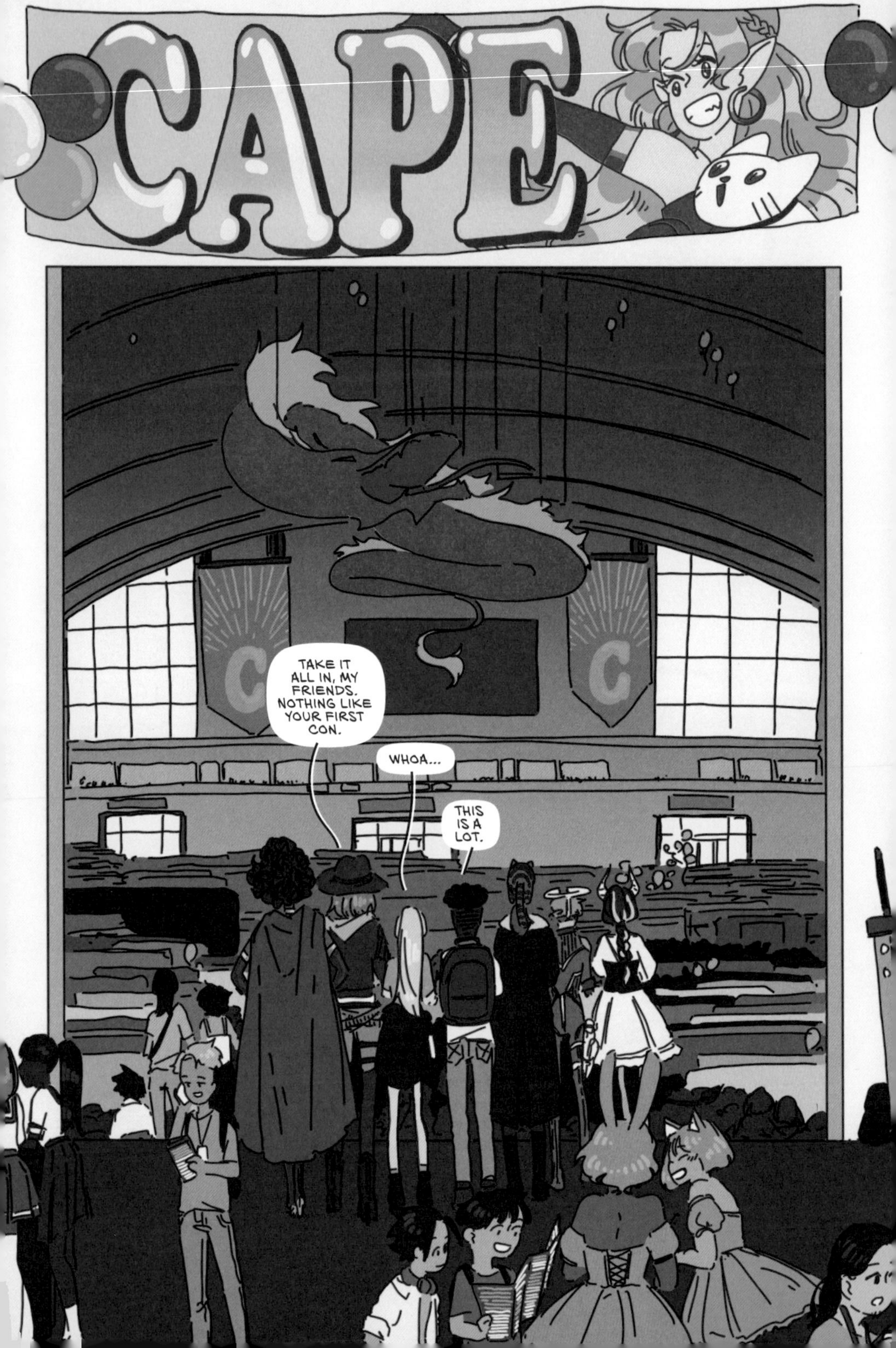
CAPE
TAKE IT ALL IN, MY FRIENDS. NOTHING LIKE YOUR FIRST CON.
WHOA...
THIS IS A LOT.

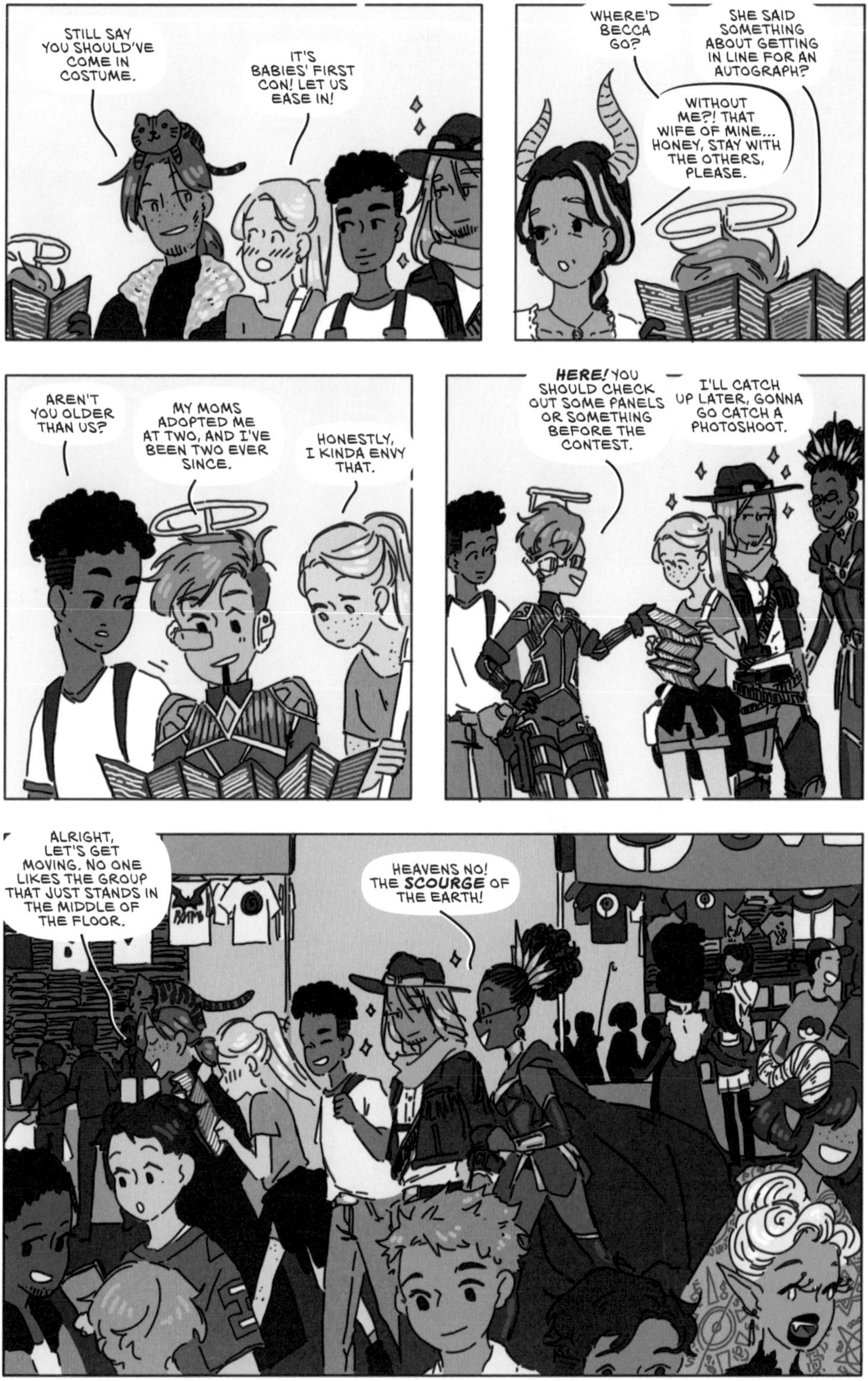
STILL SAY YOU SHOULD'VE COME IN COSTUME.
IT'S BABIES' FIRST CON! LET US EASE IN!
WHERE'D BECCA GO?
SHE SAID SOMETHING ABOUT GETTING IN LINE FOR AN AUTOGRAPH?
WITHOUT ME?! THAT WIFE OF MINE... HONEY, STAY WITH THE OTHERS, PLEASE.
AREN'T YOU OLDER THAN US?
MY MOMS ADOPTED ME AT TWO, AND I'VE BEEN TWO EVER SINCE.
HONESTLY, I KINDA ENVY THAT.
HERE! YOU SHOULD CHECK OUT SOME PANELS OR SOMETHING BEFORE THE CONTEST.
I'LL CATCH UP LATER, GONNA GO CATCH A PHOTOSHOOT.
ALRIGHT, LET'S GET MOVING. NO ONE LIKES THE GROUP THAT JUST STANDS IN THE MIDDLE OF THE FLOOR.
HEAVENS NO! THE SCOURGE OF THE EARTH!

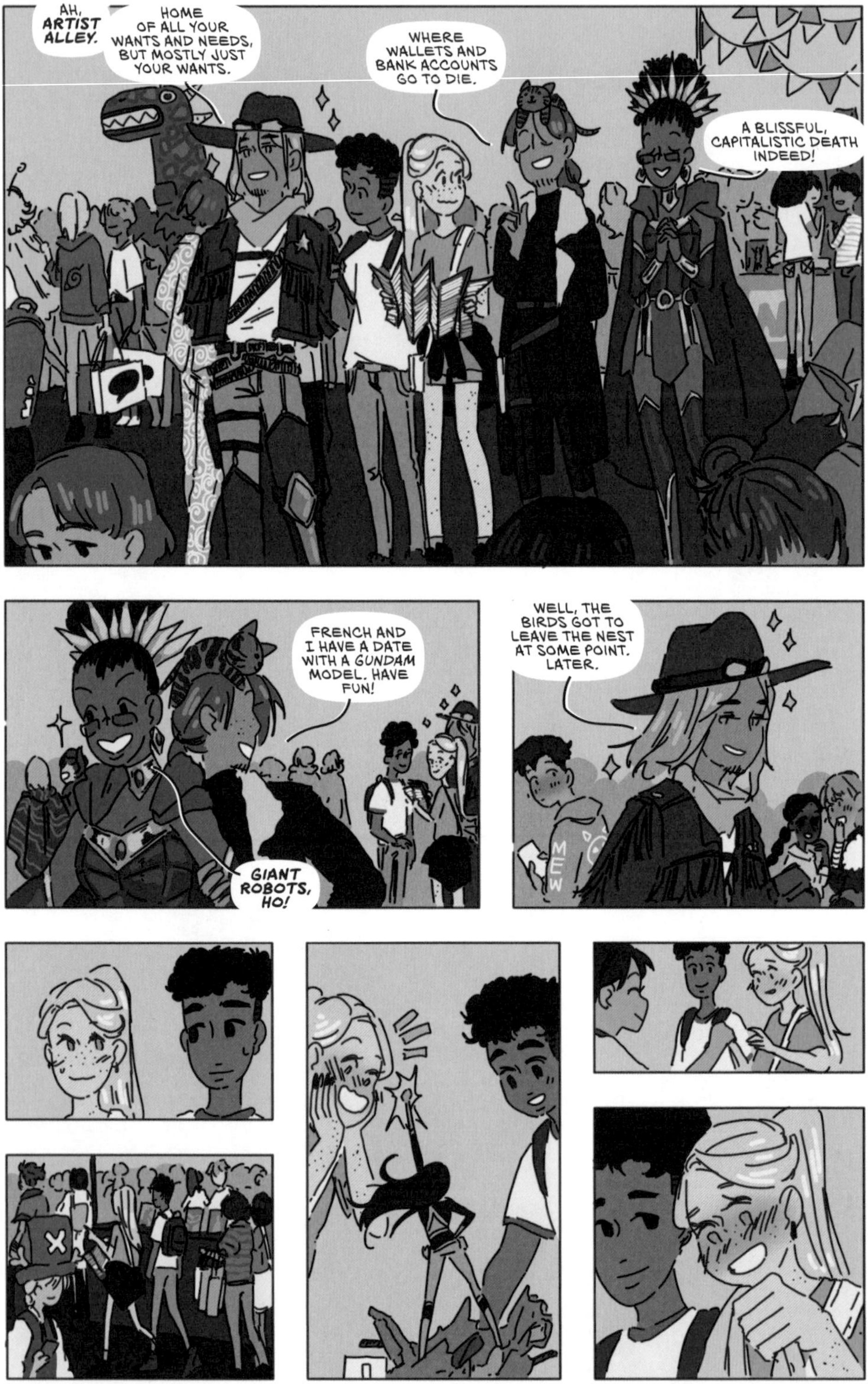
AH, ARTIST ALLEY.
HOME OF ALL YOUR WANTS AND NEEDS, BUT MOSTLY JUST YOUR WANTS.
WHERE WALLETS AND BANK ACCOUNTS GO TO DIE.
A BLISSFUL, CAPITALISTIC DEATH INDEED!
FRENCH AND I HAVE A DATE WITH A GUNDAM MODEL. HAVE FUN!
GIANT ROBOTS, HO!
WELL, THE BIRDS GOT TO LEAVE THE NEST AT SOME POINT. LATER.
MEW

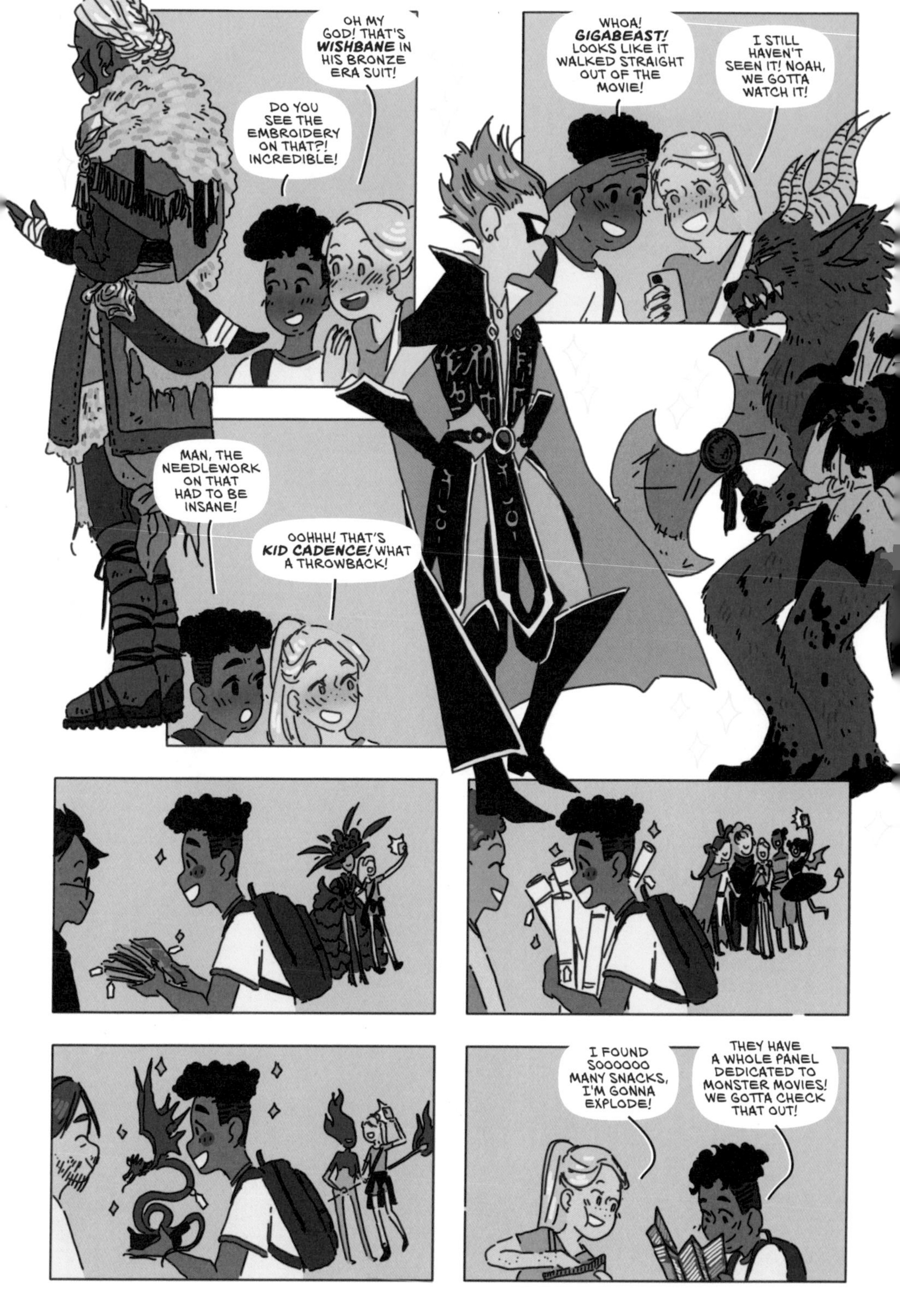
OH MY GOD! THAT'S **WISHBANE** IN HIS BRONZE ERA SUIT!
DO YOU SEE THE EMBROIDERY ON THAT?! INCREDIBLE!
WHOA! **GIGABEAST!** LOOKS LIKE IT WALKED STRAIGHT OUT OF THE MOVIE!
I STILL HAVEN'T SEEN IT! NOAH, WE GOTTA WATCH IT!
MAN, THE NEEDLEWORK ON THAT HAD TO BE INSANE!
OOHHH! THAT'S **KID CADENCE!** WHAT A THROWBACK!
I FOUND SOOOOOO MANY SNACKS, I'M GONNA EXPLODE!
THEY HAVE A WHOLE PANEL DEDICATED TO MONSTER MOVIES! WE GOTTA CHECK THAT OUT!

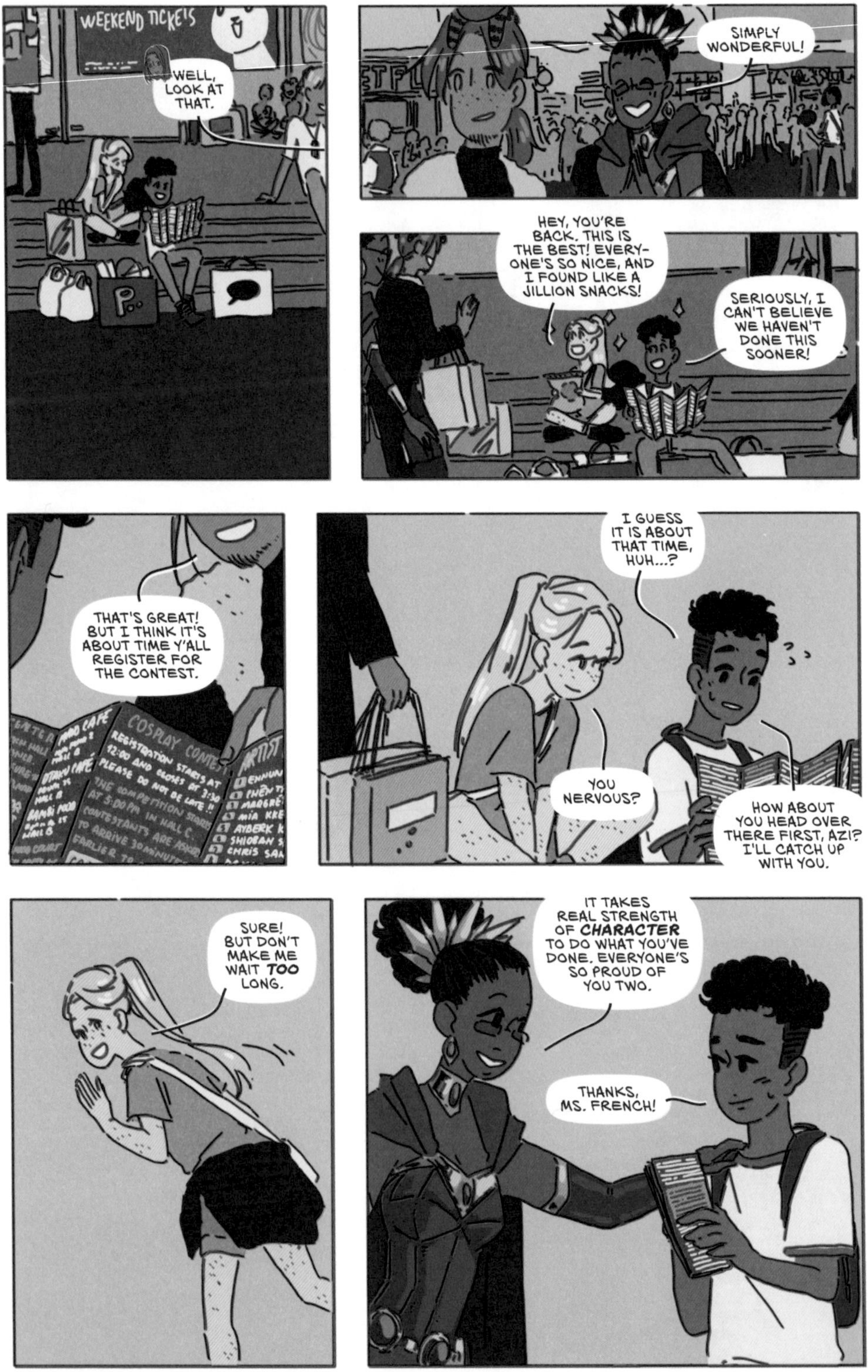
WELL, LOOK AT THAT.
SIMPLY WONDERFUL!
HEY, YOU'RE BACK. THIS IS THE BEST! EVERYONE'S SO NICE, AND I FOUND LIKE A JILLION SNACKS!
SERIOUSLY, I CAN'T BELIEVE WE HAVEN'T DONE THIS SOONER!
THAT'S GREAT! BUT I THINK IT'S ABOUT TIME Y'ALL REGISTER FOR THE CONTEST.
I GUESS IT IS ABOUT THAT TIME, HUH...?
YOU NERVOUS?
HOW ABOUT YOU HEAD OVER THERE FIRST, AZI? I'LL CATCH UP WITH YOU.
SURE! BUT DON'T MAKE ME WAIT **TOO** LONG.
IT TAKES REAL STRENGTH OF **CHARACTER** TO DO WHAT YOU'VE DONE. EVERYONE'S SO PROUD OF YOU TWO.
THANKS, MS. FRENCH!

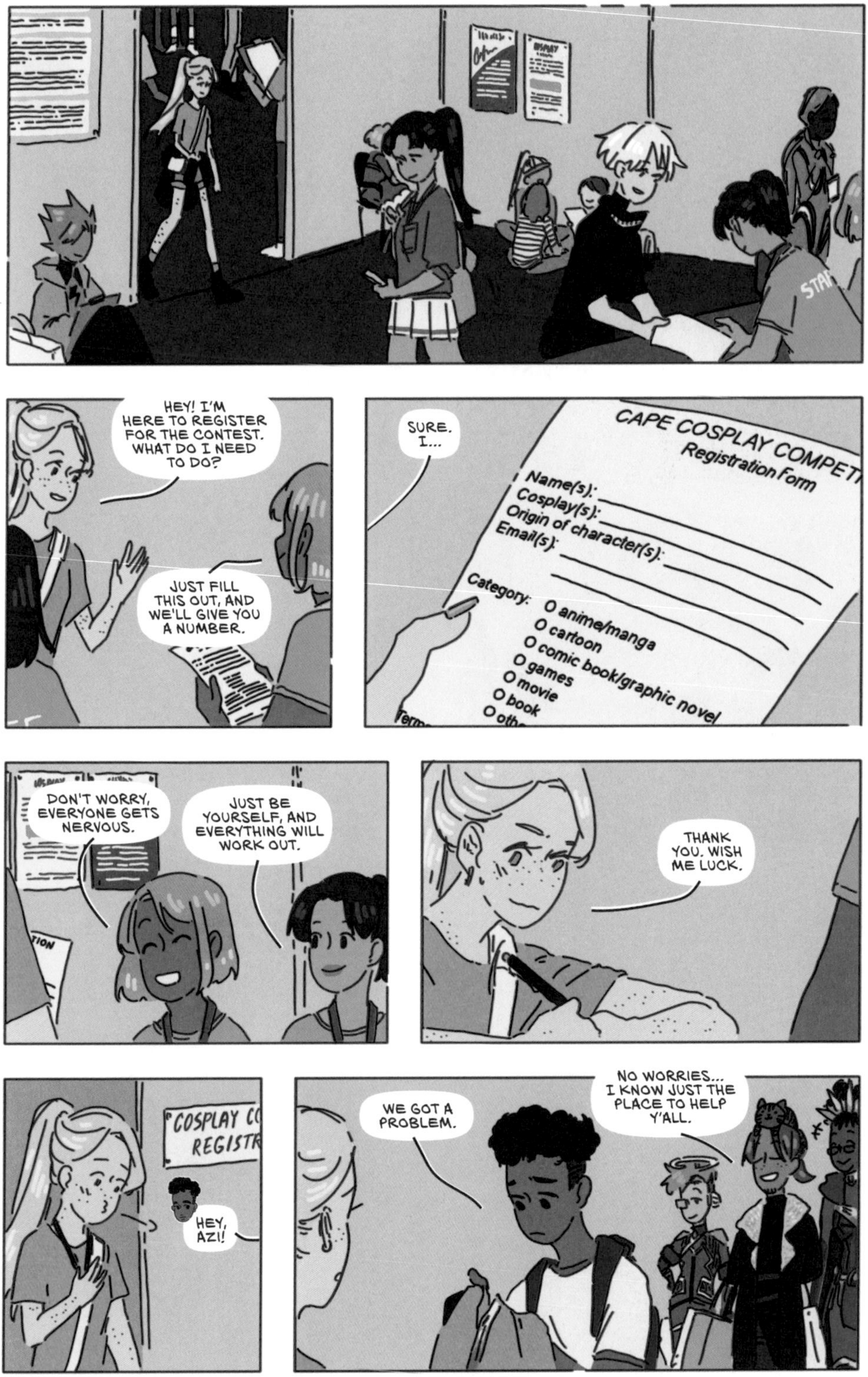

HEY! I'M HERE TO REGISTER FOR THE CONTEST. WHAT DO I NEED TO DO?
JUST FILL THIS OUT, AND WE'LL GIVE YOU A NUMBER.
SURE. I...
CAPE COSPLAY COMPET
Registration form
Name(s):
Cosplay(s):
Origin of character(s):
Email(s):
Category:
O anime/manga
O cartoon
O comic book/graphic novel
O games
O movie
O book
DON'T WORRY, EVERYONE GETS NERVOUS.
JUST BE YOURSELF, AND EVERYTHING WILL WORK OUT.
THANK YOU. WISH ME LUCK.
COSPLAY CO
REGISTR
HEY, AZI!
WE GOT A PROBLEM.
NO WORRIES... I KNOW JUST THE PLACE TO HELP Y'ALL.

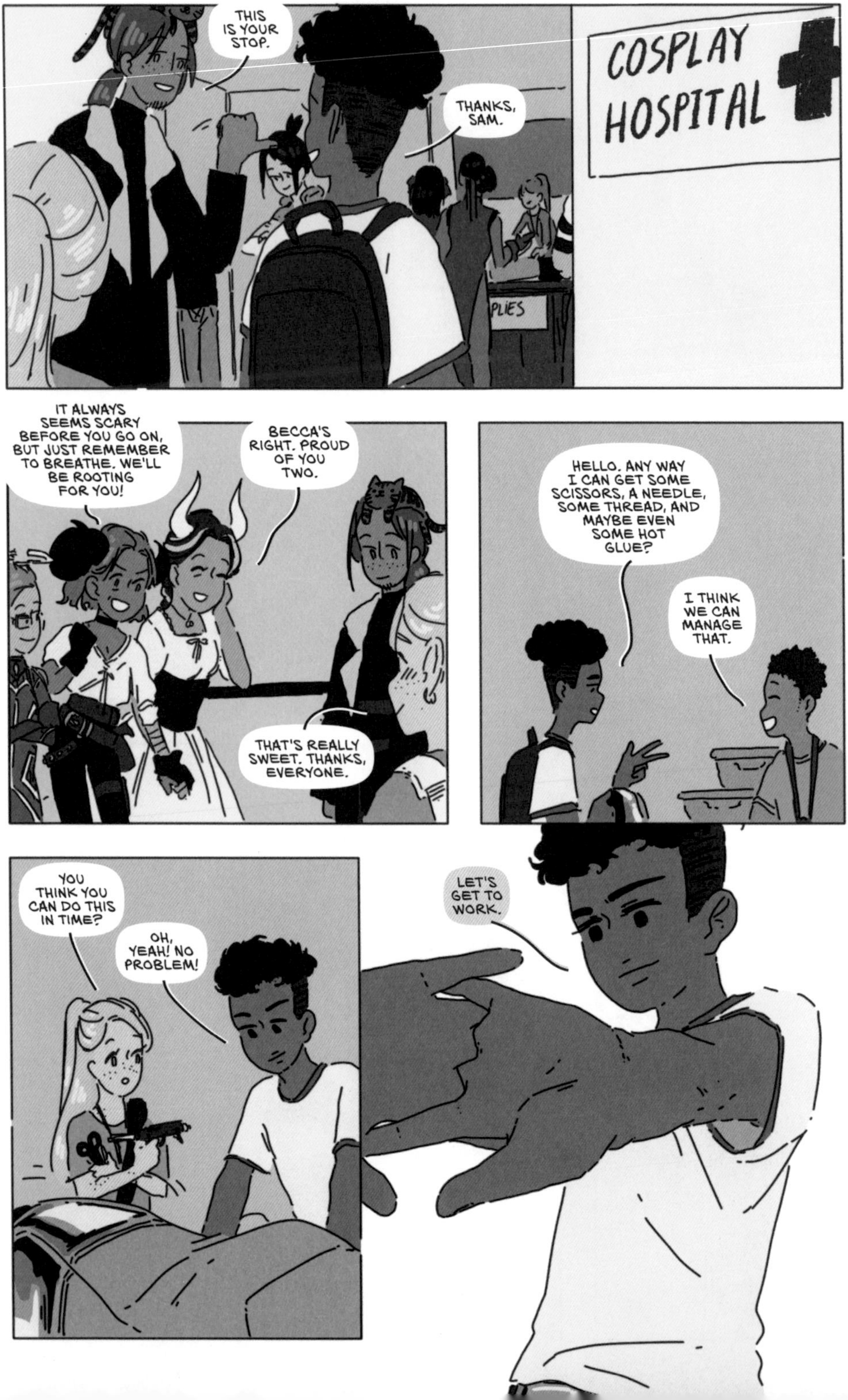
THIS IS YOUR STOP.
THANKS, SAM.
COSPLAY HOSPITAL
PLIES
IT ALWAYS SEEMS SCARY BEFORE YOU GO ON, BUT JUST REMEMBER TO BREATHE. WE'LL BE ROOTING FOR YOU!
BECCA'S RIGHT. PROUD OF YOU TWO.
THAT'S REALLY SWEET. THANKS, EVERYONE.
HELLO. ANY WAY I CAN GET SOME SCISSORS, A NEEDLE, SOME THREAD, AND MAYBE EVEN SOME HOT GLUE?
I THINK WE CAN MANAGE THAT.
YOU THINK YOU CAN DO THIS IN TIME?
OH, YEAH! NO PROBLEM!
LET'S GET TO WORK.

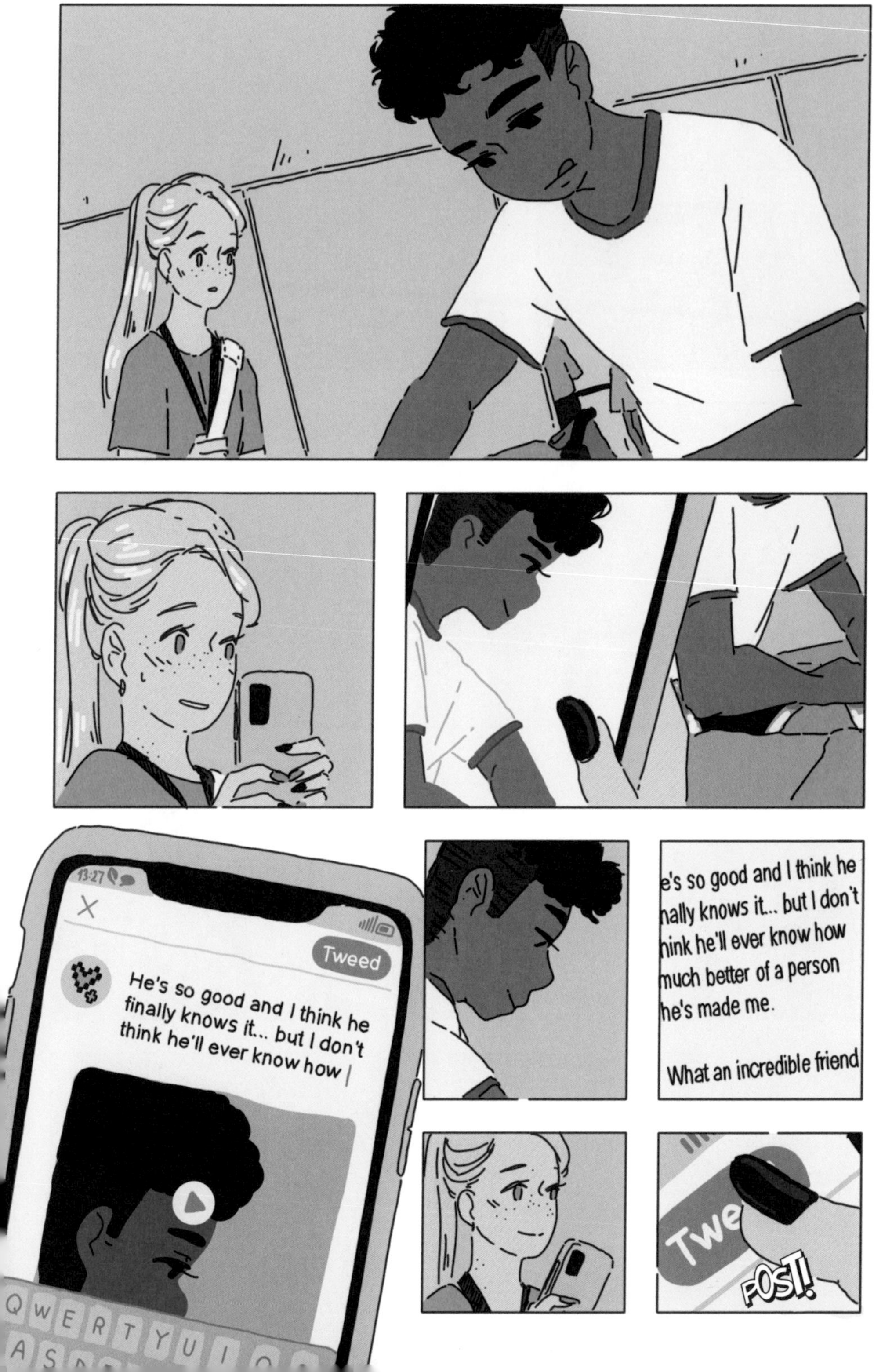
13:27
Tweed
He's so good and I think he finally knows it... but I don't think he'll ever know how
e's so good and I think he
nally knows it... but I don't
hink he'll ever know how
much better of a person
he's made me.
What an incredible friend
Twe
POST!

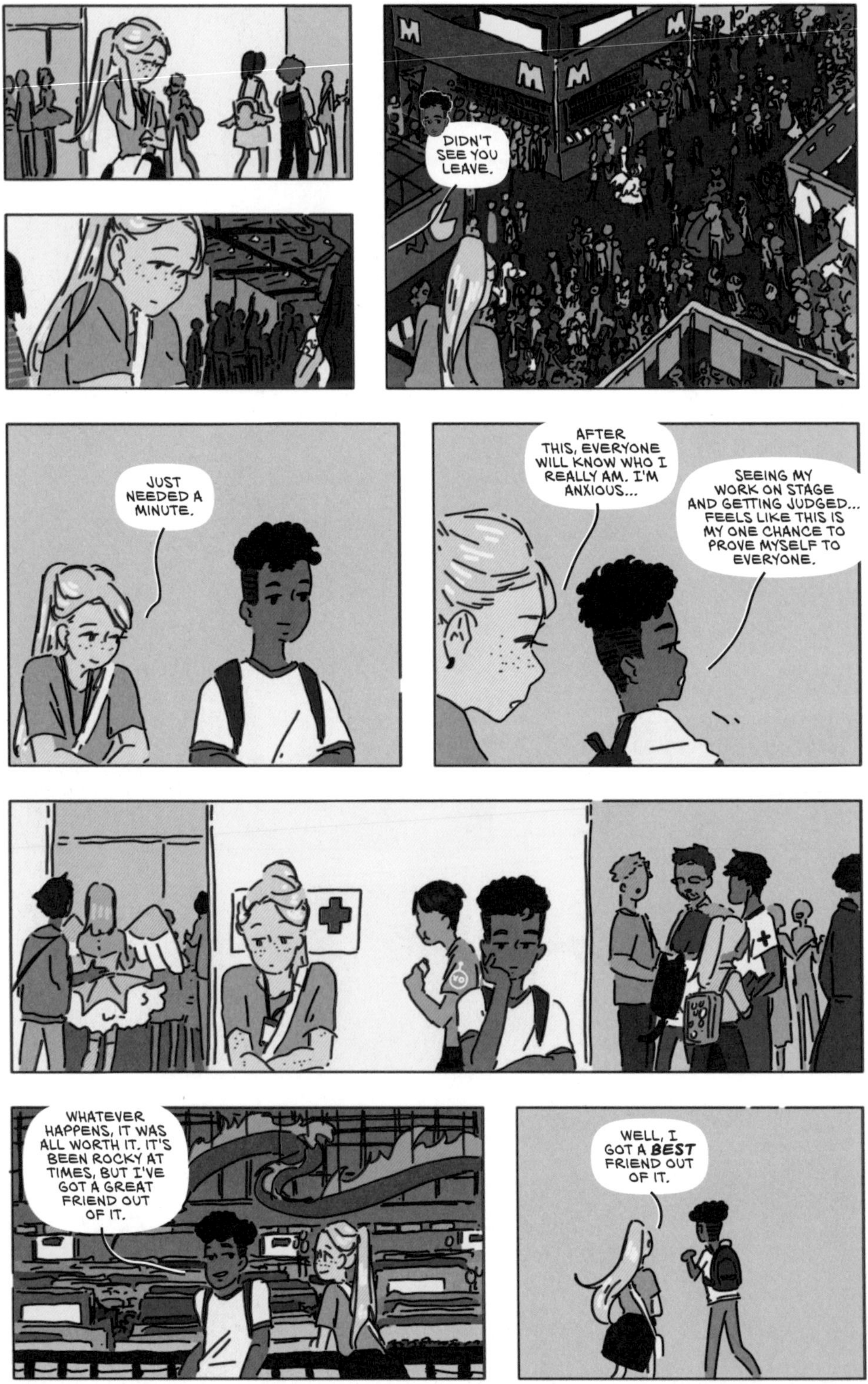
DIDN'T SEE YOU LEAVE.
JUST NEEDED A MINUTE.
AFTER THIS, EVERYONE WILL KNOW WHO I REALLY AM. I'M ANXIOUS...
SEEING MY WORK ON STAGE AND GETTING JUDGED... FEELS LIKE THIS IS MY ONE CHANCE TO PROVE MYSELF TO EVERYONE.
WHATEVER HAPPENS, IT WAS ALL WORTH IT. IT'S BEEN ROCKY AT TIMES, BUT I'VE GOT A GREAT FRIEND OUT OF IT.
WELL, I GOT A BEST FRIEND OUT OF IT.

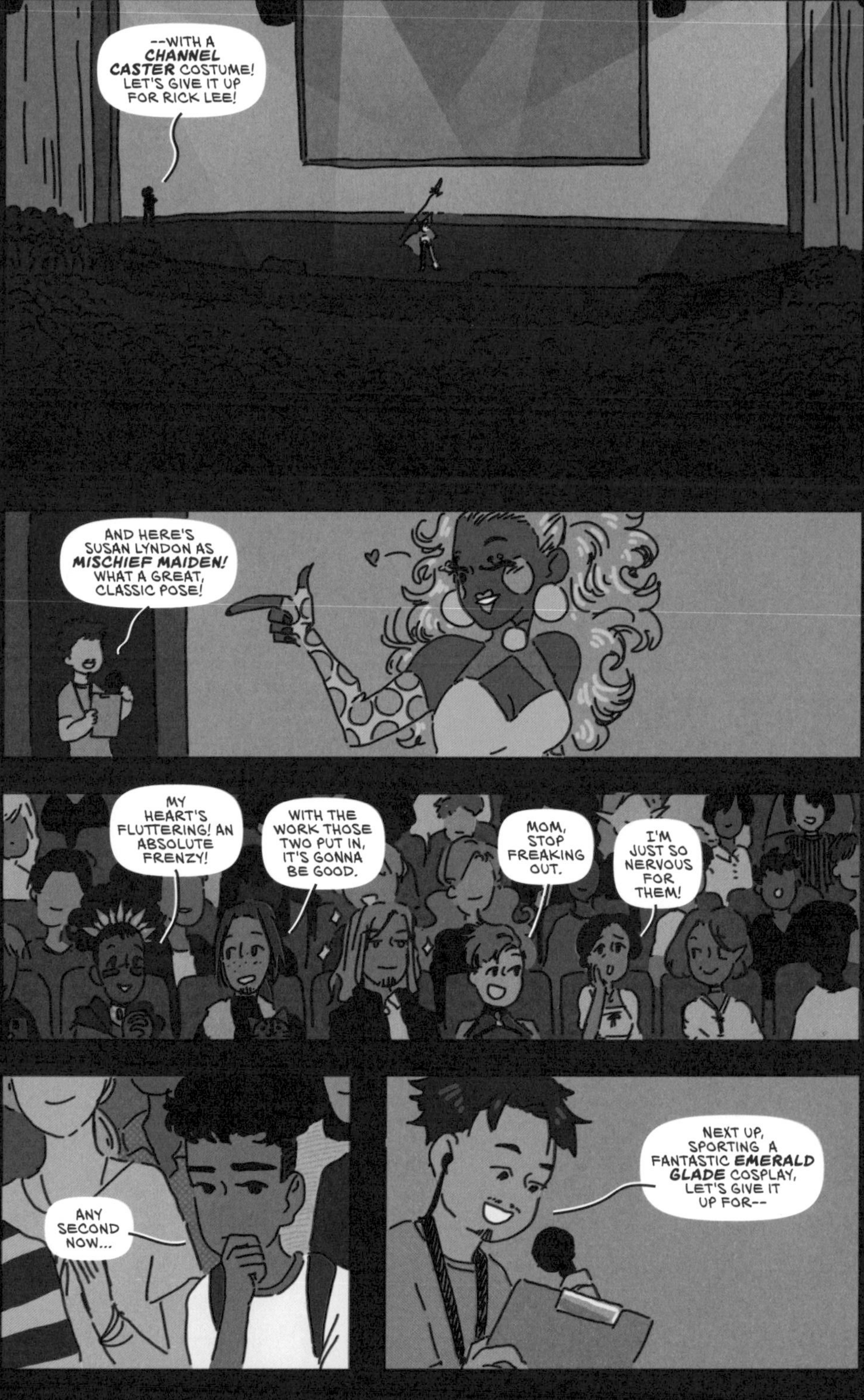

--WITH A **CHANNEL CASTER** COSTUME! LET'S GIVE IT UP FOR RICK LEE!
AND HERE'S SUSAN LYNDON AS ***MISCHIEF MAIDEN!*** WHAT A GREAT, CLASSIC POSE!
MY HEART'S FLUTTERING! AN ABSOLUTE FRENZY!
WITH THE WORK THOSE TWO PUT IN, IT'S GONNA BE GOOD.
MOM, STOP FREAKING OUT.
I'M JUST SO NERVOUS FOR THEM!
ANY SECOND NOW...
NEXT UP, SPORTING A FANTASTIC **EMERALD GLADE** COSPLAY, LET'S GIVE IT UP FOR--

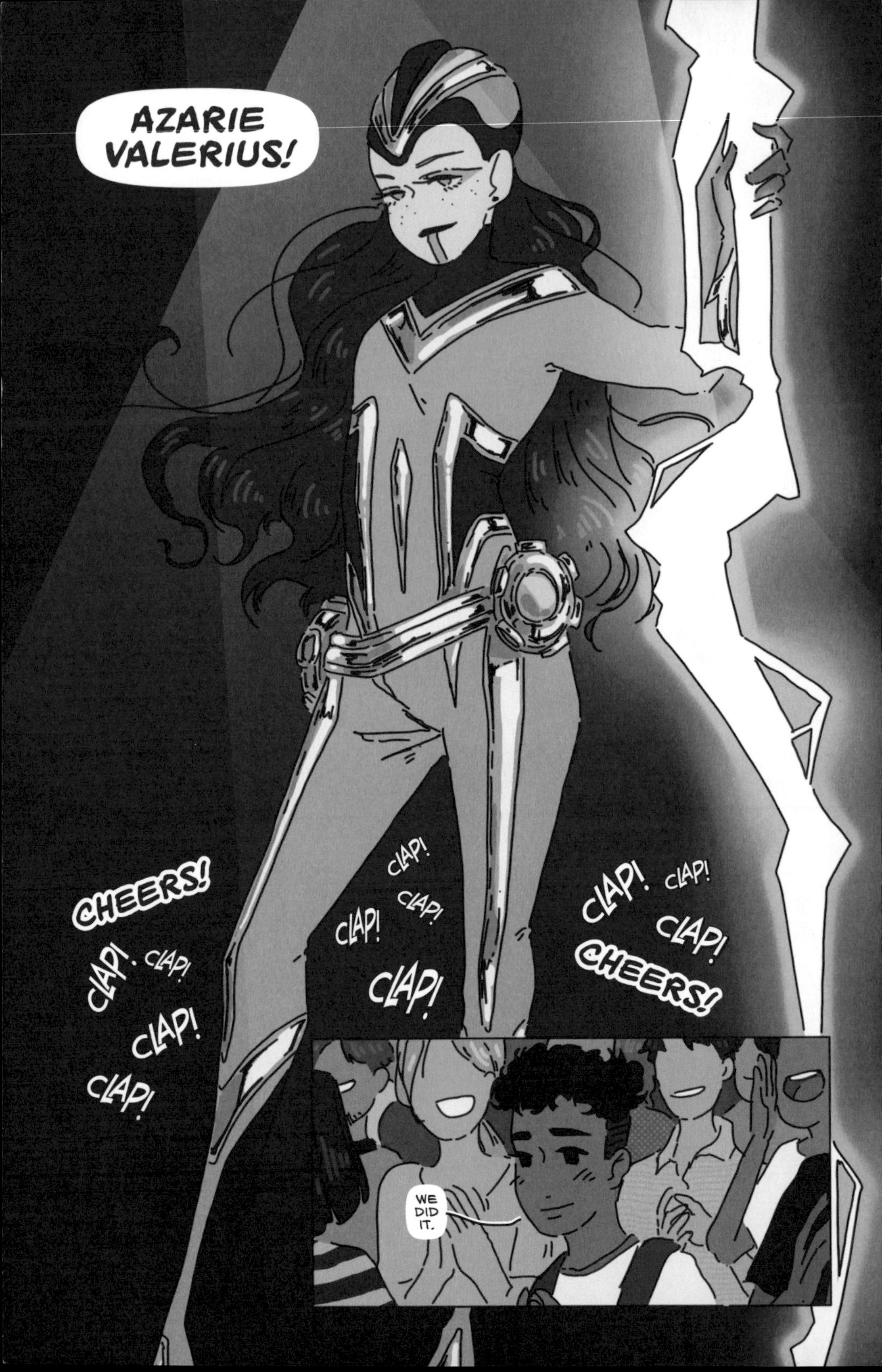
AZARIE VALERIUS!
CHEERS!
CLAP! CLAP!
CLAP!
CLAP!
CLAP!
CLAP!
CLAP!
CLAP!
CLAP! CLAP!
CLAP!
CHEERS!
WE DID IT.

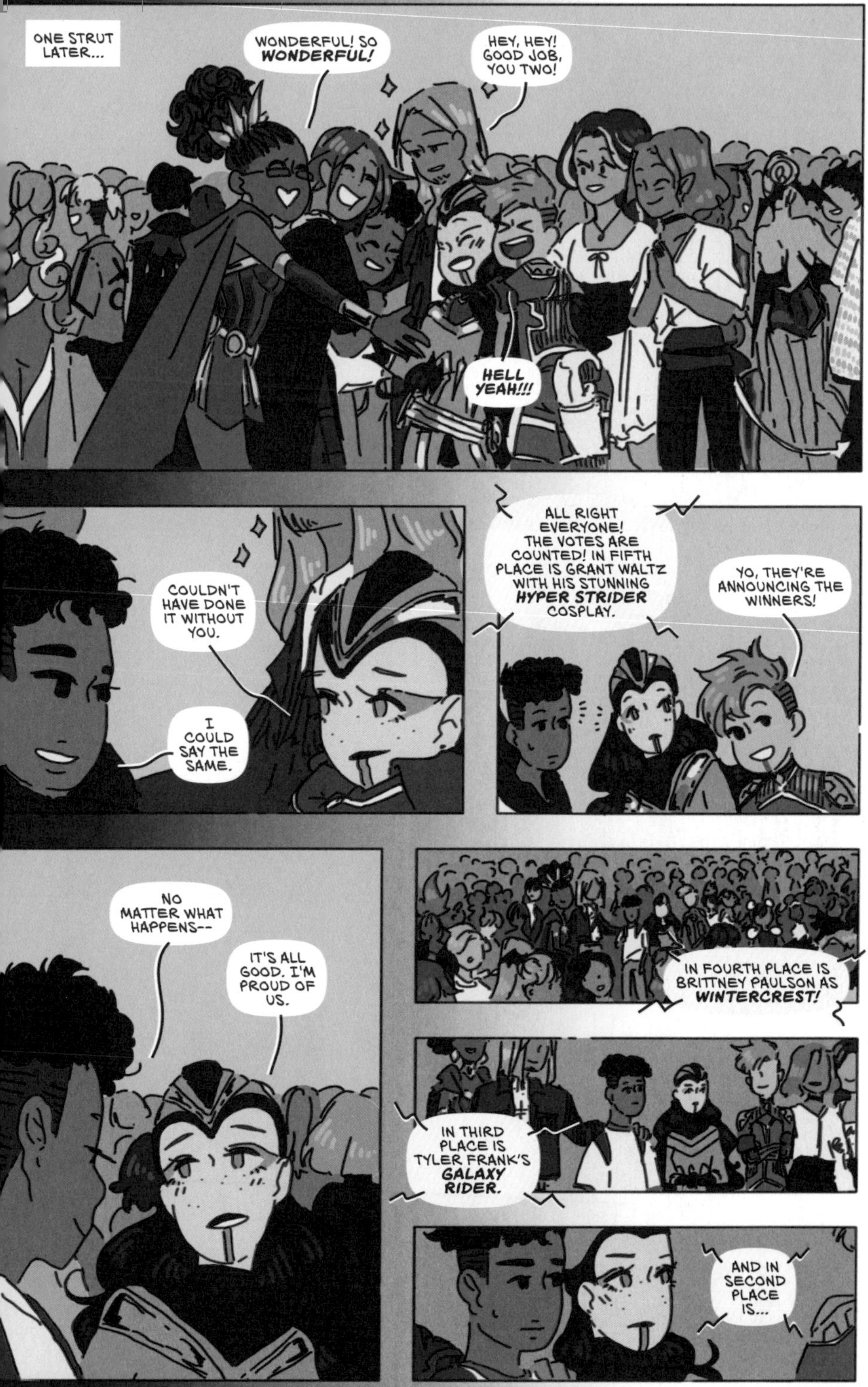
ONE STRUT LATER...
WONDERFUL! SO WONDERFUL!
HEY, HEY! GOOD JOB, YOU TWO!
HELL YEAH!!!
COULDN'T HAVE DONE IT WITHOUT YOU.
I COULD SAY THE SAME.
ALL RIGHT EVERYONE! THE VOTES ARE COUNTED! IN FIFTH PLACE IS GRANT WALTZ WITH HIS STUNNING HYPER STRIDER COSPLAY.
YO, THEY'RE ANNOUNCING THE WINNERS!
NO MATTER WHAT HAPPENS--
IT'S ALL GOOD. I'M PROUD OF US.
IN FOURTH PLACE IS BRITTNEY PAULSON AS WINTERCREST!
IN THIRD PLACE IS TYLER FRANK'S GALAXY RIDER.
AND IN SECOND PLACE IS...

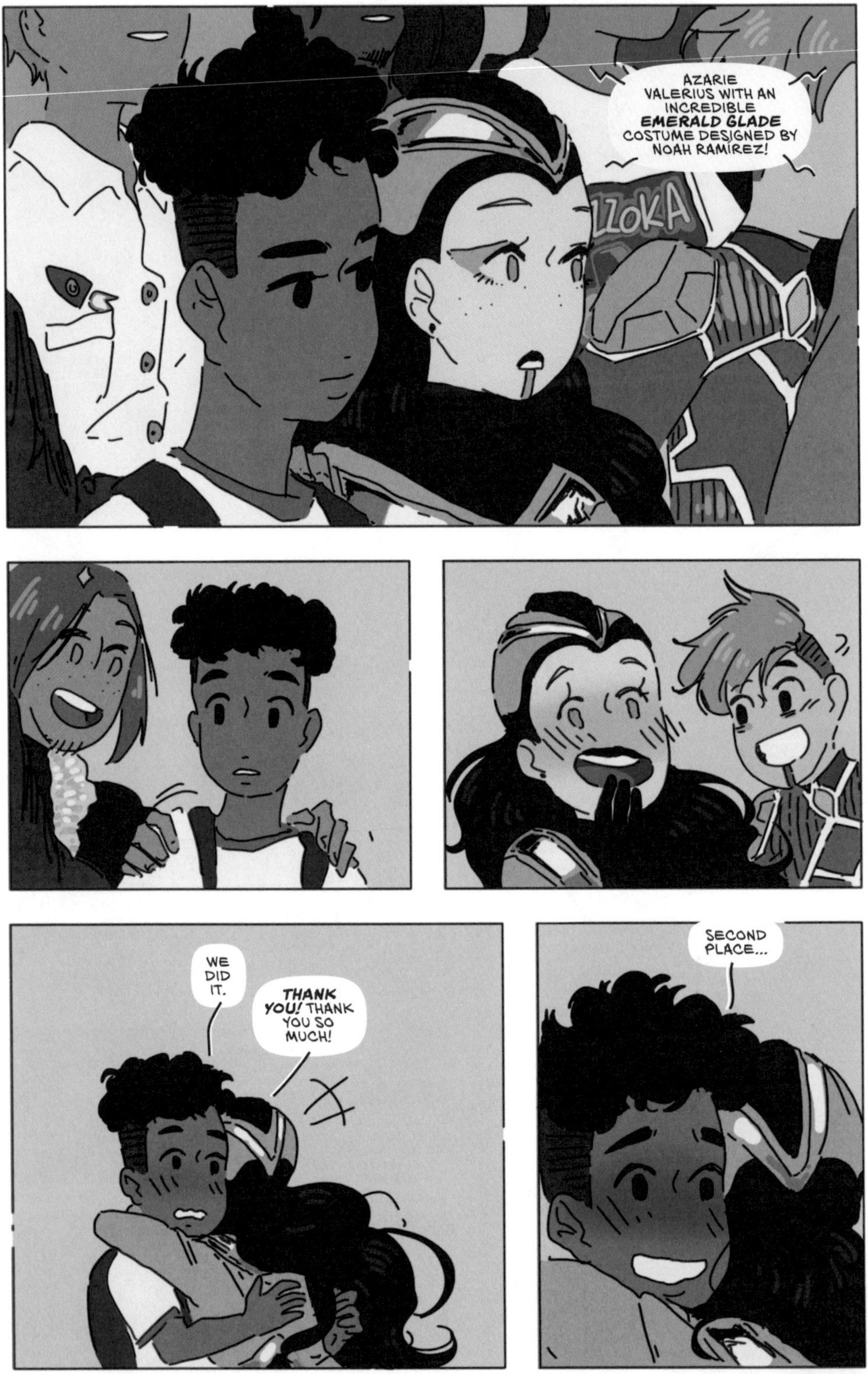
AZARIE VALERIUS WITH AN INCREDIBLE **EMERALD GLADE** COSTUME DESIGNED BY NOAH RAMÍREZ!
WE DID IT.
THANK YOU! THANK YOU SO MUCH!
SECOND PLACE...

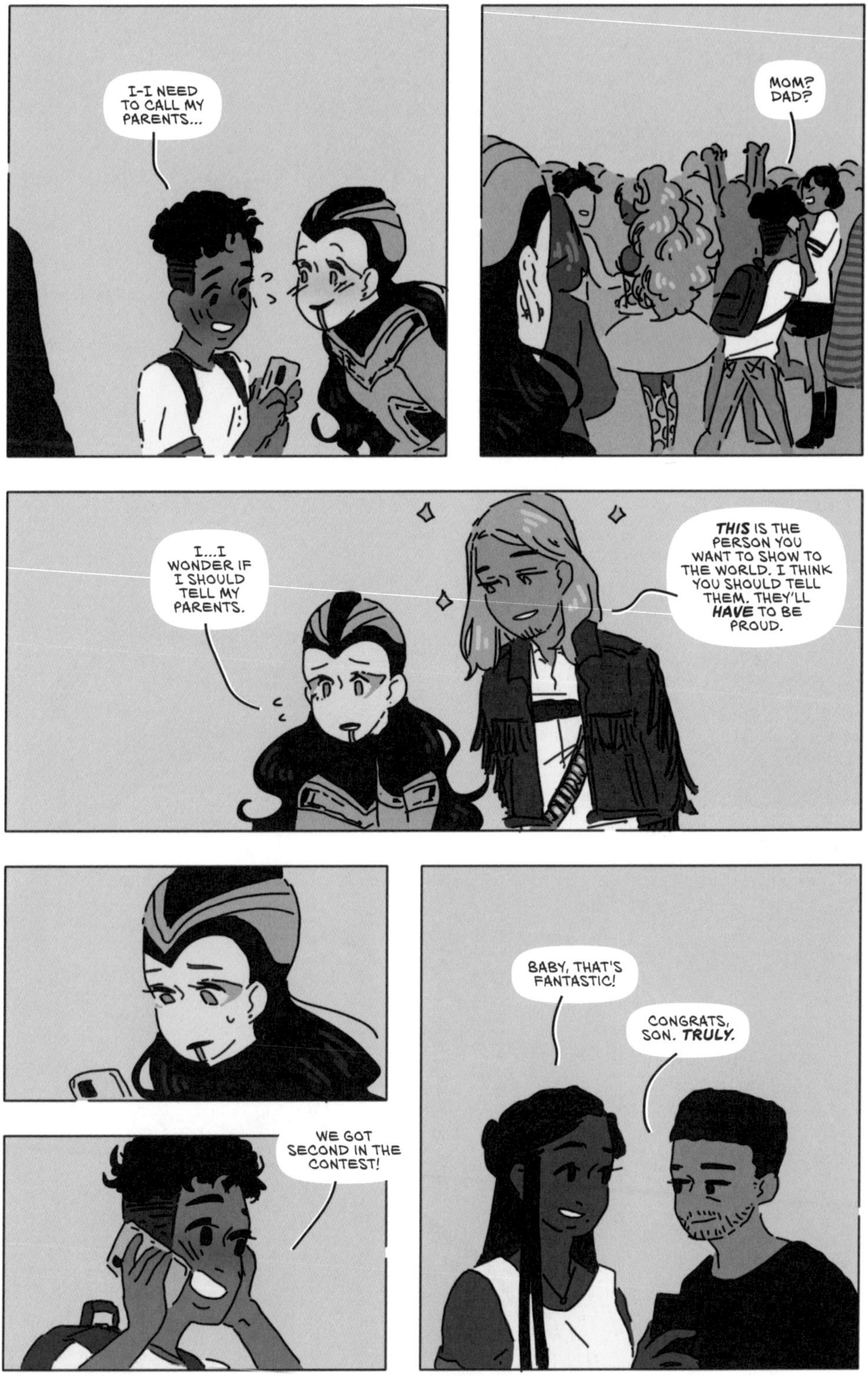

I-I NEED TO CALL MY PARENTS...
MOM? DAD?
I...I WONDER IF I SHOULD TELL MY PARENTS.
THIS IS THE PERSON YOU WANT TO SHOW TO THE WORLD. I THINK YOU SHOULD TELL THEM. THEY'LL HAVE TO BE PROUD.
WE GOT SECOND IN THE CONTEST!
BABY, THAT'S FANTASTIC!
CONGRATS, SON. TRULY.

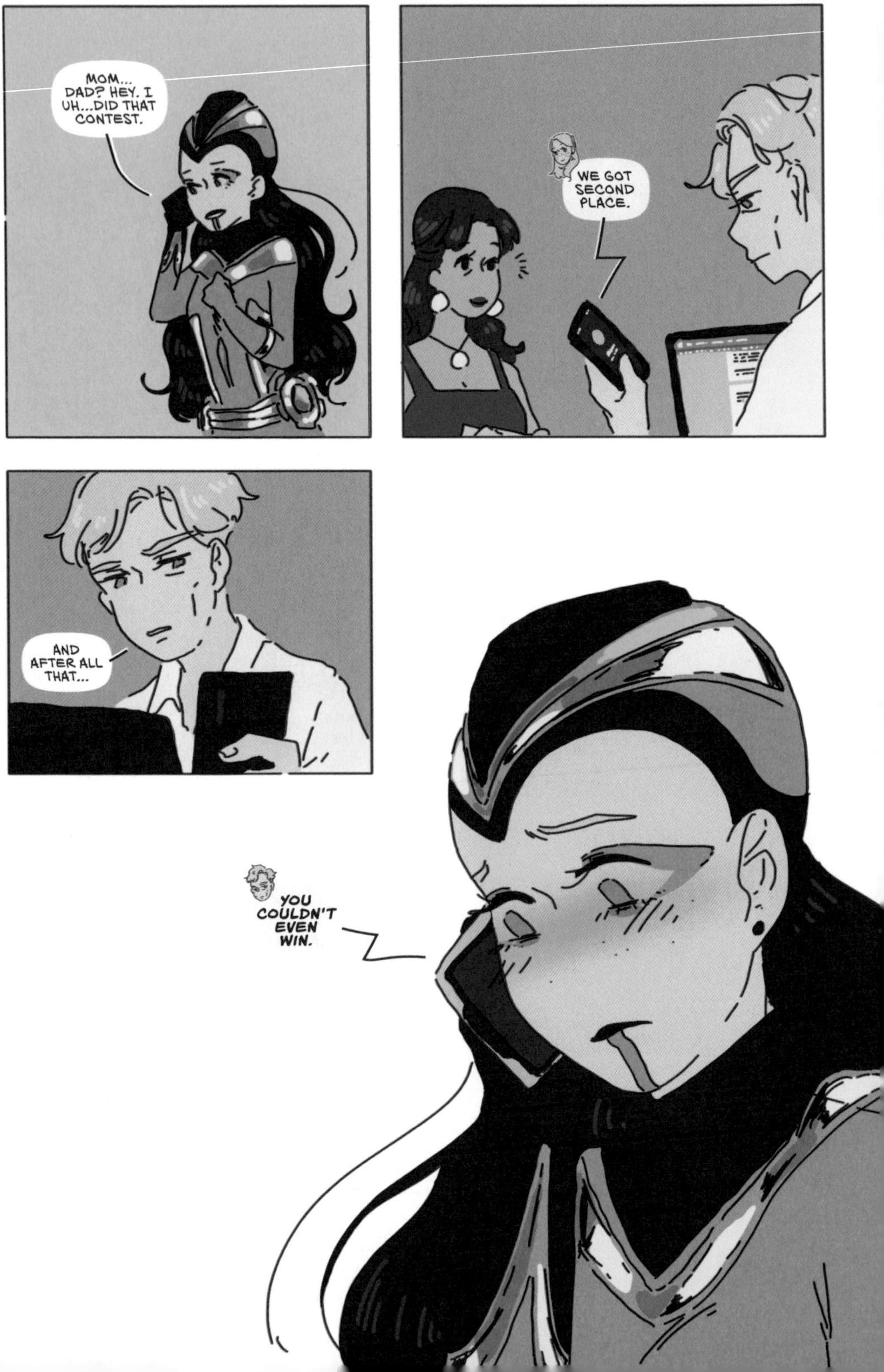
MOM... DAD? HEY. I UH...DID THAT CONTEST.
WE GOT SECOND PLACE.
AND AFTER ALL THAT...
YOU COULDN'T EVEN WIN.

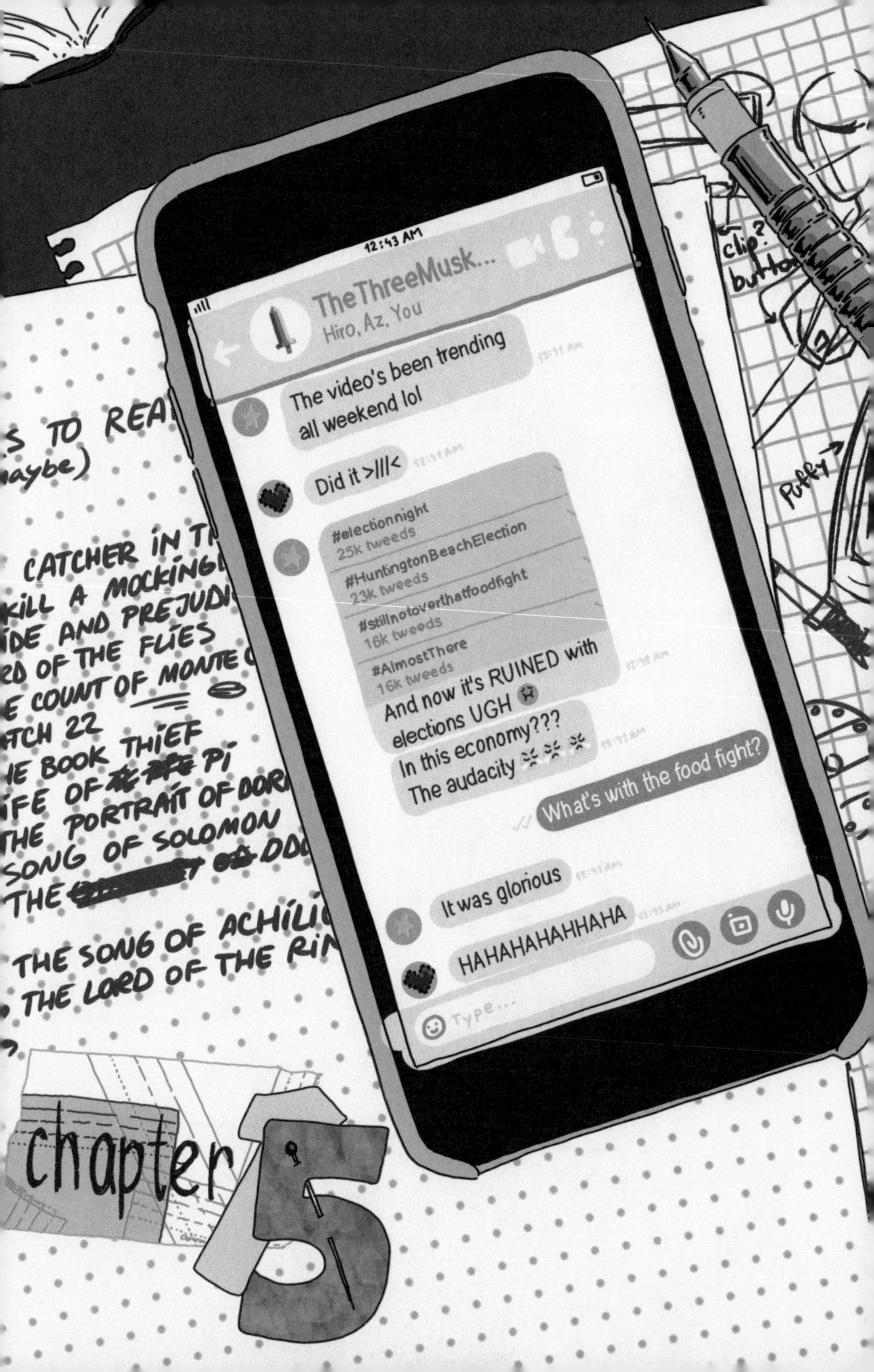
12:43 AM
TheThreeMusk...
Hiro, Az, You
The video's been trending all weekend lol
Did it >///<
#electionnight
25k tweeds
#HuntingtonBeachElection
23k tweeds
#stillnotoverthatfoodfight
16k tweeds
#AlmostThere
16k tweeds
And now it's RUINED with elections UGH
In this economy???
The audacity
What's with the food fight?
It was glorious
HAHAHAHAHHAHA
Type...
clip?
button
puffy
CATCHER IN TH
KILL A MOCKING
IDE AND PREJUDI
RD OF THE FLIES
E COUNT OF MONTE C
TCH 22
E BOOK THIEF
THE PORTRAIT OF DOR
SONG OF SOLOMON
THE SONG OF ACHILL
THE LORD OF THE RI
chapter 5

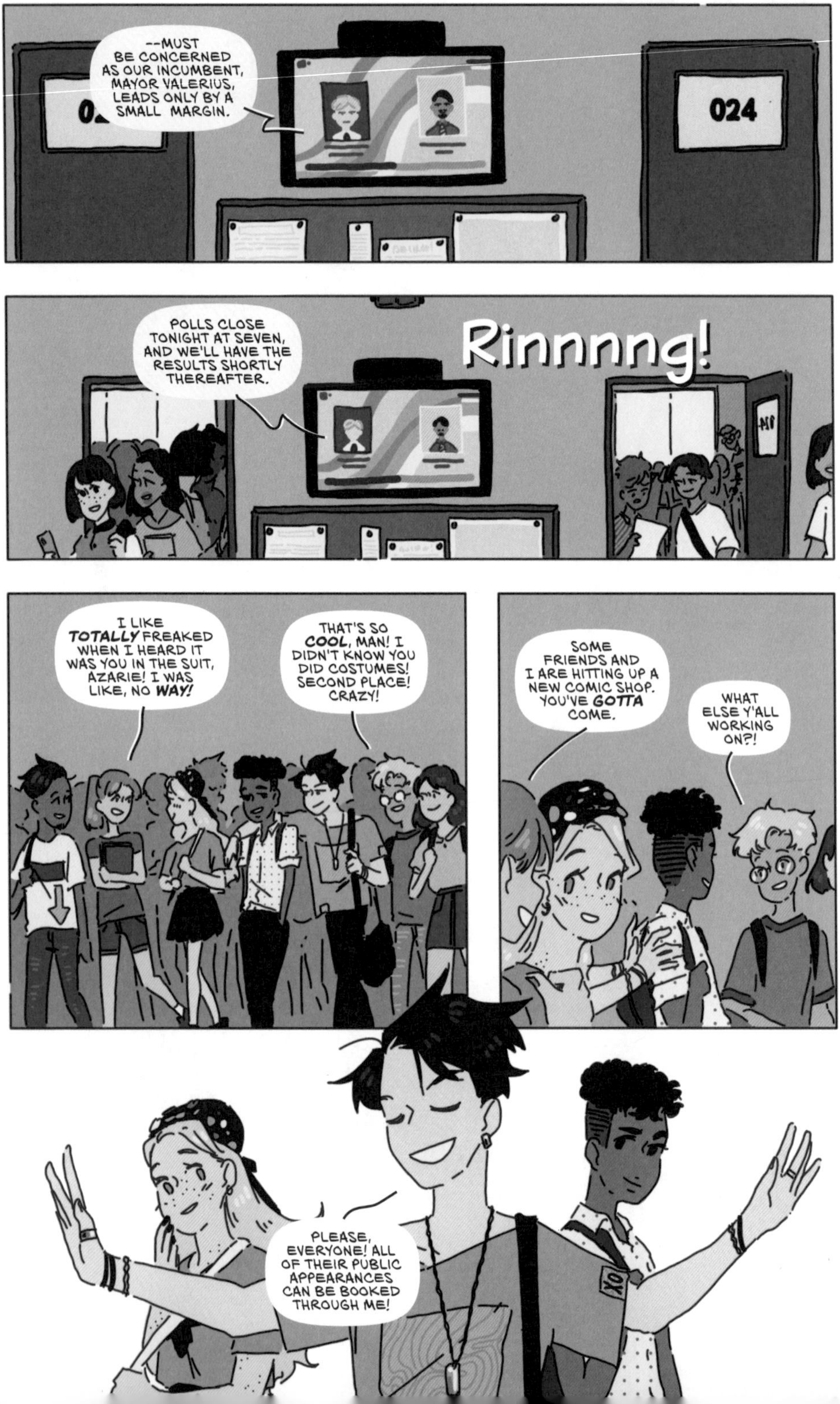

--MUST BE CONCERNED AS OUR INCUMBENT, MAYOR VALERIUS, LEADS ONLY BY A SMALL MARGIN.
024
POLLS CLOSE TONIGHT AT SEVEN, AND WE'LL HAVE THE RESULTS SHORTLY THEREAFTER.
Rinnnng!
I LIKE TOTALLY FREAKED WHEN I HEARD IT WAS YOU IN THE SUIT, AZARIE! I WAS LIKE, NO WAY!
THAT'S SO COOL, MAN! I DIDN'T KNOW YOU DID COSTUMES! SECOND PLACE! CRAZY!
SOME FRIENDS AND I ARE HITTING UP A NEW COMIC SHOP. YOU'VE GOTTA COME.
WHAT ELSE Y'ALL WORKING ON?!
PLEASE, EVERYONE! ALL OF THEIR PUBLIC APPEARANCES CAN BE BOOKED THROUGH ME!

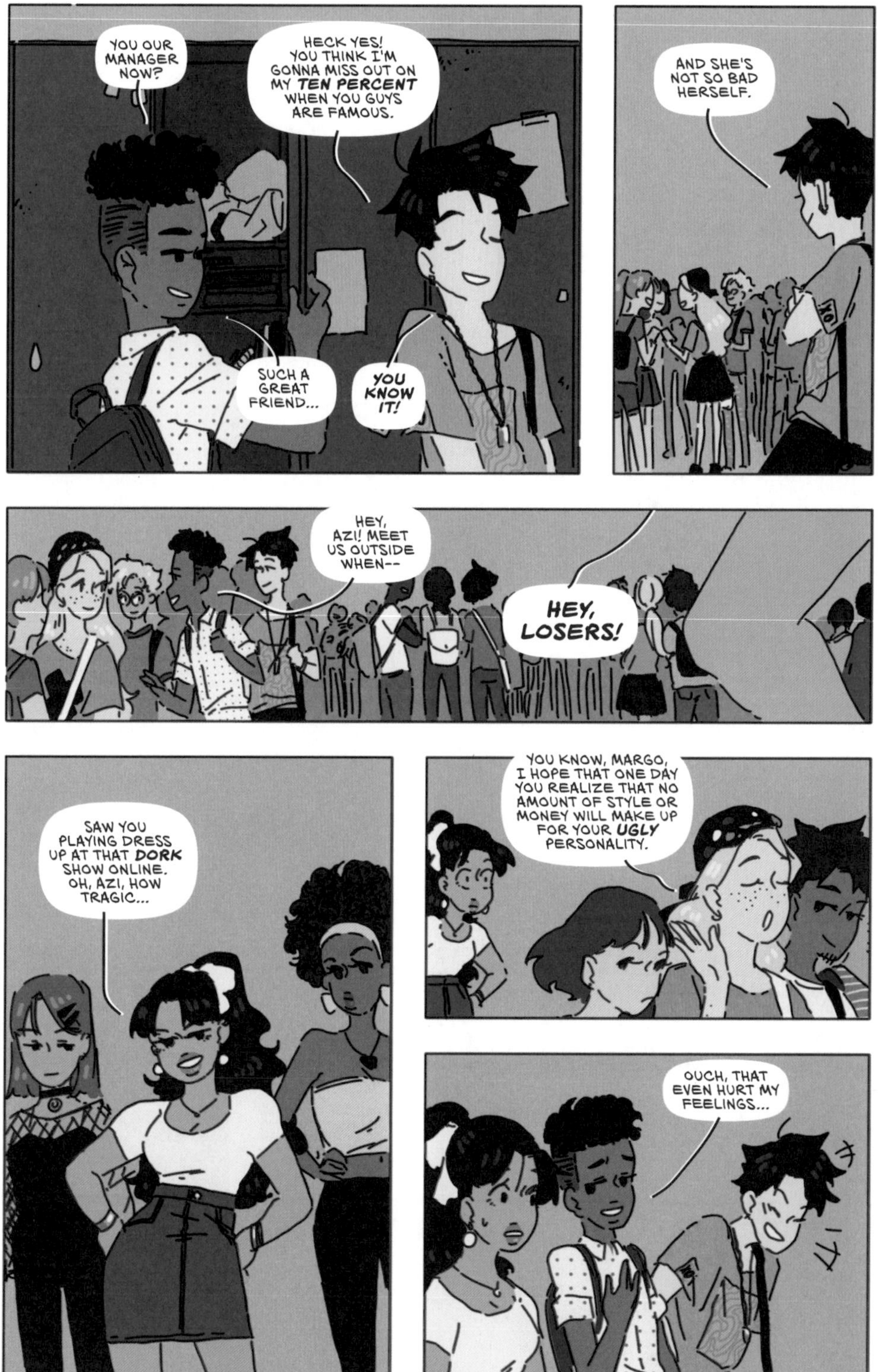

YOU OUR MANAGER NOW?
HECK YES! YOU THINK I'M GONNA MISS OUT ON MY TEN PERCENT WHEN YOU GUYS ARE FAMOUS.
SUCH A GREAT FRIEND...
YOU KNOW IT!
AND SHE'S NOT SO BAD HERSELF.
HEY, AZI! MEET US OUTSIDE WHEN--
HEY, LOSERS!
SAW YOU PLAYING DRESS UP AT THAT DORK SHOW ONLINE. OH, AZI, HOW TRAGIC...
YOU KNOW, MARGO, I HOPE THAT ONE DAY YOU REALIZE THAT NO AMOUNT OF STYLE OR MONEY WILL MAKE UP FOR YOUR UGLY PERSONALITY.
OUCH, THAT EVEN HURT MY FEELINGS...

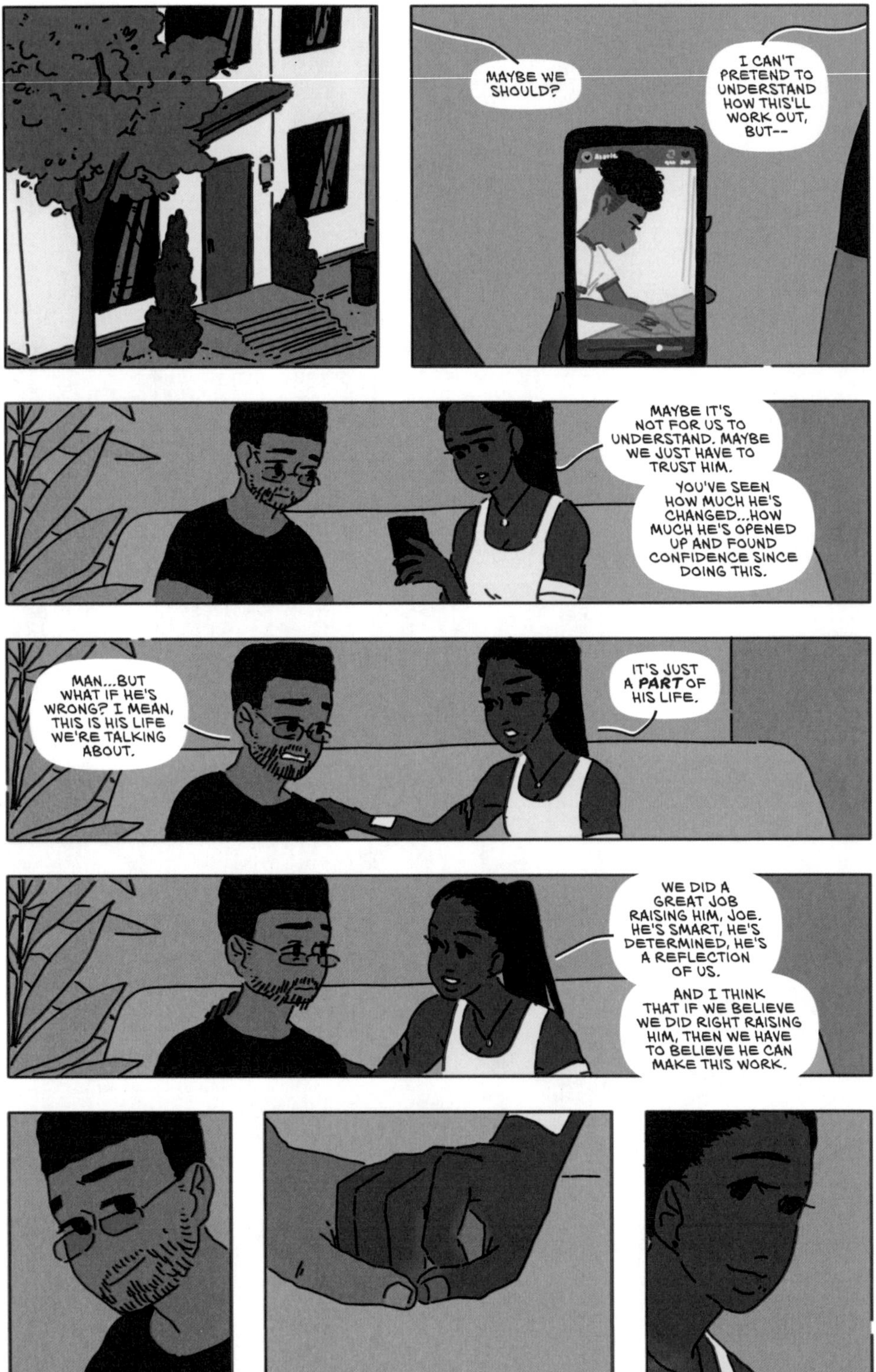
MAYBE WE SHOULD?
I CAN'T PRETEND TO UNDERSTAND HOW THIS'LL WORK OUT, BUT--
MAYBE IT'S NOT FOR US TO UNDERSTAND. MAYBE WE JUST HAVE TO TRUST HIM.
YOU'VE SEEN HOW MUCH HE'S CHANGED...HOW MUCH HE'S OPENED UP AND FOUND CONFIDENCE SINCE DOING THIS.
MAN...BUT WHAT IF HE'S WRONG? I MEAN, THIS IS HIS LIFE WE'RE TALKING ABOUT.
IT'S JUST A PART OF HIS LIFE.
WE DID A GREAT JOB RAISING HIM, JOE. HE'S SMART, HE'S DETERMINED, HE'S A REFLECTION OF US.
AND I THINK THAT IF WE BELIEVE WE DID RIGHT RAISING HIM, THEN WE HAVE TO BELIEVE HE CAN MAKE THIS WORK.

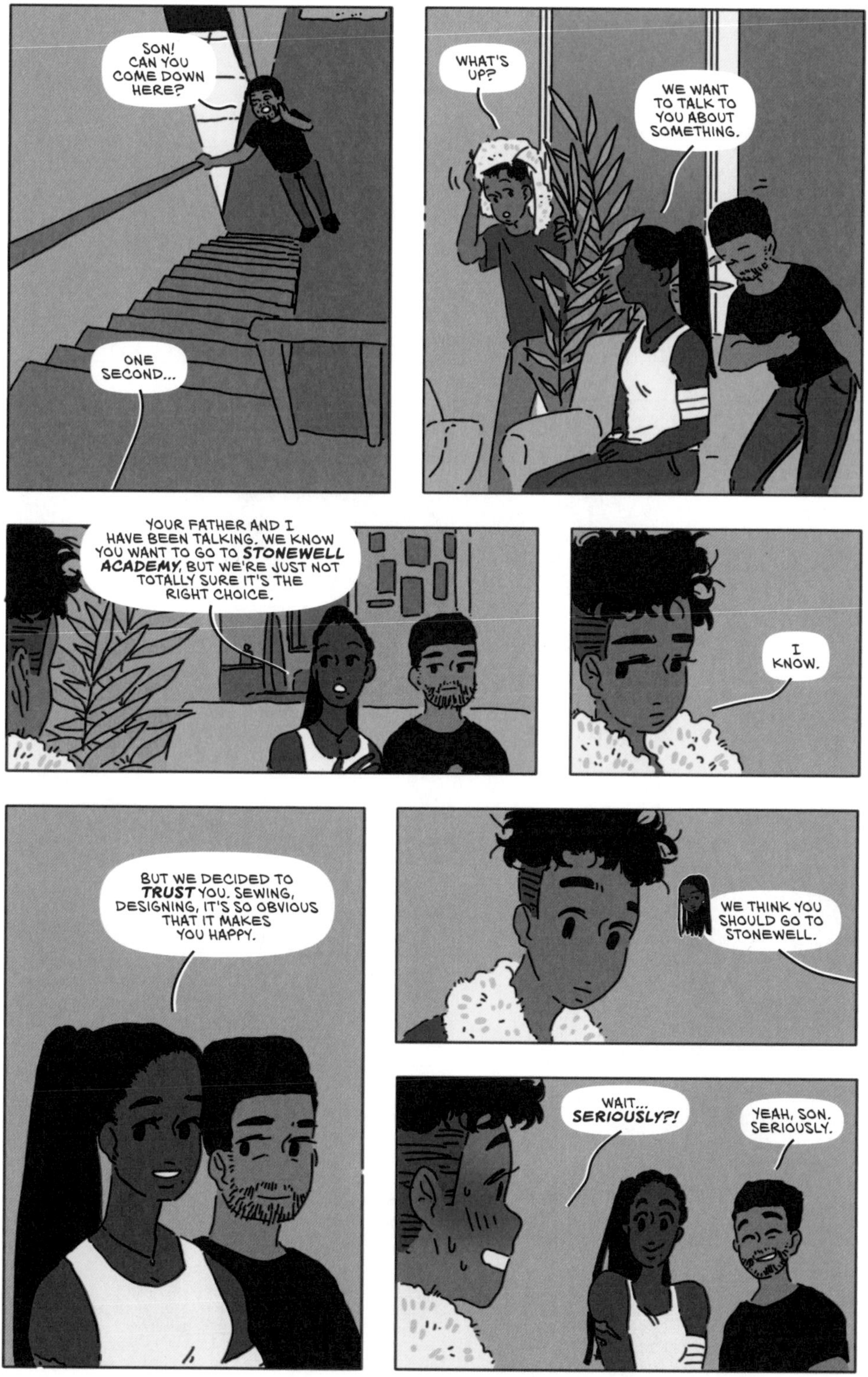

SON! CAN YOU COME DOWN HERE?
ONE SECOND...
WHAT'S UP?
WE WANT TO TALK TO YOU ABOUT SOMETHING.
YOUR FATHER AND I HAVE BEEN TALKING. WE KNOW YOU WANT TO GO TO **STONEWELL ACADEMY**, BUT WE'RE JUST NOT TOTALLY SURE IT'S THE RIGHT CHOICE.
I KNOW.
BUT WE DECIDED TO **TRUST** YOU. SEWING, DESIGNING, IT'S SO OBVIOUS THAT IT MAKES YOU HAPPY.
WE THINK YOU SHOULD GO TO STONEWELL.
WAIT... **SERIOUSLY?!**
YEAH, SON. SERIOUSLY.

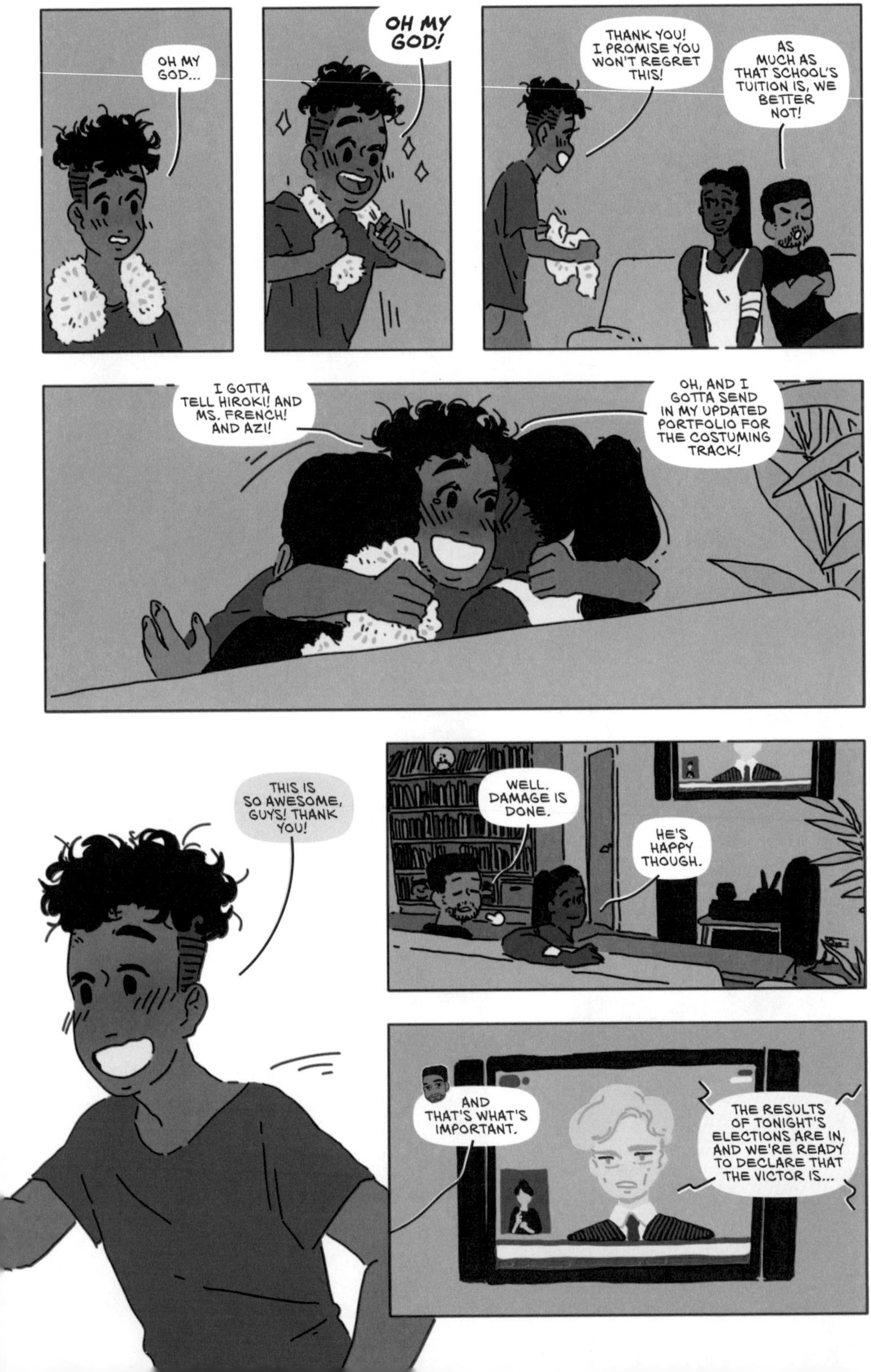
OH MY GOD...
OH MY GOD!
THANK YOU! I PROMISE YOU WON'T REGRET THIS!
AS MUCH AS THAT SCHOOL'S TUITION IS, WE BETTER NOT!
I GOTTA TELL HIROKI! AND MS. FRENCH! AND AZI!
OH, AND I GOTTA SEND IN MY UPDATED PORTFOLIO FOR THE COSTUMING TRACK!
THIS IS SO AWESOME, GUYS! THANK YOU!
WELL. DAMAGE IS DONE.
HE'S HAPPY THOUGH.
AND THAT'S WHAT'S IMPORTANT.
THE RESULTS OF TONIGHT'S ELECTIONS ARE IN, AND WE'RE READY TO DECLARE THAT THE VICTOR IS...

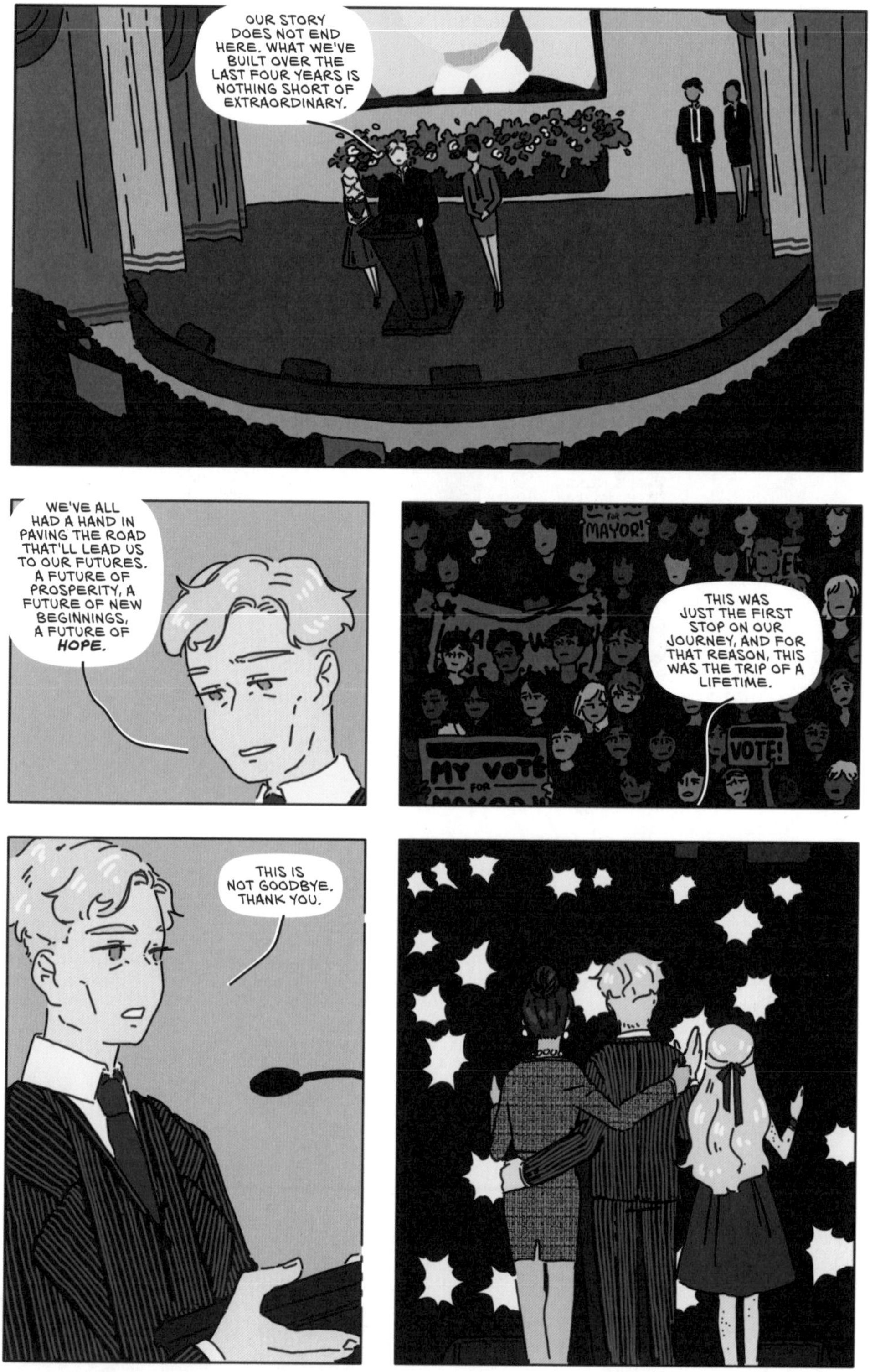
OUR STORY DOES NOT END HERE. WHAT WE'VE BUILT OVER THE LAST FOUR YEARS IS NOTHING SHORT OF EXTRAORDINARY.
WE'VE ALL HAD A HAND IN PAVING THE ROAD THAT'LL LEAD US TO OUR FUTURES. A FUTURE OF PROSPERITY, A FUTURE OF NEW BEGINNINGS, A FUTURE OF **HOPE.**
MAYOR!
THIS WAS JUST THE FIRST STOP ON OUR JOURNEY, AND FOR THAT REASON, THIS WAS THE TRIP OF A LIFETIME.
VOTE!
MY VOTE FOR
THIS IS NOT GOODBYE. THANK YOU.

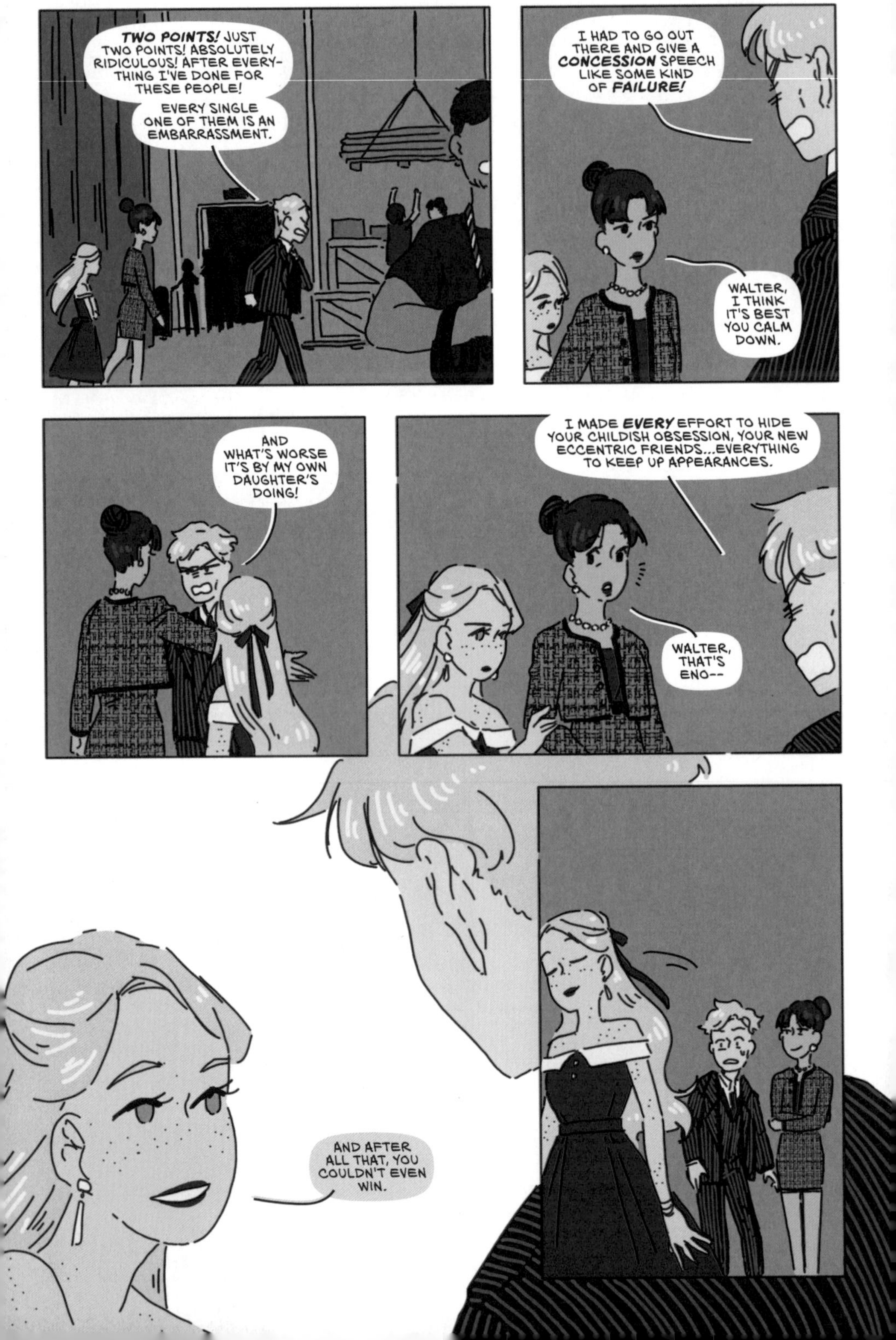
TWO POINTS! JUST TWO POINTS! ABSOLUTELY RIDICULOUS! AFTER EVERY-THING I'VE DONE FOR THESE PEOPLE!
EVERY SINGLE ONE OF THEM IS AN EMBARRASSMENT.
I HAD TO GO OUT THERE AND GIVE A CONCESSION SPEECH LIKE SOME KIND OF FAILURE!
WALTER, I THINK IT'S BEST YOU CALM DOWN.
AND WHAT'S WORSE IT'S BY MY OWN DAUGHTER'S DOING!
I MADE EVERY EFFORT TO HIDE YOUR CHILDISH OBSESSION, YOUR NEW ECCENTRIC FRIENDS...EVERYTHING TO KEEP UP APPEARANCES.
WALTER, THAT'S ENO--
AND AFTER ALL THAT, YOU COULDN'T EVEN WIN.

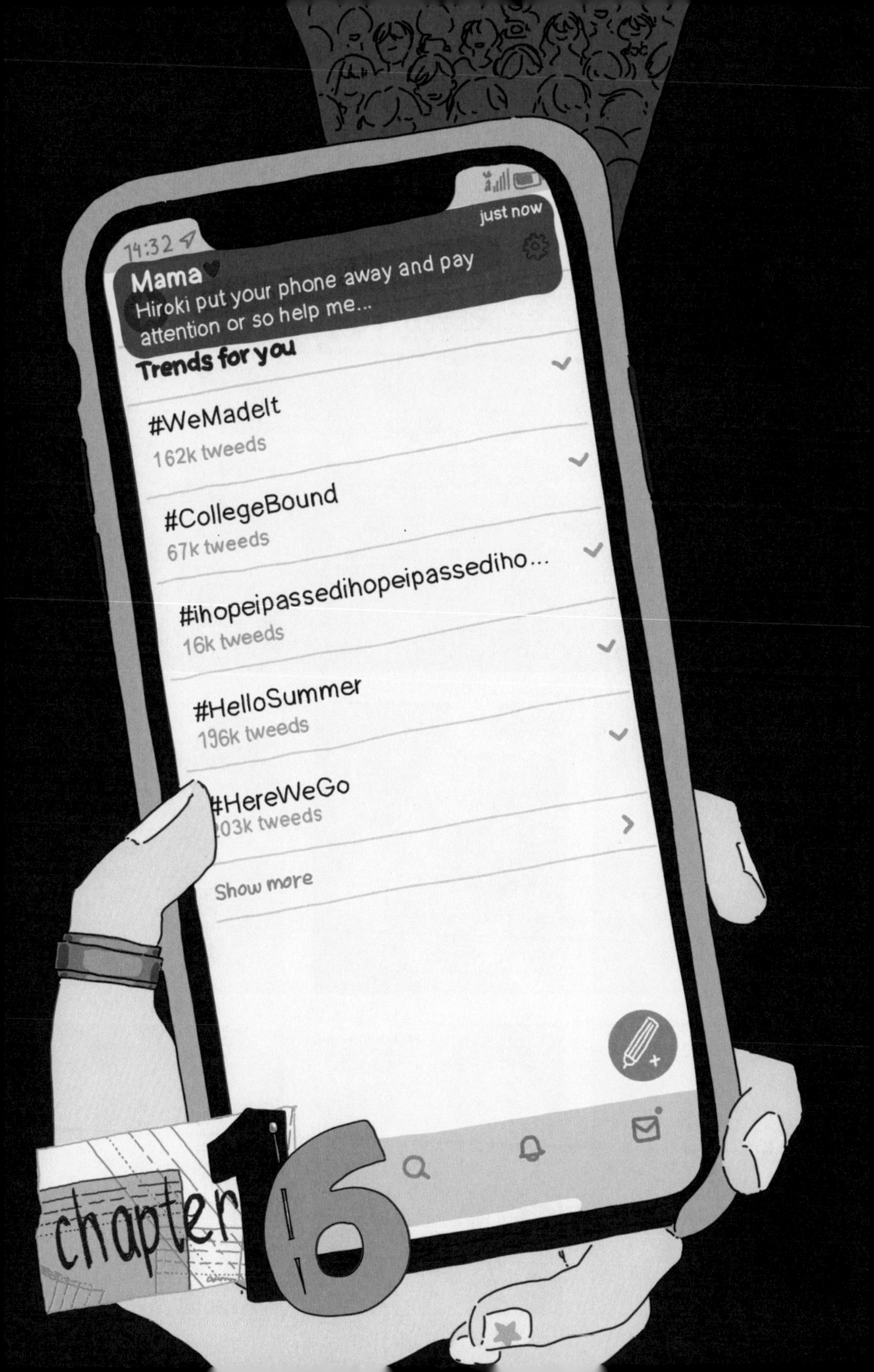
14:32
just now
Mama
Hiroki put your phone away and pay attention or so help me...
Trends for you
#WeMadeIt
162k tweeds
#CollegeBound
67k tweeds
#ihopeipassedihopeipassediho...
16k tweeds
#HelloSummer
196k tweeds
#HereWeGo
203k tweeds
Show more
chapter 16

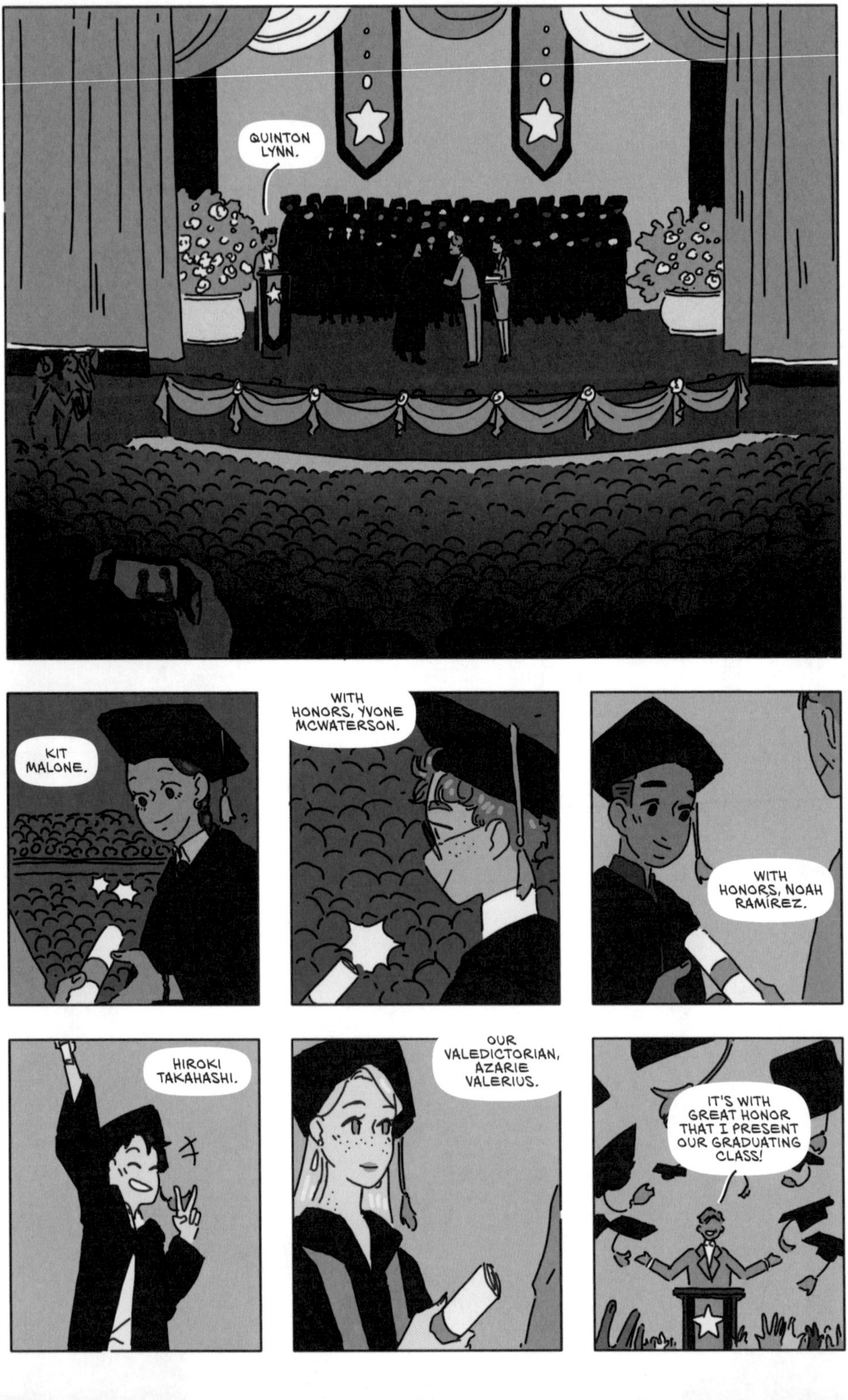
QUINTON LYNN.
KIT MALONE.
WITH HONORS, YVONE MCWATERSON.
WITH HONORS, NOAH RAMÍREZ.
HIROKI TAKAHASHI.
OUR VALEDICTORIAN, AZARIE VALERIUS.
IT'S WITH GREAT HONOR THAT I PRESENT OUR GRADUATING CLASS!

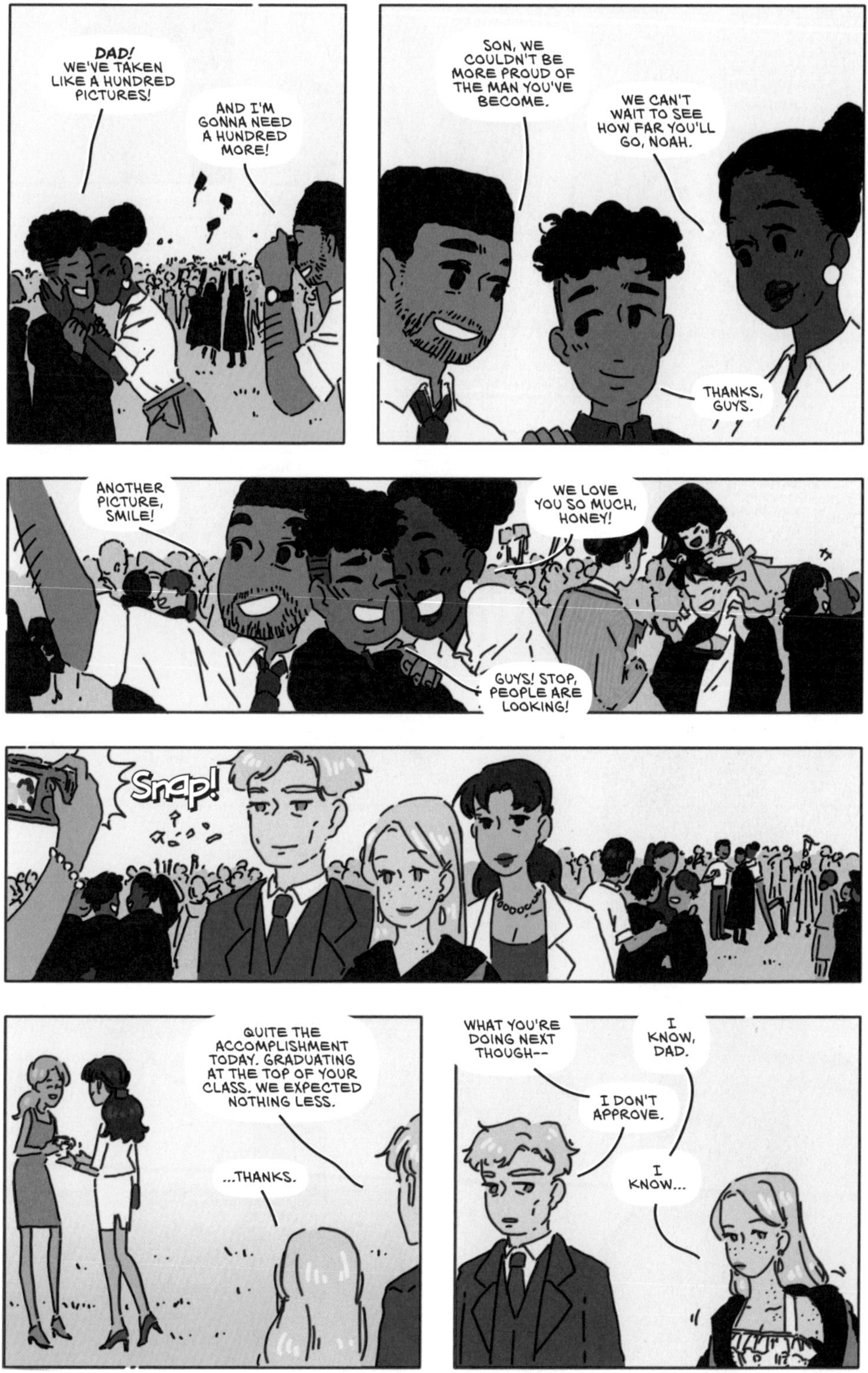
DAD! WE'VE TAKEN LIKE A HUNDRED PICTURES!
AND I'M GONNA NEED A HUNDRED MORE!
SON, WE COULDN'T BE MORE PROUD OF THE MAN YOU'VE BECOME.
WE CAN'T WAIT TO SEE HOW FAR YOU'LL GO, NOAH.
THANKS, GUYS.
ANOTHER PICTURE, SMILE!
WE LOVE YOU SO MUCH, HONEY!
GUYS! STOP, PEOPLE ARE LOOKING!
Snap!
QUITE THE ACCOMPLISHMENT TODAY. GRADUATING AT THE TOP OF YOUR CLASS. WE EXPECTED NOTHING LESS.
...THANKS.
WHAT YOU'RE DOING NEXT THOUGH--
I KNOW, DAD.
I DON'T APPROVE.
I KNOW...

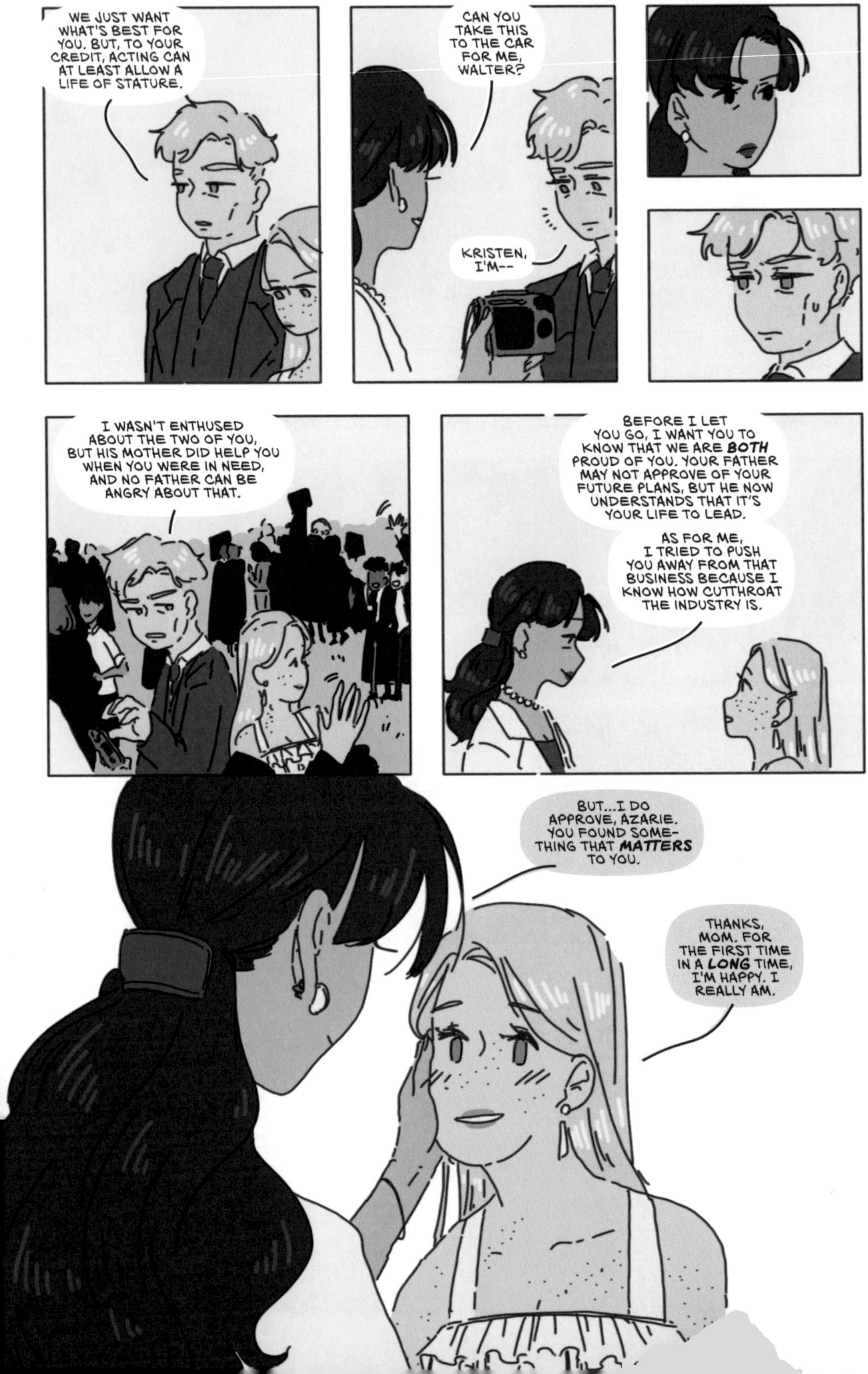
WE JUST WANT WHAT'S BEST FOR YOU. BUT, TO YOUR CREDIT, ACTING CAN AT LEAST ALLOW A LIFE OF STATURE.
CAN YOU TAKE THIS TO THE CAR FOR ME, WALTER?
KRISTEN, I'M--
I WASN'T ENTHUSED ABOUT THE TWO OF YOU, BUT HIS MOTHER DID HELP YOU WHEN YOU WERE IN NEED, AND NO FATHER CAN BE ANGRY ABOUT THAT.
BEFORE I LET YOU GO, I WANT YOU TO KNOW THAT WE ARE **BOTH** PROUD OF YOU. YOUR FATHER MAY NOT APPROVE OF YOUR FUTURE PLANS, BUT HE NOW UNDERSTANDS THAT IT'S YOUR LIFE TO LEAD.
AS FOR ME, I TRIED TO PUSH YOU AWAY FROM THAT BUSINESS BECAUSE I KNOW HOW CUTTHROAT THE INDUSTRY IS.
BUT...I DO APPROVE, AZARIE. YOU FOUND SOME-THING THAT **MATTERS** TO YOU.
THANKS, MOM. FOR THE FIRST TIME IN A **LONG** TIME, I'M HAPPY. I REALLY AM.

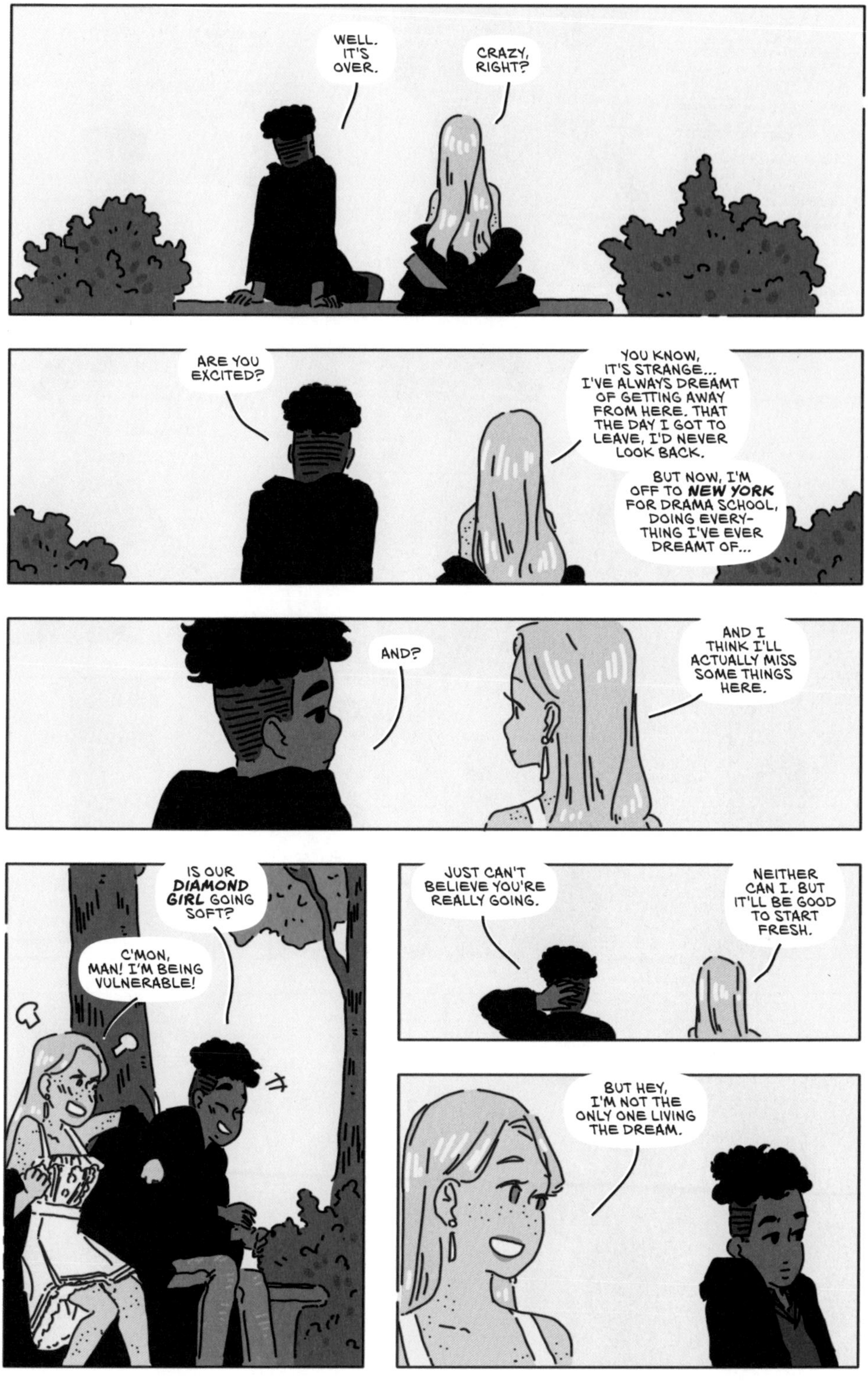
WELL. IT'S OVER.
CRAZY, RIGHT?
ARE YOU EXCITED?
YOU KNOW, IT'S STRANGE... I'VE ALWAYS DREAMT OF GETTING AWAY FROM HERE. THAT THE DAY I GOT TO LEAVE, I'D NEVER LOOK BACK.
BUT NOW, I'M OFF TO NEW YORK FOR DRAMA SCHOOL, DOING EVERY-THING I'VE EVER DREAMT OF...
AND?
AND I THINK I'LL ACTUALLY MISS SOME THINGS HERE.
IS OUR DIAMOND GIRL GOING SOFT?
C'MON, MAN! I'M BEING VULNERABLE!
JUST CAN'T BELIEVE YOU'RE REALLY GOING.
NEITHER CAN I. BUT IT'LL BE GOOD TO START FRESH.
BUT HEY, I'M NOT THE ONLY ONE LIVING THE DREAM.

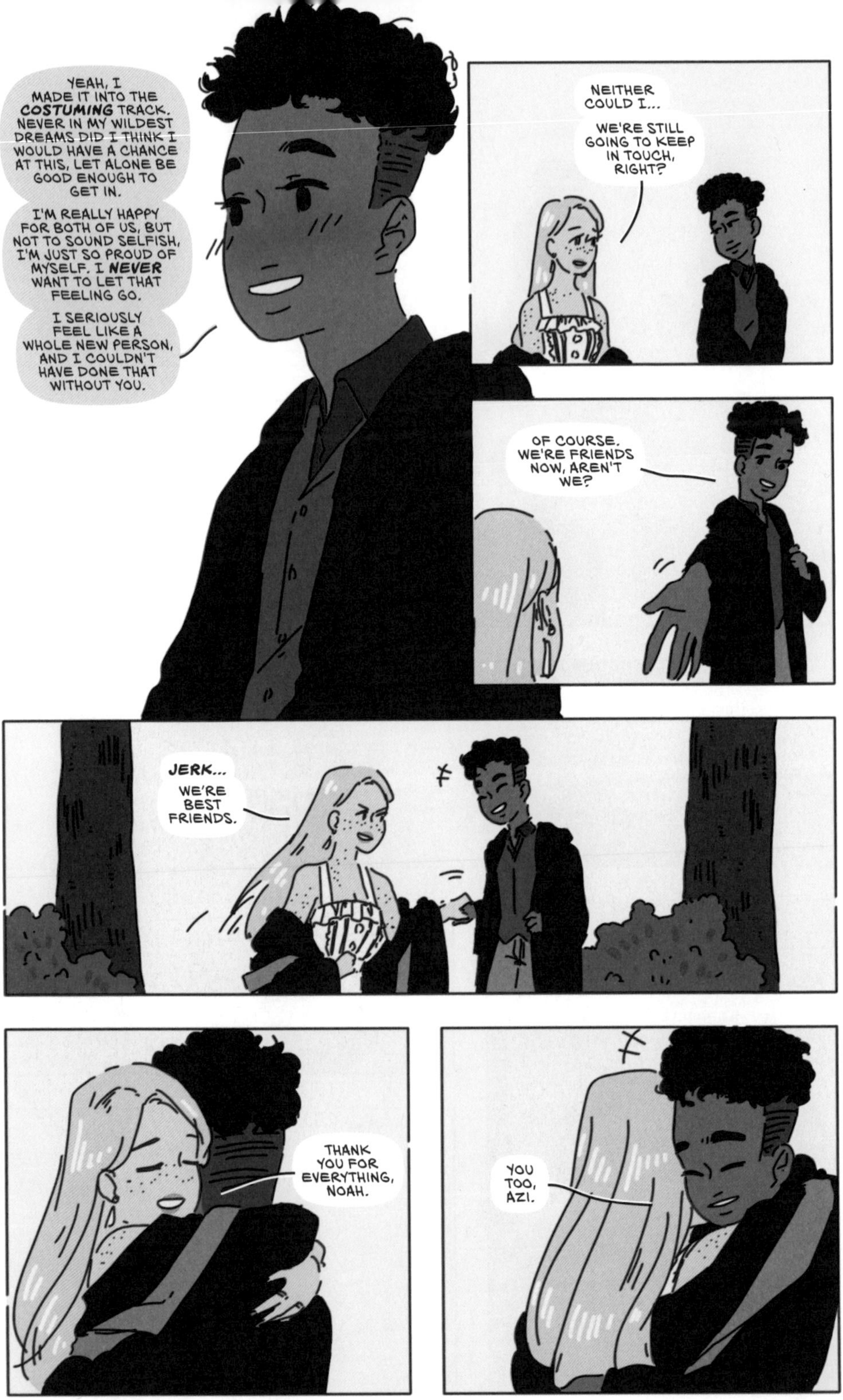
YEAH, I MADE IT INTO THE **COSTUMING** TRACK. NEVER IN MY WILDEST DREAMS DID I THINK I WOULD HAVE A CHANCE AT THIS, LET ALONE BE GOOD ENOUGH TO GET IN.
I'M REALLY HAPPY FOR BOTH OF US, BUT NOT TO SOUND SELFISH, I'M JUST SO PROUD OF MYSELF. I **NEVER** WANT TO LET THAT FEELING GO.
I SERIOUSLY FEEL LIKE A WHOLE NEW PERSON, AND I COULDN'T HAVE DONE THAT WITHOUT YOU.
NEITHER COULD I...
WE'RE STILL GOING TO KEEP IN TOUCH, RIGHT?
OF COURSE. WE'RE FRIENDS NOW, AREN'T WE?
JERK...
WE'RE BEST FRIENDS.
THANK YOU FOR EVERYTHING, NOAH.
YOU TOO, AZI.

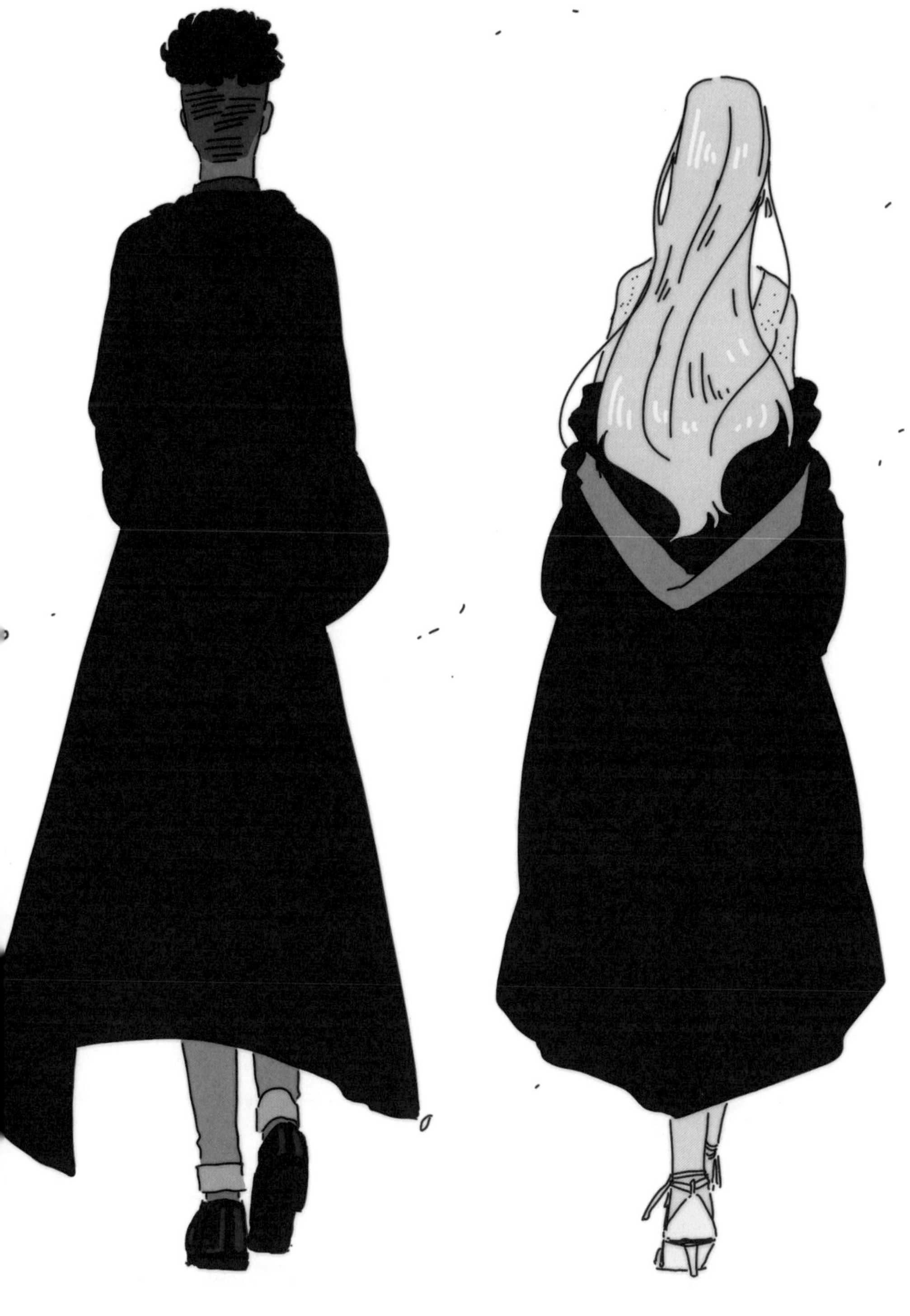

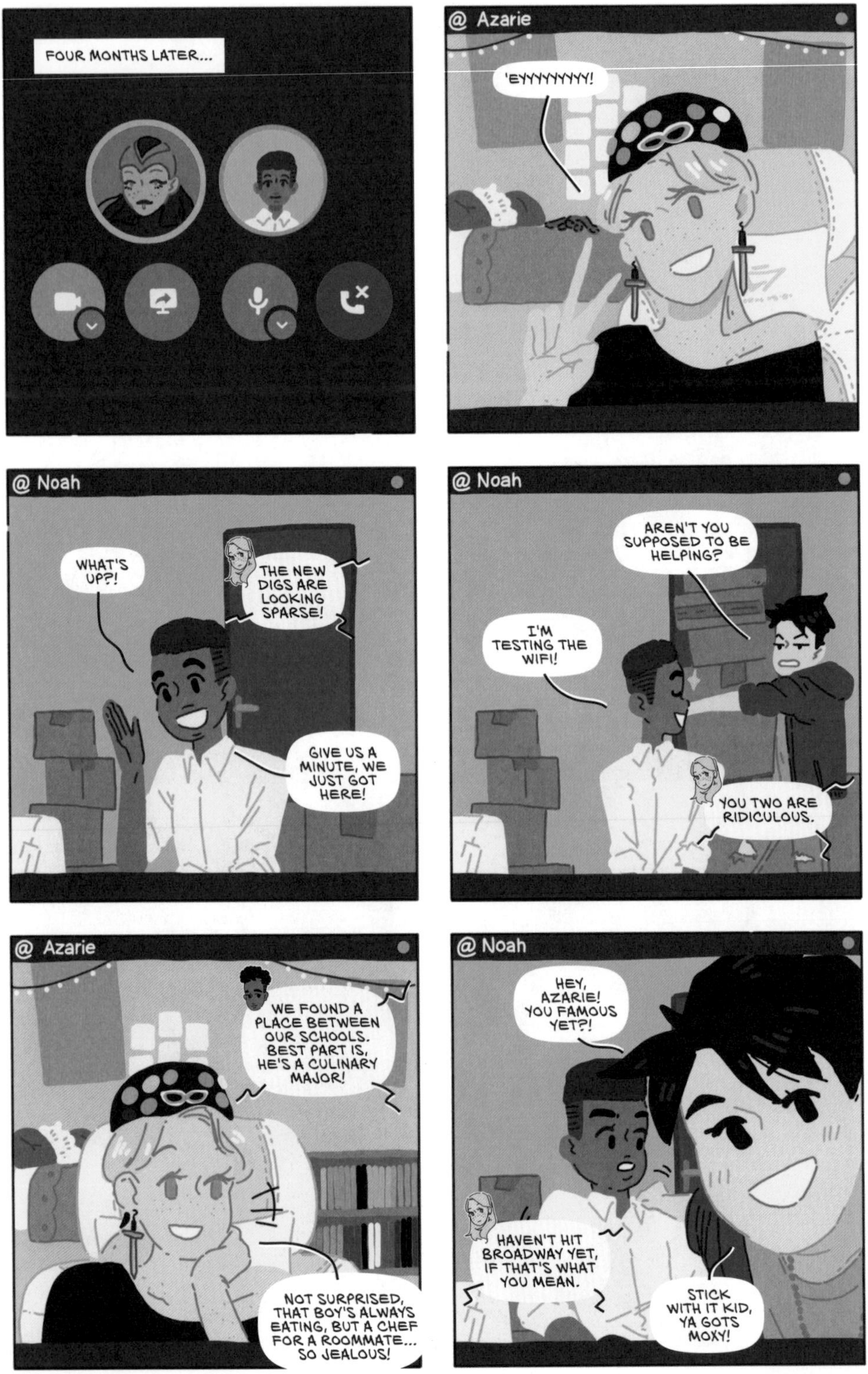

FOUR MONTHS LATER...
@ Azarie
'EYYYYYYYYY!
@ Noah
WHAT'S UP?!
THE NEW DIGS ARE LOOKING SPARSE!
GIVE US A MINUTE, WE JUST GOT HERE!
@ Noah
AREN'T YOU SUPPOSED TO BE HELPING?
I'M TESTING THE WIFI!
YOU TWO ARE RIDICULOUS.
@ Azarie
WE FOUND A PLACE BETWEEN OUR SCHOOLS. BEST PART IS, HE'S A CULINARY MAJOR!
NOT SURPRISED, THAT BOY'S ALWAYS EATING, BUT A CHEF FOR A ROOMMATE... SO JEALOUS!
@ Noah
HEY, AZARIE! YOU FAMOUS YET?!
HAVEN'T HIT BROADWAY YET, IF THAT'S WHAT YOU MEAN.
STICK WITH IT KID, YA GOTS MOXY!

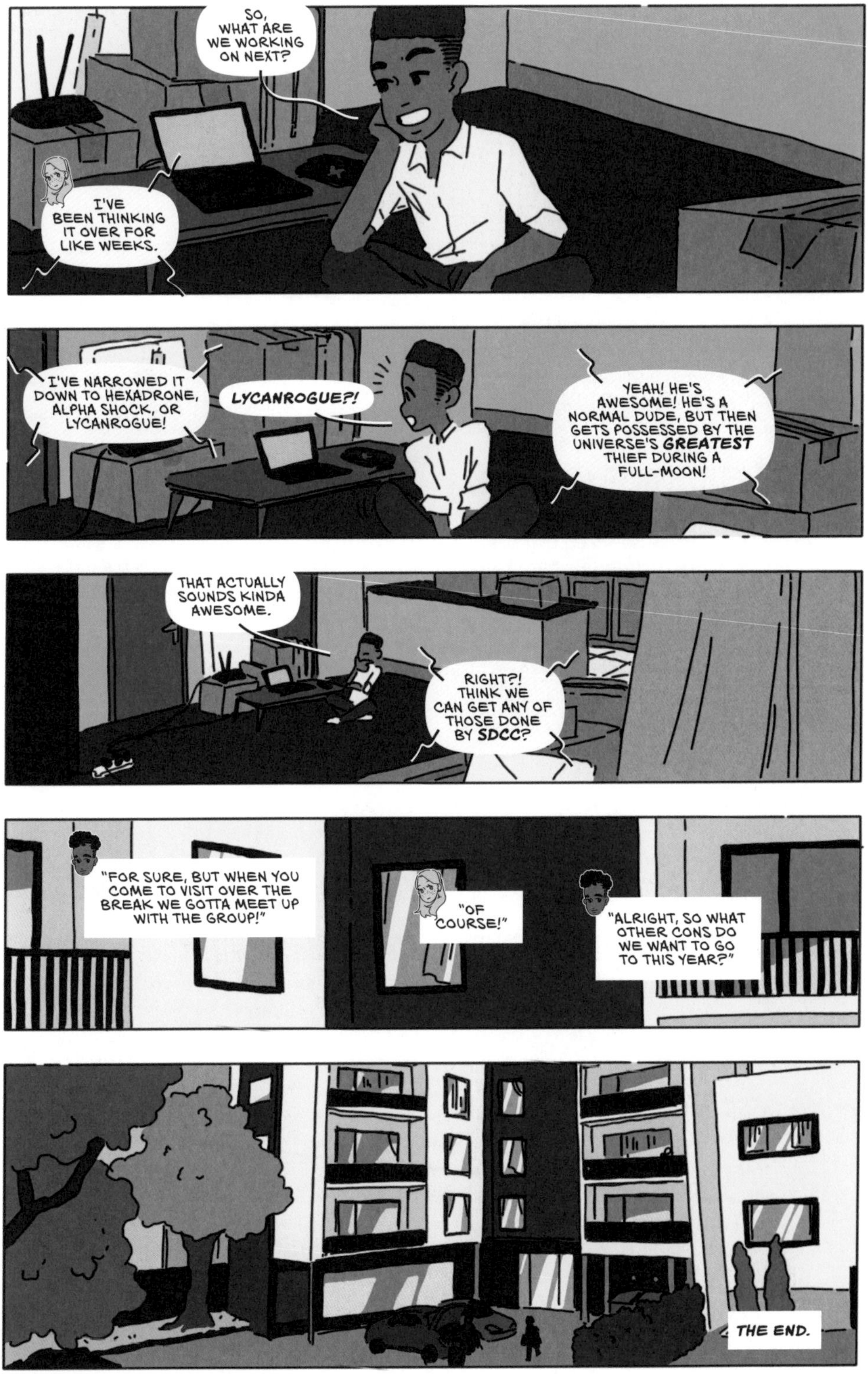
SO, WHAT ARE WE WORKING ON NEXT?
I'VE BEEN THINKING IT OVER FOR LIKE WEEKS.
I'VE NARROWED IT DOWN TO HEXADRONE, ALPHA SHOCK, OR LYCANROGUE!
LYCANROGUE?!
YEAH! HE'S AWESOME! HE'S A NORMAL DUDE, BUT THEN GETS POSSESSED BY THE UNIVERSE'S GREATEST THIEF DURING A FULL-MOON!
THAT ACTUALLY SOUNDS KINDA AWESOME.
RIGHT?! THINK WE CAN GET ANY OF THOSE DONE BY SDCC?
"FOR SURE, BUT WHEN YOU COME TO VISIT OVER THE BREAK WE GOTTA MEET UP WITH THE GROUP!"
"OF COURSE!"
"ALRIGHT, SO WHAT OTHER CONS DO WE WANT TO GO TO THIS YEAR?"
THE END.

ACKNOWLEDGMENTS

"I would like to thank my amazing parents for being nothing but supportive and encouraging throughout this whole process, as well as my brother who kept the bants going and loosened up the mood.

A great huge thanks to my beautiful, amazing bestie Margrét, who has been there with me every step of the way, for all the good and the bad. I would also like to thank Chên, Shioban, Ayberk, Mia, Riah, Mihai, Cezar, Ramona, Sarah, Dan, and everyone from Moon who helped me relax and enjoy my free time.

And of course, this book wouldn't be here if it weren't for the absolutely amazing people over at Mad Cave Studios. Huge thanks to David Pinckney for trusting me to illustrate his story, to Micah Myers for coming in clutch and doing all the letters. To Chris Sanchez, our amazing editor who put up with me and all my edits and changes, the real MVP. I would also like to thank Mark London for all of the support and trust he showed for this project, Chris Fernandez for being nothing but helpful if I ever needed anything, Jazzlyn Stone for being so amazing in helping all of us get these stories out in the world, and everyone else behind the scenes whose made this such a great experience.

Lastly, I would like to thank you, the readers, for giving our story a chance. I hope it provides you with a few good laughs, a few good cries, and an overall good time"

- Ennun Ana Iurov

"Thank you to all of my family and friends who support me in all that I do. Without them I'm sure that this book would not have been possible. Thank you to all the writers and artists that inspired me to try my hand at making comics and to try to create something that resonates with others and add something new to the world of comics.

Thank you to my editor Chris Sanchez, artist Ennun Ana Iurov, letterer Micah Myers, and each and every person at Mad Cave that helped make this graphic novel a reality. Each one of you lent a hand in making this graphic novel the best it could possibly be. And finally, thanks to everyone that picked up this graphic novel and gave it a chance. Every comic and graphic novel is made for someone and I hope this one is for you!"

- David Pinckney

David Pinckney is a long-time comic fan whose love of the medium coupled with his passion for storytelling fueled his desire for creating comics. His days are usually spent in the pages of a comic or plotting the next story.

Ennun Ana Iurov is a Romanian illustrator that is extremely pumped to have **Needle & Thread** professionally published under the Maverick imprint as her first dabble into young adult graphic novels. For over 6 years Ennun has created and self-published short comics and stories focusing mainly on empowering charity zines, working with organizations such as, Action Against Hunger, and others. Ennun's illustration skills have a wide range from folk tales to dream core to horror and more...

Micah Myers is a comic book letterer who has worked on comics for Image, Dark Horse, IDW, Heavy Metal, Mad Cave, Devil's Due, and many more. He also occasionally writes and has his own series about D-List supervillains, The Disasters.

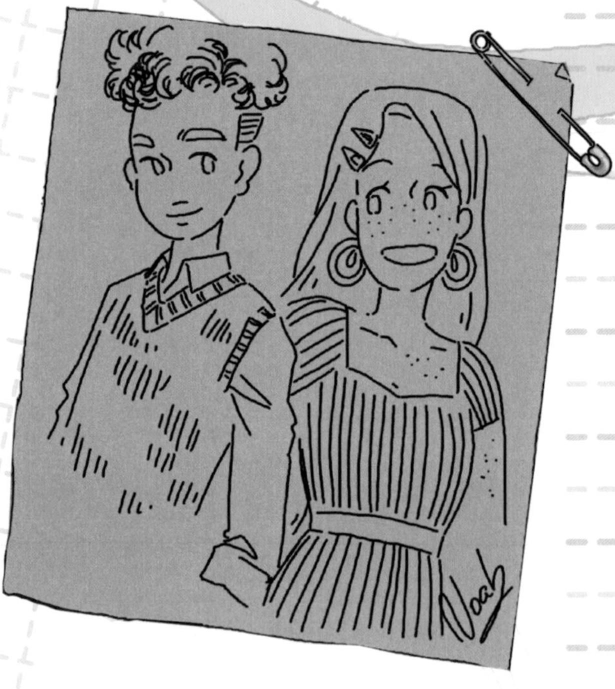

Needle & thread

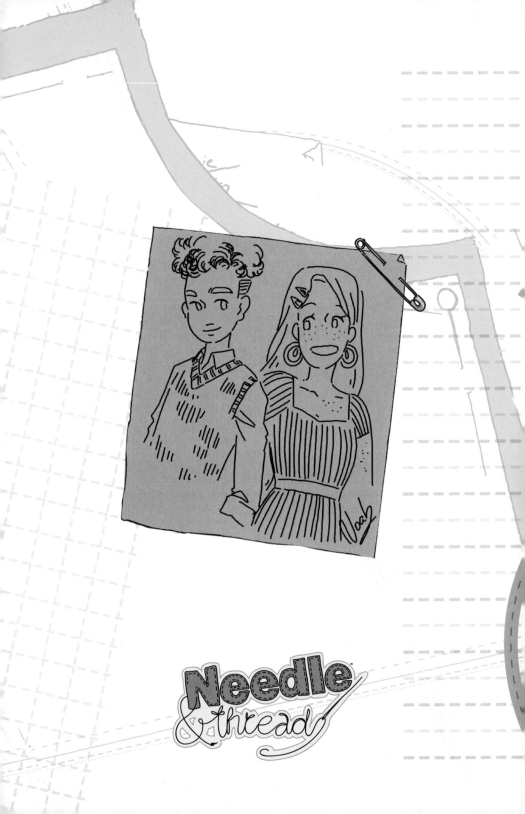